Death Descends on Saturn Villa

M.R.C. Kasasian was raised in Lancashire. He has had careers as varied as a factory hand, wine waiter, veterinary assistant, fairground worker and dentist. He lives with his wife, in Suffolk in the summer and Malta in the winter.

March Middleton, born 5th November 1862, was raised by her widowed father, a doctor, in Lancashire. She accompanied him on postings to India and Afghanistan, working as a nurse. Following his death she went to live with her godfather, Sidney Grice, at 125 Gower Street.

Sidney Grice, born 26th September 1841, attended Trinity College, Cambridge. Following a mysterious personal tragedy he disappeared for a number of years. After losing his right eye foiling an assassination attempt on Crown Prince Wilhelm, Grice returned to London to establish himself as its foremost Personal Detective.

DEATH DESCENDS ON SATURN VILLA

M.R.C. KASASIAN

HEAD of ZEUS

First published in the UK in 2015 by Head of Zeus Ltd

9 7 5 3 1 2 4 6 8

A CIP catalogue record for this book is available from
the British Library.

ISBN (HB) 9781781859711
ISBN (XTPB) 9781781859728
ISBN (E) 9781781859704

Typeset by e-type, Aintree, Liverpool

Printed and bound in Germany
by GGP Media GmbH, Pössneck

Head of Zeus Ltd
Clerkenwell House
45–47 Clerkenwell Green
London EC1R 0HT

WWW.HEADOFZEUS.COM

For Trevor Grice

Preface to First Edition

I T MIGHT SEEM vainglorious for me to write a preface to a book written to celebrate my genius but, whilst I freely admit to being vain about my many enviable qualities, there is little glory to be had by anyone involved in the events described here.

For obvious reasons Miss Middleton was not able to give a complete account of this tragic case and, after she was lost to this world, it fell upon me to finish it for her. I fear that I lack her lightness of style but at least I am able to provide some of the missing details.

I have resisted the urge to correct the many errors in my ward's account and some credit must be given to Mr Laurance Palmer (the chief editor of Messrs Hall and Co.) for bringing her notes into something approaching coherency, though I cannot help but wish that he and she had a little more regard for scientific technique and a little less interest in more sensational aspects.

It is only my wish to honour Miss Middleton's contractual obligations that persuaded me to cooperate with this account and allow it to be published so soon.

I count this as one of my very few and by far the greatest of my failures. I swore to March that I would save her but, in the end, found myself powerless to do so.

Her chair by the fire is empty and, though I craved peace and quiet while she was here and have it in plenty now, I am obliged to confess that my house is a dismal place without her.

Sidney Grice, 2 May 1883
125 Gower Street

PART I

Extracts from the Journals
of March Middleton

1

The Delivery of the Soul

THE FLAMES HAD long since died since I let Dorna Berry's message flutter into the fire, but the words still haunted me. I saw them when I tried to read Edward's letters. I saw them in the line of every book in which I struggled to bury myself. So many times I was on the brink of asking my guardian what they meant but on every occasion I pulled back, frightened that they were true.

I had never known Sidney Grice to tell a lie. What if I confronted him and he admitted his guilt? Where would I go? Who would protect me and give me shelter? Who could I trust? My father had died nearly two years ago in a walking accident in Switzerland. He was all that was left of my family, for my mother, he had told me, had been delivered of me in one breath and her immortal soul in the next.

The London of 1883 was a pitiless place and I had seen many a respectable woman reduced to poverty and the choice between immorality and starvation, for want of a man to care for her. Besides, Sidney Grice was probably – or, in his estimation, unquestionably – the foremost personal detective of the British Empire and I harboured hopes of following in his footsteps. I knew I could not let matters rest. It was just a question of finding the right moment.

7 November 1882
I am afraid for you, March. [Dorna had written] *You must leave that house. Leave it today or Sidney Grice will destroy you, just as he destroyed me and just as surely as he murdered your mother.*

2

The Portrait of Marjory Gregory

MARJORY GREGORY HAD everything. She was pretty, charming and intelligent. She married well and bore two beautiful children. She had a growing reputation as an artist, being much in demand for portraits and having exhibited at the Royal Academy.

On Christmas Day, 1876, at about three o'clock in the morning, Marjory Gregory got out of bed. Her husband stirred, but he was not especially concerned as she had long been an insomniac. She put on her dressing gown and slippers and padded downstairs. He went back to sleep.

Nobody knows what she did for the next four or five hours. Perhaps she looked at some of the paintings she had produced so long ago. They still hung in her studio, propped on easels or against walls. Perhaps she took up her charcoal. For the last seven months she had tried to draw a self-portrait every day, staring into her own eyes for hours on end but destroying the results every night.

All that is known is that as the sun rose from behind Winter Hill, Major Bernard Gregory was awoken by screams. He armed himself with his old service revolver and rushed downstairs to find his wife in her favourite wicker chair, a carving knife swinging frenziedly. It had slit her nose and gashed her lips. Her breast had been hacked wildly and he was just in time to see her stomach ripped open, whilst she writhed in unspeakable agony.

Before Bernard Gregory could reach his wife, one final stab thrust deep into her throat and was wrenched across it. The carotid artery was completely severed and the windpipe lacerated.

Marjory Gregory died, bleeding and choking blindly.

There were many strange things about her death, not least of which was that the hand that wielded the knife was her own. But Major Gregory would not accept a verdict of suicide. His wife had been murdered, he insisted, four and a half years ago.

3

The Death of Dom Hart

I T BEGAN AS it must end – with death and a priest.

The man who stood before us on that dark January morning was dressed in a black habit, the hood pushed back to reveal a mass of thick, greying chestnut hair and a rounded, rosy-cheeked face, the tip of his bulbous nose still reddened by the chill of London.

'Please,' he demurred, 'I can't take your place.'

'But how do you know it is mine?' I had not been standing by the armchair when I offered it to him.

Our visitor smiled. 'I do not imagine Mr Grice reads the poetry of John Clare.' He pointed to the book lying splayed open on the cushion.

I laughed. 'Have you come to teach us our work?'

'You will have had a wasted trip if you have,' my guardian muttered.

'Let me fetch you another chair,' I offered. But the monk put down his carpet bag and took a wooden chair from the central table, swinging it easily in one hand as he returned to deposit it facing the fireplace.

Sidney Grice and I sat opposite each other either side of the hearth as our visitor lowered himself on to his seat.

'Quite a change of career for you, from publican to Benedictine monk,' Mr G commented and our visitor tilted his head quizzically.

'It is not a giant stride of the imagination to guess my calling,' he touched the silver cross that hung from his neck, 'especially since I announced myself as Brother Ambrose. But how in heaven's name can you know my history?'

'No man can hide his past.' My guardian waved a hand. 'Though many have tried to do so. It is written in his face, his hands, his movements and his speech. Quite obviously you worked in a small establishment by the sea.'

The priest scratched his chin. 'I have not set foot in a public house nor been to the coast for over a decade. What trace of evidence can there be on me now?'

Mr G leaned back. 'I suspected it at once from your manner. You have the assured yet amiable air about you of one who serves yet remains in charge.'

'So might a head waiter,' I reasoned.

'A waiter, whatever his rank, would be more deferential.' Mr G sniffed. 'A publican knows how to be welcoming and yet remain in authority to deal with the people he has intoxicated.'

'So that is it?' Brother Ambrose was unimpressed. 'I just happen to act like a landlord?'

'It was a signpost on my road towards the truth,' my guardian told him. 'You have a well-developed torso – muscular rather than obese, though you have filled out with fat of late.'

The monk's mouth tightened at this description of himself. 'Please go on.'

My guardian put his fingertips together. 'Such a development comes of a job involving heavy lifting as a publican might in shifting barrels. You carried that chair with very little effort.'

'Many other jobs involve lifting,' Brother Ambrose objected. 'A stevedore, for example.'

'Indeed,' Mr G concurred, 'but I have never come across a dock worker yet whose back was not bent by his labours, and your right arm is much more developed than your left as results from many years of pulling pumps.'

'What if I were a carpenter? Using a saw would have the same effect,' the monk proposed.

Mr G smiled thinly. 'Your hands may have softened and lost their callouses over the years, but I have yet to meet a carpenter whose fingers are not thickened by the hard use they have been put to, and permanently scarred by splinters and deep cuts from accidents with his tools.' He leaned back to tug the bell pull twice, joggling the skull toggle.

'And how did you know my pub was small and that it was on the coast?'

'A larger establishment would have employed a potman to deal with the barrels.' My guardian flicked his thick black hair off his forehead. 'And your accent – unless my exceptional sense of hearing is deceived, which it never is – comes from or very close to Hove. Many men dream of moving from the city to run a public house by the sea but I have never known one to do the reverse.'

Brother Ambrose chuckled. 'You are an entertainment, Mr Grice.'

And my guardian inhaled sharply. 'I am neither a hurdy-gurdy man nor a prestidigitator. Tell me your business.'

Our visitor's face darkened. 'I do not know what religion you subscribe to, Mr Grice.'

'Rest assured that it is not yours,' my guardian said sharply.

'That is all to the good.'

'But why?' I asked.

And Brother Ambrose touched his crucifix. 'We want somebody who will not be in awe of our calling. A devout Catholic might hesitate to contradict or make accusations against someone he regards as his spiritual father.'

'I can set your mind at rest there,' I assured him. 'Mr Grice does not care who he offends.'

The monk's mouth twitched. 'That is what we were given to understand.'

'Then you might also have been informed that I never travel beyond the confines of this great but vile metropolis,' Mr G told him.

Brother Ambrose ran his thumb over the feet of the figure of Christ. 'You will at least hear me out?'

'It might fill an otherwise tedious moment.' My guardian stretched a hand over the back of his chair. 'Proceed.' He yanked the bell rope impatiently twice more.

'As you have observed I am a monk in the Order of Saint Benedict. My home for the last eight years has been in Yorkshire.'

'A wild place.' Mr G shivered. 'Populated by savages in tweed jackets and patterned stockings.'

'I believe it has some beautiful scenery,' I put in.

Sidney Grice shrugged. 'Nowhere is beautiful until it has been flattened and built upon.' He waved a hand. 'Recommence.'

'Claister Abbey was once one of the greatest monasteries in England,' Brother Ambrose told us, 'until it was dissolved by Henry VIII in his tussle with the Pope for supremacy. It was reopened thirty-four years ago in—'

'1849,' Mr G broke in. 'Even a non-Catholic can do that sum.'

'The monastery is a pallid reincarnation of its former self,' Brother Ambrose continued. 'Once the grounds housed three hundred monks with their own bakery, dairy, farriers and brewery – a small town in itself. Now a dozen of us crowd into a single house, surviving on the small profits of our garden produce and the printing of religious tracts, but mainly on charitable bequests.'

'No doubt from those wishing to have Masses celebrated for their souls in the belief that God judges the rich more benevolently,' Sidney Grice remarked sourly.

'Or those who have charity,' our visitor disagreed mildly. He had cut himself shaving, I noticed, and drops of blood had stained the collar of his cassock. 'But to return to the point, our much-loved Abbot, Dom Simeon, was taken by the Lord last January. We had hoped that our senior brother in Christ, Jerome, would succeed him – indeed he became temporary head – but an outsider was appointed in his place.' Brother Ambrose's strong fingers wrapped around the crucifix. 'Dom Ignatius Hart was not a popular choice. He came with a well-deserved reputation of being a mean man. He had a haughty manner, quick to take offence but dilatory to lose a grudge, and he had a flare for turning popular tasks into intolerable chores.

'Brother Daniel, the youngest of our brethren, quit his holy orders rather than face the daily humiliations heaped upon him; and many considered doing the same, but the vows of a monk bind his soul so tightly that he needs fear loosening them lest he lose it.' He pondered his own words for a while. 'The summer was hard but the winter was worse. Dom Ignatius introduced cold baths as a penance for trivial faults and there was little doubt that Brother Peter's end was hastened by such brutal treatment.' Brother Ambrose's grip tightened. 'We began to hold clandestine meetings to discuss how best to deal with our master and I have to confess that more than one man, including myself, made whispered threats in the heat of those discussions.

'Then on the fifth day of January, a wet and icy Friday morning, Dom Ignatius failed to appear for Lauds. This was very unusual, especially on the feast of the Epiphany, and an anxious discussion took place as to who, if any of us, should wake him.'

'You do not strike me as a timid man,' I said, and his hand fell into his lap.

'When you are sworn to absolute obedience to a tyrant you think long and hard before arousing his displeasure.' He grasped the end of his rope belt. 'Eventually it was agreed that we should risk his wrath and enter his cell en masse.'

'Let me guess break one of my own rules,' Mr G put in. 'Your detested master was dead.'

Brother Ambrose concurred grimly. 'We found him on the stone floor, his vomit so preternaturally black that some of my brethren feared he had been possessed by demons.' He twisted the rope around his fist. 'The police were called immediately. They are convinced we are hiding the culprit and have threatened to arrest us all and close the Order down, which is why, Mr

Grice, I have made this journey.' Brother Ambrose put a hand to his brow. 'We would like you to investigate the matter.'

Mr G looked at his watch. 'I have yet to discover any connection between what you desire and what I am inclined to do.'

Molly came in with a tray of tea, placing it warily on the table between us.

'Do I alarm you?' our visitor asked as she backed away.

'Oh, when Cook and me saw your frock when we was idling by the basement window, we thought you was her mother come back for revengeance.'

The monk chuckled. 'But why would Cook's mother want revenge?'

'Well—'

'Get out,' her employer snapped.

Molly bobbed falteringly and left.

'Mr Grice does not like leaving London,' I explained to our visitor, but he seemed unconcerned.

'I anticipated as much,' he told me, 'after I made enquiries about him. But I was given to believe that he is an exceedingly rapacious man.'

'You might also have noticed that he is still in the room,' Mr G grunted.

'I think it would take a great deal of money to lure him as far as Claister.' I poured three cups of tea.

'We are a poor Order,' Brother Ambrose said.

'Then I shall bid you good day.' Mr G rotated his cup to align the handle with the long edge of the tray.

'But you have something else to offer,' I said.

The monk nodded. 'You are a perceptive young lady,' he approved.

'If you are going to offer me Masses for my soul, do not trouble.' Mr G stirred his tea first one way and then the other. 'But I might be interested in that ancient book in your luggage.'

'How do you know it is an old book?' I asked.

'I can smell it.'

And as Brother Ambrose brought it out so could I: that unmistakeable fustiness of lightly mildewed leather and old parchment. I might have been back in my father's library.

'Mein Gott!' my guardian exclaimed. 'Jacob Cromwell's *Secreta Botanica*.'

'A gardening book?' I hazarded and the men raised their faces in mutual despair.

'The *Secreta Botanica* contains everything that was known in 1425 about the art of poisoning,' my guardian explained. 'The sources, effects, symptoms, tastes and disguising of.' He put a hand to his eye. 'It is the bible of toxicology.' His face flushed with excitement. 'It is said that Lucrezia Borgia read it instead of her breviary in church.'

'There were only four known copies in existence,' Brother Ambrose told me, 'and two of them are under lock and key in the vaults of the Vatican.'

'Have you read it?' I asked.

The monk shook his head. 'The *Secreta* has been on the Index Librorum Prohibitorum – the list of books Catholics are forbidden to read – since 1562.'

'Let me examine it,' Mr G implored, but our visitor slipped the book back into his bag.

'I might never get it back. Men have killed each other for a chance to peruse the contents of this tome.' Brother Ambrose drained his tea in one gulp. 'If, however, you were able to help us,' he wiped his mouth on the back of his hand, 'there is a space on that bookshelf which this volume might fill very prettily.'

Sidney Grice's eye fell out and he caught it without a glance. 'What if my investigations prove you and some or all of your colleagues to be guilty?'

Brother Ambrose considered the question. 'I shall have papers drawn up pledging that the *Secreta* is placed in your hands the day you reveal the culprit or culprits, whatever the result of your inquiry.'

Mr G pulled his upper and lower eyelids apart with a thumb

and forefinger. 'I shall take the case.' He forced his eye back into place.

'Good,' I said. 'I have never been to Yorkshire.'

'I regret to say that, whilst we are reluctantly admitting a self-confessed heretic through our doors, the monastery rules strictly forbid anything so impure as a woman to enter the premises.'

'Women are no more impure than men,' I retorted and our visitor smiled wisely.

'You forget, Miss Middleton, that I used to be a publican.'

4

The Dog and the Letter

WINTER HAD SET in hard and with it came the short dark days, made gloomier by the heavy yellow fogs and slushy rain. I had never yearned for my old life in India so much as I did during the long hours spent sketching by the fire or standing by the window, watching the tradesmen battle with the elements or the wandering huddles of the homeless picking putrefying scraps to eat from the filth of the pavement.

Sidney Grice set off alone the next morning.

'How long do you think you will be gone?' I rotated the brass handle to raise our green flag outside for a cab.

'I doubt it will take me more than a few days,' he said as Molly handed him his Grice Patent Insulated Flask of tea. 'The Roman clerical mind is subtle and devious and therefore much easier to fathom than the dim-witted blunderings of the common criminal. Stupidity is the only thing that ever baffles me.'

It occurred to me that, if my guardian were unable to return for any reason, I would never hear his response to the letter, but yet again I lost my nerve and only asked, 'Have you packed your toothbrush?'

'Yes.'

'And a change of shirt and collars?'

'I know you are trying to make fun.' Mr G adjusted his glass eye in the hall mirror. 'But you should know by now that I have never been cursed with a sense of humour.' He picked up his valise. 'Please do nothing to embarrass me, March.' And with those fond words he was gone.

*

I had only Molly for human company and even my kitten, Spirit, seemed lethargic, but Sidney Grice had hardly been gone an hour when we had our first caller, a Mrs Prendergast, who came to ask for help in finding her lost puppy. My guardian would have been grossly insulted, but I had nothing better to do and accompanied my sobbing client to her residence immediately. She had a nice three-bedroom house off Upper Thornhaugh Street and eagerly took me to see little Albert's bed and bowls in a cupboard under the stairs.

I was uncertain how to proceed with the investigation and so I put the age-old parents' question to her. 'Where did you last see him?'

'Do you think you might find a clue?' She took me to the basement laundry room where I spotted a black-and-tan Cavalier King Charles spaniel curled asleep under a pillowcase on top of a pile of blankets.

'Alby!' Mrs Prendergast was ecstatic and kissed the dog repeatedly on its mouth and nose until it looked almost as ill as I felt. She insisted I stayed for tea and fruit cake, and pressed five shillings into my hand as I departed. It was my first solo case, but not one I would be boasting about when I became London's first female personal detective.

The fourth post had just been delivered when I got home and all the letters were stacked on Mr G's desk, including a parcel bearing the great maroon wax seal of the King of Poland. Beside this pile were three letters for me: my dressmaker's account, which I hastily put aside; Mr Warwick, the land agent, informing me that the tenants for The Grange, my family home in Parbold, had quit the lease; and another postmarked Highgate. For lack of anything better to do, I decided to apply

my guardian's techniques when faced with unexpected correspondence and examined the envelope, holding it up to the
gaslight and sniffing it. I used one of his magnifying glasses.
There were a few faint scratches and an even fainter elliptical
grey smudge, and the ink had an unusual green tint to it, but
all in all it was just an ordinary vellum, fourpence-a-hundred
envelope.

The handwriting was a masculine copperplate in that old-
fashioned style which denotes countless raps of the childhood
knuckles with a rule and looks lovely with its extravagant curls
and swirls but is almost illegible. I hoped the contents would be
easier to read but I was disappointed. The author had used the
greater surface area available to give free rein to his calligraphic
exuberance and the words curled and swirled over and around
each other in an almost incomprehensible filigree.

I rang for tea and settled down at the desk to study it. The
signature was large and swept across the page but, for all its
skilful penmanship, I could make out no more of it than a possible Sergeant or Marquis. I went back to the opening line. The
first word, which looked like Slgf must surely have said Dear. I
sought other similar squirls for each letter and found a few possibilities which I copied on to a clean sheet of paper. The envelope
helped because I knew what that was meant to say.

Molly came in, looking as though she had slept in her clothes
and carrying a tray. When Mr G was absent I had biscuits with
my tea. He rarely ate them, having an eccentric idea that sugar is
bad for the teeth.

'Have you any idea what this says?'

Her eyes flickered. 'Is it the butcher's bill?'

'You know Mr Grice will not have meat in the house.'

Molly flushed. 'Well, what with him being away...'

I knew I had smelled sausages but I had assumed the aroma
had drifted from the house next door. 'But how do you hope to
explain the bill when it arrives?' I asked as she wrapped a strand
of hair around her thumb.

'We asked him to put it down as run-up beans 'cause his son's a greengrocerer.'

'I am very disappointed in you, Molly.' I regarded her severely. 'Going behind your master's back like that.'

Molly unwrapped her thumb. 'Please don't not snitch, miss. He'll have us out on the street before you can say gorblimey and I ain't not never had such a kind master as Mr Grice even if he does have a temper like a badger, and please don't not tell him I said that neither.'

I put down my pencil. 'I am afraid you leave me no choice, Molly.'

'Oh.' She paled. 'Oh but... Oh...'

'Unless,' I said, 'I was to get involved in your crime in which case I could not tell without incriminating myself.'

Molly chewed the strand thoughtfully, opened her mouth, closed it and recommenced chewing. 'I'll fetch you a plate,' she declared.

'And plenty of mustard.' I went back to the letter.

Dear March I translated at last. This was clearly not a formal letter but I could not think of anyone I knew in Highgate. I had never even been there. Forget – No – Forgive this – I struggled with the next word before deciding it read unsolicited. I was getting the hang of this, training my eye to ignore the ornamentation and concentrate on the core of each word: approach but...

Molly brought my bribe.

'Tell Cook to burn some cabbage with the basement door wide open,' I said and her eyes widened.

'Blimey, we'll make a criminal of you yet.'

I cut one of the sausages open. 'I hope not, for Mr Grice would be sure to bring me to justice in no time.'

Whatever people say about fruit, forbidden sausages taste immeasurably better. I had two before I went back to the letter, and the treat must have fortified my brain for I was able to get through the entire letter by the time I had consumed the last one and the first wisps of incineration were drifting up the stairs.

Saturn Villa
Highgate
Tuesday 20 October

Dear March,
Please forgive this unsolicited approach but I could think
of no better way to contact you.

Allow me to introduce myself. My name is Ptolemy
Travers Smyth.

I doubt very much that you have ever heard of me, but
the truth is that I am your father's cousin and therefore
quite confident that we are the closest and probably the
only relations that either of us possess.

I am an old man now and fear I have not long in this
world, and my only wish is to see you before I die. It
would bring me untold pleasure if you would visit me. I
am at home every day. Come for dinner today, if you can,
and – if, having met me, you feel safe – stay the night.

If you send your acceptance to the Stargate Road tele-
gram office in Highgate, I shall have my carriage collect
you within the hour.

We have a common acquaintance in Inspector George
Pound. Please consult him if you have any reservations
about my provenance or respectability.

With kind regards
'Uncle' Tolly

How the last loop of that y careered over the page. I traced it idly with my finger and it finished in the top right-hand corner but, before I had reached the end, I had made my decision. I wrote two notes and rang the bell.

Inspector Pound had worked on many cases with Mr G, but last autumn he had been sent at my guardian's expense to a cottage hospital in Dorset to recover from his wounds. Because of me he had been stabbed in the stomach and he could not easily be reached. He was a decent, honest man and we had a loose understanding, so the fact that Ptolemy Travers Smyth could use him as a reference was all the reassurance I needed.

Molly traipsed in, her apron even more crumpled than before. 'Take this to the Tottenham Court Road telegraph office – I am going out for the night.' I gave her a florin and pointed to the letter I had placed under the paperweight made from Charley Peace's patella mounted in silver. 'This is where I shall be if anybody needs me.'

'What?' she wondered. 'On the desk?'

'Just send the telegram, Molly.' I straightened her uniform as best I could, though the hat kept collapsing, and went into the hall.

'Yes, miss.' She bobbed unsteadily and dropped my note.

I left her trying to pick it up without bending her back and went upstairs to pack my Gladstone bag and change into my new dress – royal blue with cream lace trim. I looked at myself in the cheval mirror. A little rouge might have helped, but Mr G would have had an apoplexy if I had brought any into his house. I thought about letting my hair down but it was such a dull mass of mouse-brown that I left it tied back.

The smell of burned cabbage was so overpowering as I went down that I wondered if Cook had started a fire, but I decided to leave her to it and settled in the study to read an account in *The Times* of a man caught smashing plaster busts of Beethoven. When arrested he was raving something about a blue diamond. It was a curious case and I cut it out for my guardian to put into his files.

5

Past the Necropolis

I DID NOT have to wait long for the doorbell to ring and Molly to announce, in impressed tones, that my carriage had arrived.

'I am going to Highgate,' I told her and her jaw dropped.

'Oh, have a care, miss. There's dead people there what ain't even alive.' She threw out her arm as if indicating their imminent approach.

'The departed cannot hurt you,' I reassured her but she did not seem convinced.

'What about that dead damnation dog what fell on Cook's brother's head? He was unconscienced for nearly a forthnight.'

'I shall take my strongest umbrella,' I promised.

A little, pinch-faced coachman in red livery was waiting to see me into a black brougham ornamented with a coat of arms – a green oak tree with the golden letters T and S interlocked in the foreground. The front lamps were already lit.

Two students were coming out of the Anatomy Building opposite, their coats heavily stained with human fluids, which they saw as badges of honour. They were growing moustaches and whiskers but – though they must have been about my age – they still looked like children. One of them whistled as I climbed aboard and my dress rose up my calf.

'Cut up a prettier cadaver this morning,' his companion jeered.

The coachman gestured angrily and folded up the steps.

'She would have had to be dead to let you near her,' I retorted and the door closed, the driver clambering up and flicking his fine black mare to set us on our way.

This was true luxury, to be enclosed in a glazed box rather than behind the flaps of a hansom where one was exposed to the elements or forced to shelter behind a leather curtain. The seats were generously stuffed soft burgundy leather and our progress was stately, the four wheels being sprung to deaden the impact of the myriad bumps and potholes in the road.

The sun was down with the hint of an orange glow through the smoke of coal fires and the discharge of the thousands of factories labouring ceaselessly in the greatest metropolis the world had ever known.

A group of children came running after us. With their shaved heads and shapeless rags, I could not tell if they were boys or girls.

'Takin' 'er to the Tower, mister?'

'She's a wrong 'un and no mistake.'

'Off wiv 'er 'ead.'

I laughed but could not throw them any coppers from my isolated comfort.

My father had never mentioned any living relatives to me and I was always under the impression that we had none. My mother was an only child and the last family member that I knew of – my father's older brother – had been lost at sea when I was a toddler.

It did occur to me that the writer of that letter could be mistaken or lying, possibly in the hope of persuading me to support him in his old age. It could even be a cruel joke and I began to wish that I had waited for a chance to contact Inspector Pound before setting off, but I was intrigued. Perhaps Mr Travers Smyth could tell me something of the family history about which my father had always been so taciturn. He might possibly know why Sidney Grice had felt it his duty to take me into his home. I was not even aware that I had a godfather before Mr G contacted me, and he either became evasive or developed temporary lockjaw when I probed into his past.

We had a slow journey. The thoroughfares designed for a hundred thousand people now struggled to serve two million, and every omnibus, private carriage and trader's van in London had to jostle constantly with all the others to make any progress at all. Gradually, however, the roads became less congested and the rows of terraced houses broke up into semi-detached and then detached homes, set back from the streets behind front gardens. We got into a fairly steady trot, our horse tossing her head like a pit pony having its day in a meadow, as we travelled beside the high red-brick, treelined walls of the vast necropolis of Highgate. By the time we passed the entrance of the western cemetery night was falling so quickly that I could hardly make out the imposing mock Tudor gateway, flanked by Gothic-turreted chapels in black and grey brick, reminding me more of a prison than a resting place for the dead, who were unlikely to attempt a mass escape this side of Judgement Day.

We turned off the main thoroughfare and down a series of increasingly quieter lanes, which would doubtless be leafy in summer but were now bordered by the skeletons of plane trees and chestnuts, little more than angular shadows in the shadows. There were no streetlights here and the only illumination came from our twin front lamps, the crescent moon and the occasional glow from a villa where a curtain had not yet been closed.

Droplets of rain were pattering on the glass now.

We turned right down a side street, then right again and round a long curve and right again, and I had a feeling we were travelling in a circle, but then we took two left turns, by which time it was so dark I wondered how the driver could see where he was going. Our horse slowed, cautiously feeling her way as we rattled along the cobblestoned roads. I tried to work out our direction as we made a few more turns, but the moon was hidden now behind the heavy clouds and I was just realizing what a fool I had been to enter a vehicle at the invitation of a stranger when we stopped.

The night was black as a cat by now, but the coachman sounded his horn four times and all at once the scene to the left of me was transformed. A series of lamp posts lit up, starting at an open iron gate and leading either side of a long gravelled path up to a house. And a moment later the house itself burst into light from every window in the same brilliant white glow.

The coachman scrambled down, opened the door and pulled down the steps for me. 'Saturn Villa,' he proclaimed proudly. 'If you will allow me, miss.' He proffered his arm and helped me on to the pavement where I gazed in amazement at the prospect before me. 'Mr Travers Smyth likes to surprise his guests.'

'He has certainly done that.' It was as though a pocket of day had opened in the garden and I saw the copper beeches and rhododendrons and raked lawns as clearly as if it were early morning. And I was not the only one taken unawares for a tawny owl swooped startled over my head as we passed under an ancient horse-chestnut tree.

Saturn Villa was a three-storey building, a big house with an unfussy brick front and – especially with its illumination – a welcoming appearance. The driver took my bag from the luggage box at the back and I followed him, looking all about me like a child in fairyland. It certainly did not look like the residence of a man who would need to beg from me.

We climbed two semicircular steps to the white-painted entrance.

'Allow me, miss.' He pressed a polished brass button and immediately a shrill bell sounded inside the building, followed shortly by the door being opened by a young valet in red tails.

'Miss Middleton to see Mr Travers Smyth,' I told him and his solemn face cracked into a boyish grin.

'Oh yes, miss, please come in.' His hair was parted in the middle and so black that, if he had not been so young, I would have thought that he dyed it.

The hall was a high-ceilinged square with a pink-veined marble floor and pillars and white-plastered walls. The middle of the hall was dominated by a life-sized statue on a tall plinth – a heavily bearded man covered only by a cloth over his loins and holding a sickle in one hand, the other being raised, palm upwards above his head. I did not need Sidney Grice to deduce that this was the god Saturn.

The sculpture was backed by a wide stone staircase, the whole area awash in light. A glass-fronted cupboard had been built into the wall and was stuffed with Oriental bric-a-brac.

The valet stepped smartly to a double walnut door and parted the leaves with his white-gloved hands to announce me, barely having time to finish before a high voice called cheerily, 'Send her in, Colwyn. Send her in.'

Colwyn stood back and to one side. Something flitted through my mind but I shook it away and went into the room.

6

Sherry and the Magpie

I FOUND MYSELF in an oak-panelled library with glass-fronted bookcases built on to every wall.

'Welcome. Welcome.'

And I saw that the greeting came from an elderly man at the top of lofty wheeled library steps. He had a big red leather book in one hand and let go of the rail to wave with the other, leaning towards me at an alarming angle as he did so. The steps wobbled and I hurried towards him round the many bookracks and small tables that were dotted everywhere. I could not catch him if he fell from such a height but at least I could try to steady his perch.

'Miss Middleton, Miss Middleton,' the man greeted me merrily as he scrambled down with an agility which would have done credit to a metropolitan fireman. He took my hand and pumped it vigorously. 'How very, very good of you to come so soon, so soon.'

'I hope I am not inconveniencing you.'

'Not in the least, the least.' He was a tiny man, slightly bent, with a little face upturned to me, topped by a mass of thinning, wiry ginger hair that erupted from under a vermillion smoking cap embroidered in gold thread, all bordered in a frizz of whiskers ending in a long, wispy goatee. His lips were wide but thin and clean-shaven, below a narrow nose ending between big sunken eyes made all the larger by thick-lensed, wire-framed spectacles. He reminded me so much of a capuchin monkey that

I had to resist an urge to reach out and stroke his head. 'I must show you this book.' He waved it over his head like a victory flag. 'But first we will have sherry, yes, sherry.' All the time he was talking he was jigging about excitedly. 'I am so pleased to meet you, dear lady.'

'Please call me March, Mr Travers Smyth.'

His face fell. 'But I cannot do that, dear lady, unless you agree to call me Uncle Tolly. I do so hope you will.' He peered up at me like a child begging for a sherbet.

'Uncle Tolly,' I said and he rubbed his hands.

'Capital, capital. We shall be the very best of friends, March. I feel it already.' He put his head sideways. 'Do you feel it too? Please say you do, but only if it is the truth.'

There was a raised mole on his left temple, almost black, and the shape and size of a broad bean.

'You have made me feel very welcome.' I laughed. 'I have never had such a dramatic greeting.'

He furrowed his brow. 'My climbing down a ladder? I am so sorry if I unsettled you.'

'I meant the lighting.'

Uncle Tolly chortled. 'Oh yes. It is powered by,' his voice dropped conspiratorially, 'something called electricity.'

'I have seen electrical lighting before,' I said, 'but never in such quantity or brightness.'

'Ah!' He hopped from one foot to the other. 'These are the new Swan Incandescent lamps.'

'But are you not worried your house will catch fire?'

'Oh no. The conducting wires are all thickly insulated in something else called gutta percha but,' Uncle Tolly looked mortified, 'if you are concerned for your safety, I shall have the generators disconnected and light the mantles or, if you are affrighted by the thought of igniting potentially explosive gases, I shall instruct the servants to bring out the old oil lamps. Shall I do it now?'

'Please do not trouble.'

Uncle Tolly slapped his forehead. 'Oh, March – you are sure I may call you that?' I nodded and he continued. 'But I am forgetting myself. I promised you sherry and what have you had thus far? Not a drop nor a drizzle.' He rushed to the sideboard where a silver tray stood and took the stopper out of a long-necked decanter to pour two drinks, holding out a tulip-shaped glass to me and raising his own in a toast. 'Your ever so very good health, March.'

'And yours, Uncle Tolly.' It was strange to have lived two decades without having used that title before. I sipped my sherry. It was a little sweet for my taste but welcome nonetheless. 'It is so nice to find I have a living relative.' I hesitated and all at once he was filled with concern.

'But what is it? You are troubled, dear March. Have I managed to upset you already? Oh, I am such a rough-and-ready fellow, so set in my bachelor ways indeed that I have forgotten how to behave in feminine company. If I have offended you…'

I raised my hand. 'Oh no, quite the reverse. It is just… You are quite sure we are related?'

He sighed with relief. 'Oh no, dear March. I am not quite sure of it at all.'

'But—'

'I am absolutely positive.' His big eyes glittered. 'Yes, positive is the very actual word. That is why I was fetching that book when you so delightfully arrived. It is an account of the life of Samuel Travers Smyth, my grandfather and your great-grandfather, and which you may care to borrow.' He scratched under the rim of his smoking cap. 'But there again, you might not. He did little of interest to anyone other than himself and sometimes, I suspect, not even that. Still…' His feet performed a complicated shuffle. 'He is the river from which the streams of our lives have sprung. Oh, but what am I thinking of now?' Uncle Tolly swiped his brow with the ball of his hand. 'I have kept you standing whilst I chatter away like a stimulated magpie.' He guided me to a deep armchair, and we sat facing each other on opposite sides of a low table before a crackling fire.

I placed the book down. It left a fusty smell on my fingers.

'I know so little about my family,' I said and he crossed his hands over his middle.

'I am afraid to say that I am all there is to know.'

'You wrote that you are my father's cousin.'

'Do finish your sherry, dear March.' He raised his glass. 'And then I shall tell you who we are, and why I was so anxious to see you.'

7

The Donkey and the Quill

UNCLE TOLLY TOSSED down his sherry and I followed suit.

'Nectar of the gods.' He jumped to his feet and rushed to a large map table on the other side of the room near the door. 'Come, my dear lady.' I hurried to join him. 'Here we are.' He unrolled a sheet of yellowed paper, holding it down with a brass compass and an inkwell as paperweights at each end. 'The Travers Smyth family tree all the way from Great-Great-Great-Great-Grandfather Adam...' He prodded the top. 'To...' He ran his finger down. 'That handsome young fellow, Ptolemy Hercules Arbuthnot Travers Smyth, who has the honour of standing here before you today. I will set that aside for the time being.' He was bringing out other documents, some in rolls tied with red ribbon, some unfolded certificates. 'And here we have the Middleton family tree. Starting at the bottom...' Again he traced his words. 'We have you, March Lillian Constance Middleton; your father, Colonel Geoffrey Charles Pemberton Middleton, who married Constance Elsie Stopforth, your mother, in November 1861. Goodness, I believe this calls for another sherry, yes.' He fetched the decanter and recharged our glasses, and while I sipped mine he continued.

'Giles Middleton over here,' he prodded the name, 'had a second son, Gervaise, who married Beryl, my mother. And so you will see that, though I have asked you to call me Uncle, in view of the disparity in our ages, I am in fact your second cousin, Tolly.' He took a breath.

'Then I am very happy that you discovered me.' I gazed at the unfamiliar names and tried to make sense of the countless births and marriages, deaths and remarriages and progeny.

'I have a confession to make, March.' Uncle Tolly wiggled his fingers through his beard. 'I had a selfish reason for inviting you here today and I hope you will manage to forgive me for it. You see,' he teased the strands apart, 'I wished to put you to the test. Am I a terrible man?'

'That depends on how you plan to test me.'

'I am profoundly ashamed to disclose,' Uncle Tolly told me coyly, 'that I have already done so. I wanted to discover if I liked you and I am delighted to declare that I find I like you very much indeed.' He beamed before repeating it. 'Indeed. I am a mortal man, March, and no longer in the full flush of...' His voice trailed away before he regathered his mental thread. 'I have accumulated a considerable fortune in the course of my life – considerable – and nothing would give me greater pleasure than for you to say that I might leave it to you.'

I shifted uncomfortably. 'That is very good of you but—'

'Witnesses.' Uncle Tolly rubbed his hands. 'We need witnesses.' He pressed a brass button on the wall.

'You hardly know me,' I protested, but he was racing across the room and pulling open several drawers behind his desk, crying, 'Aha.' Then he rushed back with a sheaf of blank paper.

'We are flesh and blood, March, and that is enough for me.'

'But, Uncle Tolly, we have only just met.'

The maid came into the room. She was a tall girl and slim, with masses of beautiful flaxen hair piled under her starched white hat, but her face was marred by a cleft in her upper lip so wide that an upper left incisor jutted through it.

'Fetch Colwyn, Annie,' her employer instructed. 'We need him immediately.'

Annie left and Uncle Tolly hopped about excitedly. 'A pen. We shall require a pen.' He scurried back to his desk and tossed a stack of documents on to the floor. 'A pen.' He held it aloft triumphantly, an old-fashioned goose quill, as he skipped back. 'Ink.'

'You have an inkwell here.' I moved an ostrich egg out of the way. 'But what exactly are you going to do with it?'

'Why, nothing.' Uncle Tolly looked blank. 'It is you who will be using it, dear lady.'

Annie returned with a puzzled Colwyn.

'Now,' their employer cried, 'I need to ask you both an extraordinary favour.' He crooked his first finger in front of his eye. 'I want you to witness two important documents.' He dabbed his finger towards each of the servants in turn.

'Certainly, sir.' Colwyn spoke for them both.

'But where are the documents, sir?' Annie asked.

'They are in my mind,' her employer declared. 'But the wonderful Miss Middleton will transfer them from there on to pristine leaves of paper by a process known in commercial circles as dictation. If you would be so kind, my dear.' He handed me the pen. I took it uncertainly and dipped the tip into the well. 'To whom it may concern,' he declaimed and I scribbled furiously. 'I, Ptolemy Hercules Arbuthnot Travers Smyth…' He paused while I redipped the pen and caught up. The ink was very thick and tinted green. 'Being of sound mind,' he added as Annie stifled a snigger, and he continued unabashed, 'do hereby bequeath all my worldly goods to my second cousin, March Lillian—'

'Uncle Tolly,' I broke in, 'I really cannot continue with this. There must be a friend or worthy cause more deserving than me.'

But Uncle Tolly was not to be diverted. 'Please continue for we are nearly done… Middleton.'

I wrote my name reluctantly, then said, 'I cannot be a party to this.'

Uncle Tolly's lips whitened and he tugged firmly at his goatee. 'I have a solution,' he announced at last. 'If you do not agree to the terms of my will I shall leave all I own to the most undesirable cause I can think of.' He marched on the spot. 'I have it – the

Society for the Reintroduction of Slavery. I shall leave everything to that foul institution – cross my heart and hope to be unwell.'

I thought about it. 'Very well. I shall accept your bequest, but every penny shall go towards alleviating poverty in the East End.'

The blood flowed back into Uncle Tolly's lips and he reached out as if to embrace us all. 'Capital, capital,' he declared and, taking the quill from my grasp, placed his exuberant signature on his testament. 'Now you, Colwyn.'

His footman wrote his name fluently, dipped the pen and handed it to Annie, who took it in her fist, bit her extruded tongue, wrinkled her brow and printed carefully underneath.

'You said there were two documents,' I reminded Uncle Tolly and he threw out his arms, nearly striking Annie in the middle. She jumped back.

'It is a small thing,' he said, 'but important to me and concerns Jennifer.'

'Jennifer is a donkey,' Colwyn explained. There was something about the way he stressed his words that made me smile.

'Not just a donkey,' Uncle Tolly exclaimed. 'Jennifer is family. She lives in a paddock nearby and I visit her at least three times a day.'

'More like ten,' Annie teased.

Uncle Tolly's face fell. 'But she is getting old now and I fear that, if I should die, she will pine for me or that she will become ill and not receive the treatment she deserves.'

'I have no room for a donkey,' I told him. 'But I can promise to pay for her care.'

'Oh, I was so hoping you would say that.' Uncle Tolly blinked a teardrop. 'But we must make it legal. I should hate anyone to imagine that you have no rights or duty towards her. Perhaps you could write this second document too, dear March, if your wrist is not too cramped.'

'I can manage quite well,' I told him and took his dictation again.

'I, March Middleton, do hereby swear to ensure that Jennifer, Ptolemy Travers Smyth's donkey, is cared for but, if she should be suffering incurably, I will pay one hundred pounds to have her killed humanely and her body buried in her paddock under a small memorial slab of granite.'

I signed my name and the servants left after witnessing it, and Uncle Tolly blotted both documents with great care.

'Hurrah,' he cried and with a sweep of his hand toppled the inkwell, spilling its contents over his chart. He whipped out an enormous yellow handkerchief. 'Oh my goodness!'

'Do not rub it,' I warned, but I was too late. In a quick scrubbing motion he had managed to smear a large area of paper, rendering its contents illegible.

'Oh dear, oh dear, oh dear,' he flapped. 'What shall I do? What can I do? I cannot un-rub it. Oh, what an oaf I am. I hope I did not get any on your beautiful dress.'

I reassured him that I was all right. 'Perhaps we should leave the chart to dry and see how bad the damage is later,' I suggested.

'Perhaps,' he echoed so unhappily that I was afraid he might burst into tears. His big brown eyes were brimming and I did not have the heart to point out that he had ink all over his hand and on his shirt.

The door opened.

'Dinner is ready, sir,' Colwyn announced and Uncle Tolly perked up.

'Capital, capital.' He rubbed his hands in a valiant effort at cheerfulness. 'There is not a problem in the world that is not improved by a good meal.'

'Except perhaps indigestion,' I suggested and he managed a smile.

8

Guns and Pickles

THERE WAS A vast mahogany table in the dining room with twenty chairs along each of the long sides, but it had only been set at one end.

'It is a cold collation, I am terrified to confess.' Uncle Tolly guided me to the sideboard. There were rows of plates piled with carved ham, beef and mutton; a whole salmon, glazed and decorated with slices of cucumber; terrines; a dish of potato salad; a bowl of mustard. 'Do help yourself.'

'There is enough here to feed a brigade,' I said and he put his fingers to his mouth.

'Oh dear, oh dear. The truth is I am unused to entertaining.' He nipped his lower lip. 'And now I have made a complete hodgepodge of everything.'

'No, really.' He was so little and lost that I wanted to go over and cuddle him. 'This is lovely. I only mean I hope you will not be insulted if I cannot do it justice.'

'My dear March,' Uncle Tolly took a white linen napkin from the tray, 'your very presence does it justice.' He wiped the outer corners of his eyes. 'Do try some of my pickles. I make them myself… myself.'

I took a selection of food and we sat facing each other under a crystal chandelier glittering with a dozen electrical bulbs. There was a carafe of deep red wine at my side.

'Shall I pour?'

'Would you mind?' He blinked anxiously. 'Do you mind? Only I have had so little success with it in the past. I always end up spilling it over the tablecloth and then Annie gets cross and scolds me.'

'Your maid tells you off?' I could see his problem. The carafe was very heavy and the stem too thin to afford a good grip, but I managed to fill our glasses without mishap.

Uncle Tolly protruded his lower lip. 'She makes me scrub it up.'

'But why do you not dismiss her?'

'Because,' he said simply, 'she tells me I must not think of it.' And we ate for a while without conversation.

'That,' Uncle Tolly indicated over his shoulder to the portrait of a scowling wedge-faced woman over the merrily crackling fire,' is Great-Aunt Matilda.' He giggled. 'I believe she was even fiercer than she looks.'

'You have such a beautiful house. Did you build it yourself?' I asked and he twisted his lips thoughtfully.

'Yes,' he said, 'and no. I designed everything from the roof tiles to the cellar floor but other men carried the bricks and placed them one upon the other, and then another upon the other and so on and so forth, until we had run out of bricks, except for three thousand and twenty with which we built the base of a greenhouse in the back garden.'

I unfolded my napkin. 'How long have you lived here?'

'I was born here.' He spooned a hill of mustard on to his plate. 'Or on this site, for I had the old house pulled all the way down – before this house was built, of course. So I have always regarded it as my home, but I have been abroad so much that I cannot truly say that I have lived anywhere for long.'

'Where have you been?' I asked.

'China mainly.' He sawed at a thick slab of tongue. 'Yes, China. I spent a great deal of time in Hong Kong and some in Peking. The Empress Dowager Cixi was very keen to purchase modern British weapons to maintain law and order and the borders of her son's vast realms.' He put down his knife. 'Oh, I am sorry, March. Does that seem too terrible to you?'

I took a sip of wine. It made such a change to be able to consume meat and alcohol in company when my guardian forbade both. 'It is not that,' I said. 'Forgive me, but you seem so gentle a man for such a brutal trade.'

Uncle Tolly blinked rapidly. 'Oh but March, if you had seen some of the terrible wounds caused by pikes and swords, you would regard rifles and explosives as much kinder options.' His empty fork hovered in mid-air.

I saw a man without a face. It had been blown to a pulp by a musket ball at close range. I see it in my dreams and it haunts my waking hours.

'I should not judge you too harshly,' I admitted, 'for a part of my income comes from my late father's investments in armaments.'

My host raised his eyebrows quizzically. 'What a strange coincidence. May I ask which field you are involved in?'

I swallowed a pickled gherkin and hastily washed the flavour away. It was far too bitter and acidic for me. 'It is a company called Swandale's Chemicals. They started by making pesticides, which my father thought very worthwhile after witnessing the devastation and famine caused by locusts. Unfortunately, they did not have much success with that and moved on to other things. The bulk of the business in Parbold was closed down, but there is a small subsidiary which makes a constituent for cordite, I think. I am not happy with that but I cannot dispose of my shares until I reach the age of twenty-five.'

'Swandale's,' Uncle Tolly repeated thoughtfully. 'I have heard of them. They made some acidic bombs as I recall.'

'Something like that,' I agreed and he shuddered.

'How ghastly,' he said. 'I wonder…' But his voice began to reverberate and I was lost for a moment in the unhappiness of his eyes and the images taking form between us.

9

Pigs and Portholes

THERE WAS A row of portholes along the far wall of the meeting room. They were so high that I had to stand on a wooden crate to see through one, my breath misting the thick glass. I found myself looking down about ten feet into a white tiled laboratory where the gas mantles had been turned off, leaving it lit by only the portholes on the outer walls and four closed skylights.

There was a large iron-barred cage in the middle of the laboratory, containing eight pigs. I counted them, black-and-white saddlebacks contentedly chewing turnips from a trough or resting in the sun streaming through the glass. We watched them idly. One was scratching her side on a post with as great an expression of bliss as a sow is capable of.

Jonathon Pillow was standing near me. He was the chief scientist and the gas was the child of his inventiveness. His waistcoat was splashed with bleach and his hands discoloured by chemical spills. There were two brass levers in front of him at waist level. He pulled the left one down.

The pigs hardly glanced over as a metal hammer rose and fell and one of two jars suspended from the ceiling shattered. A liquid sprayed out of it over a weaner. The weaner screamed. The other pigs looked up in concern. A yellow cloud rose from the floor, mushrooming rapidly to surround them in a thick fog. And all at once they were squealing – long grating screeches, almost *human, disintegrating into choking coughs. Some of them tried to run away. One crashed blindly, shrieking, into the bars and two into each other, and a piglet was crushed beneath its tumbling mother. But none of them managed more than a few staggering steps before they collapsed, desperate for breath like old consumptive men, wheezing bloody mucous froth from their snouts and gaping mouths. They went into convulsions, legs kicking, bodies thrashing, muscles knotting in violent spasms that eased into twitches before relaxing into the final limpness of death.*

'Bravo,' Horace Swandale crowed. 'We could have killed a hundred times as many with that one bottle... probably a thousand. It will take a while to ventilate the area.'

The skylights and outer portholes were being opened. I climbed down and we went from the windows. Glasses were produced from a tall cupboard and there were brandies and sodas all round and I had a lukewarm lemonade. I leaned against a steel support column.

Major Gregory was there. Normally he would have made a fuss of me, but he looked gaunt that morning and kept in the background, sitting quietly at the big oval conference table after everyone else had quit it.

Jonathon Pillow had watched the proceedings with great satisfaction. He checked his stopwatch. 'One minute forty-five seconds from release to complete immobilization.'

Horace Swandale applauded. 'Imagine what a carboy filled with sulphur mustards could do just by smashing it on the deck of an enemy ship!' He was clapping his own words now. 'The gas is heavier than air and would sink down through the decks, poisoning the entire crew in moments. What price the heaviest ironclad then, eh, Colonel Middleton? Britannia could continue to rule the waves without ever firing another shot.'

My father was quiet as we waited for the mist to clear and the area to be pronounced safe. He looked at me and I inclined my head. I was afraid of what I would see, but even more afraid to let him see it without me.

'Bring the drinks,' Horace Swandale instructed a clerk, as if we were passing through for dinner.

The door into the laboratory opened and one of the workers provided us with wet scarves to clamp over our mouths and noses. His face was burnt as if by a fire and his eyes bloodshot and streaming. We went down a flight of steps. It was bitterly cold despite a huge stove glowing in the corner and there was still a strong, sharp smell of horseradish in the room, mingled with the stench of fresh excrement. For perhaps five minutes we gazed at the sad distorted carcasses, their skins blistered into weeping sores. Their mouths were agape and clogged with purple-black slimy spume. Their eyes were eroded and white with terror. Excrement oozed over the floor.

'Never know when we'll be at war with the Frenchies again,' Horace Swandale pronounced. 'But with a fleet of balloons over Paris you could wipe out the entire population in an afternoon. And the beauty of it is not a building would be destroyed, not a sculpture or painting damaged. Once the fog had lifted we could walk in and take their capital undisturbed.'

My father changed his spectacles and leafed through a sheaf of documents on a workbench. 'Are these your notes?'

And Jonathon Pillow rushed over. 'Be careful, Colonel. That is my only copy of the formulae.'

'Excellent.' My father swept them up.

'What are you doing?' Jonathon Pillow hovered anxiously.

My father marched to the stove and picked up a fire iron. 'Putting a stop to this... obscenity.' He knocked the latch up.

'Give me those back,' Jonathon Pillow cried. 'I must complete my work.'

But my father smiled grimly. 'Over my dead body,' he said – a phrase he used often and I hated it – and pulled on the big double doors of the stove. At that the gates of hell might have opened to spew out a demon. Jonathon Pillow became a man possessed. He hurled himself at my father, white with fury, lips pulled back in a slavering snarl. My father was a powerfully built man but he was taken by surprise by the suddenness and venom of the attack. He pitched forwards, his spectacles flying off into the burning coals and bouncing out again, one lens smashed, the papers scattering over the boarded floor as Pillow clawed at my father's face, gibbering incoherent filth and clutching at his throat.

I grabbed a whisky bottle from the clerk and ran to help, but Gregory and four other men dragged the attacker, spitting and cursing, off my father.

'I am all right,' my father said a little shakily. 'Pick up the papers, March.'

My father's collar was ripped off and his cheek bleeding. He took the bottle from me and had a long draught while I scooped them up – sheet upon sheet crammed with figures and diagrams – and handed them to him.

'No, damn you, no!' Jonathon Pillow struggled and kicked at those who restrained him.

It was then that Major Gregory came forward. He spoke quietly – I made out 'sleep on it' – and my father said, 'Very well,' and crossed to the safe in the wall, whirring the dial of the combination lock clockwise and anti-clockwise.

'We shall discuss this at the next board meeting,' he announced and deposited the documents inside. Only he and Mr Swandale knew the numbers for that lock.

There was a terrible shriek and for a moment I thought that another pig was being slaughtered. But it was Jonathon Pillow being dragged from the room.

10

Meat, Charles Dickens and Murder

THE REVERBERATIONS STOPPED and the images vanished, as if a magic lantern had been switched off, and I was aware that my relative was looking at me expectantly.

'I am sorry,' I said. 'I was daydreaming.'

'A life without dreams is not a life,' he said a little fuzzily.

The meat lay heavy in my stomach. It was a long time since I had eaten so much of it in a day.

'Why have I never heard of you?' I asked and Uncle Tolly made a wry face.

He put down his cutlery. 'I do not know how much you have been told of your mother.' His voice became clear again.

'Very little,' I said. 'But I am anxious to learn more.'

Uncle Tolly ran his fingers through his whiskers. 'Constance Stopforth was the most wonderful woman I ever met.' He stopped as if that were all I needed to know before repeating, 'Ever.'

'I have one picture of her,' I told him, 'and my father said it was a good likeness.' I unfastened the chain from behind my neck and we both half stood as I passed him the locket. We sat back and Uncle Tolly's hand trembled as he pressed the catch to spring open the lid.

'Gracious,' he murmured, holding it up to the light. 'It is a very good likeness, March, very good indeed.' He placed the locket still open on the table.

'I believe it was painted for her eighteenth birthday,' I said, and a wistfulness came over him.

'How well I remember that occasion.' His fingertips stroked a quarter of an inch above the picture. 'Lord, how she glittered.'

'The trouble is that, whilst the portrait may be a good reminder for those who knew her, it can never bring her to life for me,' I mused. 'It does not tell me how she spoke or moved or what it felt like to be hugged by her.'

'Dear March.' Uncle Tolly's pupils contracted in the bright lights. 'I cannot hope to do justice to your mother. She was a famous beauty and at least a dozen men had approached her father for permission to court her. She rejected any that he had not agreed to. She stood out in a room in a way that only the rich, famous and titled do normally – such poise, such sparkle. She had a quick wit too. Why, once, when Mr Dickens was bullying his hostess at a party, your mother told him it was a wonder Oliver, Nell and Pip had not died from blandness before they had the chance to be suffocated by the weight of coincidences heaped upon them. I have never seen such an inflated man deflated so quickly.'

I laughed. 'I wish I was more like her.'

Uncle Tolly gazed at me. 'Great beauty is a curse,' he told me. 'Be grateful that you are not afflicted.'

'I must be very blessed indeed,' I said, and he clamped a hand over his mouth and nose in horror.

'Oh, my dear March, I did not mean—'

But I raised my hand. 'Please,' I said. 'I know I am no society beauty and I am not sure that I would want to be. You are probably right and I should be grateful.'

'Oh my gracious me – gracious is not too strong a word, is it?' Uncle Tolly fluttered about. 'Have some more of this.' He picked up the dish of pickles at random and held it under my chin, and I took another slice of gherkin reluctantly so as not to hurt his feelings.

The dish tipped alarmingly. 'Mind you do not spill vinegar on her,' I cried. Uncle Tolly put the pickles carefully aside and clipped the locket shut, and I took it back.

'You have not told me your story yet,' I reminded him.

'It is one that does me little credit,' he said. 'You see, I behaved rather badly with your mother, March. I was always devoted to her and she was very kind to me, and I am afraid I took her generosity of heart as a reciprocation of my feelings. I – and I shudder to recall this now – took it upon myself, without even consulting her father, to press my suit.' Uncle Tolly blushed. 'She was very nice and listened politely, but she had the grace to interrupt before I made a complete ass of myself and explained that, whilst she was very fond of me and hoped we should always be friends, she had an understanding with an Oxford undergraduate that once he took his degree she would ask her father to look kindly upon his approach.' Uncle Tolly finished his wine and I refilled it for him, dripping a little on the white cloth. He slid a plate of ham over the stain and whispered, 'Perhaps Annie will not notice if I turn the lights off.'

'And did you stay friends?' I asked.

He lifted his glass a few inches and gazed deep into the ruby darkness of its contents. 'I never saw her again.' He sighed. 'You see, March, there is no end to my asininity. In the shock of my rejection I sought affection with another young lady, the daughter of a high court judge. It was all perfectly innocent, but she pretended to believe that we were betrothed and told several of her friends so. When I tried to put matters right she sued me for breach of promise and, with her father's connections, I was ruined. I fled the country that very day on the first booking available – a schooner to Buenos Aires – and worked my way up to Boston where I found myself working in a theatre for three years, before I realized that the world of entertainment held no place for me. I sold my share in the business to an Irish woman and moved on again.'

'You have seen a great deal of the world,' I remarked enviously.

'A great deal too much… too much.' Uncle Tolly fell into a reverie.

'Do you know what happened to the undergraduate?' I asked and he put his glass down.

'I only know,' he took up a fork, 'what an old friend wrote to tell me two years later, that your father saved your mother's life – though I do not know how – took her home that day, spoke to her father, proposed, and they were married within the month. The rest you know.' Uncle Tolly trembled. 'A terrible, terrible loss. Your father, I believe, was inconsolable.'

'Even by me,' I whispered, and Uncle Tolly harpooned a slice of ham with his fork.

'My dear child,' he said so gently that I forgot to take offence, 'you must be absolutely exhausted.'

'It has been a long day,' I agreed.

'So thoughtless of me,' Uncle Tolly said. 'So very thoughtless.' He jumped up. 'Come, March. I shall show you to your room.' He folded his napkin. 'But first I must acquaint you with the measures I have taken to prevent us,' he rolled the napkin into a silver ring, 'from being murdered.'

11

The Night Ritual

I WAS ABOUT to laugh when I saw that Uncle Tolly's expression was deadly serious.

'Are you expecting us to be murdered?' I asked, and he swivelled from side to side as if not certain that we were alone.

'I am not expecting you to be murdered, dear March,' he replied. 'Or I should never have invited you to stay under my roof, indeed I would not, indeed.'

He rose from the table and I followed him out into the hall.

'But you think you might be killed?'

Uncle Tolly chuckled. 'I do not think it. I have no doubt about it – no doubt at all.' He opened a small oak cupboard on the wall and took a bunch of keys off a hook.

'But why and by whom?'

'Two very good questions.' He inserted a key to lock the dining-room door. 'Very good questions indeed, and I only wish I had the answers. There is a secret door in the panelling, leading into a passage which goes down to the kitchen so that the servants can clear the table without entering the body of the house. The only other means of ingress is now secured.' We crossed the hall and went down a short passageway to a green-painted door, which Uncle Tolly locked with a larger key.

'Do you not trust your own servants?'

Uncle Tolly cocked his head, as if listening, before he whispered, 'With my life. Otherwise I would have my food tasted and a bodyguard.' We went to the front door, which he locked and bolted top and bottom. 'All the windows are closed with little padlocks,' he told me, 'but in case of fire there are keys in the onyx boxes on almost every window ledge. Allow me to show you to your room.' I was more tired than I thought, for the sweeping stairs were hard work and I stumbled as we reached the half-landing. 'My dear child, I fear I have overtaxed you with my chatter-chatter-chatter.'

'More likely your excellent sherry and wine,' I mumbled, for I felt quite strongly affected now.

'Oh dear me.' Uncle Tolly took my arm. 'Allow me.' He helped me up the last steps and on to a big, square, oak-floored corridor. The side facing us had windows from floor to ceiling and Uncle Tolly drew my attention to it. 'There is a fine view of the cemetery on a good day.' The left and right sides had four doors, each painted different pastel colours. 'Yours is the pink room,' he told me. 'I do hope it is to your liking.'

He opened the first door on the right and stood back.

'Thank you,' I said. 'It is lovely.' And indeed it was. There was a double bed with a floral counterpane and crisp white sheets, and the walls were papered with intertwined rose patterns. It was so clever how they flickered.

'I feel…'

He tightened his grip to steady me as the room swung towards us.

'You will be all right.' The rest of his words were lost in the roar and rush of black air and the nothingness that followed my fall.

12

The Pier and the Smoke

ON MANY SUMMER holidays we went to Southport. It was only fourteen miles away but still a great treat; even the train journey from Parbold was a cause for some excitement.

We always stayed at the Clifton Hotel, overlooking the promenade and beyond that to the sea. From my bedroom window I could watch the pleasure steamers dock at the end of the pier and the visitors disembark in their best summer clothes and make their way into town.

One year we went in the company of Major Gregory and his son, Barney, who was three years older than me. I had adored Barney ever since he had rescued Jumble, a mongrel puppy, for me from the canal, and I would follow Barney for miles on the endless golden beach and rolling sand dunes. Despite our age difference he always allowed me to join in his games and defended me when other boys mocked.

Bernard Gregory had been a close friend of my father's since they were cadets together at Sandhurst. When I was very small I had mispronounced his name and he had been so amused that he adopted 'Groggy' as his nickname.

Mrs Gregory did not come. She was at home with her daughter, Daisy, who was suffering from a nervous stomach.

On the second evening we all went to a show at the Pavilion. There were singers and dancers, acrobats and jugglers, and we *were all having a wonderful time until the magician came along. He began entertainingly enough, taking biscuits from behind volunteers' ears and producing a puppy from inside a newspaper, but then he made himself disappear. He walked round the back of his table of tricks and vanished. I still do not know how he did it and I am not sure I want to – some things should always be magical – but suddenly there was a flash and a puff and the whole stage began to fill with yellow smoke.*

The audience roared in amusement and applauded, but all I could hear were the wild frothing squeals of pigs and as the magician reappeared, running through the acrid fumes, I scrambled out of my seat, clambered over two indignant old ladies and fled.

I was gasping for breath when I made it through the foyer and on to the foot of the pier, and the seagulls' shrieks did nothing to calm me down. I put my hands over my ears but that never does any good. And then I felt a hand on my arm.

'It is all right, Marchy,' Barney said. 'It was only a trick.'

'I know.' How could I explain? At least I saw that he was not mocking me as most boys of his age would have. Barney was always protective of me and his little sister, Daisy. She was a proper girl, though, and never joined in our rough-and-tumble games.

'Thank you for caring for her, Barney,' my father said. He was probably less blithe about scrambling over people's knees and had taken a while to join us.

'I shall always care for March,' Barney vowed as a seagull swooped just over our heads. 'When we are old enough, I shall ask you for her hand.'

My father chuckled and patted Barney on the back. 'You go in and enjoy the rest of the show.'

I leaned against the railings, watching the ponies pull the shrimping wagons out into the ruffled sea.

'I am sorry,' my father said at last. The wind blew his hair back and mine over my face. 'I should never have taken you to

that demonstration. I thought they would just fall asleep.' His shoulders dropped. 'That is what I was led to believe.'

From the corner of my eye I saw Barney go inside.

'Perhaps having me there helped you to see how horrid it was,' I said. 'I am glad if it did.'

'Damned fool,' he grunted and I knew he meant himself.

He was a wise man and foolish, and the finest man I knew.

*

The next day I was taken to meet the magician. He was a kindly soul and gave me two bottles of the liquid that he used to make the smoke.

'Play with zem when you get 'ome,' he invited me in an unconvincing French accent. 'It will 'elp you be not afraid.'

I took the bottles back to The Grange and hid them in the cellar, terrified that they would explode and fill the house with fumes. My father said he would get rid of them.

13

Solid Shadows and White Slave Traffickers

SOMETHING BUMPED.

I did not open my eyes at first. The bed was so comfortable and the pillows so soft. But where was I? Not in my childhood bedroom at the top of Parbold Hill where the mattress sagged in the middle and the boards creaked like a ship when I shifted, and I had left it, I remembered, after my father died. Not in 125 Gower Street where the mattress was hard and the throb of the city never ceased. Not in India under mosquito netting with the suffocating heat and the bugle blowing reveille.

I opened my eyes. A flame ran along the top of a broad wick in the smoky glass chimney of an oil lamp and I did not recognize the room, but the paper seemed familiar with its bright pink roses and criss-crossing lines of leaves. I lay and studied it and tried to remember.

I was thirsty and there was a washstand against the wall with a floral jug. I struggled to sit up but my limbs were weak and numb, and so I rolled to the side and managed to swing my legs over the edge. How much had I had to drink? Had I had anything to drink? I managed to push myself up and waited for the room to stop spinning in all three dimensions. It took a long time and I thought at one stage that I would vomit.

It was then I realized that I had been lying on top of the eiderdown. I did not remember getting undressed. Was I was still fully clothed with my boots on?

How cross my father had been when I did that after a ladies' night in the officers' mess. We were supposed to be ruling India by dint of our moral superiority. What kind of example was I setting the natives who so loved and admired us? But I had learned enough Hindi to know what lay behind the bows and smiles of those we so benevolently oppressed.

Cautiously I lowered my feet to the ground and realized that they were bare and that I had my nightdress on.

First and foremost I needed to slake my thirst. I hauled myself to a standing position, leaning heavily on the side table, nearly tipping it over with my weight and only just managing to catch the lamp as it slid towards the edge. I let go, stumbled three steps forward and grabbed a solid shadow that had loomed before me – a wardrobe. My sight was very blurred.

For a moment I forgot where I was going, but my thirst reminded me and I let go of my security and launched myself at the washstand, tumbling to my knees on the fringe of the rug just in front of it, and it flashed through my head that I was in church.

I was not sure I could get up without tipping the stand and so I reached, both hands in supplication, bringing them together until they closed on the jug. I put it on the floor but, sweeping over the cool marble top, could not find a mug. I raised the jug to my lips and tilted it. The rush of icy water over my face, into my open eyes and up my nose shocked me into choking consciousness.

I clambered to my feet. My nightdress was soaked. I took a hand towel off the hook on the side of the stand and mopped myself down as best I could. I felt a little steadier now and tipped the jug again, but more carefully, to take a long drink. The water was dusty and lay chilly in my stomach, but I felt awake enough to wonder exactly where I was. A strange bedroom was as far as I got.

I remembered tales of white-slave traffickers kidnapping girls to sell to wealthy desert sheikhs or Turkish sultans, and made an unstable rush for the door. To my relief it was not locked and, peeping out into the moonlit corridor, nobody appeared to be guarding me.

I took a breath and somebody screamed. I leaned against the doorpost, my mind tossed about and the corridor going dark as a cloud drifted over the moon, and then another scream and a voice shrill with terror.

'No... Oh no... Please, no.' And a wail of such anguish that I put my hands over my ears and cried out for pity, but I should have known better than to hope for that.

14

The Howls and the Porcelain Handle

THE HOWLS STOPPED and, as my eyes became accustomed to the dark, I saw a light creep weakly from under a door next to the end window on the opposite side of the corridor.

Please God, let this be a dream – mine or that of the person who made those terrible sounds.

I was just beginning to tell myself that I had imagined it when another scream cut my hopes to shreds. And, as I made my way towards the light, it was apparent that I was getting closer to the source of screams.

I came to the door but I did not want to open it. I knocked. 'Are you all right in there?'

I thought I heard a whimper and pressed my ear to the wood-work. A harsh exhalation.

'Have you been having a nightmare?'

Please say yes. Please open the door and say you are sorry to have disturbed me, whoever you are.

But then I heard another cry, long and shuddering. I put my hand to the porcelain handle and turned it. If only my guardian had been with me. He was a small man but strong and I had never seen him show any sign of fear. I pushed on the door, half-wishing it would be bolted, but it swung open two or three inches.

'Are you all right?'

Another whimper.

'I am coming in. Do not be afraid.'

I think I said those last words more to myself than the occupant of the room.

'Uncle Tolly,' I remembered as I stumbled in.

15

The Taste of Murder

THE ROOM WAS lit by a single gas mantle on the wall turned very low. For some reason it fascinated me, that blue-centred, deep yellow glow, not exactly pushing the night back but oozing into it until the colours leached away. I did not want to take my eyes off it and see what lay before me.

I felt the wooden shaft in my hand suddenly heavy and the sweat trickle down my breast, and my heart pounded up my neck through my ears and into my head, not drowning out but magnifying the cries.

I raised the axe and the man on the bed whimpered as it fell. I felt it judder in my hand and up my arm and felt the splatter on my face.

He was clutching a soaked sheet in his fist – as if it could protect him – and holding it to his mouth. His skull was split wide like a pomegranate after a thunderstorm, revealing the bright red seeds of his mind. I could have reached in and touched the glistening flesh within.

There was so much blood on him and on me, my arms and my nightdress, and on the walls, blacker even than the shadows. I looked at my hands, sticky with spilled life, and opened my fingers, and the axe fell heavily on to the floor and stood on its head for a long time before it toppled jerkily and more slowly than is possible, hanging, almost stopping before it landed on the floor, the impact reaching my ears in dull parcels of sound.

The man shot up... or rather the bed he lay on shot up... or rather the floor as I hit it with my shoulder. It did not hurt, though I fell like a pole, but it knocked the wind out of me. The sound boomed across the room. I curled up my legs and lay still, hugging my knees and knowing that, even if I awoke, the taste of what was happening would never leave me.

16

The Hanging Hand

SOMETHING JUMPED INSIDE me. Had I been asleep? I realized that I was wet. Something to do with a jug? My nightdress clung to me. I grabbed the end of the bed and got on to all fours like when I used to give Maudy donkey rides on my back. I savoured the memory and rose to my knees, and then it slammed into me. Uncle Tolly, his skull cracked open so wide that I could see his brain, the rippling ridges and deep meandering valleys of his mind.

He was crumpled back on the bed, half-sitting in his striped sodden nightgown, drawn back against the corner of the splattered walls, clutching the curtain in his right hand. His mouth was agape with terror and his front teeth had been smashed, presumably by the same blow that chopped off his nose and shattered his lower jaw. The top of his face looked odd, intact but hanging awkwardly. And the wetness on me and on the rucked sheets was the blood of his life.

I have seen death a hundred times and never let it destroy my judgement. What is different?

His left hand dangled by the skin from his gashed wrist. Presumably he had raised it in a hopeless attempt to defend himself.

Now I remember. It is me that makes it different.

The axe had been in my hand when Uncle Tolly cowered back. I felt the heavy metal head fall. It was no dream. The proof lay hacked before me.

17

◆━◆◆◆━◆

The First Mrs Rochester

I FORCED MYSELF to think. First I needed to get dressed. But I was covered in blood. I took the water jug from his washstand and made my way back to the room I had woken up in. I was still a bit unsteady and sploshed water on my feet. Who had undressed me and put me in my nightgown and to bed? Surely not Uncle Tolly? But there had only been the two of us in the main body of the house and the servants were locked out – or so he had told me.

I untied my gown at the neck and pulled it over my head, smearing the warm stickiness over my face. I dropped it on the Turkish rug and stepped out of it, a crumpled ring of black cotton. I poured the whole jug of water over myself, trickling it over my forehead, my shoulders, all down myself, seeing the clearness turn red and splash on to the bare boards and drip between them and through a knothole, rising as marsh mist around my ankles.

I dried myself on a towel that had been folded on a blanket box at the foot of the bed. It was stained when I had finished and I was still wet. I ripped the sheet off my bed and rubbed myself with that.

My clothes were in the wardrobe, hanging like flayed skins, and I did not want to touch them but they were soft when I did. I put them on and caught a glimpse of myself in a cheval mirror – the first Mrs Rochester newly escaped from her prison – staring

59

eyes and wild-haired. I wrenched my hair back and tied it up, but the reflection's hair still hung like kelp in a rock pool. I reached inside to rake it away. Her eye oozed cream and her lips were rotted into a black-toothed snarl.

'Murderess,' she hissed.

I leaped away and tried to calm myself. Her hair was tied up when I steeled myself to look again.

Concentrate.

Five long, slow breaths and I stepped back into the corridor. Dawn was seeping through the big windows at the end. There were pigs in the garden. I did not need to look to see them snuffling in the earth.

The end door on my side was saffron. It had two bolts. I drew them back and it opened outwards to reveal a narrow flight of uncarpeted stairs going up to what must be the attic.

'You!' A mad woman hurtled down, dress in flames, knife raised in clenched fist. I yelped and cowered but there was no one, only a dead moth on the fourth step up, and no footprints in the thick dust. That mattered but I could not think why. I closed up and re-bolted the door. The paintwork was unmarked.

The pigs were still grunting outside.

One by one I went through the rooms. The blue first. It was very like mine but decorated in cornflowers, wafting in the wallpaper when I blew on it. I searched in the wardrobe and under the bed. There was no one. I went through the other four – all empty – before I braced myself to revisit Uncle Tolly's room. The door was still ajar and I pushed it fully open. I had an insane hope that he would just be sleeping but I smelled the death, sweet and cloying, even before I entered, and he was still there, mutilated, with his butchered face and gashed head and severed left hand. His right hand on the sill clutched the curtain.

The blood glistened and oozed down him, but it did not flow from his wounds. I knew there was no point but I made myself take his right wrist. It was still warm but not a thread of life beat through it. I put it in his lap.

There was a little copper lever on the wall near the door. I pulled it up but nothing happened.

The axe lay on the floor, long-handled, its blade caked in clots, a sliver of skin and strings of hair that matched the dead man's. The wardrobe was packed tight with everything from tweeds to tails, one dusty brown and six highly polished black pairs of shoes lined neatly on the base with their toes facing outwards. I went on my haunches beside the glistening pool and reached across it to lift the sheet and peer under the bed – an unused chamber pot but nothing else. The pool shimmered and I knew that if I slithered into it I would sink, thrashing in my own death struggle, drowning in the gore I had spilled. I edged away.

There was a key on a hook, brass with a latticework on the handle that reminded me of the carpet beater we used when we spring-cleaned The Grange. I took it, went back into the corridor, shut the door and locked it.

'For the love of God, help me!' Uncle Tolly's plea sliced through the wood between us. 'Oh my dear God, March, please help me.'

I dropped the key and watched it drift down side to side like a lost coin in a lake. It seemed so far away when I leaned to retrieve it and the lock was spongy as I twisted it back, and he was still there, Uncle Tolly, slumped in the corner, his hand on the sill grasping the curtain, unmoved, not a glimmer of life about him. I stood a long time watching from the sloping threshold but there was nothing, not even the hope. I slammed the door, secured it, and slipped the key into my dress pocket where it clinked against my lucky sixpence.

'My lucky, lucky sixpence,' I whispered as I crept away.

The stairs were steep and stretched forever down to hell. I put a foot on the first step. It gave a little beneath me so I adjusted my weight and took the bannister rail, twisting and scaly as a snake writhing between my fingers, but I grasped it hard and tamed it.

'See how it dances to the charmer's flute,' my father said.
The flute had a swelling near the mouthpiece mimicking
the hood of the cobra rising and swaying with the music.

Everything undulating, I made my way down tentatively, trying
to recall going up. Was it really only last night? I remembered
stumbling halfway up and Uncle Tolly taking my arm, and I
stumbled again now, toppling helpless on to the storm-tossed
deck as we sailed round the Horn on our way to India.

I clung to the post until the dizziness subsided and looked
around the hall – the same square with the pink-veined floor and
pillars and white-plastered walls. I went round the leering Saturn
and checked the doors. They were all locked except the double
walnut door into the study. I entered and glanced at the charts
spread over the map table and the fire gone to ashes in the grate.

Was that another cry?

I went back into the hall and called out Hello, but only the
reverberations of my voice answered me. So many echoes.

'How ghastly,' Uncle Tolly said. 'I wonder…'

The ring of keys was still in the box. I took them down and tried
two before I found the one that opened the dining-room door.
Annie the maid was dusting the flame-shaped leaves on a flower-
less aspidistra. She greeted me brightly. 'Oh, miss, you're an early
riser. Mr Travers Smyth doesn't usually breakfast until eleven
o'clock. Would you like me to get you something?'

Everything looked so normal, even the portrait of Great-Aunt
Matilda rolling her eyes and huskily repeating every word: '…
get you something?'

'No,' I said. 'Thank you.' The secret door was open in the oak
panelling behind her, not secret anymore. 'Did you hear anything
unusual last night, Annie?'

'Unusual,' said Great-Aunt Matilda.

She lowered her duster. 'Why, bless you, miss, I don't hear

nothing in the night. It's all I can do to stop myself falling asleep before I get to bed. Mr Travers Smyth is a kind master but a domestic's day is too long and too hard for a body to deal with, without listening for noises.' She crinkled her forehead. 'What sort of thing do you mean?'

'Mean,' said Great-Aunt Matilda.

I pointed to the panelling. 'Are there any other secret passage-ways in this house?'

'Why no, miss.' She pulled out a broken feather. 'But Mr Travers Smyth will be able to tell you that for he designed and built this house himself, so I believe. Did—'

I slammed the door and locked it.

18

The Frozen Bicyclist

I HAD NO idea what to do next. Sidney Grice would have known. He would have been upstairs sniffing around Uncle Tolly's body, probing wounds with his steel spatulas, inspecting the axe through his pince-nez, putting samples of hairs into his envelopes and blood clots into his test tubes, scrutinizing hand marks on the wallpaper, tapping about with his cane. I could not even face going up those stairs again.

I paced to and fro, much steadier on my tingling feet now. I have never been afraid of a corpse. The soul has departed and the shell it has quit can no more do me harm than it can do me good. One might as well be frightened of a log. The human body deserves reverence for what it once contained, but it should not instil terror.

And yet I was afraid. Was it because I could not face the consequences of my actions? Was I terrified by what I had done? What had I done? I had been half-aware of a tapping, but then it became four sharp knocks and a man's voice called out, 'Miss Middleton? Are you all right? Is Mr Travers Smyth there?'

I opened the door again to see Colwyn in his shirt and waist-coat, but his jacket over his arm and his cravat hurriedly arranged.

Great-Aunt Matilda glared at his back.

'Fetch the police,' I said. 'Something has happened.'

His face was all concern. 'To my master?'

'Yes.'

He automatically straightened his cuffs. 'Can I be of assistance to him?'

'He is beyond assistance,' I replied, and found that I could not meet his eye. 'I am sorry, but he has been murdered.'

'Murdered?'

'Murdered,' Great-Aunt Matilda suspired.

'Be quiet,' I told her. 'Yes.'

Colwyn looked perplexedly about him, then to Annie, who had dropped her duster. 'Fetch the police.' She hesitated. 'Hurry, girl.' And Annie ran through the secret door and disappeared, her boots clattering and quickly fading down the wooden steps. He turned back to me. 'But how, miss? What's happened?'

I felt hot and nauseous. 'I cannot say.'

Colwyn shook out his jacket and slipped his arms through the sleeves. 'I must go to my master.'

'No.' I held his gaze this time. 'You must wait for the police. I have locked the door.'

'Then I must ask you for the key, miss.'

'The body must not be disturbed,' I demurred, wondering how I knew such a thing.

'I do not understand.'

'Neither do I.' I was feeling dizzy again. 'But I think I might have killed him.'

Colwyn took a step forward ready to catch me, his eyes wide with consternation.

'Allow me to escort you to the study, miss.' I did not want to play the swooning girl, but I felt so unsteady that I was obliged to take his arm and be guided back into the library and the armchair where I had sat the night before facing Uncle Tolly. 'May I offer you a drink, miss… something to steady your nerves?'

'Gin,' I said, 'if you have any.'

Colwyn went to the sideboard and took the stopper out of a square decanter. 'And tonic water?'

'No, thank you.' I had had enough quinine in India not to regard its consumption as a pleasure.

He brought me a large tumbler two thirds full and I took it from the tray. The glass felt woolly in my grip.

'While we are waiting for the police, miss.' He hovered by my shoulder, 'Is there anything you can tell me about how Mr Travers Smyth was killed?'

I took a drink. 'Is there anything you can tell me? Did you hear or see anything unusual last night?' I felt as if I were reciting the lines of a play. The curtain would close soon but no one would applaud.

Colwyn lowered the tray. I glimpsed myself in it but could not remember how I got there.

'Nothing until Annie told me you had locked her in.' He hesitated. 'I have followed your guardian's career with some interest, miss, and I recall in the Adventure of the Frozen Bicyclist that he was able to bring the murderers to justice simply by getting all the witnesses to write their recollections of events and comparing the different versions. If I may venture to make a suggestion, it might help the police if you were to make a written record of what you know whilst the memory is still fresh in your mind.'

I got to my feet and went to the desk, the long grass brushing my dress, a thousand blue swallowtail butter-flies flitting around us as Edward struggled with the hamper behind me.

There was plenty of paper, a box of goose quills and an almost empty bottle of ink. I dipped the pen and began, my words having the same odd tint of green as Uncle Tolly's letter had shown to me when I lived in another world. I, March Middleton...

Where to start? I made a few notes while Colwyn busied himself building the fire.

'Not usually my job.' He snapped a length of kindling. 'But I suppose I do not have a job now.'

'I am sure you will have no trouble finding another position,' I said as he hung the tongs back on their stand.

I continued: ... of 125 Gower Street, London. But I could not write that I thought I might have murdered him.

Colwyn glanced back at me, and for an instant I saw a little boy crouching as he struck a Lucifer, but I shook the image off as one dries an umbrella.

'Boys love to light fires,' I said, and he shot a glance at me as if I had said something very peculiar.

I made a few notes about how Uncle Tolly had contacted me and how I had never heard of him but, even as I wrote, I knew that I was jumbling things up. Why was I writing about pigs?

Colwyn had the fire going and was tidying up some books.

'It would be better not to disturb anything.' My voice came from very far away, from another room in another house.

'Very well, miss.'

The valet stood back as I crossed the room, folded the page and thrust it into the coals which were just starting to glow. The embers rose and floated prettily down and I remembered another letter I had committed to the flames when some of the world seemed sane.

I am afraid for you, March.

The doorbell rang.

'Excuse me one moment, miss.' He went into the hall and I heard the bolts drawing back but they seemed nothing to do with me.

Sidney Grice will destroy you.

Colwyn returned with a uniformed constable close behind.

'That was quick,' I commented.

'What's all this about then?' the policeman asked.

'This lady says that Mr Ptolemy Travers Smyth is dead,' Colwyn announced in shocked tones, 'and that she might have killed him.'

Destroy you, she said.

19

——◦•※•◦——

Musical Mice

THE CONSTABLE REGARDED me doubtfully. 'Do you have anything to say, miss?' His cape and helmet were wet.

'He was my second cousin.' I tried hard to get to the point. 'And he has been murdered.'

'How?'

I supported myself on the desk. 'With an axe.'

'No!' Colwyn breathed. His face blanched.

'Did you do it?' the constable asked.

'I am not sure what happened.'

The policeman took his helmet off and tucked it under his arm, the Brunswick star glowering like a Cyclops' eye. 'We had better take a look at the body then.'

'You will need the key.' I delved into my pocket and placed the hot metal in his hand, and the policeman huffed.

'Is this an attempt to bribe me?'

He held it under my nose and I saw that I had given him my lucky sixpence. I took it back and handed him the key.

'Allow me to show you the way,' Colwyn said.

The constable shuffled his surprisingly dainty feet. 'You won't try to do a runner?'

'I am not sure I can even walk.'

'I don't think Miss Middleton will try to get away,' Colwyn vouched and the policeman brightened up.

'Never caught a murderer before,' he confessed modestly. 'Could be a promotion in it for me.'

'It is probably all a misunderstanding,' Colwyn said.

'The police should be here soon,' I contributed before discovering that they had gone. I got up. The desk was tilted and slippery and the floor gave way, like soft sand beneath my feet, but I made it to the fireplace. The fire was burning well now and white mice scampered between the coals, singing a very high and haunting tune.

Annie came into the room and viewed me warily as I tried to sing along.

'I do not know the words,' I confessed.

The mice started glowing.

Part of my notes fluttered on to the hearth, my name still visible on the carbonized page.

One of the mice began to smoulder. It squeaked and burst into flames. I tried to pick it out, but the fire was too hot and pouring out thick yellow smoke. The other mice were starting to steam.

'We must do something,' I cried and pushed her aside to get the tongs, but the mice were all catching alight now and the smoke mushroomed, fused and floated towards me, and I knew that if I stayed any longer something terrible would happen.

'Too late.' I do not know which of us said that.

I threw the tongs aside, for I knew now that these were not mice but tiny pink pigs and you cannot pick up pigs with tongs. Annie snatched up the poker and waved it nervously, standing well back.

'The policeman said you might turn violent.' She was trembling as she spoke. 'Please don't try anything on me, miss.'

'I am not the one who is armed,' I reasoned and she giggled uncertainly.

It was then I realized that the pigs were only small because they were far away but they were growing now, which meant they were getting closer, a whole herd of wild hogs thundering along the tunnel that led into the fireplace.

'I've heard that is how mad people try to get you off guard. I don't suppose poor Mr Travers Smyth,' Annie fought back the tears, 'knew you were dangerous.'

The room was filling with fumes and I could already hear the squeals and see those pink eyes blister, opaque with pain.

I am afraid for you, March. You must leave that house.

Their trotters crunched in the glowing embers as they hurtled along. The first pig leaped out, trotters skidding on the bricks as it scuttled past me, snorting and chomping its salivating jaws.

'I have to get out of here.'

'I am sorry, miss.' Annie darted in front of me, the poker raised. 'But I have been told to keep you here.'

You must leave.

An old sow was squealing, mouth agape, her yellow teeth bared, her tongue coated in green slime.

'But they will kill us both.'

Leave.

I could even smell them now, the acid and the mustard and the excrement. I tried to step aside but a shrieking, slavering hog lunged at me, sabre tusks slashing, and I toppled into Annie but she stood her ground. Perhaps she was trying to fight the pigs off, but the poker passed through their bodies as it rained upon my head.

20

The Land of Angels

I RAN. I STAGGERED into the hall, shielding my head, and snatched my cloak, sending the stand crashing over, forgetting that Colwyn had said that the door was locked, then recollecting where the keys were kept, fumbling with the ring. So many little keys and one big one.

There was a rush and I thought the pigs were following, but it was only Annie. 'Help, she's getting away.'

'That must be it.' I slipped it into the hole, steadying my right hand with my left, the lock turning easily. 'Yes.' I slid back the bolts and flung the door open.

Feet thundered on wood deep inside the house – animal or human, I did not wait to find out.

I jumped down the two semicircular steps and along the drive, my boots sinking into the gravel, the ground rising black with white crests breaking around me, almost knocking me off my feet. I got to a vertical section of drive and scrambled up it, toppling over the edge and landing heavily on the other side. My palms stung and the pain helped me concentrate. I got to my feet and staggered on and heard a shout behind me. Stop. But it only spurred me on and I found that if I leaned forwards I could run much faster.

I was on the pavement now and something rushed past – a rippling block of brown followed by a wall of grey with massive trundling spokes – a carriage going along the road to my left, and I was frightened of it so I went right. There were feet crunching on the loose stones far away, but they were getting louder and therefore closer and I knew that I could not outpace them. I went right again and left – I think – up another driveway towards a turreted brick house, except it had an arch which seemed familiar and so I rushed through the massive open gateway and down a path with neatly trimmed high hedges, and then another narrower way which meandered between bushes where a dog crouched frozen and colourless at its master's frozen and colourless feet. There was a crashing through the undergrowth and voices nearby, and the ground disappeared and I fell.

I fell like Icarus, his waxen wings melted by the sun, like Alice down the rabbit hole, like…

The ground reappeared and hit me very hard, knocking the wind out of me and making my teeth clack, and I lay trying to quieten my breathing, quite sure that my heart was booming loud enough for anyone to hear. There was a rustling close by. Somebody tripped and hissed, 'Shit,' but seemed to move off in another direction, and the following footsteps became fainter and a man called, 'I can't see her.' And another replied, 'Don't worry. We know where she's going.' And I lay still, wondering how they could possibly know that when I had no idea myself.

I waited a long time, face down, listening to the sounds dying. Where do sounds go when they die? My breathing and pulse slowed and quietened but still I did not get up. The earth was comforting. The smell and firmness of it made me feel secure. I half rolled and found that I was in a shallow trench with very straight edges. I crawled out on my knees towards two angels, white skin and hair and robes, wings folded and heads bowed towards each other, their faces steeped in sorrow.

I stood up. There was a marble child nearby with the marble kitten in her arms going green. I walked round her and found myself in a long straight alley bordered by pebbled rectangles with upright granite slabs at the far ends and separated by well-tended lawns. A lady was kneeling, placing a holly wreath in front of a Celtic cross. She jumped in alarm.

'Are you all right?'

'I fell into a grave,' I told her, as if it were the most natural thing in the world. 'Luckily, it was only half dug.'

I recalled a woman trying to push me into her brother's grave once but I could not recollect why.

The lady surveyed me with revulsion as I leaned against a yew tree.

'Stimulated,' she shuddered, 'at this hour.'

I wondered what would have been a better hour to be intoxicated and realized that she was not addressing me but somebody behind.

A man's face appeared indecently close to mine. 'She don't smell of drink.'

'Does not,' I corrected him absent-mindedly as the circle of light contracted around his weather-torn features. 'And stop sniffing me.'

The lady's face reappeared, hovering over me with a tortoise-shell-handled lorgnette.

'My goodness.' She recoiled. 'Regard the presentation of her. She has had a calamity.'

'She needs a doctor,' the man decided. One of his eyebrows was singed.

I was always told it was rude to talk about people as if they are not there but I let it pass.

'I just need a cab,' I assured them as I scrambled to my knees. 'If I can get home I live near a hospital.'

And they must have helped me to the road for I was clambering into a hansom and croaking, '125 Gower Street,' to the driver.

'Blimey, that's where old Rice Puddin' lives,' he called down as I fell on to the seat, and the next thing I knew Molly was answering the door.

'Oh goodness, miss, you look horrenderous. I thought you were a mongerel's dinner when you set off in that dress what

74

you've still got on, but you look much worserer now. Your face looks all bashed in.'

'I think it is,' I told her wearily.

'Oh.' She took my cloak. 'Was it the lady from number 115 'cause you said her bonnet looked like a compost heap?'

'I do not think she had heard me.' In the mirror I saw the mud on my cheeks, a graze on my nose and a large contusion on my forehead. My nose was bleeding.

'Oh, don't worry, miss. She didn't not.' Molly hung my cloak on the rack. 'But I accidently told her.'

I made my way to the study, slumped into the chair behind the desk and took a sheet of paper. 'I want you to take this to the telegraph office immediately.'

'A pen?'

'I haven't written it yet.' I found the address in Sidney Grice's card index box. 'What is Inspector Pound's surname?' I heard myself muttering before I worked out the answer for myself.

'Not immediantely then,' Molly mumbled as she watched me print it out.

DO YOU KNOW PTOLEMY TRAVERS SMYTH QUERY I MAY HAVE KILLED HIM STOP MARCH.

I thrust the note into her hand with a few coins from Sidney Grice's change bowl.

'Go,' I said. 'And on the way back fetch a doctor.'

'A docker, miss?' Molly queried. 'I think you are more in need of a doctor.' Her lips moved as she perused what I had written. 'And a solossiter.'

21

The Quirry

'THERE IS A *creature at the bottom of the quarry called the Quirry. It lives in the hollows, beneath the stagnant pools and in the cracks that go down to the centre of the earth. At night it creeps out and feeds off any living creature it can find, like a spider sucking the insides out of a fly.'*

Barney laughed, but Maudy Glass paled and looked about her in alarm. She was the same age as me but always seemed younger, and so I stopped my story and we finished the dregs of our lemonade, chewing the shreds of rind thoughtfully. Maudy had to go and help her mother and the sun was sinking, and so we set back.

The edge of the sandstone cliff had crumbled and a dead tree trunk tilted almost horizontally over the side.

'Bet I could walk on that,' Barney speculated.

Maudy begged him not to, but I bet him tuppence he couldn't. I lost my bet for he clambered over the tangle of roots and strolled easily along the trunk, arms outstretched – as we had seen a tightrope walker do when Silcock's Circus came to the village – twenty feet to the last broken branches. Maudy could not watch but I applauded. I would have tried it myself were it not for the ridiculous layers of clothing that society decreed I must wear.

'Come back now, Barney,' Maudy begged, but he was enjoying her terror.

'Watch this,' he called and stood on one leg, but the bark was wet and his foot slipped. Barney wobbled and slid sideways. He managed to snatch at a bough but it was rotten and snapped. Barney seemed to hang for an age. His mouth opened but no sound came as he fell.

I rushed to the side, grabbed on to a root and looked down in time to see Barney bounce off a rocky projection and land spread-eagled on his back on the quarry floor a hundred feet below.

'Get help,' I shouted at Maudy. 'Run to The Grange and tell my father.'

Maudy hesitated. 'What will you do?'

But I did not have time to explain. I was ripping off some of those swaddling petticoats.

'Go. Just go,' I yelled.

Maudy headed back up the track, past Swandale's – which was deserted now – and went out of view. It was probably two miles down the side of the quarries and back up to where Barney lay. The side was not quite sheer and there were ledges and a few jutting bushes, and a huge boulder to squeeze round.

A broken child lay on the quarry floor in more pain than I had ever seen. His eyes flickered and his pale lips parted.

'Don't leave me, Marchy,' he sobbed. 'Don't let me die.'

I held his hand and swore, 'I won't.'

22

The Kidney Dish and the Ring

'OUCH.' I TOUCHED my brow and wished I had not.

'Does it hurt very much?'

I knew that voice, but I did not know to whom it belonged and I could not see anything. I put my hand up again but gingerly this time.

'Careful, March. They have bandaged your head and face.'

'Who?'

'The nurses.'

'Where am I? Who are you?'

'You are in University College Hospital, March, and I am George Pound.'

I remembered the hospital and the nurses, and of course it was the inspector, but it was he who should be in bed with me bringing him meat pies and jugs of beer after he was stabbed because of me.

'What am I doing here?'

'That's what I hope to find out.'

'Uncle Tolly!' I tried to sit up.

'You must lie down.' He – at least I assumed it was him – restrained me with a hand to my shoulder. I touched that hand and knew it for his beyond doubt. He squeezed my arm and I sank back. 'Who is Uncle Tolly, March?'

'He is dead.' The bandage slipped and I could see bits of the inspector through a slit.

He brought a telegram from the inner pocket of his overcoat. 'Ptolemy Travers Smyth?' He read and I nodded and realized that I had a headache, a bad one. The inspector clicked his tongue. 'Was he your uncle?'

'He said he was my second cousin and that you would vouch for him.'

'I have never heard of the man. Where did he live?'

'In Highgate, in a big modern house near the cemetery.' My hand was still on his. 'And I might have killed—'

The squeeze became urgent. 'Don't say anything else, March. Remember what I am.'

I knew what he did but I was not at all sure what he was – to me. The bandage slipped and I was blinded again.

'You are supposed to be recuperating.'

'I got your telegram.' His voice still sounded weak, but I was pleased that he had recovered from my attempts to trim his moustaches when he was the patient and I the visitor.

He said something else but I was drifting again. I listened to strangers talking and a wheel squeaking and somebody crying noisily and being shushed, and I closed my useless eyes and when I woke up again he was still holding me.

'Your mother's ring,' I said. 'You gave it to me for safekeeping. Perhaps you should look after it while I am here.'

The grip slackened. 'I would rather risk it being stolen while you are asleep than have you return it.'

I put my right hand to my breast and felt the hard metal on the chain around my neck. It seemed to be the only solid thing I had. I did not know what else to say.

'I have sent a telegram to Mr Grice,' Inspector Pound told me. 'He should be back soon.'

'But he will be furious,' I protested. 'He is on an important case.'

'Not as important as yours.'

'I did not know I had a case.'

'You must not overtire Miss Middleton,' a woman scolded.

'I shall go in a moment,' he promised.

'Very well. Then make yourself useful and hold this bowl.' There was a tugging around my temple. 'Raise your head.' I did and felt the bandage being unwrapped. My vision was blurred on the right-hand side but I could see her face well enough, a nurse with a dry sunken face and a grim expression on her downy lips. 'I think we need to let the air get to it.' She tossed the bandage into a kidney dish.

I looked at the hand holding that dish and followed the dark grey sleeve up to the lapel and the white shirt and charcoal tie, and the face above with its neatly clipped moustaches was smiling reassuringly, but the clear blue eyes winced in undisguisable horror at what they saw.

23

Chimpanzees and Emetic Tartar

T HERE WAS A fuss at the door but I could not see it because they had put a screen round the dead patient in the bed next to mine and it blocked my view.

'You can't come in here,' a woman insisted.

'My dear, yet dispiritingly dowdy Matron.' I knew that voice and I had never been so glad to hear it. 'You have no conception of my capabilities. I am perfectly able to walk into this fetid misconstruction of a hospital ward as I am about to demonstrate.'

'Visiting time is at six o'clock.'

'I shall file that information under ACICT for Almost Certainly Irrelevant and Certainly Tedious,' he told her, 'for I am not a visitor. I am me.'

'Are you a doctor?'

'I cure more ills than you can possibly imagine.'

'Oh,' the matron said. 'I am sorry.'

'Always apologize. Always explain,' my guardian said, and after a short pause he appeared, hat in one hand and cane in the other, and tossed them both on my bed. 'For goodness' sake, March. I leave you alone for...' he glanced at his watch and reeled out how many thousands of minutes it had been, 'with strict instructions to stay out of trouble and what do you do? You go clodhopping into it up to your scrawny and unnecessarily elongated neck the moment I am out of the borough.'

'Dom Hart,' I remembered.

'Oh that.' Sidney Grice spiralled a hand above his head. 'A simple matter. All men have their vices and the late Abbot was a secret drinker. One of the older monks, Brother Jerome, put potassium permanganate in his wine – hence the black vomit. It was not in my remit to discover his motive, though I should like to have had time to have done so.'

His eye slid inwards.

'I am sorry.' My tongue was dry and clicked on my palate.

'Then stop grinning like a demented chimpanzee.'

'I am pleased to see you.'

Mr G grimaced. 'I shall decide whether I am pleased to see you or not after you have answered the first two of the eighty-nine highly intelligent questions with which I intend to confront you over the next two days. Who is or was Mr Ptolemy Travers Smyth?'

'My second cousin.'

'Is he dead?'

'Yes.'

'Did you kill him?'

'I do not know.' The blanket was tickling my chin and I pulled it down a couple of inches.

Sidney Grice grunted, 'Then I shall draw the provisional con-clusion that you might not have.' He pulled the blanket back up just below my mouth. 'Let us hope for both our sakes that my investigations do not prove that conclusion wrong.'

'Your sake?'

He unhooked his left cufflink. 'Think what an embarrassment it would be for me if you were convicted as a murderess.'

The word murderess wrapped itself around me so tightly that I could hardly catch my breath, but Mr G was humming now, eight rapid random notes over and over, as he clipped his pince-nez on to his elegant thin nose, bending over me to scrutinize the damage.

'Ummm,' he said, as if appreciating a fine delicacy. 'Ah-ha.' He brought out a short steel ruler and held it close to my brow, turning his measure ninety degrees before tutting and scribbling something on the inner surface of his cuff.

'Do you not have a notebook?'

'Of course I have a notebook.' He drew back indignantly. 'Can you imagine me without one?'

'Was that one of your questions?'

He sniffed. 'It was rhetorical.' He delved into his satchel. 'Even in your more than usually befuddled state I think you will notice that the cover is brown whereas this case cries out to be bound in blue, and you could hardly expect me to waste a book which might be better suited to investigating the defenestration of a university don.'

'Why blue?'

'Blue is a recondite colour. It feels scratchy and smells of burnt gunpowder.' He fell back to humming and made a few more measurements. 'The next three questions are outside the scope of my agenda but pertinent to your inconvenient situation.' He prodded my nose with his little finger. 'Does that hurt?'

'Not much.'

'Pity.' He whipped off his pince-nez. 'What about that?'

'Ow! Yes.'

'Excellent. Who presented you with your injuries?'

'Annie, Uncle Tolly's maid.' I closed my left eye but the lightning flashes continued. 'With a poker.'

He rested one foot on the bedside chair as if expecting me to polish his boot. 'Before, during or after the slaughter of her employer?'

'Afterwards.' I remembered some pigs.

He thrust his notebook back into the satchel still on his shoulder. 'Time to come home, March.'

'Has the doctor said I can go?'

He dusted the toe of his boot with an edge of the sheet. 'I have no idea and little interest in what conversations he may have had, for he has had none with me.'

'But surely—'

'Tut-tut, March. You cannot spend your whole life idling in bed, especially when we have your alleged act of dynastic homicide to investigate.' He glanced about. 'Where are your clothes? And do not pretend you do not know. I can accept that you may not know if you have killed a man, but every girl always knows where her clothes are.'

'If I were a girl that might be—'

'No time for that nonsense.' Mr G refastened his cuff.

'In my bedside cabinet.'

'Good.' He pulled down his coat sleeve. 'This screen will serve.' He took hold of an upright pole.

'There is a dead woman behind it,' I protested.

'Then she has no need of it now.' He dragged the curtains out and round us.

'I shall wait in the corridor for eight minutes.'

'Eight minutes,' the old woman whispered as she came though the screen. 'That gives me plenty of time.'

I was surprised that my guardian had not noticed her as he stepped out, closing the gap behind him. There were sharp footfalls and the matron angrily demanded, 'Have you no respect for the dead?'

'None at all,' he replied cheerfully, 'and precious little for you.'

'How dare—'

The old woman was pedalling a grinding stone. It creaked reluctantly at first but she soon had it turning.

'I dare,' Sidney Grice's voice faded as he quit the ward, 'because it is quite obvious from the most cursory glance that you are attempting to murder your father-in-law, and I would advise you to cease immediately as I have no more desire to waste time giving evidence at his inquest than I imagine you have to dance your way to perdition on the looped end of a hempen cord.'

'I don't know what you are talking about.'
'Emetic tartar.' His voice carried from afar.
'This is an outrage.' But the matron's voice faltered.

'Time for what?' I asked the old woman. She was pedal-
ling hard now and the wheel was whirring.

'To kill you,' she said, though her lips had been sutured
together. Her skin was pocked and discoloured like old
orange peel and her hands were gnarled talons, but she
held the carving knife dexterously enough as she ran the
blade over the spinning stone, the steel squealing and the
sparks flying as she worked. 'Nice and sharp to cut out
your heart, cut out your heart, cut out your heart,' she
sang as she worked. 'Nice and sharp to cut out your heart
on a cold and frosty morning.'

I thought that she was wearing smoked glasses, but as
she turned her head to me I saw that they were pennies
on her eyes. I tried to roll away but the terror bound me
so tightly that I could not move.

'Lovely.' The old woman whisked round and ripped
back my sheets.

'What on earth are you doing?' Sidney Grice demanded.
'Get her away from me.'
'Who?' Sidney Grice glanced about the empty cubicle but I
was not that easily fooled. I could smell the decay and the sparks
still danced in my eyes.

24

The Amber Book

IT WAS JUST after midday when we left the hospital. Straight ahead and set well back was the imposing white dome of University College. We turned right and walked the hundred yards to number 125 with me leaning heavily on my guardian's arm, for I was much more unsteady than I had realized. Sidney Grice rapped on the door with his cane.

'Is the bell broken?' I asked and he furrowed his brow.

'I have no reason to suspect so.'

'Then why—'

Mr G rounded on me. 'You think your return is an occasion for joyous chimes?' He rapped again. 'Perhaps you are expecting fire crackers and a military band.'

Molly admitted us. 'Oh, miss, if I'd known you were coming out today I'd have got you a bottle of your secret gin.'

'Tea.' Mr G plunged his cane into the stand like a matador finishing off his bull. We went into his study, me to my chair on the right of the fireplace and he to his facing me. 'Oh, March.' He regarded me solicitously. 'I do not suppose you feel like talking about it.'

'Well, not at the moment.'

Mr G gestured compassionately. 'I quite understand.' He popped his eye out. 'Nevertheless, you shall.' He slipped the eye into a silk pouch and tied on his patch. 'Let us start with an easy one. What on earth do you think you were up to?'

I put my hand to my brow but even the lightest contact sent a pain shooting through it. 'I think my skull is fractured.'

'No doubt.' He opened the lowboy beside him. 'But that does not answer my question.'

'I had a letter.'

'A letter?' he repeated, as if he had never heard of such a thing. 'I am sorry, March Lillian Constance Middleton, but this sounds increasingly like a yellow case.' He ran his finger along a row of notebooks and drew out an amber book, much thinner but taller than the rest, with several orange marker ribbons looped through it. 'I receive, on average, forty-two letters and seven parcels a day without becoming the sole suspect in a murder inquiry or engaging maids in near-lethal combat with cast-iron fireside companions.' He whipped out his engraved Mordan mechanical pencil. 'What exactly was so intriguing about this correspondence that you felt compelled to act?' He jabbed the pencil towards me. 'And you may save your indignation for your silly and sensational diary. Confine your answer to the facts.'

'I only wish I could.' My left hand in my lap was twitching as if it were playing a Scottish reel on the violin. 'But I am bewildered.'

He raised the pencil towards the ceiling. 'Do you seriously imagine that your not knowing things will save you?' He straightened his arm, his pencil aloft like a regimental standard. 'If so, I must rapidly disabuse you. Ignorance is not bliss, March. It is the quickest route to prison and the execution yard.'

'They cannot hang me for something I might not have done.'

Mr G snorted. 'Many a man – though not as many as I would like – has been executed for something he could not possibly have done. Might not having done something is just not good enough.' His arm shot down and he entered something in his book in his tiny shorthand code. 'Let us change tack and assume that you did it.'

I swallowed. 'All right.'

'The fact that you did not instantly deny it is the first point in your favour,' my guardian commented.

'So you think I did not do it?'

'Dear March,' Mr G spoke tenderly, 'I think you may be telling the truth that you do not know if you did it – whatever it may be.'

Molly came in and put a tea tray on the table. 'Cook said I was very rude to say that about your dress the other day, miss.'

'It does not matter,' I told her.

'I just wanted to make it clear,' she continued. 'There wasn't not nothing wrong with the dress. Anybody else might have looked pretty in it.'

'Thank you, Molly.'

'And—'

'Get out,' her employer commanded, 'before Miss Middleton attacks you as she allegedly did the last maid who crossed her path.'

'Oh, miss.' Molly put her hand to her mouth. 'I never even knew you had a path. I hope I never allegingly cross it.'

'Go,' her employer snapped and she did, and I wondered why he had not commented on the pennies of her eyes.

I dabbed my forehead with a napkin and saw a smear of fresh blood. 'The letter came from Ptolemy Travers Smyth,' I began but, seeing my guardian wince, corrected myself. 'It was signed in his name and I assumed it came from him.'

'All assumptions are dangerous,' Mr G pronounced, 'unless you know them for what they are, in which case they may be useful rungs as we clamber our way ever upwards in search of that elusive creature popularly known as the truth. What is the address on the letterhead?'

'Saturn Villa, but I do not know exactly where it is. It was dark and I got disorientated,' I said, and Sidney Grice cocked his head to one side like an intelligent spaniel but said nothing, so I continued. 'I sent my reply to the Stargate Road telegram office.'

'Why?'

'It was the only address he gave.'

'And that aroused no suspicions?' My guardian made a putting noise like water being poured from a carafe. 'And where is the aforementioned letter now?'

'I think I left it at his house.'

He regarded me. 'That was stupid of you.'

'I was not expecting any of this to happen.'

Sidney Grice pressed the dimple on his chin with the joint of his left thumb. 'Why not?'

'Nobody goes into a house expecting their host to be murdered.'

'I do.'

'Nobody normal.'

'If you want to be normal find employment in a hat shop.' He gestured towards the tray. 'Pour the tea.'

The pot seemed much heavier than usual and my right wrist ached as I filled our cups. 'I thought he was the uncle I never knew I had.'

Mr G crossed out a line of notes. 'What do you think I would do if a letter arrived in four minutes' time purporting to be from Abigail, a niece who does not exist, inviting me to meet her up an unlit alley in Limehouse after midnight?'

'You would make some enquiries first,' I conceded and then remembered, 'but he said Inspector Pound would vouch for him.'

My guardian stirred his black sugarless tea. 'And did that moderately capable and exceptionally honest officer do so?'

'No.' I dug my spoon into what I supposed to be the sugar bowl but it came out writhing with maggots. 'I have been a fool.' They wriggled up the handle. I stifled a cry, threw the spoon in the fire and brushed them off my fingers.

Sidney Grice raised an eyebrow. 'Not in itself a crime,' he conceded, 'though it should be.'

'The handwriting was very difficult to decipher,' I recalled. 'So I made a copy.'

'And?' He shook his spoon dry.

'It is in my room.'

A darkness was lurking under my chair.

He put the spoon in his saucer as if afraid that both would shatter. 'Then trot up and get it.'

I closed my eyes. Even the grey daylight was painful to them. 'I do not feel like running.'

'And I do not feel like wasting my time on this case. For goodness' sake, March, the wording of that letter may save you from a fate no worse than death.'

The darkness was gathering around my feet now.

'Very well.' I struggled to my feet. The room swayed and the blood rushed through my head, and I was dimly aware that the darkness had clambered on to my lap and was rushing up to swallow me.

25

Christmas

I FOUND MYSELF lying on my back on the floor, feet together, my dress pulled modestly down to my boots and my arms crossed over my breast as if I had been laid out for my wake.

Sidney Grice was perched on the arm of his chair, surveying me over his cup. 'You do not paint your face?'

'Not since I was Minnehaha in a village play.' My guardian dipped a corner of his napkin into his tea and dropped to his knees to vigorously wipe my left cheek. 'That hurts.'

'I am very sorry,' he said softly, 'that you are making such a fuss.' He clipped on his pince-nez and leaned down until his nose almost brushed mine. 'Keep your head still and look to your left... Now your right... Interesting.' He pulled away quickly. 'You have a slight green discoloration of the skin, which was not apparent while you were flushed but is obvious to my acute observational powers whilst you are pallid. It is also evident in your sclera and the beds of your fingerplates. Do you desire a glass of water?'

'Yes, please. I am very thirsty.'

He leaped to his feet. 'Splendid. Any other symptoms you wish to report?'

'Apart from the pains in my head—'

'Of course,' Mr G broke in. 'But we cannot spend the rest of our lives – especially as yours may be violently curtailed very shortly – gossiping about that.'

'My feet and hands tingle.'

He started to pace round me. 'Why did you say feet and hands? Most people talk about their hands and feet?'

I felt giddy watching him. 'I suppose my feet feel worse than my hands.'

'Do your boots feel too tight?' He stopped at my head and peered down at me.

'A little.'

'Good.' Mr G clicked his fingers. 'You may arise now.'

I managed to get on to my elbows as he marched off towards his bookcases. 'A helping hand might be nice.'

He watched my struggles. 'For you perhaps, but not for me,' he decided, unlocking a fruitwood casket and sliding out a familiar thick, stained leather-bound tome. 'The *Secreta Botanica*,' he declared, fired with a strange passion and laying it reverently upon his desk as he sat in his captain's chair, gazing at it with something approaching awe.

I remembered something about a monk. 'Is that…?'

'Be silent.' He donned a pair of white cotton gloves and opened his prize, turning the pages with great care, then began to read. 'As I thought.' He made a note on his blotter. 'Exactly as I thought.'

I got myself into an awkward sitting position. 'What is?'

He tilted sideways to open a lower drawer. 'But thinking things is little use without proof.' He rooted about. 'Close your eyes, March.'

'Why?'

'The reasons are dual. First, because I have commanded you to – and do not trouble to feign indignation – and, second, because I have prepared a surprise for you.'

'You make it sound like Christmas.' The dull January light was giving me a headache so it was something of a relief to obey.

'Nine similarities instantly occur to me.' I heard the drawer shut. 'Shall I enumerate?' The voice came nearer.

'Please do not trouble.' I was feeling sleepy.

'It would perturb me very little to do so.' His knees clicked. 'In fact I have a predilection for explaining things which is frequently useful in my profession.' He took hold of my wrist and rotated it. 'Especially when I have solved a case.' He tapped the back of my hand gently. I found it rather soothing. 'Which I almost invariably—'

'Bloody hell!' I tried to pull away but he had a firm grip on me.

'I shall not have the language of the conduit in this house.' Mr G was more shocked than I had ever seen him, even when confronted with a mutilated corpse. 'Keep still.'

'It hurts.'

'Yes, but only you.' He pulled back the plunger and slipped the needle out.

I sat up. 'In what way was that like Christmas?'

'Well, you did get a surprise.' Sidney Grice got to his feet.

'Apart from that?' I clamped my thumb over the freely flowing puncture wound.

He squirted my blood into a test tube and placed it in a little wooden box, scrunching up some newspaper as wadding. 'Second, it was not the actual birthday of Jesus the Christ.' He put three rubber bands round the box. 'Third, it ended in tears – yours. Fourth—'

'When did you last sharpen that needle?' I asked and he took hold of the bell rope.

'That presupposes that I have ever sharpened it.' Molly must have been standing in the hall for she answered his summons almost immediately. At least she had taken the pennies off this time, though there were still white rings around her eyes. 'Take this box to the University College building,' her employer commanded. 'The one down the road with the big dome – I take it you know what a dome is – and give it with this concise note to the desk porter.'

'Give the dome to the porter, sir?'

'Box and note to porter.' He shooed her away. 'Now.'

I leaned back against the side of my armchair. 'Do you think I might have been poisoned?'

He wiped the needle. 'How?'

'By eating cacti.'

'That is possible.' He put the syringe away. 'Except that even you would never do anything so reckless.'

I cleared my throat. 'Well…'

26

The Man with the Twisted Ear

I WAS LYING, propped up, on my bed, reading through my account of The Man With the Twisted Ear, when a child came into the room. I lowered the manuscript.

He was twelve or thirteen years old, I estimated, and his frock coat must have been a hand-me-down from an older brother, for the shoulders jutted out and it hung halfway down his calves. His hair was black, parted in the middle and gummed down, and he wore spectacles with thick round lenses.

'Have you come to amuse me?' I asked. When I was eight I was sent to sing to an elderly lady who lived on Tan House Lane, but luckily for us both she died before I got there.

'I am here to cure you.' He had adopted that thinly booming tone which boys sometimes imagine sounds grown-up.

Sidney Grice appeared behind him, a head and half a neck taller. 'Miss Middleton, this is Dr Crystal.'

I looked at the flamboyant yellow polka-dot bow tie and asked, 'Are you a magician?'

And the boy coloured shyly. 'Some say I perform miracles.'

'Dr Crystal is the best available authority in alkaline toxicity in the empire,' Mr G assured me.

'Available?' Our visitor wrinkled his glossy brow indignantly.

'As you are aware,' my guardian explained unabashed, 'Professor Cornelius Latingate is serving a short custodial sentence in Oslo.'

'And well deserved.' Dr Crystal licked his lips. 'Latingate is an unscrupulous scoundrel.'

'And I have had a disagreement with Dr Wembley over his wife's death,' Mr G continued. 'He insists that he murdered her whereas I am certain that he did not.'

'How old are you?' I broke in and Dr Crystal looked down, as if the answer were pencilled on his palm.

'Forty-two,' he told me.

I stared at him. 'Really?'

He blushed. 'And a quarter.'

'I am sorry,' I said.

'My age is not your fault,' he assured me.

My guardian strolled to the far side of the bed and rested his palm on my Bible as if taking an oath. 'Dr Crystal has discovered a possible antidote to the poison you so stupidly and ravenously devoured.'

'I only had a couple of slices out of politeness,' I protested and Dr Crystal put a hand on his head and asked, 'Am I to understand that you took poison rather than cause offence?'

'I did not know it was poison.'

Both men laughed, Mr G in a low sniff through his nostrils and Dr Crystal high and toothy like a beagle.

'How could she not have known?' Dr Crystal deposited a heavy brown bag on my shins.

'Her ignorance knows bounds, but they are breathtakingly wide,' Sidney Grice told him with perhaps a hint of pride.

'I did notice it was bitter,' I defended myself.

'All alkaloids are bitter,' Dr Crystal informed me.

'The problem is,' Mr G explained, 'that, whilst Miss Middleton's senses are young and acute, she stubbornly refuses to interpret correctly the messages they send to her brain.'

'Lots of things are bitter,' I objected. 'Coffee and quinine, for example.' But Dr Crystal was unclipping the tarnished brass catch and opening his bag. 'What is that?'

He had produced a small clear bottle three-quarters full with a fluorescent yellow liquid.

'The antidote.' He brought out a long metal box and opened it to reveal a syringe with an alarmingly long and fat needle.

'It may have some unusual effects,' he warned. 'I have only ever tried it on a border collie.'

'Will I develop a cold wet nose and a compulsion to round up sheep?' I enquired.

Dr Crystal considered the question. 'I think that unlikely.'

'Or thick glossy hair? I should not mind that.'

He pursed his lips. 'On the contrary, almost all my subject's hair fell out within two days.'

I sat up. 'Did it grow again?'

He patted his cheek. 'I cannot say. The creature died a week later – but not of the antidote; at least I do not think so. Roll up your sleeve.' The liquid was so viscous that he had great difficulty in drawing it out of the bottle. He held the syringe up and pressed the plunger to expel the air. At least the needle looked sharp as a glutinous blob appeared, hanging tenaciously to the tip. He took off his spectacles. 'This will hurt,' he told me as he inspected my left arm, flicking it with his fingertip, but did not add a little. He found a blue cord under my skin and gouged the needle into it. I yelped. 'Shush.' He gripped my wrist and I saw his thumb blanch as it fought to expel the liquid.

The plunger jumped down the barrel and the antidote spurted into me.

'Streuth!' I cried out. He might as well have injected paraffin and put a Lucifer to it.

'I must apologize,' my guardian said, but Dr Crystal shrugged and told him, 'I have heard much worse. Blimid, for example.'

'I will thank you both—' Mr G began.

'Or Frebbing,' Dr Crystal continued.

The ball of fire stretched lazily, creeping up under my sleeve, burning a map of its progress along the vein. An inch or so along it forked and then again until my whole arm had a frame of white hot wires. I grabbed my elbow and squeezed hard in an attempt to create a tourniquet but the pain gathered speed, racing to my shoulder.

Every curse I knew streamed out of me as I jumped off the bed, nearly knocking our visitor over.

'I have not heard that one before,' Dr Crystal conceded as a furnace ignited in my chest, my heart fluttering in a futile attempt to beat out the flames.

'You have killed me,' I cried and my guardian frowned.

'The very fact that you can say that is evidence that he has not,' he argued as I toppled forward. And the last thing I remember was Sidney Grice adding, 'Yet,' and Dr Crystal stepping smartly aside so as to avoid having to catch me.

27

Anthrax

I WAS BACK in bed when the door opened.

'Feeling better?' Sidney Grice came into the room. He had a canary waistcoat on with bright silver buttons and an immaculately arranged yellow cravat.

'I think so.'

'Good.' He clapped his hands. 'Get up then.' He made to leave.

I started to rise but my left arm was stiff and sore.

'Who undressed me?'

'Why, Molly, of course,' Mr G called over his shoulder.

'No, I meant...' But the door closed. 'Uncle Tolly,' I whispered.

I looked at my bedside clock. It was ten o'clock so I would have missed breakfast. I put on my peach dressing gown and went across the landing. The bath water was warm as I lowered myself stiffly into it.

I dried myself and went back to my room, and saw myself in my dressing-table mirror. My face was that of an unsuccessful prizefighter. My hair – never my crowning glory – was dull and straggly and it stubbornly resisted my attempts to brush the knots out. I had lost many battles in my life but I was determined not to lose this one. Once, as a child in Parbold, I had got so cross with the tangled mess that I took Cook's bone scissors to it. My father chuckled and said I reminded him of a fox terrier after a day's ratting. Today I scraped at it doggedly and pulled it back with a navy ribbon.

The doorbell rang. I dressed and went downstairs, and before I had entered the room I heard voices.

'Leave the magistrate to me,' Sidney Grice was saying, 'and I will see you there at noon.'

'Miss Middleton.' Inspector Pound rose to greet me, wincing with the effort, and I took his hand and remembered.

'You are supposed to be convalescing,' I scolded.

'I could hardly stay idle in Dorset once I knew you were in trouble,' he said reasonably. 'Besides, grateful though I am, I have had enough of being treated like a spoiled child and admiring the view. Never saw the point in scenery, myself. What can you do with it?'

I laughed. 'You sound like Mr Grice. He is never interested in anything that is not a clue.'

'Not true,' Mr G grunted. 'I have sixteen other interests. Shall I enumerate?'

'Perhaps after I have gone,' the inspector put in hastily, and eyed me with concern. 'But never mind my health. Are you well enough to be out of bed?'

'That does not matter,' my guardian pronounced. 'It is sufficient that she is here.'

The inspector saw me into my chair. I was glad to rest my legs for they felt quite weak.

'Thanks in part to the attentions of Dr Crystal,' I said.

Pound tipped his head back. 'Dr Grant Crystal?'

'The very same,' my guardian confirmed. 'You know him?'

'I came across him when our mounted branch thought two of their horses had anthrax.'

I turned to my guardian. 'Dr Crystal is a veterinary surgeon?'

'The second best,' he confirmed.

'You had Miss Middleton treated by a horse doctor?' Inspector Pound asked indignantly.

'We can all sleep easy,' Sidney Grice smoothed back his thick black hair, 'knowing how rapidly the police can establish a fact.'

The inspector bristled.

'Whatever he is, he seems to have done the trick,' I said hastily.

'What trick?' Mr G glanced about suspiciously.

Inspector Pound went carefully down on his haunches and gazed into my eyes. 'Miss Middleton, there is something I must say.' His face was pale and for a moment I thought he had requested my guardian's permission and was going to propose marriage, so I was both disappointed and relieved when he continued, 'Mr Grice has asked me to tell you one thing and made me promise to tell you nothing else. It took a little longer than I expected because it is not known locally as Saturn Villa, but we have discovered the residence of Mr Ptolemy Travers Smyth.'

28

Umbrellas and the Double-headed Fox

SATURN VILLA WAS not such a welcoming sight this time. It loomed grey at the end of the long drive, dissolving into the thick morning air.

'It might have speeded the police search if you had told them about the electrical lighting.' Sidney Grice clinked a lamp post with the ferrule of his cane.

Did I not? I thought about it as we set off up the drive.

'It was quite beautiful last time,' I recalled.

'I have no interest in beauty other than the foolish things people do when they think they perceive it.' Sidney Grice rooted through the gravel with the toe of his boot.

'Why only think?' I wrapped my cloak tighter around myself.

'Because there is no means of measuring beauty and that which has no dimensions can only exist in the imagination and therefore not at all.'

Nonetheless, the dewdrops glistening on cobweb veils in the rhododendron bushes seemed very pretty to me.

We reached the end of the drive and I pressed the bell button. 'It is operated by electricity also.'

'How foolish,' Mr G muttered. 'Is it not enough that we run poisonous, explodable gases into our homes without streaming highly charged particles of atoms into them as well? Imagine the carnage if it leaked into the street.'

A moment later the door was opened and Colwyn stood before me. I stepped back warily.

'Miss Middleton!' His face broke into a boyish grin. 'How good it is to see you. We have been so worried.'

'Why?' My guardian shouldered his cane.

'Because Miss Middleton was so distressed when she left us.' Colwyn peered out into the gloom. 'Mr Grice,' he said. 'I recognize you from your portrait in *Foul Murder Monthly*.' He stepped aside. 'Please come in.' The fog followed us a little way into the hall, condensing on the marble floor.

'Wie lange haben sie im Gorizia-Tyrol gewohnt?' my guardian rattled out.

'Dreieinhalb Jahre,' Colwyn replied without a blink.

'Sie sprechen aber gut Deutsch.' Mr G inspected himself in the mirror.

'Merci Vielmol.' Colwyn bowed. 'You are as observant as your reputation, sir.'

I looked at the footman closely and he returned my gaze with untroubled eyes.

'I shall tell my master you are here.'

'You have a master?' I asked and he grinned.

'As you can see for yourself, I have not been dismissed yet, miss.' Colwyn went into the library.

'I do not understand,' I told my guardian. 'The last time I saw that footman I was a suspected murderess.'

'Never mind that for the moment,' Mr G said and swept his arm. 'What has changed?'

'Nothing.'

'Now you are being obtuse.' He tapped his toe. 'Were those muddy footprints there last time?'

'Of course not,' I said. 'We have just made them.'

'Then look more carefully,' he urged, 'and tell me one thing that is different.'

I surveyed the walls and ceiling and the dissolute marble god reaching for the heavens. 'The lights are off.'

'We have already established that.' He whipped off his wide-brimmed, soft felt hat and tossed his gloves into it.

'It is all the same.'

'Nonsense.' Mr G leaned towards the hallstand. 'Everything changes all the time. Were there the same number of umbrellas,' he supressed a shudder for he had a fear of such devices, 'when you first arrived, and are they in the same order now?'

'I did not notice.'

Mr G huffed. 'If there were prizes to be had for not noticing or comprehending, your display cabinet would be the envy of all London.'

'Just to demonstrate my ignorance further,' I said, 'what were you talking to Colwyn about?'

'I asked how long he had been in Gorizia-Tyrol and he told me it was three and a half years. I said his grasp of German was good and he thanked me.'

'But how on earth did you know that he had been there?'

'Simplicity itself.' Mr G gave his attention to the statue rising before us. 'His accent has a faint Germanic tinge and he wears a signet ring with the double-headed fox that is the Adler-Haussmann insignia and was only given to trusted retainers.'

'I noticed something odd about the way he spoke,' I said, 'and he has a blister on his left hand near the knuckle.'

'Undoubtedly a clue.' He walked round the plinth. 'Filth.'

'Some might say it was art,' I objected and he shrugged.

'I am referring to its upturned hand.' He unscrewed the spherical brass handle of his walking stick and deposited it into his pocket. He inverted the cane and a corked test tube slid out of the hollowed core, followed by five more which he slipped one by one into his waistcoat top pockets where they jutted out in two rows. 'The Grice Patent Specimen Storage Stick,' he announced.

'Would it not be easier to keep the tubes in your satchel?' I wondered.

Mr G tutted impatiently. 'The additional bulk of padding required would leave little space for other important items such as my flask of tea. Apart from which I could not patent that idea.' He stretched up and scooped some dust into one of the tubes, resealed it and inserted it back into his cane.

'Who is Colwyn's master now?' I wondered aloud. But I did not have to wait long for an answer as the library doors burst open with a violence that made me jump and Sidney Grice raise his hat like a shield.

'My dear, dear March!' Uncle Tolly rushed into the hall, his arms outstretched, his face aglow. 'How wonderful to see you, wonderful. I have been beside myself.' He grasped my hands, almost dancing with delight as he repeated, 'Absolutely beside myself, with anxious anxiety.'

29

The Death of Hope

S IDNEY GRICE SURVEYED my relative coldly.

'And you are?'

'This is Uncle Tolly,' I burst out in astonishment.

'Who can, as he has already demonstrated, speak – though rather annoyingly – for himself.'

Uncle Tolly let go of my hands and straightened his blue smoking cap, which had slipped forward during his exuberant greeting. 'Forgive me, Mr Grice, but I am so thrilled to find your ward safe and well, though naturally I am distressed to see her so battered and bruised.' He thrust out a hand which Mr G took suspiciously. 'I am Ptolemy Travers Smyth, though my friends call me Tolly as I hope you will too.'

'How easily the hopes of fools are dashed,' Mr G retorted, but instead of releasing Uncle Tolly's hand he bowed as if to kiss it, in reality scrutinizing the fingerplates. 'Your skin has been discoloured by Fretwell's Lime Ink and you are wearing differently coloured stockings. Why are you not dead?'

Uncle Tolly laughed uneasily. 'Your guardian has an unusual sense of humour,' he told me.

'My dog is livelier than my sense of humour and I do not even keep a dog,' Mr G told him. 'Kindly answer the question.'

Colwyn was still hovering in the background and his jaw jutted forward.

Uncle Tolly exuded bewilderment. 'I am not dead because I am alive. What more can I tell you?'

Mr G released the hand and wiped his own on a big white handkerchief. 'Do you have or have you ever had an identical twin brother?' He glanced at the handkerchief. 'Or even a brother whom fate has cruelly formed to resemble you?'

'I have never had any siblings,' Uncle Tolly replied. 'Have you?'

Sidney Grice snorted. 'It is my place to ask pertinent questions and yours to answer them.'

Uncle Tolly twitched like a nervous mouse. 'They seem more like impertinent questions to me, if I may make so bold.'

'You have already done so.' My guardian turned his back on him and inspected me. 'It would appear that you have deceived me.'

'I do not understand.'

And Mr G sniffed. 'Your display cabinet is stuffed to bursting – speaking of which,' he leaned towards a glass-fronted cupboard, 'where did you get that Liu Song jade belt clasp?'

'You know your jade, sir.' Uncle Tolly simpered like a proud father.

'It is not mine.'

'Xining, in China,' my relative recalled dreamily. 'It—'

'And did you visit the Longgong Caves whilst you were in that area?'

Uncle Tolly clasped his hands. 'Oh yes, indeed, indeed. They were magnificent. The—'

Sidney Grice put up a hand and addressed me. 'Speak.'

I looked again at Uncle Tolly and there was no doubt that it was he. His appearance, his voice and his manner were all exactly as I remembered them. 'I saw you dead.'

Uncle Tolly gawped. 'I do not know what to say.'

'Tea,' my guardian said.

And Uncle Tolly fiddled with his tassel. 'A capital idea,' he murmured. 'Yes, tea. Please take our visitors' overcoats, Colwyn, and then we shall have tea.'

'In the library,' Mr G added firmly.

'Indeed,' Uncle Tolly agreed weakly.

Colwyn took my cloak and hat.

'This hallway was polished this morning,' my guardian observed, keeping hold of his satchel and cane.

'It is polished every morning, sir,' Colwyn informed him and Mr G raised one eyebrow.

'Remember that, Miss Middleton, if that is not demanding too much of your faculties. It is the most important clue so far.'

'Clue about what?' Uncle Tolly asked as he guided us into his library.

'Your murder,' Mr G replied and Uncle Tolly shivered.

'But I have not been murdered.'

'Nobody has been murdered until they are,' Sidney Grice assured him. 'Tell me what happened, Miss Middleton.'

'Uncle Tolly was up his ladder,' the steps were still in the same place, 'getting a book down.'

'*My Interesting Life and Interesting Times*, a biography with inspirational verses,' Uncle Tolly confirmed. 'It was written by—'

'Samuel Travers Smyth,' my guardian broke in, picking the book up to leaf through a few pages. 'What next?' He replaced the book with great precision.

'We sat by the fire and had sherry and then we went to that map table for Uncle Tolly to show me the family tree, and he spilled ink over it.'

'Why?' Mr G demanded.

'It was an accidental accident,' Uncle Tolly quavered, raising his hand for inspection. 'I have tried scrubbing it.' The stain had faded but was still visible, an old treasure map stretching from the side of his little finger and curling on to his palm, the creases transformed into a river delta. 'I am not sure why I am being asked these questions.'

Sidney Grice strolled round my relative. 'I take a dim view of the obscurance of evidence.' He tucked his handkerchief to flow foppishly from his breast pocket, 'Proceed, Miss Middleton.'

'And then Uncle Tolly got me to write a will in which he left me everything,' I recalled. 'Colwyn and Annie, the maid, witnessed it.'

'The same Annie who clubbed you with a fire iron?'

'Surely not,' Uncle Tolly protested.

'It seems very like,' Mr G told him, 'you wanted to be murdered.'

'Why on earth would I want that?' Uncle Tolly fingered his beard nervously.

'That is what I intend to find out.' Sidney Grice kneeled to peer under the table as Annie came in with the tea.

She put the tray down stiffly and looked at me with concern, but did not speak as she left the room, blushing under my guardian's open stare.

'Am I going mad?' I asked and Mr G gazed at the hearth.

'Of course not,' he reassured me, 'though it is possible that you have already done so.

30

The Six Dwarves of Streatham

W E SAT AT a games table, the top inlaid to create an ivory and ebony chessboard, and I poured our teas.

'Dear March,' Uncle Tolly said, 'I am at a loss as to what happened when you came here last. We were getting along famously, I thought, famously, and then you became unwell. Perhaps you were unused to consuming alcohol.'

My guardian snorted. 'Miss Middleton is more unused to not consuming alcohol.'

'I helped you upstairs and you passed out on the bed. I checked you an hour later and you had changed into your night-gown and were fast asleep on top of the bed, so I went back to my study.'

'What time did you go to bed?' I asked.

'At about five of the clock.' Uncle Tolly blinked. 'I am a crea-ture of the night and work best when the rest of the world is quiet.'

'What species of work?' Mr G touched all the uncovered black squares.

'I study and I scribble,' Uncle Tolly told him. 'Botany is my great love. I grow exotic flowers in my conservatory. It is a sepa-rate building in the grounds.'

'Why?' Mr G snapped.

'To keep it out of the shadow of the house,' Uncle Tolly replied. 'Many of my plants require maximum sunlight. I can shade those that do not, but I cannot create sunshine for the ones that do and they do not like artificial light. I have asked them.'

Sidney Grice ran his tea around his mouth, sucking air over it before he swallowed.

Uncle Tolly held out a plate and pulled a face. 'Would you like a biscuit, March?'

'What is wrong with your arm?' Mr G asked. 'You are holding it oddly.'

'I fell and sprained my elbow,' my relative told him.

'Poppycock.'

I took a slice of Garibaldi but Mr G declined.

'I rarely consume sweetmeats but I should like some of your pickles.'

Uncle Tolly frowned and then smiled. 'March has told you about them – a little hobby of mine.' He stood and went over to the bell pull. 'But I have never thought to offer them with tea.' The maid came in. 'A dish of my pickles for Mr Grice, please, Annie.'

'One moment, Annie,' I called as she made to leave.

'Yes, miss?' She hovered under the lintel.

'I shall not be angry if you tell me the truth,' I promised, 'but did you strike me with a poker the last time I was here?'

'If you did not, then somebody went to the trouble of attaching a small blood clot and five dull brown hairs to it,' Mr G observed.

Annie ran her tongue through the cleft in her lip before bursting out with, 'Well-they-said-you-was-mad-and-had-killed-Mr-Travers-Smyth-and-I-thought-you-was-going-to-attack-me-with-those-tongs-and-escape.' She took a deep breath and continued more slowly. 'I only meant to tap you but you struggled and I had to do it you a couple of times.'

'There are the signs of four,' my guardian told her. 'That will be all.'

'Thank you for your honesty,' I said as Annie backed into the hall.

My guardian produced a small telescope, extended it full-length and scanned the room slowly before settling upon my relative, who shifted uncomfortably under the long wordless scrutiny.

'How many servants do you keep?' Sidney Grice adjusted the focus a fraction.

Uncle Tolly counted them off on his fingers. 'Colwyn and Annie you have met. Then there is Cook, a kitchen maid and a boot boy and a boilerman. Outside I have a head gardener, a—'

'You are boring me now,' Mr G complained. 'How and where is your electricity manufactured?' He lowered his telescope and Uncle Tolly perked up.

'There is a boiler in an outhouse which turns a generator. I call them Billy and Danny.'

'Which is which?' Mr G snapped.

'The boiler is Billy,' Uncle Tolly replied. 'The generator is—'

'I think I can make an educated guess.' Mr G compressed the telescope smoothly.

'Does it matter?' I asked.

'The truth always matters.' My guardian raised a foot to tidy his bootlace. 'Though it may not be relevant.'

Uncle Tolly fiddled with his goatee. 'Why are you asking me these questions?'

Mr G sat back. 'I wanted to see if you are as twitchy talking about seemingly irrelevant household matters as you were when I mentioned your murder, and I am interested to note that you are.'

'You have thoroughly unsettled me.' Uncle Tolly slopped tea into his saucer. 'If I had known you would be put into the care of such a man, March, I should have applied to be your guardian myself. Indeed I should.' The saucer tipped and stained his cuff and his indignation was all at once deflated. 'Oh dear.'

I handed Uncle Tolly a napkin and he took it blankly.

'It is just Mr Grice's way,' I tried to comfort him as Annie brought a silver tray bearing a small glass jar and a silver fork.

Mr G opened the jar. 'Are these the pickles you so rashly consumed?'

'I think so.'

'The very same,' Uncle Tolly affirmed. 'Slices of Indian Comb.'

Mr G leaned forward. 'Otherwise known as achycereus pectin-aboriginum.'

'You know your caryophyllales too,' Uncle Tolly approved.

'And yours,' Mr G affirmed.

'Cacti?' I clarified.

'Why yes,' Uncle Tolly agreed enthusiastically. 'I have a special hothouse for them in the grounds. Would you like to see it?'

'Do not accept that invitation, Miss Middleton,' my guardian warned.

'You can come too,' Uncle Tolly assured him, but Mr G stiffened.

'If I could be diverted in the course of my investigations that easily,' he sniffed the vinegar, 'I should not have rescued the six dwarves of Streatham High Street.' And picking up the fork between his thumb and forefinger, he plunged it into the jar and withdrew a speared, elongated oval of dripping sliced cactus. 'Perhaps you would like to sample this for us, Travers-Allegedly-Smyth.'

'With my morning tea?' Uncle Tolly held up his hands. 'I think not, Mr Grice.'

'Some might find your refusal suspicious.' Mr G laid the fork on a saucer, tines down. 'But I do not.' He deposited the slice in another test tube and slid it into his cane.

Uncle Tolly blinked like a sleepy owl. 'I do not understand.'

'There appears to be a familial predisposition towards incomprehension,' my guardian told him, and Uncle Tolly scratched his jaw.

'We shall see upstairs now,' Mr G announced, but my uncle bridled.

'You go too far, sir.' Uncle Tolly stood and reached for his bell pull.

'I am sorry, Uncle Tolly,' I put in hastily.

Uncle Tolly paused uncertainly. 'I do not like your guardian's manner.'

'I have yet to meet anyone who does,' I assured him.

'I should be alarmed if they did,' Mr G muttered.

'Perhaps I could explain exactly why we are here,' I suggested as my uncle wavered.

'Very well, March, but I have just discovered that there is a limit even to my patience and your guardian is testing it severely.' He twisted his chair in a little sitting jump a fraction away from Mr G but towards me, and sat back in it.

'I have jumbled memories of when I was here last,' I began. 'I know that I was taken unwell as you showed me to my bedroom, and I do not think that I was drunk.'

Uncle Tolly found a wrinkle on his cheek and pinched it. 'If you had food poisoning I do not fancy you could have acquired it here so suddenly, especially as we ate the same things.' He puffed out his cheeks and swallowed nothing as if it were a hard lump. 'You think,' he swivelled his head towards my guardian like an angry hen, 'that there is something wrong with my pickles?'

Sidney Grice placed his fingertips together. 'It is a possibility.'

'This is an outrage,' Uncle Tolly blustered, but was all at once deflated. 'But then perhaps it is not.'

'Explain.' Mr G jabbed at him with the fork.

'It is the one thing I did not eat,' Uncle Tolly told him miserably. 'But only because I have had a slight stomach – and I apologize if that is too vulgar a word – complaint. Perhaps the cactus has gone off.'

'Perhaps.' Mr G tapped his telescope. 'Or perhaps the plant itself contains toxins capable of confounding one's mental processes. Fortunately for us and possibly unfortunately for you, the thoroughfare on which I reside is also occupied by the finest medical and scientific institutions in London and, therefore, the world. We shall soon find out.' Mr G stroked the teapot handle regretfully. 'But we are wasting time with these pleasantries.' He flicked his head. 'Ring for your agreeable footman and well-presented maid to accompany us. We shall inspect Miss Middleton's sleeping chamber first.'

31

The Dead Moth and the Dust

UNCLE TOLLY LED the way, scrambling up the stairs, with Sidney Grice close at his heels and the servants following me.

The landing was just as I remembered it, large and square with three coloured doors to either side and a massive window filling most of the end wall – though there was still not much of a view out through the fog.

The first door on the right was pink and the wallpaper flowery.

Sidney Grice paced the bedroom like a caged bear. 'What have you done to this room since Miss Middleton quit it?' He wagged a finger at Annie and she flinched.

'Why, just my job, sir. I cleaned the room.'

'What state was it in?' He picked up the water jug, sniffed it and tipped it upside down. It was empty.

'A very bad state, sir.' Annie avoided my eye. 'There was water sploshed all over – that rug was sodden – and the jug had been broken and there was a nightdress on the floor, sopping and stained.'

'Stained with what?' He replaced the jug.

'Why, blood, sir – and water.'

Mr G polished his pince-nez. 'And where is it now?'

'In here, sir.' Annie pulled open the top drawer of the chest to reveal my long white cotton nightdress, pressed and neatly folded.

'Can you identify the garment with complete confidence?' My guardian poked at it with his cane as if expecting a venomous snake to slither from underneath.

I took it out and unfolded it. 'It is very like mine. The tag has my name on it... and there is a small repair on the hem.'

'So either yours or a painstaking forgery.' He stepped back. 'Hold it up to the window, Miss Middleton.'

The daylight shone weakly through. 'There are still some faint stains,' I observed.

'Blood is difficult to get out,' Annie said.

'Do you do the laundry?' I asked.

'Oh no, miss. A Spanish girl from abroad – though she lives in Dartmouth Park – comes every Thursday.'

'I believe Maria is actually Maltese,' Uncle Tolly chipped in, but my guardian ignored him.

'And does it where?' Mr G clipped on his pince-nez.

'Why, in the laundry room in the outhouse, sir.'

Sidney Grice began to hum. He was almost getting into a tune when he broke off and whipped round with a grace and speed that would have done credit to a ballet dancer, knocking Uncle Tolly's cap off with a swish of his cane.

'Have a care,' Tolly protested, his head suddenly small as he bent to retrieve his cap.

'I intend to,' my guardian assured him. 'Where might one most conveniently gain admittance to your attic?'

Uncle Tolly was crumpled as he stuffed on his cap and led us back into the corridor and to the light saffron door at the end. Mr G pushed through us and ran his index finger lightly over the top bolt, held it up and sniffed it. 'This has not been oiled.'

'It does not need oiling,' Uncle Tolly objected.

'You would be wise to think before you speak,' Mr G advised as he pulled his coat sleeves up to bare his wrists and drew back the bolts. He opened the door a crack to peek through. 'Stand back,' he barked and flung it open so violently that it crashed against the wall.

'Was that really necessary?' I asked. But Mr G dropped on to his knees below the first step and enquired, 'Was it like this when you saw it?'

'The dust was there and that dead moth.'

'Nobody has been up there for months,' Uncle Tolly said.

Mr G hummed seven notes, picked up the moth delicately by one wing and whispered, 'Cossus cossus.' His voice rose as he declaimed, 'The goat moth.' He laid it respectfully aside. His tweezers appeared and he picked something like half a shrivelled pea to drop into a test tube. 'I must have some of this dust.'

'Shall I have it sent round?' Uncle Tolly asked with newfound spirit.

'That is a generous offer – though I am always suspicious of kindness, however it presents itself.' Sidney Grice used the edge of a plain postcard to scrape a sample into an envelope. 'Remember thou art dust,' he told his sample as he folded the flap over. He got to his feet and regarded his trousers in dismay. 'I must design an overall suitable for criminological investigations.' He patted himself down. 'Your bed chamber, Mr Travers Smyth,' he announced. 'I shall examine that now.'

Uncle Tolly prickled timorously. 'I am not sure that I want you poking about in there. A gentleman's bedroom is private.'

Mr G smiled thinly. 'Not if he is murdered in it.'

'But I...' Uncle Tolly wiggled his fingers through his beard. 'But I...' He flapped his hands in confusion before steeling himself to make a decision. 'I think you had better go now, Mr Grice.'

'What you think is of little interest to me,' Mr G informed him cheerfully, and I noticed Colwyn bulking out his chest. 'It is what Miss Middleton has or has not done that commands my attention at present.'

'Mr Travers Smyth has asked you to leave,' Colwyn reminded him with a steely edge to his voice.

'Not so.' Mr G looked him up and down as one might a

garish painting whilst wondering if it is really art. 'Your employer expressed an opinion as to what might be best. It is a subtle difference which might not be apparent to one in servile employment.'

Colwyn towered over Sidney Grice.

'Please forgive my guardian, Uncle Tolly,' I said hastily. 'He means no offence.'

'Whatever gave you that idea?' Mr G pondered.

'Uncle Tolly,' I continued. 'I do know what happened when I stayed here, but I had an overpowering impression that you had been murdered and possibly by me.'

Uncle Tolly fluttered his arms. 'But as you can see, dear March, I have never been less murdered in my life.' He revolved to demonstrate that he was alive from every angle.

'I know that now,' I said. 'But it might help me to dispel the images that still trouble me if I could see that your room is not the death chamber of my imagination.'

Uncle Tolly pushed his little finger through a buttonhole in his coat. 'I will do anything I can to help you do that.'

'Thank you.'

Uncle Tolly struggled to extract his digit as we crossed to the blue door. 'Here we are.' He wrenched himself free and reached towards it.

'No,' Sidney Grice snapped. 'Let her do it.'

Uncle Tolly put his head to one side. 'Very well.' He moved away and I took hold of the handle.

'The door was shut?' Mr G asked.

'Yes. I knocked and called out.'

'Then kindly do so now.'

Feeling more than a little foolish, I tapped and called, 'Are you all right in there?'

'Did anyone reply?' Mr G was watching me intently.

'I thought I heard somebody whimper but I could not be sure, so I called Have you been having a nightmare? And somebody cried out so I went in.'

'Show me.'

I took a deep breath and turned the porcelain handle and the door swung open.

32

Shrews and the Submariner

IT TOOK EVERY ounce of willpower I possessed not to close my eyes. I knew, of course, that my relative was alive and well, but nothing I told myself could dispel the expectation of being greeted with the sight of him lying on that bed, axed to death.

The fog was lifting and sunlight filtered a little more strongly through as we entered the room. The bed, I was relieved to see, was unoccupied and neatly made. It was pretty for a man's room – cornflower wallpaper with matching curtains, a washstand with a white bowl and jug, a light oak dressing table and wardrobe, both carved in swirling interlocked T's and S's similar to the shield on the carriage that had first brought me there. The general effect was airy and cheerful and quite unlike the slaughterhouse that I thought I recalled.

'Did you go straight in?' Mr G asked.

'I peeped round the door and sort of stumbled.'

'How can you sort of stumble?'

'I tripped.'

'On what?'

I slid my boots over the threshold but they did not snag. 'I do not know. Perhaps just my own feet. I was very unsteady.'

'Enter the room.' He followed me in. 'What is different?' My guardian craned his neck as the others filed in behind us.

I thought about it. 'It is difficult to say.'

'The fact that something is difficult should not prevent you from doing it.'

'It was dark and I was confused.'

Mr G wagged a finger. 'It was unwise of you to be so at such a time. What did you see?'

'I thought—'

'I did not ask what you thought.'

I tried again. 'This sounds—'

'I shall decide how it sounds.'

'I saw Mr Travers Smyth on the bed.'

'How did you know it was him?'

'It looked like him – even that mole on his temple.'

'I was born with it.' Uncle Tolly touched the mark to confirm it was still there.

'You told me it was dark,' Mr G objected.

'It was dark in the corridor but the gaslight was burning on the wall there. It dazzled me for a moment but then I saw quite clearly.'

'I always have it on at night,' Uncle Tolly concurred. 'Billy and Danny are prone to overheat and could catch fire if unattended, and so I have the electricity off.'

'The mantle is fifteen inches from the wall,' Mr G estimated, 'and the pipe has been extended recently. Explain.'

Uncle Tolly twiddled through his beard. 'I wanted it to be overhead for reading at night.'

Mr G glanced about. 'I see no literary materials.'

'I usually bring a book up from my library and take it down to continue over breakfast.' Uncle Tolly scratched his pate. 'I have just finished *Lichens of the New Forest* by Professor David Corless.'

'Which edition?'

'The third.'

'An excellent choice.' My guardian beamed. 'His observations on lecanorineae are second only to my own.'

'You have made a study of pezizomycetes?' Uncle Tolly's eyes lit up.

'I dabble,' Mr G acknowledged with unusual modesty.

'Perhaps I could show you the paper I am preparing for the Highgate Scientific Society,' Uncle Tolly ventured.

'I am sorry to interrupt,' I said, 'but is any of this relevant?'

Both men eyed me with distaste.

'He who is bored with symbiosis is bored with life,' Mr G opined. 'But you are right, Miss Middleton. I must not let the fascinations of phycobionts divert me from your selfish concerns.' He sighed wistfully. 'So what did you see?'

'Mr Travers Smyth was sitting up in bed. His right hand was raised defensively and his left hand was partially severed.'

'Get on to the bed,' Mr G instructed.

Uncle Tolly twitched. 'This is most irregular.'

My guardian stuck his thumbs into the lower pockets of his waistcoat. 'If the matter were regular I should not be here. Hop on.'

And Uncle Tolly, with an ever greater air of bewilderment, clambered on to his bed.

'You were huddled back into the corner,' I told him and he leaned back obligingly. 'The lower third of your face was smashed.'

Uncle Tolly shrank. 'I hope you are not going to re-enact that.'

'The top of your face was odd,' I said, 'but I cannot remember why.'

'Odder than it is now?' Uncle Tolly chittered.

'It moved oddly,' I recalled.

'An odd face is doubtless of paramount importance.' Sidney Grice rubbed his hands. 'It was crucial in the case of the snub-nosed submariner. What next?'

'The curtains,' I said. 'They were closed but Mr Travers Smyth grasped hold of this one.'

'Do so,' Mr G commanded and Uncle Tolly started to shuffle over.

'You were still in the corner,' I said and he slid back. Uncle Tolly put out his arm, but no matter how much he stretched he could not reach the curtain.

'I do not understand.'

'Your lack of comprehension is of vital significance.' My guardian scribbled a note in his yellow book and indicated towards my relative. 'You may disembark now.'

Uncle Tolly scuttled off the bed and watched bemusedly as Sidney Grice fell to his knees. Mr G ran his hands over the square Persian rug and scrutinized his palms through a magnifying glass. He lifted the rug, sniffed the undersurface and let it fall.

'Was this revoltingly lurid example of Persian wool here that night?'

'That or one very like it,' I said.

'It has been there for eight years,' Uncle Tolly told him, 'except when it is beaten every spring. And it is a remarkably fine example of tight-weave turkbar.'

'Nonsense.' Mr G lay on his side. 'The knotting is farsbaf.' He lifted the blue striped counterpane to inspect under the bed and swept his cane to and fro.

'Not a speck of dust,' he commented.

'Why, thank you, sir.' Annie glowed with pride.

'That was not a compliment.' He picked at something with his tweezers. 'Indeed it may indicate a staggering degree of care-lessness.'

'I do not see how,' I objected.

Mr G shuffled out and sat up. 'What do you make of those?' He held out his palm.

I bobbed down to get a better view of his find. 'They look like two eyelashes.'

Mr G snorted. 'Even your bristly lashes are not that coarse.' He deposited them into one of his test tubes.

Uncle Tolly bent over. 'What have you found?'

'Perhaps the most important thing I have found was a silver pig,' Mr G replied, 'but that was many years ago.' He pointed. 'There are three scuff marks on the ceiling which could not pos-sibly have been caused by you being murdered in the manner described by Miss Middleton.' My guardian got on to his knees.

'They are therefore of inestimable value.' He bounded to the wall and began to tap it with the silver handle of his cane. 'As clues.'

'Have a care with the paper,' Uncle Tolly protested and Mr G spun round, his face inches away from my relative's.

'You need have little fear on that account, Mr self-proclaimed Ptolemy Travers Smyth,' he hissed. 'I am about to pay very close attention to it indeed.' He pirouetted away again and rested his nose on a flower, inhaling deeply as though the print might have a fragrance. His hand plunged into his satchel and drew out an intricately carved ivory handle. 'The paste smells old.' He pressed a button and a blade shot up.

'Goodness!' Uncle Tolly jumped backwards.

Sidney Grice ran his finger down a seam and slipped the point of his knife underneath it, lifting an inch of paper away from the wall. He wiped the blade on his handkerchief and inspected the white cotton.

'Please do not do that any more,' Uncle Tolly reproved mildly.

My guardian waved the handkerchief in a fond farewell. 'This room was decorated more than six months ago.'

Uncle Tolly counted on his fingers. 'Seven months,' he concurred.

'Which most competent mathematicians would calculate is greater than six.' My guardian went to the window, bent and sniffed the sill and brought out his knife.

'I trust you are not going to damage my paintwork,' Uncle Tolly ventured and Sidney Grice flicked the blade out.

'Your trust is not misplaced.' He ran the edge of the blade around, scraping some white flakes into a test tube. 'Tell your man to bring me a candle.'

Colwyn coughed politely. 'I do not believe we have any in the house, sir.'

'I cannot think that we do,' Uncle Tolly concurred. 'We have more than a sufficient number of oil lamps for use in the event of a concurrent electrical and gas failure. I find they give a much stronger light and are not extinguished so easily by draughts.'

'I shall provisionally accept your word for that.' Mr G tested the window catch. 'Where is the passepartout, maid?'

Annie's eyes drifted about blankly.

'The key,' I translated.

She moved to the dressing table. 'There should be one in that.'

'Deliver it to me,' Sidney Grice commanded, 'without delay or subterfuge.'

Annie took the lid off the onyx box and held out the key. He snatched it from her, inserted and rotated it, his ear close to the lock as it clicked open. He reached up and heaved the lower sash, which slid smoothly up. Mr G stuck his head into the chill air.

'Curious,' he proclaimed. 'This window has not even been tampered with.' Sidney Grice stepped back into the room and tidied his hair. 'Remarkable.'

'What is?' I asked.

My guardian tilted his head a little to the right. 'I have never been in a house in which there is so little evidence of a criminally induced death having occurred.'

Uncle Tolly beamed. 'I am delighted to hear it.'

'So am I.' Sidney Grice returned his jubilation blankly. 'For it gives me hope that a murder took place or shall take place very shortly.'

Billy, Danny and Exotic Plants

ANNIE EMITTED A tiny squeak, shut the window and locked it again.

'We shall continue our tour now,' Sidney Grice announced, 'since you appear to have no intention of offering us any more tea.'

'I am not sure I feel very hospitable,' Uncle Tolly admitted and my guardian snorted.

'I am quite sure that you do not.' Mr G put an ear to the wall and tapped the chimneybreast with his knuckles. 'Why have you no fireplaces in the bedrooms?'

'I like to be cold, especially at night.'

'I rarely sleep well unless I can see my own breath,' Mr G enthused. 'Where would you like to show us next? The choice is yours, Mr Ptolemy Travers Smyth.'

Uncle Tolly brightened. 'A man with your scientific bent should find the electrical generating machines of interest, of very great interest indeed, indeed.'

'My thoughts precisely.' Mr G clapped his hand. 'It is strange – is it not? – that Miss Middleton and I can occupy the same house and investigate the same crimes without having anything whatsoever in common, and yet I can come into your home and find so many shared interests that I scarcely know where to begin.'

Uncle Tolly beamed and fluffed up his beard. 'I knew we should be friends.'

'And I knew immediately that we should,' Mr G smiled, 'not. Lead the way, my good fellow.'

Uncle Tolly flinched at the slight but meekly obeyed, and we followed him out of the room, down the stairs and back along the hallway to a small side door which led along a low passage-way – windowless except for two skylights – to an end door.

Inside was pitch-dark but the heat hit us immediately. Uncle Tolly reached in, pulled something, and a dazzling light came on immediately, flickered and dimmed.

'Bother.' Uncle Tolly tisked. 'One of the globes has expired and I have no spares. I shall have to contact Mr Swan for another.'

The remaining light source was still bright enough for us to see as we entered a large brick building where a massive furnace stood, cast iron and sprouting several levers and dials. It reminded me of the time I was allowed to stand in the cab of the train to Wigan and help the fireman shovelling coal into the blazing fire. I ruined my best frock but it was great fun. This time the door to the firebox was closed. The boiler was connected at the side to some sort of steam engine with pulley belts running down to another machine in the far corner. Judging by the piles of rubbish against the wall, the floor had been swept but it was still carpeted in ash and pieces of clinker.

'Why is the generator not turning?' Mr G banged a pipe with his cane.

Perspiration mushroomed on my forehead.

'We turn Danny on intermittently to charge the cells which store the electricity and release it when required,' Uncle Tolly said.

I hoped I was not as purple as I felt. 'Then why do you have the boiler going?' I asked.

'An intelligent question,' Uncle Tolly commented and, unusu-ally for a man, did not add for a girl.

'Then answer it.' Mr G crouched and tugged at his bootlace.

I fanned myself with my hand.

'It takes a long time to build up heat and pressure.' Uncle

Tolly's visage glowed with pride. 'Any excess steam is vented off to heat my exotic plant house.' He patted a gauge affectionately. 'Also, we had some rubbish to get rid of.'

Mr G, who seemed unaffected by the heat, was shuffling his feet side to side through the ashes, like a novelty dancer. 'And if I wished to put out the furnace in an emergency?' He executed a half-twirl, sending clouds of dust over his trouser legs.

'Why, you would close this valve here to cut off the oxygen supply.' Uncle Tolly touched a red-painted iron wheel which had a black handle projecting from it. 'The fire would go out quite quickly then... What are you doing?'

Mr G strode over and pushed him aside. 'Following your advice.' His face was still pale and dry as he vigorously rotated the wheel.

'But really there is no need,' Uncle Tolly assured him. 'In fact I would prefer it if you did not. The fire can be difficult to reignite once put out, very difficult indeed.' He waved his arm anxiously, almost mirroring my guardian's action.

Colwyn hurried up in concern. 'Shall I stop him, sir?'

'You will not be able to.' Mr G crouched to adjust his bootlace. 'I am trained in the ignoble Oriental arts of offence and have had recourse to them on twenty-nine occasions, always to my opponents' shame and chagrin and, in three instances, permanently extinguishing their vital signs.'

'I think you had better not try, thank you, Colwyn,' Uncle Tolly decided nervously.

Sidney Grice jumped up. 'If any one of you attempts to interfere with that valve I shall have him or her charged with obstructing the police in the course of their duty.'

'Police?' Uncle Tolly quavered.

'Police,' my guardian repeated. 'You may expect them in,' he made a great display of checking his hunter watch, 'three minutes.'

Colwyn addressed Sidney Grice. 'I am sorry to speak out of turn, sir.' He glared indignantly at the little man before him. 'But

Mr Travers Smyth has shown you nothing but courtesy since you arrived uninvited at his home and you have persisted in taking advantage of his kind-hearted and – if I may say so – timid nature.'

'I am timid,' Uncle Tolly confessed.

Annie placed herself protectively in front of her master. 'You are a bully, Mr Grice.' Her voice quavered.

My guardian wiped his hands on a handkerchief. 'I flatter myself that I am. Unlike most bullies, however, I am not a coward and I never bluff.' He shook the handkerchief out vigorously.

'But why should the police be coming here?' Colwyn braced himself as if expecting them to hurtle through the door at any moment.

'To investigate the murder, of course,' Mr G explained impatiently.

'But whose murder?' Uncle Tolly asked anxiously and my guardian glared at him.

'Have you not been paying any attention?' He jiggled his hand in irritation. 'Your murder, of course.'

'Oh my goodness.' Uncle Tolly covered his mouth with the fingertips of both hands. 'Whatever—'

'Hark.' Sidney Grice leaned towards a distant sound and put his hand to his ear as if in a melodrama.

'The front door.' Annie hesitated, uncertain if she should answer the faint shrill ring.

'Ask not for whom that bell tolls, Mr Ptolemy Hercules Arbuthnot Travers Smyth,' my guardian proclaimed.

Uncle Tolly trembled. 'They will probably go away.'

'They are more likely to break your door down,' I warned.

'I had better go and deal with them,' Colwyn decided.

Sidney Grice held up his hand. 'We shall all go,' he declared and marched jerkily out of the room with the rest of us in his wake.

34

Soppy Girls and the First Baron Lytton

THE RINGING HAD become insistent and piercing by the time we reached the hall.

'Perhaps you should wait in the library, sir,' Colwyn suggested solicitously.

'Library?' Uncle Tolly dithered. 'Yes, indeed, thank you, Colwyn.' And he wandered away uncertainly.

Annie smoothed down her apron and put a hand to her hair.

'You go downstairs,' Colwyn instructed her. 'I'll deal with this.' He stepped smartly forward and opened the door.

Inspector Pound was on the top step in his second-best suit, looking very businesslike. 'Mr Travers Smith, if you please.'

There was a Black Maria on the drive with the back door open. Three constables and a balding sergeant were milling round it.

Colwyn stood to attention. 'My master is not at home.'

Pound's mouth tightened. 'He is at home to this.' He held up a folded sheet of paper and Colwyn put out his hand but the inspector kept a firm grip on the document. 'I shall not hand this to anybody other than your master.'

Colwyn frowned. 'One moment.' And he went to close the door.

But Pound put out a foot. 'It is an offence in law to shut out or attempt to shut out a police officer in the execution of his duty.'

'Very well, but you may not enter until you have shown Mr Travers Smyth your authority.'

'You know your law,' the inspector remarked. 'Been in trouble with it, have you?'

'Not yet.' Colwyn marched off into the library.

We heard low voices and a moment later Uncle Tolly appeared, his velvet cap tilted forward and to one side.

'Mr Ptolemy Travers Smyth?' the inspector asked.

Uncle Tolly went to the threshold and cleared his throat. 'I am him, that is, of course, to say he.'

'I have here a warrant signed by a Justice of the Peace, authorizing me to enter and search the premises and grounds of the property known as Saturn Villa for the purposes—'

'An Englishman's home is his castle,' Uncle Tolly said with a fire I had not witnessed in him before. 'His castle.'

'No man is above the law,' Inspector Pound told him, 'and I must advise you that it is an offence—'

'Yes, yes,' Uncle Tolly broke in. 'I suppose I have no choice, no choice in the matter at all.' He stepped aside and Colwyn, who was hovering behind, whispered something in his ear. 'Quite so.' Uncle Tolly walked his fingers up his jacket front. 'Does your warrant authorize Miss Middleton and Mr Grice to ransack my house also?'

'No, it does not,' Inspector Pound admitted and glanced down at me. 'I am sorry, but he has every right to ask you to leave.'

'Oh, I would never turn my own flesh and blood away.' Uncle Tolly folded his arms. 'But I shall not extend any more hospitality to her horrid godfather today.' The long black cap tassel fell over his right eye.

Sidney Grice considered the situation. 'I shall wait in the police van and rattle my halfpennies.' He pointed his cane, rapier-like at my relative's throat. 'But I warn you, if anything happens to my ward whilst she is under your roof I shall hunt you down and slay you like that man in the stupid book by the man that she was wittering on about the other week.'

'Edward Bulwer-Lytton,' I clarified.

Mr G edged sideways to the door as if unwilling to turn his

back on them. 'I am fascinated by the contents of the generator furnace,' he told the inspector, handing him the last test tube from his waistcoat. 'And any small items of hardware in particular.'

Sidney Grice whirled on his heel. He did it elegantly as always – whereas I should probably have fallen down the steps – but he cut a forlorn figure hobbling alone down the gravelled path.

At a signal from his superior officer the sergeant donned his helmet and the men lined up behind him.

'You know what to do,' Pound told them. 'Sergeant Mahoney will take Constable Lovell to check the contents of the boiler. Constable Brierley will go round the back to make sure nobody tries to sneak anything out. Constable Perkins and I will search the attic.'

I recognized Perkins as one of the men who had dragged the canal for a body in the Ashby case. He had called me a soppy girl and then been made to look foolish because of his efforts with a grappling iron, but I bore no ill-will and, from the hint of a wink he gave as he came in, neither did he.

Inspector Pound addressed Uncle Tolly. 'We shall try to disrupt your household as little as possible, sir. Perhaps your servants could show us the way.'

Uncle Tolly ran a hand over his brow. 'Very well, but I do not know who will make Miss Middleton's tea.'

'Unlike Mr Grice, I can probably survive without,' I assured him.

'Sherry then,' he said as the policemen dispersed and he went into the study. 'Or Colwyn told me you like gin.'

'I would love a gin,' I agreed and followed him through. 'Especially as I have brought my own.'

35

Mr Snuffly and the Skull

UNCLE TOLLY GAVE me a tumbler and, while I half-filled it from my flask, poured a sherry for himself.

'Dear March.' He ushered me into an armchair and sat cautiously on the edge of his seat opposite. 'Your face is so serious that I feel we must be seated before I swoon in terrified terror.'

The fire glowed cheerfully today, but I could not help remembering when my words burned and filled the room with yellow smoke.

I took a good swig of my gin and watched Uncle Tolly – so little and frail – sipping with quick dips of his wispy head.

'Do you really have no idea what happened the night I stayed here?' I asked eventually and he opened his sunken eyes wide.

'I only know that I am very glad to have made your acquaintance, March, very glad indeed. But, goodness, what a topsy-turvy world has resulted from that meeting. I hardly know what to think any more and now my home... my lovely home...' His voice wandered away and was lost. 'My private things,' drifted across the space between us. 'Strangers...'

'I am sorry,' I said and we fell silent again.

I heard heavy footsteps in the hall and Inspector Pound being summoned, but I resisted the temptation to investigate.

Uncle Tolly fumbled in his trouser pocket and dragged out a red and white checked handkerchief. 'I do not suppose you meant to bring this trouble upon me.'

I took a breath. 'Some very strange things happened when I first came here and I do not pretend to understand them.'

Uncle Tolly dabbed his eyes. 'It is sometimes better not to pretend.' He tied a knot in one corner of his handkerchief.

'Those cacti,' I said. 'Did you pickle poisonous ones by mistake?'

'I know that Mr Grice suggested as much.' Uncle Tolly knotted the opposite corner. 'But three days ago I was desperately desperate to try my new batch of pickles so Colwyn and Annie and I consumed an entire jar.' He patted his middle ruefully. 'I had a bad tummy – I can say tummy, can I not? – and Annie felt what she described as collywobbly and Colwyn said he never wanted to eat another pickle as long as he lived, not even if I doubled his salary, which, I am ashamed to admit, I have not. But none of us had any bad dreams as a result.'

'It was not a dream,' I insisted. 'I saw you murdered.'

Uncle Tolly waggled his head as vigorously as a puppy imagining a glove to be a rat. 'But we have discussed this, March and, as you can see…'

'What did I see then?'

'Who can say?' Uncle Tolly bowed his head. 'The night brings strange fancies to us all. I well remember the faces I imagined in the recesses of my room when I was a child.'

'But I am not a child,' I protested. 'And what I saw was no shadow. I lifted the axe. I felt it solid in my hand, the weight and smoothness of the handle.'

He tied another knot. 'What can I tell you, dear March?' His eyes glistened in the gaslight. 'I heard nothing amiss and I saw nothing amiss.' He folded his handkerchief and for a moment I thought he was going to do a trick as my father used to when he made Mr Snuffly, the cotton mouse.

There were more footfalls and men talking, and the door opened.

'The inspector would like a word, sir.'

Uncle Tolly stuffed the handkerchief away. 'You had better send him in then.'

Inspector Pound's usually immaculate hands and cuffs were grey and he was carrying a shallow wooden box, the sort that might be used for seedlings in the garden. 'I should like you to take a look at this, Mr Travers Smyth.' He put the box on to the table.

Uncle Tolly arched forward. 'What is it?'

There was a piece of sacking over a domed object, and the inspector lifted the cover away to reveal the upper jaw and part of the vault of a human skull. Uncle Tolly made a mewing sound and put his hand up, tilting his cap to the left.

'Oh my goodness.' He cupped his face in both hands. 'I had hoped he would be completely burned by now and he would have been if that nasty Mr Grice had not extinguished the furnace. Oh dear, oh dearie me. You have found the remains of Geoffrey.'

36

Empty Sockets

INSPECTOR POUND BROUGHT out his notebook and a wooden pencil. 'Geoffrey who?'

'Umm.' Uncle Tolly twiddled at his beard. 'Umm, just Geoffrey, I'm afraid. I never knew his real name and so I called him Geoffrey. It was just an affectionate nickname really.' He shivered. 'I should have buried him, I suppose, but I hated the idea that somebody might be digging about and find him – poor, poor Geoffrey.' He exhaled.

'How did he die?' Pound asked.

And Uncle Tolly stroked his beard. 'I am sorry, I cannot help you there, Inspector.'

Pound sat on the arm of a small leather sofa close by. 'It will go all the worse for you if you do not cooperate with my enquiries, sir.'

Uncle Tolly chewed his lower lip. 'Oh dear-dear-dear.' He let go of his beard. 'I would love to be able to help you more, Inspector, honestly I would, but I really have no idea how he died. I know he did not have any major head injuries.'

Pound watched him quietly. 'What was he to you? A friend? A servant?'

'A sort of friend, I suppose.' Uncle Tolly giggled. 'But he would not have been much use as a servant.'

'I am glad you find it so amusing, sir.' Pound shut his notebook and Uncle Tolly's face fell.

'Whatever must you think of me?' He sighed. 'Am I a very bad person, Inspector? I do not mean to be.'

Pound tapped the box. 'Can you make anything of it, Miss Middleton?'

'Not much.' I picked it up. 'He was obviously a mature adult – the bones are fused and the wisdom teeth are fully erupted. His right canine is missing and the gap closed.'

'I estimated he was about fifty,' Uncle Tolly agreed chattily.

'When did he die?' I tried, and Uncle Tolly scratched the side of his nose and said, 'I am not sure, March.'

'That's enough.' Pound banged his book on his knee. 'If you don't start telling us the truth I will take you to the police station, where my colleagues won't be quite so gentlemanly about the way they ask questions.'

Uncle Tolly's eyes welled up. 'Oh but, Inspector, I have told you nothing but the truth, I promise.'

I tried again. 'Uncle Tolly, you must realize that having human remains in your furnace and admitting that you knew they were there is highly suspicious.'

'Suspicious?' Uncle Tolly's mouth fell open. 'Suspicious of... oh my goodness me, I understand now. You think I murdered Geoffrey?'

'If you didn't kill him, who did?' Pound snapped.

'I am not sure that anybody did.' Uncle Tolly took off his glasses and his eyes shrank from capuchin to fledgling. 'I believe that most of these people die of illnesses and have no families to claim them.'

The light dawned on me. 'Geoffrey was a skull.'

'He still is.' Pound scratched the back of his hand.

'No, I mean he was just a skull,' I said.

'Well, actually he was an entire skeleton,' Uncle Tolly informed us, 'when I bought him from Dr Kershaw's widow.'

'So you're telling us that this is the skull of an anatomical skeleton,' Pound reiterated sceptically. 'Then why the hell didn't you say that in the first place?'

'I assumed you knew that.' Uncle Tolly hurred on his lenses. 'And I thought I was in trouble for not giving him a proper funeral.' He polished the glass on his cravat.

'But why did you want to get rid of him?' I queried, and he hooked the wires over the backs of his ears.

'He frightened me,' he said simply. 'I kept looking inside his head and wondering what thoughts had been there, and if they were still in there and thinking ill of me. I could not bear those empty sockets staring at me and those teeth always grinning, grinning, grinning, and so I put him in a canvas bag. But then I worried about what he was grinning about in there. And then you had your terrible dream that did not seem to be a dream, March, and I wondered if Geoffrey were playing tricks on you. The day after you ran away Annie thought she saw him creeping about this library when I was in my greenhouse, and so I decided he had to be destroyed – cremated. I am sorry.'

Inspector Pound stood up. 'I shall want proof of purchase.' He towered over us both.

'I do not have a receipt,' Uncle Tolly faltered, 'but I believe I would have heard if Mrs Kershaw had died. She will vouch for the truth of what I say – about purchasing Geoffrey from her, I mean. She cannot bear witness about my fears, my fears, because I never discussed those with her or anybody else at all.'

'I am not satisfied.' Pound picked up the box, sprinkling ash on the table. 'But I need to get back to my men.'

'Oh dear,' Uncle Tolly whispered when the inspector had gone. 'I think I could do with another drink.'

'Would you like a cigarette?' I offered and his hand tremored as he took it.

37

Charred Bones and Vices

W E SAT AND drank and smoked, and I thought how much more pleasant my life would be if Sidney Grice would join me in what he regarded as my vices, or even allow me to indulge in them openly. There were voices outside the door and somebody clomped up the stairs and somebody else down the hallway. I had finished my cigarette and tossed the stub into the fire before Uncle Tolly spoke again.

'Do you think I shall be in trouble, March?'

'Not for burning Geoffrey,' I reassured him, 'if you are telling the truth.'

'Oh, I always do that, dear March. It is too, too complicated not to.' He held his cigarette like a piece of chalk and drew pictures between us. 'I get confused enough as it is.'

'If your conversation with Inspector Pound is anything to go by, I can see your problem.' I lit another cigarette and watched him through the smoke.

Uncle Tolly fluttered his eyelids. 'Oh, it is too awful,' he moaned. 'All these strange officials rummaging through my life, confronting me with Geoffrey as if I was – Oh, March, what have I done?'

The door opened and Colwyn showed Inspector Pound back in. 'We have finished upstairs, Mr Travers Smyth,' he announced. 'They found a few more charred bones in the boiler room so, as I said, we shall need proof of where they came from.'

Uncle Tolly quivered. 'So you are not arresting me?'

Inspector Pound frowned wearily. 'Not today, sir.'

'And did you find what you were looking for?' I asked.

'I assume this is what Mr Grice wanted.' He held out the test tube for my inspection. It held three ash-caked woodscrews.

'What is it?' Uncle Tolly straightened his spectacles.

The inspector shrugged. 'Not very much to me, sir, but I have known Mr Grice solve a case on the strength of one crushed peppercorn.'

'The Musty Grave Ritual.' Uncle Tolly shuddered. 'I have read about that.'

38

Shelley and the Seagull

ONE OF THE constables fetched us a hansom while Sidney Grice examined their finds.

'Not a bad morning's work,' Mr G commented.

'Where do you think the skeleton came from?' I grasped the front fender to steady myself on the slippery footboard, but the horse moved and I slithered into the running gutter.

'I do not know… yet.' My guardian watched me struggle to my feet and into the cab. 'But I do know there is a nice little cafe three hundred and forty-four yards from here.'

'But I cannot go in a cafe like this,' I objected. 'I am splattered in mud.'

'You could wait outside whilst I have a quick pot,' he suggested.

'I am not going to stand on a street corner dressed like a vagrant,' I protested and Mr G huffed.

'Very well,' he grumbled. 'Though I never thought, when I took you in, that it would come to this, being denied refreshments because of some silly fuss about your apparel.'

'For pity's sake.' I slammed my hand on the seat between us. 'I have just been trying to console my only relative, who may or may not be a murderer, and all you can worry about is your precious tea.'

'It was not worrying enough about tea that led to—'

'Why do you always dredge up obscure cases whenever I say anything?'

'Roger Spedding's untimely death,' he continued.

'Stop it,' I shouted and the hatch opened.

'Can't stop on this corner,' the cabby said.

'I was not talking to you.'

The driver winked and tapped his nose. 'Being a naughty boy, is he?' And the hatch slid shut.

'What a peculiar reversal of roles,' Mr G called up, 'when the dumb animal drives and the more intelligent one pulls the cab.'

'Whoah.' The driver hauled on his reigns, and apparently we could stop there after all. 'Apologize or get out.'

'The second option is preferable to me. Keep the change.' Mr G tossed up a coin.

'What on earth was the point of that?' I asked as we stood on the pavement near the cemetery gates, watching our hansom speed away, almost running over a small boy. 'It will take ages to get another cab here.'

'About twenty minutes,' my guardian estimated. 'I shall give that malodorous child thruppence to summon one for us, which should just give us time,' he tilted his head towards Becky's Coffee House across the road, 'for a quick cup of tea.'

'You planned that,' I accused, and Mr G whistled a jaunty discordance as we crossed over.

There was a flower stall nearby.

'What good are roses to a dead body?' Sidney Grice wondered loudly as we entered.

The interior was packed with people in various stages of mourning.

'You might as well ask what good a coffin is,' I retorted quietly. 'Why not use a sack?'

'Why not indeed?' He selected a seat by the window for he always liked to look out at the streets. 'A corpse is just as comfortable in one as the other.'

'I shall remember that when arranging your funeral,' I warned.

'First, although you are younger than I and the female of the species – if she survives her childbearing years – has a longer life expectancy than the male, you are unlikely to outlive me.' There was a fork on the table and he swept it clattering on to the floor with his cane. 'I am far too intelligent to die before you.'

'If a good brain is what keeps you alive, why did Shelley die so young?' I argued.

He snapped his fingers for service. 'Percy Bysshe Shelley could have been of use to the world, mutilating people as a surgeon. Instead he frittered his life addressing Greek pots.'

'That was Keats,' I corrected him.

'And ended up being outwitted by water,' he persisted. 'That does not sound like an especially good brain to me.' He clicked again and called out, 'Two teas, hot and fresh with a pot of steaming water.'

The young waitress had something of the look of a seagull about her. 'Yes, sir, but I am just serving these gentlemen.'

Four undertakers were mulling over a plate of garishly iced cakes.

'Have some sense, woman,' he exclaimed and the room went quiet. 'If you waste time fussing about their order I shall have to wait longer for mine.' She put the plate down for them to continue their selection and went out through the back doorway, and gradually people stopped staring and started talking again, though several angry glances came our way.

'So,' Mr G asked me as the waitress approached with a tray, 'what did your second cousin have to say about the presence of human remains in his outhouse?'

The waitress started.

'His name was Geoffrey,' I said, 'and Uncle Tolly claimed that he only incinerated him because he grinned a lot and the maid thought that he crept around the house.'

She unloaded the tray warily.

'His teeth were broken in an interesting way,' Mr G pondered. The waitress froze.

'It is all right,' I told her. 'We are actors discussing a play.'

She giggled uneasily. 'I knew that, miss, from the fake blood on your costume.' She edged away and I spoke to my guardian again.

'I know it sounds stupid—'

He raised his hand. 'Then why say it?'

'I think Uncle Tolly is very naive,' I said. 'I do not think he could have killed a man and burnt his body.'

'That sounds very stupid indeed to me.' Sidney Grice motioned for me to pour.

*

'Do not speak,' Sidney Grice commanded as we set off in a cab.

'You need time to think?'

Mr G closed his eyes. 'It was not a difficult instruction,' he said.

And so I did not say anything when I saw a man coming out of the New Imperial Hotel. He was tall and sinewy and I should not have paid much attention were it not for the way he carried his cane, pointing backwards in his gloved fist. He barged a little girl aside and was soon swallowed in the swamp of humanity, but I could almost have sworn that it was Jonathon Pillow.

I was sitting on my favourite log in the shade of the old apple tree reading Vanity Fair for at least the third time and imagining myself as Becky Sharp when the gate opened. As he rounded the yew tree I saw that it was Jonathon Pillow. He must have come up the hill from Swandale's and he marched past, twenty feet from me, staring fixedly ahead.

He was a tall sinewy man and he carried a blackthorn stick pointing backwards in his fist. He went to the side door and rapped hard upon it and I saw him go into The Grange.

The windows were shut, but I could hear the raised voices and was just about to investigate when the door crashed open.

'Be grateful that I did not press charges,' my father said loudly but calmly.

'They are my papers and I shall have them,' Pillow bellowed, raising his stick like a cudgel.

'Over my dead body,' my father swore.

Pillow brought the stick back as if to strike him but my father did not flinch.

'As you wish, Middleton,' Pillow scowled, 'as you wish.' And he stormed away.

Georgina the hen ran flapping towards him and Pillow aimed a kick at her, but Georgie was too quick and Pillow stumbled on a stone. I giggled and he turned on me in a fury. 'You'll laugh on the other side of that pole face when you're an orphan.'

39

Trombones and Liver Flukes

SIDNEY GRICE BRUSHED the rim of his soft felt hat and tossed it on to the hall table.

'I still do not understand what happened,' I said once we were installed in the study.

My guardian rang for tea. 'I am in little doubt that a terrible crime has been or shall be committed,' he said as he went to his armchair.

'You are referring to the skull?' I suggested and Mr G yawned behind a loose fist.

'Let us hear whether or not the police can verify its alleged provenance before we get too excited about that discovery.'

He bent to fiddle with his boot again.

'Perhaps you should invent a new kind of bootlace,' I suggested.

'I had this footwear modified by the finest mousetrap manufacturer in England,' he grumbled, 'but the mechanism is sticking.'

An omnibus came to a halt opposite our front window with a solitary passenger on top, trying to punch the dents out of his stovepipe hat.

'Please do not tell me you are trying to catch mice in your boot.'

The man gave up and hurled his hat furiously into the road.

'An interesting idea.' My guardian spread out his copy of the *Bloomsbury Echo* on the floor. 'Though I suspect you were attempting – and failing, as always – to be humorous.' He put his foot on the paper, jerked the lace and there was a click. 'The heel of this boot has a compartment with a sliding, spring-loaded hatch in the base.' He stamped and a pile of ash spilled out over an advertisement for stronger, longer-lasting moustaches wax. 'At last.'

'That was why you were doing that shuffly dance.'

As if in hope of accompanying him, a trombone played outside – the opening bars of 'You Can't Take Your Donkey on the Bus'. I remembered Edward trying to entertain the mess with that song at a Christmas party and getting as far as It put its blinking hoof straight through the blinking roof before he fell off the table to wild applause.

'I was collecting evidence.' Mr G kneeled beside the newspaper. 'Fetch me my brass-handled magnifying glass and the silver one for yourself. We shall also need the letter opener and the penknife.' Mr G wrinkled his brow as he took the glass and knife from my hand. 'I have divided the pile into two smaller yet nearly equal piles. The one furthest from me is for you.'

I went on my knees opposite him, no easy feat in a bustle. 'What are we looking for?'

'I am looking for clues.' He levelled his pile out with the blade of his penknife. 'And I suggest you do the same.'

I flattened my little heap with the letter opener and raked out the ashes – shapeless specks of grit and soot, smudging over the story of how a little boy's tortoise was rescued by a quick-witted barber. Mr G began to hum with his usual lack of melody while the trombonist played the chorus with gusto.

'Cement and coal,' he remarked contentedly, and I was reminded of when Maudy, Barney and I had searched for gold nuggets in sludge from the banks of the River Douglas. Barney had made a special sieve – he was always making things in his father's workshop – but the most exciting thing we found was a snail.

Something caught my eye. I flicked the surrounding particles away, blew very gently to clear the rest, and examined it under my glass.

My guardian stopped what he was doing. 'What have you discovered?'

'I am not sure. It is a bit—'

'Blue,' Sidney Grice finished my sentence and, before I could examine it any more, he had licked his finger and dabbed my find away to inspect it more closely. 'Paint.' He scraped it into an envelope and made a note on the flap. 'And doubtless an important or irrelevant find. Now…' He folded the newspaper around the rest of his sample and weighed it down with a copy of *The Nine Plagues of Ashby-de-la-Zouch*. 'Let us examine that other sample of dust.'

'Oh, do let us.' I jumped up in mock delight and he eyed me balefully.

'You seem to forget that a few hours ago you faced the prospect of judicial execution,' he scolded.

'I am sorry.' I avoided his eye. 'But now I do not even know what we are investigating.'

'According to the Bible you lay so much stock by,' Mr G climbed to his feet, 'it was only man's curiosity about the unknown that enabled him to escape from the Garden of Eden.'

'I believe Adam and Eve were driven out as a punishment,' I informed him.

'Punishment?' Mr G went to a wooden rack on his desk. 'Is not the prospect of eternal happiness terrifying enough without having to endure it in this world?' He lit a miniature oil lamp and placed it in front of his microscope, dipped a steel spatula into a test tube and sandwiched a pinch of its contents between two glass slides. 'Interesting.'

'Is anything not interesting?' I queried.

'Music,' he responded without hesitation, 'and there is a device manufactured in Rotterdam which is tedious beyond words.' He tipped the mirror a fraction. 'What do you make of that?'

'Is this what you found on the statue's hand?'

'I do not find clues.' Mr G frowned. 'That conjures up images of me stumbling over them by mere happenchance. I detect them.

That is what a good detective does and – and there is no point in being modest about it – I am the best.'

I went over and adjusted the focus and the trombonist started 'The Man Who Married Mary'.

'Amorphous inanimate specks and tiny bundles of fibres – fine particles of wood – sawdust,' I diagnosed and was rewarded with a mildly impressed pulling down of his lips. 'I used to study all kinds of things under my father's microscope until I broke one of his prize specimens of a sliced liver fluke.'

'I am surprised he did not disinherit you,' my guardian said gravely.

The clock struck. 'Anyway, it must be time for lunch.'

Mr G winced. 'What is lunch?'

'An abbreviation of luncheon.'

He put his microscope away. 'Next you will be calling break-fast brek, supper sup or dinner din.'

'And I trust you will remember who suggested it if I do.'

He closed his eyes in despair.

Luncheon was vegetable stew with a difference, the difference being that it was hot.

40

Pistols and Lies

INSPECTOR POUND CAME that evening, tired and holding an arm protectively over his wound.

'I sent a sergeant to see Dr Kershaw's widow,' he announced, 'and she backed up Mr Travers Smyth's account of purchasing a skeleton from her. It was written in her accounts book for eight guineas.'

'Assuming it was the same skeleton,' I pointed out and my guardian pursed his lips approvingly.

'I am prepared to make that assumption for now,' our visitor said as I fetched a mahogany chair.

'I have a bone to pick with you, Inspector,' I challenged as he lowered himself on to it. 'Why did you not tell me you knew that Mr Travers Smyth was alive before I set off for his house?'

Inspector Pound pinched his philtrum. 'Mr Grice wanted to see your reaction.'

I fiddled with the cording on the arm of my chair. 'And so you went along with it.'

The inspector's clear blue eyes flicked away. 'He made me promise.'

'How?' I demanded. 'Did he point his ivory-handled pistol at your heart?'

'What a ridiculous question.' Mr G plonked himself into his chair without offering our visitor one. 'It is not a pistol. It is a revolver.'

I refrained from reminding my guardian that he had recently blown his only friend's brains out with that very weapon.

Inspector Pound straightened. His finger and thumb parted, running along the lower edge of his neatly trimmed moustaches. 'He told me that he needed to see how you and your uncle greeted each other.'

A clump of soot splotted into the grate, bursting into a miniature black snowstorm over the hearth.

'I hope I performed satisfactorily.' I glared at Sidney Grice but he was serene.

'Your performance has not been satisfactory,' he told me, 'from the day you clomped into my house dressed like an agricultural labourer in brown shoes and a coat he might wear to feed the geese.'

I sat up. 'That coat cost me five guineas.'

Molly arrived with a loaded tray.

And Mr G retracted his shirt cuff. 'A horse blanket would have cost less and been smarter.'

The inspector laboured to conceal his amusement. 'Perhaps I should leave you both to quarrel about that later.'

'I don't not know why horses have blankets.' Molly put the tray down. 'They don't not never go to bed.'

'Get out, you blockheaded lumpen serving wench,' her employer ordered.

'Don't not go to mine much neither,' Molly mumbled as she departed.

'You will stay for tea,' I invited and Inspector Pound fetched an upright chair from the round central table, sucking in sharply as he lifted it.

He sat down gingerly. 'The important thing is that you are no longer in danger of being accused of murder.'

'Sloppy logic,' Sidney Grice snorted. 'My ward might be accused of a different murder committed some time ago or on a future and interesting occasion, but I concede that she is unlikely to be accused of the killing of Mr Travers Smyth in the early hours of Friday last.' He put a finger on his glass eye to control its inward drift. 'Also, it is only the third most important thing. The second being that I may not have to be embarrassed by this affair much longer.'

'And the first?' I enquired and he tapped the pot.

'This tea is doing two things that I prefer tea not to do. It is stewing and cooling and therefore presents us with our most urgent challenge.'

'I think I can rise to that.' I took hold of the handle, which was still quite hot, and poured three cups. 'So what did my reactions tell you?'

'That you were probably telling the truth.' Mr G centred the tray.

'Only probably?' I splashed a little milk into my tea and a lot into our guest's but Mr G put milk quite high in the long list of things he detested.

He stirred his drink six times clockwise, though he abhorred sugar also. 'You invariably exhibit three signs when you are trying to deceive me and, since none of them was evident, I shall assume that your surprise was genuine.'

'What three signs?' A long time ago I used to cross my fingers behind my back and Edward used to claim that I blushed, but I do not think I did.

My guardian stirred vigorously anti-clockwise. 'If I were to tell you that, you would change your habits and I should have to search for new ones.'

Pound helped himself to the sugar. 'Perhaps you could tell me some time.'

'I have never lied to you, Inspector.' I caught his eye. 'Well, not about anything important.'

'The truth is always important.' Mr G gazed so intently past me that I wondered if he were seeing it somewhere behind my left shoulder.

'I still do not understand what happened.' I took the bowl back. 'And please do not mention display cabinets, dear Godfather.'

The inspector looked quizzically from one to the other.

'Luckily we have a witness,' Mr G reasoned. 'That is to say, you.'

'Yes, but I do not know what happened,' I objected.

'I suspect,' my guardian dried his spoon as if shaking the mercury down in a thermometer, 'and it is my job to suspect things – that you do know what happened but are confusing fact with fancy. What – apart from the usual female aberrations of your mental processes – do you suppose might have caused that?'

'I was drugged by the pickled cactus.'

'Was that what your uncle gave you?' Inspector Pound asked.

'He gave me two helpings of it.'

The inspector rubbed his chin. 'Perhaps I should pay this gentleman another visit.'

'It is not actually an offence to feed someone with unusual vegetables unless you can prove intent to kill or cause bodily harm.' My guardian closed his eyes.

Inspector Pound sipped his tea. 'Possibly not,' he conceded, 'but he must be guilty of something.'

'I do not suppose it is an offence to pretend to be murdered either,' I pondered, 'especially as he did not even waste police time by summoning a real constable.'

'Impersonating an officer is illegal,' the inspector said, 'though it is hardly worth pursuing the matter if it was just some kind of prank.'

'Prank?' I was incredulous. 'I was terrified almost out of my mind.'

'Hardly a prank to kill a man,' Mr G said quietly.

'But Uncle Tolly is still alive,' I protested, splashing my tea over my wrist.

'Yes, but is it not obvious even to you?' Sidney Grice cried. 'The evidence that no crime was committed lights our way so clearly that we are in peril of being blinded by it. We should be proud of Miss Middleton, Inspector.' He put a finger to his eye. 'She has been a witness to one of the finest murders not committed.'

41

Violins, Coffins and Toothache

INSPECTOR POUND'S EYES widened fractionally but his expression remained impassive.

Sidney Grice's hair had fallen foppishly forward. He flicked it back with a jerk of his neck and inhaled heavily like a man enjoying the sea air.

'At the risk of appearing to be the simple child you believe me to be,' I said, 'I should be grateful if you could explain that last remark.'

Mr G blinked. 'What did you not understand? Of the thirteen words I used in my last sentence only four of them were longer than one syllable.'

'It is not the words but the way you assemble them that baffles me,' I replied and my guardian huffed.

'I hope you are not going to ask me to explain,' the inspector lowered his cup and saucer on to his lap, 'because I fail to see how you can witness something which has not happened. I would be laughed out of court if I gave that as evidence.'

'You think Miss Middleton dreamed it all?' My guardian clicked his fingers as a man might summon a waiter.

'No, but I thought we had agreed—'

'I have not agreed to anything.' Mr G brought out a tiny coffin from his waistcoat pocket. It was a snuffbox, though he had only ever taken any once to clear a cold.

'Heaven forbid that he should be agreeable,' I muttered.

Sidney Grice pressed a cross on the side of the coffin and the lid sprung open, though he did not dip into it. 'I met a man today claiming to be Travers Smyth, but I have long found it a useful rule of life never to trust a man with a criminal record, a violin or a name which should be hyphenated but is not. First, we only have his word for it that he is who he claims to be, though I have an unfounded suspicion that he might be. I shall employ the services of Turpin, Turpin and Turpin, the genealogists, to investigate that. And, second, I did not say that nothing occurred.'

'Then what do you think did happen?' the inspector asked.

'I have absolutely no idea.' Mr G hinged the lid back down. 'But I could give you an almost interminable list of things which did not.'

'And you prefer this to scenery?' I asked the inspector and his eyes crinkled.

My guardian drained his tea. 'If you took as much interest in studying nature as you do in reading trite poems about it, you might be a bit more useful to me and yourself. Remember how my examination of cobwebs helped me to solve the Foskett case? And it was my detailed knowledge of the nocturnal habits of tapeworms that saved the ninth Earl of Rattingdon from a very long custodial sentence indeed.'

Pound put a hand into his pocket. 'I should quite like to have Mr Travers Smyth down at the station.' He brought out his pipe, though he knew better than to light it. 'He strikes me as a man who would crack quite quickly under pressure.' He blew down the mouthpiece. 'Though I can hardly take him in without any evidence of a crime.'

'I could always allege one,' I suggested.

And the inspector smiled. 'We'll make a policeman of you yet, Miss Middleton.' He clenched his pipe between his teeth and sucked on it wistfully.

'No need for that.' My guardian leaned back. 'I have asked him every relevant question.' He reached over his shoulder to grasp the skull on his bell rope and Pound tensed his arms.

'You will stay for more tea,' I urged as he began to rise.

'I cannot.' He struggled to his feet.

'Good,' Sidney Grice said.

'I will show you out,' I offered and went with him into the hall.

'I have missed you,' I whispered as I handed him his hat.

He touched my face and I reached up to stroke his, taken aback at how hot it felt.

'Can I see you?'

'Of course you can see her.' Molly appeared from nowhere with a dustpan in her hand. 'It ain't not that dark.' She took his coat from the stand. 'Blimey, have you both got toothache?'

And our hands dropped guiltily away.

42

Facing the Wall

I WAS READING *in the library when my father came back from Southport. There was a grimness in him that I had never seen before and he poured himself a large brandy before he sat at the table with me.*

'It is very bad, March.' His voice was croaky. 'Little Daisy had a fit in the night.' He tossed half the drink down and cleared his throat. 'She did not survive.' His breath shuddered. 'There was nothing I could do.'

'Oh, poor Daisy,' I cried and my father put a hand heavily on mine.

'Marjory has gone into shock.' He finished his drink. 'I do not know if she will ever come out of it.' He stood abruptly and strode back to the side table.

'Barney must be...' I could not think of a word to describe it.

My father had his back to me as he refilled his glass. 'Barney is very ill, March. They took him to Southport for his weak chest.'

'But Barney has quite recovered from his fall. He is—'

'Very ill,' my father insisted, though Barney had raced me up Sparrow Hill the day before they left. 'His weakness has turned into consumption.' The stopper rattled back into the decanter. 'I am going to arrange for him to be admitted into a sanatorium abroad. The sea air did him no good so we will try the mountains.'

And still my father faced the wall.

43

The Stolen House

A S USUAL SIDNEY GRICE was in the dining room before me the next morning, dipping into his bowl of prune juice sprinkled with charcoal and surrounded by fragments of eggshell.

'March.' He tossed aside a copy of the *Manchester Guardian*. 'I am afraid you will have to breakfast without the benefit of my jolly banter this morning. I am required in court as a professional witness for a freemason who found someone had painted his study in scarlet.'

'Sounds serious.' I helped myself to the teapot.

'It was.' He threw his napkin on to a pile of crunched-up and torn newspapers. 'When he stepped out of the room to find the rest of his house had been stolen.'

I sniffed the tea. 'I did not read anything about that.'

'The government is trying to hush it up.' He ripped out a column of print and stuffed it into his pocket. 'But I suspect it will be all over London by this evening.'

'Just as his house may be,' I suggested.

Mr G gave me an atrophying look and stood up.

'And you will have a quiet morning in.'

'Will I?'

'Yes,' he said firmly and was gone, rattling down the stairs and shouting to Molly for his flask, and how was he supposed to know she had already done it when she never has before?

I poured myself a tea and sifted through the wreckage of his morning's papers. There was an article about a new hat shop on Regent Street, but he had torn out the middle for a stabbing on the Gray's Inn Road. I found another about a possible new suspect for the slaughter of the Garstang family in Burton Gardens, but it was easy to see why my guardian had not thought to save it. It was written by Trafalgar Trumpington – a journalist Mr G detested – and padded out with a neighbour's unfounded conjectures.

Molly trudged upstairs. 'Letter by special messengerer,' she announced with a despairing glance at the debris of her employer's activities.

Even as I took it from Molly I knew whom the letter was from. I had corresponded with the inspector whilst he was in the nursing home and I would have recognized that solid square handwriting anywhere. I unfolded the single sheet of white paper.

My Dear March,
How it cheers me to call you that.
  Can I see you alone? There are so many things I want
to say to you. Will you come to the El Cabala at ten
o'clock? If it is difficult or SG is suspicious do not trouble.
I shall wait one hour.
  Yours affectionately
  GP

I did not need to think twice about it. My guardian could hardly object to my meeting a trusted police officer in a public place. I went back up to my room and changed, saw myself in the cheval mirror and changed again – my blue and white dress from Madame DuPont's. It was not a new outfit but I did not want to be too dressed up for an informal cafe.

I did battle with my hair, won a Pyrrhic victory and hurried downstairs.

'I am meeting Inspector Pound at the El Cabala Cafe,' I told Molly as I raised the flag. 'Please do not tell Mr Grice unless there is some emergency.'

'Oh lor', miss.' She dropped my umbrella and stepped back as if expecting it to bite her ankle. 'I don't not think the master will be very happy when he finds out you've gone and went out. He'll be like flea with a sore head.'

'Bear,' I corrected her.

'Flea with a sore bear,' she tried uncertainly as I trotted down the steps.

I saw no reason to take a cab. It was a five-minute walk to Upper Montague Street and a hansom would probably take four times that long in the ever-heavy traffic.

'Any spare dogs?' a young lad begged and, seeing my puzzlement, explained, 'Cats and dogs is pets. Pets is cigarettes.'

'You might as well say fish,' I reasoned. 'Fish get caught in nets. Nets are cigarettes.'

He wrinkled his nose. 'Nah,' he decided as we crossed the road together. 'Don't fink so.'

I flipped open my father's silver case and gave him two Virginias.

'Ain't you got no perks?' he complained and I gave him a Turkish as well. 'Got an 'orrible?' I knew that one – horrible fright/light – and struck a Lucifer for him. He sucked in deep and broke into a raucous coughing fit. 'Gawd, that cleared the tubes.' He spat into the gutter and I walked on.

The fog was very patchy, poisonous strands lacing the air and curling around the pedestrian's legs, while a black-and-white terrier jumped through a stray wisp, trying to snap it up. I was amazed it had the energy for I could see every one of its ribs.

I passed into Upper Gower Street and went left up Francis Street.

'Missus, come quick.' A girl, probably no more than eight or nine, with only a few tufts of ginger hair on her enlarged square head, ran up and snatched at my sleeve. 'Please, missus, it's my likkle sister and she's 'urted bad.'

I had not seen this child before. Her cherub eyes looked up at me pleadingly as she trotted bow-legged at my side.

A man in black knee breeches and ivory stockings wobbled wildly on his velocipede and snatched a lamp post to save himself.

'Where? What happened?'

She had a tight grip on me now. 'We was muckin' out and the 'orse kicked 'er. She's gone all white and funny.' She pulled me towards a narrow mews.

'Where did it kick her?' I asked, allowing myself to be led past a row of closed stables and an inquisitive pony tethered to the wall.

'In the stomick,' she told me.

We came to an open door and I squeezed past an old van parked in the alley and almost blocking it.

'In here?'

She stood, white with fright. 'She ain't dead, is she?'

There was a bundle of rags in filthy straw under an empty manger in the gloomy far corner.

'Where is the horse?' I wondered, stepping in.

There was a rushing and something swooped from behind, came over my head and swept down my body, rough, opaque and damp.

'What?' was all I managed before I was bowled over, crashing on to the cobbles, and I felt a tightness as a rope was tied round my ankles. There were two sharp cracks in rapid succession.

'Gotcha.'

I screamed and something smashed into my left cheek.

'One more sound and I'll cave yer face in.'

'Who are you?'

My face was struck again.

'Can't you 'ear me in there?'

I nodded, uncertain if the man could see my movement inside his sack, and the rope wound around me. He raised and dropped me as he worked it up until it gripped my throat like the noose I had put round other people's necks. My head fell back on the stones. I yelped involuntary, to be rewarded with a kick in the back.

I felt myself being hauled up by the shoulders and dragged, heels scraping through the mucky straw, back into the street. There was a slight change in the light but nothing more.

'Grab 'er feet.'

I was lifted at both ends, swung and dumped down on to a wooden floor, and I knew they must be putting me into the van.

'What you doin' wiv 'er?' It was the little girl.

'Take yer money and scarper,' a man growled, but not, I thought, the man who had hit me.

'Get Sidney Grice,' I called. It was better to risk a beating than to be at their mercy. The doors slammed. 'I will pay you ten times what they gave you – and a new dress,' I yelled, though I knew it was unlikely that she could hear me.

44

Harems and Hunting Dogs

W E SET OFF, juddering over stones and potholes, each lurch tossing me about. I tried to sit but only succeeded in bruising myself more as I toppled over, and so I rolled. It was difficult to bend my legs, but I managed a few kicks at the side and shouted as loud as I could and repeatedly. 'Help. Help. I am in the black van.'

But I could hardly hear myself above the crashing of wheels and the squeal of a rusty axle, and I knew there was little hope that my voice would carry through the sacking and the planks over the roar of the traffic and shouts of the sellers.

We had swung to the left, stopped, and then jolted to the right, and I judged we must be making our way along Tottenham Court Road. But I was thrown about so much I could not tell if we were taking another street or going round obstructions.

As the bustle gradually decreased and our speed picked up, I ceased my attempts. The rope was digging into my ankles and every move I made tightened it round my throat. I would save my energy, I decided, and lay still and quiet. A clock struck ten. Inspector Pound would be at the table, waiting to greet me. My guardian would be in court. I did not know where I was now, and then we stopped and I listened. The bolts were being knocked back and the two back doors squealed reluctantly open.

Somebody took a fistful of sack tangled with my dress and hauled. When we were young, Maudy Glass and I used to read stories about girls being kidnapped and sent to harems. It did not seem so romantic now. I had also heard of girls being dropped in the river when they were with child and wanting support, and it occurred to me this might be a case of mistaken identity.

'I am March Middleton,' I said as steadily as I could, steeling myself for a blow which did not come. 'If this is a mistake, take me back and leave me and you will hear nothing more about it. I have no idea who you are.'

I was being lifted at both ends again.

'Blimey, she's 'eavy for a scrawny one.'

'If you expect a ransom, I have some money,' I tried again.

'That's 'cause she's a dead weight.'

'She don't sound dead to me.'

'It's an expression.'

'If you kill me, Mr Sidney Grice will hunt you down and have you both executed,' I warned, my voice rising as they lumbered along.

We were inside again, I judged, going along a passageway, because the man at my feet was shuffling backwards and once I was bumped against a wall.

'Open the frebbin' door then.'

There was a struggle to hold me in one arm while he rattled at a handle.

'It's locked.'

'No, it ain't.'

More rattling. 'Oh no, it's open.' He readjusted his grip and we went on. Then another door and more fuss.

'Blimey, I'm fit to drop.' I could hear wheezing.

'No far now.' More shuffling. 'Here it is.'

Another door opened. 'There you are, gov.' And I was deposited on the floor.

'What is it?' a man asked. I knew that voice.

'It's the girl.'

'Uncle Tolly,' I yelled. 'Is that you?'

45

Dogs and the Art of Persuasion

A CHAIR SCRAPED back.

'Dear God! Dear God!' Uncle Tolly cried out. 'What have you done?'

I heard a throat clear. 'You told us to bring 'er 'ere.'

'Not like this, like this.' Uncle Tolly's voice was shrill. 'Have you hurt her? Have they hurt you, March?'

'Just knocked 'er abart a bit to keep 'er quiet.'

'You hit her? My God, if I were thirty years older I would thrash you to within an inch for that, half an inch.'

'Just give us the money and we'll go.'

'Money?' Uncle Tolly repeated incredulously. 'You were told to persuade her to come here, not bundle her up like a sack of kittens.'

The two who had brought me grunted something then. 'But that's what p'saude means where we comes from.'

'Get out!' Uncle Tolly screeched. 'Get out now before I summon the police. If my niece is injured in any way you will be punished, punished with the full severity of the law, the law. Get out.'

More mumbling. 'Don't think you can get out of payin' us that easy.'

'Out!' Uncle Tolly howled. 'Before I set the dogs on you.'

'We'll be back.'

'Then I shall greet you with my shotgun.'

A long hesitation. 'Right then.' Heavy feet, the sound of a door being flung open, and then another one slammed.

'Can you get me out of here, Uncle Tolly?' I asked.

'Out?' I could picture him twiddling with his beard. 'Out... Yes, of course, of course.'

'The knot is tied round my ankles.'

'Knot? Oh yes, knot.' He crouched beside me. I heard his knees click twice and felt them press into my shins as he struggled with it. 'Goodness, it is complicated.'

'Do you have any scissors?'

'Did I hear somebody at the front door, sir?' Annie asked. 'Oh my goodness!'

'It is Miss Middleton.' Uncle Tolly rested a hand heavily on my knee.

'Is she doing a novelty escape act?'

'No, I am damned well not.' I was very hot and cramped. 'Just untie this sack.'

'Why don't I have a go, sir, while you ring for Colwyn?'

'An excellent idea.' The pressure on my knee increased as he got up, and I heard Annie's dress rustle.

'Don't you worry, miss. We'll soon have you out of there.' More poking and pulling about. 'It's very tight.'

'Just rip the sack then.'

More wrenching around. 'I'm sorry, miss.' Yet more and then, 'Oh no, I've chipped a tooth.'

'Get some scissors or a knife.'

I knew I was not but I felt like I was suffocating. Footsteps approached and stopped.

'Good heavens,' Colwyn exclaimed.

'It is Miss Middeltone,' Annie told him.

'Ton,' I corrected. 'Middleton.'

'Oh dear, oh dear,' Uncle Tolly twittered helplessly.

'Let me have a go,' Colwyn said. 'I'm good with knots from helping my mum save string.' Annie moved away and was replaced. 'Now, let me see. The trick is to find the end and work it backwards.'

'Just cut the bloody rope,' I bawled.

'Mr Travers Smyth does not like bad language,' Annie told me.

'And I do not like being tied up in sacks,' I retorted. 'I will swap places if he likes. He can be tied up and I will listen to the curses.'

'Here we go,' Colwyn said. 'Now that I've got that first bit through it's just a question of untwisting this, so, and working that... so... and...' And then triumphantly, 'Yes!' And the tightness was released from my ankles and then my legs, and I found myself being sat up. 'If you could be so kind, sir.'

'What? Oh yes, of course.'

And then there were two of them hauling me to my feet.

'Do not let go,' I begged. My legs were paralysed with pins and needles and could not support me.

'Close your eyes,' Annie instructed, though I did not know why until she added, 'I'm going to pull the bag up and her dress will be disarrayed.' More fussing about and I felt the sack rising and my dress – as she had predicted – partly with it. 'Let go of that arm for a minute. Hold tight, Colwyn. Now, you take her please, Mr Travers Smyth. Can you hold her?'

'I shan't let her fall,' he announced valiantly, as if defending a bridgehead, and his fingers dug into my arm.

'Nearly there,' she announced and whipped the sack off as my hair collapsed around my face. 'Keep those eyes closed, you two.' It was only then I realized I had shut mine as well, and I opened them to see Uncle Tolly and Colwyn supporting me on either side and Annie kneeling to arrange my dress over my ankles. 'You can both open your eyes now.'

'Goodness!' Uncle Tolly viewed me in shock.

'Perhaps you would like to sit, miss,' Colwyn suggested and guided me into the nearest upright chair.

'Call the police,' I said.

'The police? Oh dear, oh dear.' Uncle Tolly had his red smoking cap on, but it had been dented on top.

'First things first,' Annie said firmly. 'You men leave the room while I make Miss Middleton more presentable.'

Colwyn bent to pick up the sack and rope.

'Leave those,' I said. 'They are evidence.'

'I do hope...' Uncle Tolly tightened the belt of his red silk smoking jacket and started again. 'I do hope they won't want to trespass in my house again.'

'The police and a cab,' I called as they left the room.

'My carriage is always at your disposal.'

'A cab,' I insisted.

Uncle Tolly gripped his shawl collar like a man about to make a speech. 'I really...' But his voice trailed away and so did he.

'Now.' Annie crouched at my feet. 'Let's get you straightened up properly.'

'Is my face very bad?' I felt it gingerly. It was sore but did not seem to be bleeding.

'Just a bit more bruised.' She reached up to tug my underskirts into some sort of order. 'It'll go down. Oh, your poor legs.' She raised my left foot and I bent over and saw that my ankle was indented by angry rope marks. 'Let me rub them better.'

She had lovely light yellow hair tied in a neat bun behind her hat and her fingers were long and soothing.

'My toes are numb.'

She changed to the right leg and massaged the front of my shin, and I tried not to remember when another human being had last touched me so intimately. I would have done anything for a stiff gin, but I was frightened to eat or drink in Saturn Villa now.

I came out of my brief reverie. 'I must go now.'

'It will take a while for Colwyn to get you a cab,' Annie forecast. 'I'll just tidy your hair a little while we wait.'

Annie stood up and went round behind me. She took my stray tresses and combed her fingers though them, gently teasing the tangles apart. 'I always wanted a lady to brush her locks and talk about dresses and the like. Mr T is very kind but he don't have much hair and he don't know the first thing about fashion.'

I laughed. 'I do not suppose he does.'

'It's good to hear you laugh,' she piled my hair up, 'after all you've been through.'

I tried to stop myself shaking. 'What have I been through, Annie?'

And Annie tensed. 'I don't know, miss.' She retied my ribbon and whispered, 'I wish to God I did.'

And it occurred to me that I was not the only one who was trembling.

46

Pounce and the Dandelion Clock

FTER ANNIE HAD done her best with me, Uncle Tolly returned.

'Have you summoned the police?' I asked, but the fact that Colwyn came in sheepishly behind him showed that they had not.

'I am frightened of what they will do.' Uncle Tolly ran in a circle.

'You are frightened?' I said scornfully. 'I have been duped, smothered, tied up, beaten, thrown in a van, dragged across London and dumped on your floor, not knowing what was going to happen to me but dreading the worst, and you are frightened?'

'If I might explain.' Colwyn patted the air with his palms to try to pacify me.

'No, you may not.' I waved him away with a gesture that might have been Sidney Grice at his most imperious. 'You may go out and fetch a policeman.'

The valet looked askance at his employer, who chewed at the end of his cravat miserably. 'You had better do as she requests, Colwyn.'

'Do not trouble with the cab,' I instructed. 'I shall wait for the police.' My cheekbone was throbbing and my back was stiff from the kick. 'Thank you for your kindness, Annie, but you may leave now. I wish to speak to your master alone.'

'Oh, but…' Uncle Tolly's fingers seemed to have a life of their own now.

'Alone,' I said firmly as Annie left us. 'Sit down,' I instructed. 'I am not in a mood to be towered over.'

Uncle Tolly slumped meekly in a balloon back, side-on to me, and I was struck by how receded his chin was. Those who believe in such things would have claimed it proved his weak character, but I found it difficult to believe that a man's bones reflected his personality.

'Explain,' I commanded, even sounding like my guardian now.

'It is all my fault.' Uncle Tolly gripped his seat. 'I was so upset by what has occurred between us...' His hands splayed rigidly.

'What has occurred between us?' I asked.

The fire was dying.

Uncle Tolly tucked his legs under the chair. 'I wish I knew.' He tilted his face towards me like an anxious child hoping for reassurance.

'That is one thing we have in common,' I conceded.

He brightened briefly. 'Shall I ring for tea?'

'You shall not,' I responded and his light was extinguished. 'You shall explain exactly what has happened.'

'It is all my fault,' Uncle Tolly repeated, his fingers going limp. 'I wanted to see you again. You are my only flesh and blood, March, and that may mean nothing to you because you are young, but when one's life nears its natural span one starts to think of what one will leave behind.' His bush-baby eyes welled up.

'Family means a great deal to me,' I said, 'but you still have not explained anything.'

'I am trying.' He wrapped his feet behind the front legs of his chair. 'I wrote you letters but they did not say what I wanted them to. I asked Colwyn to plead my cause but he said you would not trust him after he tried to stop Mr Grice and the police. I begged Annie but she reminded me that she had hurt you. I spoke to Cyril...' He wiped his eyes with the back of his hand.

'Who?'

'My coachman.' Uncle Tolly showed me his profile. 'He said he knew two men who could persuade you for ten pounds. It seemed rather steep to me but, if they could bring you back to me and give me a chance to make amends, it would be money well spent. I cannot tell you how shocked I was when I found what they had done.'

A grandfather clock chimed the hour from another room.

'You do not really have any dogs to set on people, do you?'

Pound would have given up waiting by now. I hoped he would not think I did not care. He probably assumed that Mr G had detained me.

'No,' he admitted, 'but I have always found that ruffians are afraid of them.'

The wind was rising. I could hear it moan over the chimney top.

'Or a shotgun?'

'No.' He checked his half-hunter against his grandfather clock and clucked. 'One is slow or the other fast.' He put his watch to his ear. 'Or mayhap one is slow and the other fast.'

'Where is Cyril now?' I paddled my feet up and down, hoping it might get the blood flowing properly. 'The police will need to speak with him and I would certainly like to hear what he thought he was up to.'

Uncle Tolly rattled his watch. There were silver charms on the chain – a horseshoe, an old boot, a rabbit's foot. 'He has gone to see his niece or aunt or sister-in-law, I think.' He patted his waistcoat. 'Now what did I do with the winding key?'

'Never mind about your watch,' I told him. 'Exactly where is your coachman?'

He found the little key and held it up with a cry of triumph but, catching my expression, put it sheepishly away.

'I do not know exactly,' he mused, 'not exactly.'

'When is he expected back?' I would have given a gold sovereign to be able to kick off my boots and scratch my feet.

Uncle Tolly took one last lingering look at his half-hunter and dropped it back into his pocket.

'I do not know exactly,' he repeated, 'not exactly.' But seeing that his answer was not satisfactory, he explained. 'I rarely use my carriage so when I need Cyril, I send a note to Black's the Ironmongers. I believe the shop is owned by his brother, and Cyril helps out there when he is not here. He usually comes within the hour.'

'Excellent.' I rubbed my legs surreptitiously against each other. 'Then I suggest you do so now.'

'Shall I wind my watch first?'

'Now.' I shook my finger sternly and Uncle Tolly leaped out of his chair as though it had been set on fire and there was a pail of water behind his desk.

'I shall need a pen.' He rifled through the clutter. 'Here we are. And ink… yes, yes, and paper.' He opened and shut a few drawers before coming out with a solitary creased sheet. 'Yes… What shall I write?'

'What do you normally write?'

He sucked the feathered end of his quill. 'I always put Dear Cyril,' he declared.

'And then?'

He picked a fragment of something from the tip of his quill and launched into, 'I trust this finds you as well as I find myself, which is tolerably good. I hope your aunt or niece is—'

'Just put Cyril, come urgently.'

'But that will make him anxious,' Uncle Tolly protested, putting the quill back in a brass stand.

'The man had me kidnapped,' I shouted. 'Write it.' I got up painfully.

Uncle Tolly shuddered, snatched his quill from its stand and plunged it into his inkstand. 'Dear…' He scratched out something. 'Dear… Oh dear, shall I just quickly wish him the very best to start with?'

'Cyril, come urgently.' I hobbled over.

'Indeed, indeed.' He redipped his pen. 'Please... come... urgently.' He wrote very slowly and with great deliberation as if carving his words into marble. 'How shall I sign it?'

'In your usual way.'

His usual way took a considerable time and I leaned across to see what he was doing. He was drawing squirls and ornamentations all around the page.

'Oh, this is difficult.' He reached for a cardboard box with pounce pencilled on the side, took off the lid and sprinkled a thick layer of the cuttlebone powder all over his letter to dry it. The pounce must have been used for blotting before as it was already blackened. 'Oh, that is much too much.' Uncle Tolly picked up the sheet of paper and blew, and the powder flew into his face and over my dress. 'Oh, I am so sorry.' He looked about and offered me a grubby cloth.

'Do not worry,' I assured him. 'I have a handkerchief.'

'But it will be ruined.' He crooked a finger. 'I have the very thing. Wait there, March, and do not move or it will spread all over you. Oh, this silly, naughty stuff.' He stepped out and tossed the box into the fire and it flared with an audible whoomph. 'One moment, one moment.'

Uncle Tolly scampered across the room to behind his map table and bobbed down, and I could hear him rooting about underneath it.

'Can I help?'

A flame shot up the chimney. It crackled and cascaded sparks before it died.

'No, thank you, March, I have found it.' He bobbed up like a jack-in-the-box, his cap tilted forward and his hair strands poking out like a dandelion clock. 'Here we are.' He waved it triumphantly – a massive and ancient service revolver.

'Is that loaded?' I asked warily and he peered down the barrel.

'It certainly is. In fact I loaded it myself last night.'

'Be careful,' I begged and he lowered the gun to point straight at me.

Uncle Tolly giggled. 'Oh, March, it is perfectly safe – unless I pull the trigger.'

'Then please don't,' I beseeched.

His hand was steady now. I stepped to one side and it followed me.

'I should like to tell you how Geoffrey died,' he chattered. 'He was on his knees at the time, imploring me.' Tolly's voice rose into a mocking shriek. 'No, please don't shoot me, please. And I put the gun to his heart like this and he screeched again – No, please. I don't want to die. But I pulled the trigger like this.'

He fumbled with the safety catch.

'Uncle Tolly,' I cried out. 'For heaven's sake—'

I saw the finger tighten and blanch. The trigger must have been very stiff and at first I thought he could not manage as he strained to pull it, but then I saw the trigger move. It was only a fraction of an inch but enough for the hammer to click back and fall.

47

The Drowning of New York

EVERYTHING WAS STILL. Uncle Tolly stood with a smoky haze hanging in front of him.

I cried out. I know I did but I could not hear it.

And Uncle Tolly moved. He saw the blood gushing though the padding of his smoking jacket and mouthed something. It might have been Mother.

'Gosh,' Uncle Tolly said. I heard that as if through cotton wool. He snatched at the table to support himself. The slap of his hand was quite clear.

I rushed towards him but at that moment the door flew open and Colwyn stood there.

'Help me,' Uncle Tolly gasped, swivelling round and staggering two paces back and one forwards. 'Mar—' He fell on one knee and, letting go of his desk, toppled on to his side behind it.

'Uncle Tolly!' I ran forward but Colwyn was there before me.

'Shit.' Colwyn kneeled beside his employer in the three-foot gap between the table and the wall. He rolled Uncle Tolly on to his back and I saw the black cavity in my relative's chest, and two pumps of blood, then one last welling flow.

Uncle Tolly's legs jerked and his lips struggled around a foaming word that was never to be formed. He was lying on a large map of a coastline with the words New York in block capitals before the dark fluid drowned them.

'Do not disturb him,' I warned and stepped forward.

'Let him alone.' Colwyn got up, his trousers and coat drenched and his hands dripping.

'Get a towel – anything – take off his cravat. We might be able to staunch the bleeding.'

There was a rasping sigh.

'Too late for that.' He eyed me venomously.

'I have experience with wounded men.'

'I'll bet you have.' Colwyn snatched up a letter opener. 'Get out of this room.' His voice was as hard and sharp as the steel he held.

I have fought a few men in my time and occasionally bettered them. They expect me to be weak and timid and I am neither. But the assured way the valet handled that knife – his knees slightly bent and his intent gaze – was enough to convince me that I stood no chance against Colwyn. I backed out into the hall and he followed, shutting the door behind him and standing with his back to it.

'Go over there.' He jerked his head at the statue and I edged towards it. 'Well, miss,' the last word was delivered with a sneer, 'looks like you've really done it this time.'

'Colwyn,' I said. 'You must listen to me. Your employer shot himself.'

Colwyn cackled mirthlessly. 'And why would he do that?'

'I do not know. He just did.' I took a step towards Colwyn but his raised left hand was enough to halt me. 'There is a faint chance he might still be alive.'

'And there is a faint chance you might get out of here alive, but I would not wager on either event.'

I tried again. 'I used to be a nurse. I want to help him.'

'Or finish him off.'

'Why on earth would I kill him?'

Colwyn shrugged. 'Perhaps that cocky little glass-eyed man you dragged along last time can tell us, but Mr Travers Smyth's last will and testament seems like a damned strong reason to me.'

'I am quite well off—'

'You are now,' he agreed grimly, 'for all the good it will do you.' He reached out and pressed the button on the wall and a distant bell vibrated.

I knew there was no point in pleading with him so I stood as tall as I could and said, 'Colwyn, I believe that you care about your master and, though I hardly know him, so do I. So I am going back into that room to see if there are any signs of life and if I can staunch his bleeding.' I looked him in the eye with much more confidence than I felt.

Annie came into the hall.

'Fetch a doctor and the police,' I commanded.

Her hand went to her mouth. 'Colwyn! What has she done to you?'

'It is Mr Travers Smyth,' he told her in disbelief. 'Run out, Annie, and get the police... Use the front way for cripes' sake.'

Annie rushed out, the wind gusting sycamore leaves on to the floor.

'Have you forgotten that I was brought here by force?' I reminded the valet, but he waved the knife furiously.

'So you say. How do I know that you did not arrange the whole thing?' He lowered the knife to hip height. 'How do I know that you did not arrange that yourself to get in and give yourself an excuse to kill him? He would never have had you brought here like that – never.'

'I cannot debate this with you now.' I walked up to Colwyn, so close that the tip of his knife brushed my dress. 'I am going back into that room,' I vowed. 'If you want to stop me, you will have to stab me and try explaining that to the police.'

Colwyn ruminated. 'Very well,' he said at last and went to open the doors.

48

The Black Pool and the Terrible Crater

IT WOULD ALL be a trick again, I knew that. Uncle Tolly would be sitting by the fire, savouring his amontillado. He would spring up with the tassel of his smoking cap dangling and declare, 'March, how lovely to see you.'

But there again was Uncle Tolly on his back in a black pool with that terrible crater in his breast.

I kneeled in that stickiness and took his wrist and pressed my fingertips to it and put my ear to that gaping mouth, but I was playing a part. When you have seen death often enough, you know it. You know it by the glazed eyes and that awful emptiness that turns a man into a husk. A dead man is more motionless than a boulder for the rock never moves and so shows no lack of it.

His cap had come off and lay knocked over like a begging bowl in its owner's gore. The gun was still clenched in his right hand and I noticed the smell of gunpowder now.

I got up. What else should I be looking for? I could not think.

Colwyn was crouching now. He had thrown the knife down and I surreptitiously slid it under the table with my toe.

'Leave him alone,' I warned, but he was straightening his master and folding the arms over the chest.

'It is about something you can't understand,' he muttered. 'It is a question of respect.'

'It is also a question of not interfering with evidence,' I tried to reason and Colwyn bowed his head.

'This is not a clue,' he said quietly. 'This is Mr Ptolemy Travers Smyth, one of the finest gentlemen who ever lived.' He passed his fingers over Uncle Tolly's eyes to close them but they crept open again.

'I have some coins,' I offered.

'Blood money,' he spat and got to his feet.

I wandered over to the desk and picked up the letter with its final exuberant flourish.

Colwyn crossed himself.

'You said that your master was very upset and anxious.' I put the letter down. 'Did he ever threaten suicide?'

Colwyn grasped furiously at nothing. 'Don't you try that one on me.' His fists tightened. 'Murdering whore. I should have stabbed you out there in the hall.'

I fixed his eyes with mine. There was a rolling rule on the desk and I rested my hand on it without taking my gaze off him. It was good solid mahogany and might at least help me to defend myself. My fingers closed over it and Colwyn glanced down.

'Think that will save you?' He snatched up a bronze paper-weight and hurled it just past my head into a bookshelf. 'I could tear you apart with my bare hands and not a soul would blame me.'

'I might.' A tall, heavily built young constable came into the room. 'I may be new to this job, sir, but I'm pretty sure that shredding young ladies is contrary to Her Majesty's penal code.' He saw the body and winced. 'Your maid wasn't making it up then.'

I remembered the last policeman I had met in that room and asked politely, 'May I see your warrant card?'

The policeman's eyes twinkled. 'Think this is a fancy-dress costume?' But he reached into his cape pocket and held one out for my inspection.

'Thank you, Constable Sedgemoor,' I said. 'I am Miss March Middleton and the deceased is my second cousin—'

'Ptolemy Travers Smyth,' he said. 'We go – used to go – to the same church and I know your name from somewhere too.' He clicked his fingers. 'The lady who works with Sidney Grice.'

'Hold on,' Colwyn said bitterly. 'This is getting a bit too cosy for my liking.'

Constable Sedgemoor put his card away. 'And you are?' he asked coolly.

'Colwyn Blanchflower, Mr Travers Smyth's valet.' He tidied his cravat automatically. 'And this woman murdered him.'

Sedgemoor leaned over. 'Well, he is certainly dead. What makes you think Miss Middleton did it?'

'It's not complicated,' Colwyn told him. 'She was the only one in the room and he shouted out No, please don't kill me. I don't want to die. I heard it loud and clear in the hall.'

'It was actually No, please don't shoot me, please. And then No, please. I don't want to die,' I corrected.

'It was something like that,' Colwyn snapped.

'It is important to get these things right,' the policeman told him.

'Quite so,' I agreed. 'I should not like to be executed because you have no ear for dialogue.'

Colwyn banged the side of his fist on the wall. 'The point is that there was a shot and I ran in to find Mr Travers Smyth dead on the floor and this woman standing over him, putting the gun into his hand.'

'That is a lie,' I insisted. 'The gun was already in his hand and you took it out to rearrange his body when I told you not to. I was standing over there by the desk when he did it.'

Colwyn quaked with indignation. 'Then how did all that gun-powder get on your dress?' he challenged.

I picked a few grains off and held them out. 'That is pounce.'

'What the hell is pounce?'

'It is ground cuttlefish bone,' I told him. 'It used to be very popular for drying the ink on—'

'Blotting paper,' Colwyn shouted. 'There you are again, caught out by your own lies. My master used blotting paper. You saw him use it yourself when you tricked him into writing a new will in your favour.'

'Excuse me, miss.' Constable Sedgemoor leaned towards me and inhaled. 'But that smells like gunpowder to me.'

'This is ridiculous,' I protested. 'The whole room stinks of it. I imagine you do by now. Shall I sniff at your uniform like a bloodhound?'

'Where is his pounce jar then?' Colwyn spread out his hands as if to prove he did not have it.

I marched to the fireplace. Perhaps there would be something of the box with some of its contents left but, when I thought about it, the whole thing had gone up like gunpowder. I poked about with the fire iron but there was nothing recognizable left.

Colwyn rammed a chair aside to get closer but the policeman held out a warning arm.

'She is a mad woman,' Colwyn raged. 'She came here the first time claiming that she had killed him when all the time he was asleep in bed. Then she brought the police and accused Mr Travers Smyth of murdering a scientific sample. Then she came here—'

'Came here?' I repeated indignantly. 'I was kidnapped, beaten and dragged here.'

Colwyn gripped his fists in frustration. 'And then she tried to make out that Mr Travers Smyth had arranged it all.' He strained over the outstretched arm without actually touching it.

'One moment.' Constable Sedgemoor licked his finger. 'Pardon me, miss.' He ran it lightly over my sleeve, picking up several black grains on the tip which he put on to his tongue. He mulled the grains around his mouth like a wine taster. 'Gunpowder,' he pronounced.

'I told you,' Colwyn insisted. 'She shot my master in cold blood. Give me five minutes and I'll get the truth out of the murdering bitch.'

'Be quiet,' Constable Sedgemoor ordered. 'And step away from my suspect.'

'Suspect?'

'Do you have anything to say, miss?' I shook my head and the policeman inhaled heavily. 'Then I'm afraid I must ask you to accompany me to the station.'

'Are you arresting me?'

Constable Sedgemoor's countenance was bleak. 'Yes, miss, I'm afraid I am.'

49

Resisting Arrest

I WEIGHED UP the situation. I could hardly hope to overpower or outrun both men and what would be the point? They knew who I was and where I lived.

'I should like to see Mr Grice first,' I said.

'I'll bet you would,' Colwyn jeered. 'That nosy little cripple has caused enough trouble here already. Take her away, Constable.'

Constable Sedgemoor bridled. 'All in good time.'

I stood as tall as I could, which is not very tall. 'I never go anywhere without my handbag.' I went briskly towards the map table. Uncle Tolly's feet projected from the end.

Too late, Colwyn realized. 'You didn't have one when I got you out of that sack.'

'She's after the gun!' Sedgemoor yelled.

The revolver lay on the top where Colwyn had placed it. He lunged at me and I dived, scattering a metal rack, books and maps before me as I scrambled desperately over the table, stretching every sinew to reach the weapon and tumbling sideways to crash on to the floor, just managing to struggle to my feet as he grabbed at the hem of my dress.

'Release me.' I kicked at Colwyn's hand and he let go.

I straightened myself up a bit. My hair had collapsed about me but there was nothing I could do about that.

'Don't be silly, miss.' Constable Sedgemoor was strolling

towards me, apparently as unconcerned as if he were taking the country air.

'I am often silly,' I aimed the gun at the ceiling, 'as my guardian will vouch when he gets here.'

There was an upright wooden chair with its back to the front window and I edged crab-like towards it.

'Mr Grice can come to the station,' the policeman reasoned. 'I'm sure he knows the way.'

'I want him to see the scene before it is disturbed any further.' I sat in the chair to try to stop my legs shaking, but I could see them quiver below the blue fabric and I was sure he could too. He had big brown eyes that took everything in.

Colwyn rubbed his knuckles, which I was pleased to see were raw. 'It's a criminal offence to threaten a police officer, isn't it, Constable?'

'It is,' Sedgemoor concurred. 'Be sensible, miss. You are only making things worse for yourself.'

I lowered the gun. It was sticky with Uncle Tolly's blood. 'But I am not threatening you.' I put the muzzle to my temple. 'I am threatening myself.'

'Let her do it,' Colwyn urged. 'Go ahead, Middleton, and save us all the bother of a trial.'

I ignored him and told the policeman, 'If you try to drag me out of here I shall pull the trigger. If you summon Mr Grice I shall go as meekly as a lamb.' I almost added to the slaughter.

Constable Sedgemoor put out his hand for the gun. 'It is also an offence to resist arrest so, even if you are not guilty of killing your uncle, you could end up in prison.'

'You are very logical,' I told him, 'and I am sure Mr Grice will appreciate your sound common sense when he gets here, but I am not resisting arrest either. You are perfectly at liberty to detain me, though you may have to scrape some of my head off the wall.' I shuddered at my own image.

'Blow your brains out, see if we care,' Colwyn exhorted.

'If I did that I should not be here to see whether you care or not.' I rested my elbow on the arm of the chair to keep my hand steady. The revolver was very heavy. 'I would prefer to wait for Mr Grice.'

Constable Sedgemoor narrowed his eyes determinedly.

'I'm afraid you will not be able to shoot yourself, miss.' Sedgemoor forced a little smile. 'You see, the safety catch is on. So why don't you just give me the gun and we'll forget all about it.'

He had me rattled for a moment.

'This is a Wagstaff-Turner six-shot revolver,' I bluffed. 'There is no safety catch. If you think there is, take it off me and let us hope the gun does not fire in the struggle.'

Constable Sedgemoor weighed his options.

'I think we shall sit this one out.' He pulled up a chair to face me.

'Send a message to Mr Grice. In fact send two,' I suggested. 'He may still be at the Old Bailey or he may be at home.'

'Are you deaf?' Colwyn mocked. 'Nobody is sending any messages.'

'Watch my finger,' I told the constable and tightened it on the trigger.

The policeman made a fist. 'Do it, man,' he commanded. 'Don't argue. Just do it.'

'You'll pay for this,' Colwyn swore and stormed off.

My finger relaxed and the constable pushed his chair several feet back.

'Lower the gun,' he said. 'You're making me nervous.'

I did as he bade. 'Not nearly so nervous as I made myself,' I said.

'Ever play poker?' he enquired.

'Yes.' I put the revolver on my lap but kept hold of the handle. 'And I usually win.'

50

Cleopatra

WE DID NOT speak for ten or more minutes. Constable Sedgemoor toyed with his handcuffs, shutting and locking and unlocking and opening them again so often that I was beginning to get annoyed.

'Now that we're alone,' he broke the silence at last, 'and you have had a chance to cool down, suppose you tell me – just between ourselves – exactly what happened.'

I tried to summarize my first visit and why I fled. I told him about the police search and he listened without making notes.

'So what is that sack for?' It still lay on the floor but had been kicked to lie half under an oak bookcase. 'Were you planning to dispose of the body?'

'I was brought here in it and tied with that rope.'

'Sounds a bit like Cleopatra,' he remarked coolly.

'Except that she did it of her own accord and was not assaulted first.' I indicated my injuries. 'Where do you think I got these from?'

Sedgemoor rested his right ankle on his left knee. 'Maybe your uncle put up a fight.'

'And I have rope marks on my legs.'

'Could be self-inflicted.'

I tried again. 'Uncle Tolly shot himself. He wrote a letter, sprinkled a lot of black powder on it and blew some on me. He went to the map table, saying he was getting me a cloth, ducked down and came up with a gun, shouted out and shot himself.'

Constable Sedgemoor pondered my words. 'It doesn't sound very likely, does it?'

'It sounds extremely unlikely to me,' I agreed, 'and most policemen would pour far more scorn on my story than you have.'

Sedgemoor hung his handcuffs back on his belt.

'I know officers who would have slapped you by now,' he admitted, 'especially if you were not a lady.'

'You are better spoken than the average constable,' I observed, 'and I do not think many of your colleagues would have even heard of Cleopatra.'

'I could have gone in much higher with my background,' he admitted. 'But I want to be a proper policeman first.'

We fell silent again and Sedgemoor began to whistle brightly between his closed teeth, a brisk version of 'Who Stole the Sweet From My Sweetheart?' complete with all the trills after 'I used to be the happle of 'er eye'.

Eventually he tired of that and started on 'Polly of Petticoat Lane' which he ran through twice, though a little mournfully, before Colwyn returned.

'So she did not shoot you?'

'If she has, I did not notice,' the constable replied drily. 'Where are the other servants?'

'There's only me and Annie, the maid, who live in. Cook leaves us cold scraps on her days off and this is one of them. Annie will be in the kitchen, I should think, keeping warm by the range.' Colwyn's shoes were splattered with mud – three different types to judge by their hues, and I wondered what Sidney Grice would have made of that.

'Go down and tell her to stay there. Then come back and sit in the hall,' Sedgemoor instructed. 'Any chance of a mug of tea?'

'Go hang yourself.' Colwyn left the room.

'I think that means no,' I told the constable and he shifted in his chair.

'You can tell me, now that you've got what you asked for. Would you really have shot yourself?'

'No,' I said.

'But your finger tightened on the trigger.'

'I saw how much Uncle Tolly's blanched when he pulled it.'

Sedgemoor rested his right ankle on his left knee. 'It was still a big risk. The trigger might have pulled more easily after it had been used.'

I held the gun up and turned it round for him to see. 'The safety catch was on.'

Constable Sedgemoor chuckled. 'You had me there,' he conceded. 'It'll take a while to live that one down.'

'I shall not tell anybody,' I promised and plonked the gun on the occasional table at my side. The catch slipped. I felt it move in my palm and the hammer fell and the gun jumped, and all of hell burst out of that barrel.

Constable Sedgemoor had sensed it coming. He uncrossed his legs and twisted away, but as the raised edge of the table erupted into smoke and splinters I saw his body jerk and he fell forwards, toppling on to the floor between us.

51

The Confines of a Bullet

CONSTABLE SEDGEMOOR'S HEAD hit my leg and bounced away. I fell to my knees. His eyes were still open. A shadow became solid and I felt my arm gripped hard and wrenched back and saw Colwyn distorted by fury, his fist pulled back. I ducked and he punched the back of my head twice. Sedgemoor's arm came up.

'No,' I heard as the reverberations died away. 'I am all right.'

'She tried to kill you too.' Colwyn shook me as I had seen a mongoose do with a cobra.

'Leave her be,' Sedgemoor shouted fuzzily.

Colwyn threw me aside and stepped back as I disentangled myself from the policeman.

'If you had not thrown yourself down...' I pulled my curtain of hair back.

'I could not have been quick enough to beat a bullet.' Constable Sedgemoor clambered back up into his chair. 'Luckily for me, it was pointing over that way.'

There was a splintered hole big enough to put my boot through in the side of Uncle Tolly's desk.

'Thank God.' I tucked my hair as best I could behind my ears, but the clips had gone everywhere and I could not find the ribbon.

The revolver had kicked back off the shattered table and lay on a rug, mercifully pointing towards the wall because I was too terrified to touch it now. I sat down gingerly.

'You might have had some trouble explaining that one.' Sedgemoor slumped into his chair.

'I think I could have explained it easily enough,' Sidney Grice declared as he came into the room. 'You would be safer trusting a fox with chickens than a girl with a gun.'

'Oh, Mr G,' I cried and rose to greet him. 'Thank God you are here.'

'I wish I could say the same.' He halted me. 'Sit back down. Good afternoon, Charley.'

'Mr Grice.'

'You two know each other?' I returned to my seat.

'I am not in the habit of addressing strange policemen as Charley,' my guardian said. He had removed his Ulster coat and wide-brimmed hat before he entered, but retained his satchel and cane.

'I do not remember, of course, but my mother told me Mr Grice used to rock me off to sleep,' Sedgemoor admitted.

In spite of everything that had happened, or perhaps because of it, I laughed. The image of my guardian fondly dangling a baby on his knee was incongruous with the man I knew.

'How is your mother?' Mr G asked. 'No, do not trouble to answer that. I am not interested and only asked in a regrettable lapse into courteousness.' He prodded a forefinger towards me. 'If you wish to see the year out you will say nothing unless it is in direct response to my enquiry. Is that instruction firmly embedded in your crude facsimile of a brain?'

'Yes,' I said.

'And will you obey it?'

'Yes.'

'Good.' He thrust his cane and satchel at me. 'Then I can entrust you with these. How did you get gunpowder on your dress? And I am not talking about that resulting from the presumably accidental near-assassination of this worthy and well-connected constable. I refer to the stale gunpowder which was ignited outside the confines of a bullet at least two weeks ago.'

'How can you possibly know that?' Sedgemoor rubbed his grazed chin.

'The grains are swollen from absorbing atmospheric humidity.' Mr G flicked some from my left sleeve with the tip of his pencil on to a blank page of his notebook. 'Whereas these,' he picked a few off my right sleeve, 'are hotter, smaller, crisper, blacker and therefore fresher. The old grains are not all burnt either as would happen if they had been in a bullet.'

'Uncle Tolly blew them on me,' I explained. 'I thought it was pounce. He threw the cardboard box with the rest of it into the fire.'

'And you did not think it odd he stored his pounce in such a container rather than a pot?'

'He was a strange man.'

Mr G grunted. 'You will relate eight illustrations of similar behaviour to me when I have exhausted all other possibilities for mental stimulation. It is low-grade powder and contains non-ignited particles. Did you not notice the flare and sulphurous aromas?'

'I did, but I did not think anything of it,' I replied.

My guardian rolled his eye. 'I have spoken to you before about not thinking anything of things. Kindly commence thinking something of things at your earliest convenience. That was not a question. Do not respond.'

'Why are you wasting time listening to this?' Colwyn railed at Constable Sedgemoor. The valet was striding about the room.

'Because I want to find out the truth and Mr Grice seems to be getting there,' Sedgemoor responded, then added, 'In the meantime, you shall stand still and be quiet, or I shall put word about that you have taken an interest in the wife of Gipsy James Mace.'

'The prizefighter's wife? I've never even met her,' Colwyn protested.

'The very words of Harry Napoli as they carried his broken body out of the Flying Horse,' the constable recollected and Colwyn closed his mouth.

'And you, Miss Middleton, shall stay there.' Mr G limped slowly back to the map table and peered round it. Constable Sedgemoor got up and followed.

Mr G hummed loudly as he cast his eye over the scene. 'I am delighted to note that a great many things have been disturbed. One gets so tired of solving crimes at a glance.' He stood at Uncle Tolly's feet. 'It is obvious that Miss Middleton kneeled pointlessly beside the cadaver in a futile attempt to detect a pulse and that the hitherto pleasant valet who glories in the name of Colwyn walked round and kneeled beside it after-wards, but which of you rolled it from its left side on to its back and removed the revolver from the right hand? I have strong reasons for supposing it was the masculine party that did so in both cases.'

Colwyn crooked his lip contemptuously but did not reply.

'You may answer,' my guardian told me just as I was about to anyway.

'Colwyn,' I cleared my throat, 'though I told him not to.'

'That was stupid, even for a servant.' Mr G jumped twice on the spot, dashed sideways, put his ear to the oak door and scratched at it like a dog wanting to be let out.

Colwyn rounded on him angrily. 'It was a question of respect.'

'To the deceased or his murderer?' Constable Sedgemoor enquired.

'I have no respect for her,' Colwyn spat and I bit my tongue.

My guardian folded his arms behind his back and leaned so far over the body that I feared he would topple on to it, clipped on his pince-nez and crouched to peer under the table. He got up almost reluctantly, then ran round to the other side and tilted his upper half to view the body over the table. Mr G exhaled longer and harder than seemed humanly possible.

'How humdrum,' he pronounced at last. 'He shot himself.' His shoulders sagged with disappointment.

Colwyn let out a cry of disbelief. 'Himself? You are all in this together. You killed him and you can't pin the blame on me so—'

'If I chose,' Mr G stated flatly, 'I could have you convicted and strung up for this before you had a chance to snivel, but, fortunately for you, I value the truth more than the pleasure I would get from seeing you hang. This absurd little man killed himself.'

Constable Sedgemoor fiddled with his baton. 'How can you decide that so quickly?'

'Consider where the blood is,' Sidney Grice insisted.

'It is everywhere,' Colwyn said and Mr G snapped his fingers.

'Blood is never and can never be everywhere. None of it is daubed on the absurd structure of Saint Paul's Cathedral, nor is any to be found bespattering the ugly hillsides of Provence, to give two of the uncountable examples. A lot of it is on the floor, especially that graphic misrepresentation of the lost colonies of the Americas.' He swept his cane in the general direction. 'And a great deal of that has been smeared about by you and my goddaughter, but most of it and that which was propelled from the thorax with the greatest effect is on the top of this vulgar reproduction of a mid-Jacobean map table.' He tossed his head proudly.

'So the fact that he bled more on the table than the floor shows that he pulled the trigger himself?' Constable Sedgemoor summarized sceptically.

'I like a man who listens.' Mr G clapped his hands together once. 'The first flow of blood from a ruptured thorax is always the greatest. The human body is not an inexhaustible source of gore. Its supply is generally depleted after a gallon at most. So each succeeding beat of the punctured heart expels less of its contents. Plus the heart itself does not enjoy being perforated and weakens with each succeeding contraction.' He put his pince-nez away unused. 'The late and surpassingly irritating Mr P. T. S. was standing facing the desk four inches away from it when the leaden projectile was introduced into his person, hence the lagoon of blood over the top and the cavitation produced in the poor-quality Canadian oak-wood panelling behind him by the escape of that ballistic device though his left scapula.'

'His what?' Colwyn was incredulous.

'His shoulder blade,' Constable Sedgemoor explained. 'The bullet passed straight through him.'

'Not perfectly straight,' Mr G corrected him. 'No doubt the skeletal structures diverted its journey a little, plus the rifling of that aged weapon would send any projectile on a highly erratic journey.'

'I'll get it dug out later,' the constable declared and my guardian eyed him with almost paternal pride.

'This table is approximately six foot and seven inches deep,' Sidney Grice continued. 'How could anybody – least of all Miss Middleton with her dwarfish proportions and stunted arms – reach across it and put the muzzle to his chest? The burns on his garish smoking jacket illustrate the latter point. She could not have climbed on to the desk as the ornamentations had not been disturbed at the time.'

'This is ridiculous.' Colwyn flapped his hands. 'The orna-ments are everywhere.'

'Another inaccurate use of everywhere,' Mr G reproved. 'But leaving that aside – as I fear we must – they were all knocked over after Mr T. S. died. The blood sprayed on to what has become undersurfaces and sides now, and the spillage on the table top has been disturbed quite markedly on that side of the desk.'

'Miss Middleton dived over it to get the gun,' Constable Sedgemoor confirmed and Colwyn howled in frustration.

'She killed him. I know she did.'

'How?' Mr G responded with interest. 'There is no trapeze on which she could have propelled herself towards him. She could not have crawled under the table. The floor is too stacked with undisturbed geographical books and papers, a great many of which I possess or should like to possess copies of.'

'Maybe she will let you read them when she inherits the place,' the valet jeered.

'A pleasant prospect,' Mr G murmured. 'But let us not permit it to divert us from the task in hand. Nobody else could have shot this tidily composed corpse, ergo the wound was self-inflicted.'

'So it was suicide?' Constable Sedgemoor clarified.

'Suicide?' Colwyn yelled in disbelief. 'Then how come I heard my master calling out No, March, please do not kill me?'

Mr G wiped his hands on a cloth from his satchel. 'Firstly, I do not know that he did.'

'Miss Middleton admitted as much herself,' the constable confirmed.

'That is not quite true,' I piped up and my guardian rolled his eye despairingly. 'His exact words were No, please don't shoot me, please, and then No, please. I don't want to die.'

'Did I ask you a question?' Sidney Grice rubbed at a stain on his coat.

'You did not.' I rubbed my back and wondered if my left kidney were damaged.

'Secondly,' my guardian continued, 'it is enough that I have determined what happened without troubling myself to wonder why.'

'Yes, but I want to know.' Colwyn slammed the side of his fist into the wall behind him, rattling the gas mantle so hard that the flame dipped momentarily and tossed a dark gauze across Uncle Tolly's face.

'Then find out.' Mr G walked past the valet to where I sat and bent to pick up the revolver. The shadows skittered about before they went to rest.

'Be careful,' I warned. 'The safety catch is faulty.'

'It is not I who needs lectures on the handling of firearms,' he remarked. 'What you take to be the safety catch is an adjustment for the tension. You have it on what I believe is referred to in sensational novellas as a hair trigger.'

'My God,' Sedgemoor breathed, 'and you squeezed it with the barrel to your head.'

Sidney Grice put a finger to his eye. 'Lucky there is nothing of use in there then,' he said coolly, but his face was drained. 'To continue…' His right eye was watering badly. 'I did not say it was suicide, merely that he shot himself.'

'Now you are quibbling,' the constable protested.

'There are at least nine other possibilities.' Mr G spun the bullet chamber. 'Perhaps it was an accident. We know that the weapon is faulty. Perhaps he was under the illusion that his heart was on the other side of his body. Perhaps he thought his skin was harder than a bullet.'

'Now you are being stupid,' Colwyn complained.

'The last time I counted I was one thousand, four hundred and nineteen different things. Stupid was not one of them.' He broke the gun open. 'You have no conception what strange ideas otherwise seemingly sane people can adopt.' Mr G peered at him through the opened barrel. 'Jeremy Noble, the respected astronomer, believed that he was made of paper and would rip or blow away in a breeze.' He emptied the remaining four bullets into his palm. 'Unsurprisingly, he did not.'

'So that's it, is it?' Colwyn shouted. 'She kills a man and walks away, just because of who she is and who you are, and being such great pals with the police?'

'Of course not,' Sidney Grice clamped the revolver shut. 'First—'

'And don't start all that first second stuff again.' Colwyn was purple.

'I am not pals with the police or anyone.' Mr G aimed at the valet's head. 'I like nobody and nobody likes me.' He cocked back the hammer.

'I do a bit,' I said. 'Sometimes.'

'And second—'

Colwyn snarled.

'Second…' My guardian pulled the trigger. The hammer snapped home and Colwyn winced but stood his ground. 'I believe,' Mr G continued, 'that Constable Sedgemoor has already arrested Miss Middleton and he must – as all men in uniform should but often do not – do his duty.'

Not for the first time I wondered if Sidney Grice had gone mad, and the constable was visibly taken aback.

'You are suggesting that I take your ward into custody for an offence you have just proved she could not have committed?' He pulled his jacket straight and checked the button of his collar.

'I am suggesting that you formally release her or she will still be under arrest.' Mr G allowed himself a tiny smile. 'Not that that worries me especially. It is just that, if I take her home I shall be harbouring a fugitive.'

I went close to Sedgemoor and gazed up into his big brown eyes. 'Go on then,' I urged.

'You are free to go without charge,' he mumbled.

'Thank you,' I said and walked out of the room.

52

The Tortured Tree

SIDNEY GRICE DID not speak as I scurried down the drive after him.

'Thank you,' I said to his back and he grunted.

'I am sorry,' I added as we boarded a hansom, and he snorted.

'I must congratulate you, March.' He plucked at the fingers of his gloves to straighten the seams. 'Apart from Delilah Swan, the untalented but reputedly attractive actress, you are the only woman I know who has stopped the traffic in central London – not that it was moving very fast.'

I cupped my face in my hands and failed to work out what he meant. 'How did I do that?'

'Inspector Pound and I did it on your behalf.' He rattled his flask hopefully. 'Jane Dozer.' He spoke the name as if it had mystical significance. 'And before you ask who lays claim to that title, she is the odoriferous and diseased gutter child who lured you into the stable on Bentley Mews under the impression that it was a romantic tryst.'

'So she told you I had been kidnapped.' I resolved to reward her at the first opportunity.

Mr G wrinkled his brow. 'If she did my memory is failing me. She called at the house demanding money. The vile urchin told Molly and when Pound called on some pretext – but really because you had missed an illicit assignation with him – Molly told him. He sent word to me. Luckily, I had finished giving evidence, and between us and a gang of twenty-four constables and three sergeants we brought the flow of vehicles to a halt whilst we searched every black van – and there are an astonishing number of them – for over an hour until I got bored, and two runners came simultaneously bearing the announcement that, not content with being abducted, you had butchered your exasperating relative in his own home.' He shook a few drops into his tin cup. 'Really, March, you have excelled yourself today.'

'I did not know any of this would happen.' I fought back my tears. 'I was just going for a cup of tea with the inspector and I tried to help a little girl.'

Sidney Grice drank his trickle of tea. 'I have warned you before about being kind. These are not people like us, March. They are creatures of darkness who—'

'For pity's sake, they are children,' I cried. 'That girl was tricked into luring me there and did what she could to save me.'

'In the expectation of a bounty,' he said. 'If somebody had offered her more not to let me know, she would never have set foot on my doorstep.'

'Have you any idea what I have been through?' I raged. 'No, do not answer that. I cannot argue with you any more.'

My guardian's expression was fixed into one of mild puzzlement and he did not hum or tap his cane annoyingly as was his habit. At 125 Gower Street he disembarked, leaving me to pay the fare, and was knocking on the door before I reached the pavement, and hammering by the time I had joined him.

'Oh, sir, it's you.' Molly flopped in relief. 'From all that banging I thought it must be somebody important.'

'Tea,' he snapped and strode jerkily into his study.

'I shall go and change,' I announced, but he had shut the door before I finished.

'I've just finished polishing Spirit's claws,' Molly declared as I mounted the stairs.

Once in my room I took off my blood-caked dress and laid it on the floor. My lower legs were gouged and raw from being bound so tightly and there was a rope burn across the left side of my neck just above the chain, and the ring had dug into my breast. My face was not as badly marked as I had feared, but by using my hand mirror and the cheval I could see a large purple area on my lower back.

Whilst the bath filled, I smoked a cigarette out of the window. The water was tepid as I completely immersed myself. I soaped all over, pulled the plug with my toe and let the bath drain, refilled it and lay still. The water was cold this time but I did not care. I drank a very large gin from my father's old hip flask and let the alcohol seep through me. I did not want to get out of that bath ever, but I was shivering so badly that I had no choice.

If there was one luxury Sidney Grice never stinted on, it was towels. We always had a plentiful supply of fluffy Indian cotton bath sheets. I wrapped a big one around me and made a turban of a smaller, then went back to my room for another cigarette. I had left the window open. I leaned out and glanced down. My guardian was sitting on the little bench below the twisted cherry tree, one hand clawing around his empty socket, the other clutching his wounded shoulder.

'Damn damn damn.' His body contorted like a rabid beast tearing at itself.

I could not call out. He would not have wanted me to see him like that and I could not bear to watch. I put on my light ochre dress and was tying up my hair when Molly came panting up.

''Spector Pound to see you,' she announced, and I was past her and galloping down as fast as several yards of cloth would allow me.

At the bottom of the stairs I composed myself and went into the study. Pound and Mr G were standing behind his desk scrutinizing something but, the moment I entered, the inspector started towards me. 'Miss Middleton...'

My guardian put down his brass magnifying glass. 'I am going to do something in another room,' he declaimed, as if reciting the lines of a play. 'It will take me two minutes and fifty seconds.'

He marched stiffly out of the room and Pound stood uncertainly for a moment. I rushed towards him.

'Thank God you are safe.' He turned up my face towards his. 'I will hunt them down, March. I swear it.'

'Just hold me,' I said and he put his arms round me.

'They didn't…?'

'No.' I buried myself in him, breathing the coal tar and pipe tobacco which seemed as much a part of him as his voice or his strength. I rested my head on his breast, and he stroked my hair, his heart beating hard and steady.

'Thank God,' he whispered.

'I saw little sign of him today.' I closed my eyes to hold back the tears.

Pound bent and nuzzled the top of my head. 'You have been in the jaws of hell and you would not have found him there.'

'Perhaps your mother's ring kept me safe.'

His hold tightened and his voice caught. 'I want to talk to you about that.'

The door handle rattled for longer than could possibly have been needed and Sidney Grice returned to find the inspector by the window and me ensconced in my armchair, flicking through the first journal that had come to hand, *The Parasite Periodical*.

'We are in for a blowy night,' Pound forecast.

'There is a storm brewing,' Mr G concurred grimly. His skin was sallow, I thought.

53

The Listener

G ROGGY CAME THE *night before my father left. The two men sat a long time by the fire, drinking whisky and reminiscing half-heartedly for my benefit. Eventually I took the hint and rose to go.*

Groggy had aged dramatically in the last few years. The death of Daisy and his wife and the continuing ill-health of Barney had dealt him savage blows. He managed a smile, though, and squeezed my hand when I wished him a good night.

I am ashamed to say I eavesdropped from the landing. It was obvious that they were going to discuss something important and I felt old enough to know what it was.

My father talked in a low voice about assessing somebody and then Groggy said, 'I know I promised to look after March should anything happen to you, Middlers.'

I smiled, for nobody else addressed my father in such a familiar way.

Groggy continued, 'But the fact is I am unlikely to outlive you—'

'Nonsense,' my father broke in.

'Even so,' Groggy continued, 'it might be a good idea to look for somebody else.'

'All you need, my good fellow,' my father assured him with forced gusto, 'is another whisky.' I heard glasses clink and my father added more seriously, 'We will talk about it when I get back.'

'There will be much to talk about then,' Groggy said, 'one way or another.'

A wet log cracked in the fire and I jumped back and went to bed. Who else would take me, I wondered. My father and Groggy apart, there was no one.

54

The Shade of Merry Murray

I WENT TO bed early that night and, somewhat to my surprise, had a long dreamless sleep and, when I awoke, the sun was struggling through one of the thinner clouds into my room. I had forgotten to draw my curtains. It must have rained in the night for the panes were heavy with drops. I lay on my back and listened to the confusions of city life – millions of people battling for the space to move; tens of thousands of horses dragging heavy loads; countless men, women and children imploring people to buy their wares – and the next I knew Molly was shaking my foot.

'Mr G sent me to check you ain't not died.'

'Well, as you can see, I have not.'

Molly eyed me uncertainly. 'In "The Shade of Merry Murray" what you told to me and Cook, Merry Murray talks to the red-hooded highwayman for nearly an hour before he finds out she is a dead,' she recalled. 'Oh, me and Cook couldn't not sleep when we was supposed to be polishing cutulery for weeks after that.'

'Merry Murray could walk through walls,' I reminded her. 'I can only bump into them, but I am not going to demonstrate.'

'I hope not.' Molly went pink. 'I hate it when Mr Grice demonstates with me.'

'I think you mean remonstrates.' I was getting a bad headache. 'Anyway, "The Shade of Merry Murray" was a made-up story.'

Molly puffed contemptuously. 'No, it wasn't not. 'Cause the red-hooded highwayman says at the end This is a true story.' She flung her unanswerable logic at me so confidently that I saw no point in telling her it was a story I had made up for Maudy Glass and Barney when we were children.

'I shall get up in a moment.' I stretched and yawned. 'What time is it?'

'A quarter before lunch,' she told me.

I dragged myself into a sitting position. 'Please do not tell me it is leeks again.'

'I won't.' Molly picked up my boots. 'But it is,' she added as she left the room.

*

Sidney Grice lowered his slender new book and slid his pince-nez to the tip of his nose.

'You seem refreshed,' he commented. 'It is most unbecoming.' He marked his page with a knife.

A grateful client, knowing Sidney Grice's vegetarian habits, had given him a consignment of leeks from his cold store, and Cook had made good use of them with a gallon of leek broth which she reheated twice a day. This was the fourth meal we had begun with her creation and I had not especially enjoyed it the first time.

'You are very jaundiced.' I picked at a dry slice of bread. 'And I do not mean just your manner.'

His skin was a distinct mustard colour.

'It is a minor bout.' He wiped his mouth on his napkin.

I skipped the soup course, cleared our bowls, put them in the dumb waiter and rang the bell.

'Bleedin' 'eck,' a voice came up the shaft, 'can't a woman get any rest.'

'There are plenty of beds in the workhouse for unemployed cooks,' my guardian bellowed.

'Ruddy 'ell,' Cook said. 'D'you fink 'e 'eard us?'

'I shouldn't not think so,' Molly reassured her as the dumb waiter began to descend.

I went to the window. The clouds were so heavy now that it might have been night-time and the rain flung itself so hard that the panes rattled. A black pigeon huddled on the sill, desperately seeking shelter, but I knew better than to draw it to my guardian's attention.

'I know you do not like theories,' I began.

'I do not like unfounded ones,' he agreed.

'But can you think why Uncle Tolly shot himself?'

'I could speculate but I shall not.' He flattened a crease in the tablecloth. 'I can tell you one thing. Whilst Turpin, Turpin and Turpin, the genealogists, have confirmed that your second cousin was who he claimed to be, much else about him was fraudulent. When I engaged him in conversation he claimed to have visited the Longgong Caves from Xining, whereas they are a good two thousand miles apart by very difficult roads.'

The dumb waiter rose with three covered bowls and two unwarmed plates, and I put them on the sideboard.

'He told me he had fled there after my mother rejected him and a judge's daughter sued for breach of promise.'

My guardian's eye fell into his glass of water. 'You cannot know how ironic those lies are.' He fished it out with a dessert spoon. 'Converse and Bligh, the penal investigators, sent me their report today. Ptolemy Travers Smyth travelled no further than a cell in Brixton Prison, where he served twenty tears for robbery with violence.'

I knew that Mr G would only mock if I protested that Uncle Tolly had seemed such an innocent, so I said, 'He changed before he killed himself.' I put a boiled leek on his plate, where it sat in a light green puddle. 'He became hard and menacing, like a madman almost.' I gave him three potatoes and a boiled onion that sagged in the middle with a cloudy tarn on top. 'He said that Geoffrey had begged for mercy and then he shot him.'

'There are too many third-person singulars in that last sentence for it to be unambiguous,' he scolded. 'But it is an interesting piece of information, thank you.' He looked at the offering I had placed in front of him and rubbed his hands. 'Leeks.' He beamed in delight. 'Anyway, why are you clearing and serving?'

I gave up trying to drain my vegetables and settled for one of each.

'I wanted to save Molly the trouble with all those stairs.'

'The point of servants is to save us trouble.' He mashed his onion with the back of his fork into a beige pulp.

'But why would he say that?' I persisted.

Mr G opened his book. 'The mind of a man is a mystery even to himself,' he philosophized, and immersed himself in his reading – *Finger Smudges, the Eighty-Four Variations In Their Patterns.* 'Tosh.' He tore out the upper half of a page and let it drift to the floor. 'Twaddle.' He ripped the lower half out and rolled it as one might a cigarette before wedging it behind his ear.

'If you could have seen him,' I persisted.

'I should not have permitted his actions,' he mumbled. 'Shush now.' He whipped out his pencil. 'I am getting to the good part.'

Sidney Grice shovelled a mound of squashed leek into his mouth, chewing it thirty times as he scribbled a comment in the margin.

*

We had hardly got into the study before the doorbell rang and Molly cantered down the hall to answer it.

'Mrs Prendergast to see Miss Middleton,' she announced, presenting me with the silver tray.

'Well done, Molly.' I took the card. 'You got her name right first time.'

Molly grinned. 'I did what Mr Grice advised the other day and cleaned out my ears with carbolic. You wouldn't not belief the muck that came out.'

Mr G paused from shredding his book. 'Who is Mrs Prendergast?'

'A private client,' I told him. 'I helped her with a case whilst you were in Yorkshire.'

His eye narrowed. 'What category of case?' He took off his patch.

The rain had stopped now but there was still very little daylight. I turned up the gas.

'She had lost her dog,' I confessed.

Mr G polished his eye and forced it home. The lids were very inflamed.

'And how much did you charge her?'

I rubbed the back of my neck. 'Five shillings.'

'Excellent.' He clapped his hands together. 'At thirty per centum I shall expect one shilling and sixpence for use of my facilities.'

'Ask her to come in,' I told Molly.

'Mrs Pound O'Glass,' she proclaimed proudly as the lady bustled in, her dress sopping and her bonnet disarrayed.

'Oh, Miss Middleton,' Mrs Prendergast cried. 'It is Albert, poor little Alby.'

I tried to usher her to my seat, but she was pacing the floor in agitation.

'Has he gone missing again?' I asked.

Mrs Prendergast bit her lip and sobbed.

'Have you searched the laundry room?' I suggested.

Mrs Prendergast burst into tears. 'It is worse than that,' she cried. 'Much worse. Albert has lost his reason.'

I forced myself to keep a straight face.

'He has not joined the Liberal Party, has he?' my guardian enquired.

'If only he had,' Mrs P wept. 'At least they know how to bombard the Egyptians. No, Mr Grice, Albert has gone stark staring mad.'

Mr G leaned forward. 'How intriguing,' he said. 'Well, Miss Middleton, it appears you have another case.'

*

For once Sidney Grice was wrong. We were welcomed at the door by Mrs Prendergast's maid, smiling broadly.

'Oh, madam,' she said, 'it is quite miraculous. Come and see for yourself.'

I followed them both through into the drawing room and there was Albert, a blue ribbon in his hair, wagging his tail and jumping up excitedly at his mistress.

'But what happened?'

Mrs P swept her little dog up and rubbed her face on his head. 'Squidgy-widgy-woo.'

'He was sick, madam,' the maid said, 'all over the scullery floor, and straightaways he was back to his old self.'

The maid had a sweet face, almost classical in profile, and masses of blonde hair.

'He probably ate something that disagreed with him,' I suggested, and Mrs P projected her jaw.

'It's that boy from number 6,' she asserted. 'He gave Albert a sweet this morning after I told him not to. Boys have very dirty hands and pockets.'

'Well, I am glad he is all right.' I made to leave.

'But you will stay for tea.' Mrs P kissed Albert on the nose. 'Who's Mummy's googly-woogly-poogly boy?'

From the way he enthusiastically licked her mouth, I assumed Albert knew that he was.

'I will not, thank you,' I decided. 'I have just had some.'

'A little bit of cake,' she pressed. 'Wazoo feeling poorly-woorly?'

I recoiled. 'We shall be having dinner soon.'

'Take a little home,' Mrs P urged. And before I knew it the maid was passing me a packet of greaseproof paper, which I stuck into the pocket of my cloak.

I refused payment – though I felt sure my guardian would not have – and walked home. I needed the closest London could offer to fresh air, for I was feeling a little sicky-wicky.

*

'An easy five shillings,' Sidney Grice commented when I had told him about my visit.

'I did not charge her.' I nibbled a slice of bread.

'That was foolish. You will have all her friends queuing down Gower Street with their sick pets, and put Dr Crystal out of business.' He blew on his soup, presumably in an attempt to warm it up, and smacked his lips. 'Do you think Cook has been taking lessons?'

'Not in cookery.' I pushed mine away.

55

—◦•❈•◦—

The Bloomsbury Butcher

UNUSUALLY SIDNEY GRICE was proved wrong again the next morning. There were no queues of anxious pet owners down the street. He spent the morning devising a formula for the calculation of the volumes of ink of each colour used in a tattoo. He could not explain why it mattered but was convinced that it would one day. All truth matters was one of his favourite maxims, and he trotted it out again as he dipped his needle in red ink and stabbed at the sample of pig skin pinned out in a tray on his desk.

'I have received a report from Artemis Rosenberg's, the plebeian genealogy experts.' He dabbed the puncture wound with a rolled cloth. 'And they are in no doubt that Ptolemy Hercules Arbuthnot Travers Smyth, Esquire, was, as he laid claim to be, your second cousin.'

'So I have found a relative only to lose him again.' I opened my journal, the one I did not mind him seeing. 'What do you think will happen to Uncle Tolly's estate?'

'If the coroner is satisfied as to the cause of death you might inherit it.'

'Why only might?'

He selected a green ink. 'His last will and testament would have to be proved.'

'But why should it not be?' I took up a pencil to sketch my guardian.

'The signatures might be forged.' He dotted the pelt.

'Mine certainly was not.' I was having trouble with his nose. It was long and thin and straight, but my effort bore a striking resemblance to Mr Punch. 'And I watched the others sign their names.'

'Yes.' He dabbed his handiwork and wrote down a figure. 'But did they use their normal signatures? If they wrote in a strange hand they might pretend that the document was counterfeited. Who knows – ouch.' He shook his finger.

'Are you all right?' I started again on a new page.

'Of course I am,' he snapped and squeezed the wound. 'I always suffix knows with ouch, or at least I shall in future.' He sucked the finger. 'And do not dare pick me up on that.'

'It will be difficult not to,' I forecast. 'I suppose if the servants were mentioned in a previous will, they might be tempted to do that.'

'Precisely.' He picked up a magnifying glass. 'The dye has not taken, thank goodness. I should hate my decomposing body to be identified by a stain rather than by the abundance of cerebral tissue contained therein.'

I tried his nose again but now he resembled a dolphin.

*

I decided to go out for lunch rather than face another leek and called at Huntley Street to see if my friend Harriet Fitzpatrick was in town. I had met Harriet on the train the day I first came to London and she remained my staunchest ally. She almost always came on the first Tuesday of every month, and often on other days, to escape her humdrum life in Rugby. But Violet, who ran the ladies' club, answered my three quick rings in her sequinned red gown and told me that my friend had not been in for over a fortnight.

'Come in anyway,' she invited me, with great wafts of eau de cologne, but I declined and made my way down Capper Street to Brown's Grill House. There a resentful waiter in a grubby white jacket found me a table at the back of the restaurant where I could smoke. I ordered lamb chops, and Porter in two half-pints because they would not serve pints to a lady.

'What vegetables?' the German waiter snapped.

'None.'

'Very good.' He snatched the sauce-stained menu back.

'I do not care if you think it good or not,' I said, a little taken aback by my own abruptness, and the waiter scowled.

'Neither do I,' he said. 'I am hating this job. I am wanting to be an engineer in the army but I breaked my back spine and now I am waiting tables.'

'If you give me two extra chops, I will give you a fifteen per cent tip.'

'Twenty-five.'

'Fourteen.'

'One moment.' He flicked something squashed off his notepad. 'This is not how you are splitting the difference.'

'I do not split differences.'

'Very well, twenty,' he bid again.

'Thirteen,' I renegotiated. 'But I will make it fifteen for ease of calculation. If I go to twenty I might as well pay the extra bill, and I should like a very large gin.'

'We do not serve the spirits to the ladies.'

'As you have probably guessed, I am not a lady.'

He grimaced. 'I am sorry, but they will be sacking me.'

'Then serve it to me,' the young man on the next table instructed, 'and I will pass it over. You won't stop me doing that, will you?'

'I am beginning to like the English.' The waiter bowed from the waist. 'But not very much.'

'Donald Livingstone,' the man introduced himself, but I did not reply. I was not that much not a lady.

*

There were three letters for me when I returned home: one inviting me to visit a new haberdasher's on Oxford Street, but rather spoiled by addressing me as Dear Sir; another complimenting me on using their genuine whale-oil hair restorer, which was the first I had heard of it but also the first time anyone had said anything nice about my hair in years; the last was from Mrs Prendergast and my heart sank as soon as I saw the name. I had no desire to be remembered as the first detective to specialize in neurotic animals.

> *Dear Miss Middlington,* [Not the best of starts, I thought.] *I should like to apologize for wasting your time on the two occasions you have visited Alby and me. I cannot begin to express my gratitude for your patience and kindness...*

I skipped a couple of paragraphs.

> *I have bought you a present and would be honoured and delighted if you would call on me at four o'clock today to accept it.*

I showed it to my guardian.

'I see she went to Hempleman's College,' he said. 'Only Miss Beetle would teach a girl to cross her H's like that.' He held the paper up. 'This ink has not been produced for eight years now. Either she purchased a prodigious quantity of it or she writes very few letters.'

'I wonder how many tattoos she could get out of a bottle of that,' I murmured and he perked up.

'An interesting question. Perhaps you could ask her to give you a sample.' He mopped his glistening brow. 'Oh, I see, you were being sarcastic.' And he looked so wounded that I felt guilty, until he added, 'They say it is the lowest form of wit but I am not convinced that it is wit at all.'

*

I walked to Mrs P's and two children broke off from throwing a dead rat at passers-by to walk with me.

'Penny for a bowla soup.' The boy prodded my sleeve.

I gave them tuppence each.

'Is it true old Puddin' guzzles blood for dinner?' the girl asked.

'Every day,' I told her. 'And if you try to put your hand in my bag again, he will drink yours tonight.'

'Sorry, I was tryin' to shut it for you.' She mimed what she imagined to be an appearance of innocence.

There were patches like kettle fur on her eyes and the left eye was almost covered. Bitot's spots – my father had told me – were keratinized plaques. I had seen them in the poorest parts of India and now in the wealthiest city in the world. If I did get Uncle Tolly's money, I resolved, I would do something to help.

They skipped on either side of me.

'You off to catch a murderer?' The girl dipped to pick a scrap of something off the pavement.

'I hope so.'

'Can we 'elp?' She popped it in her mouth and chewed.

'Yes.' I tapped her hand away from my purse. 'If you wait outside our house and shout miserable old gizzard when Mr Grice appears, he will know it is a code and that I am on the trail of the Bloomsbury Butcher. But you must run away afterwards because he will pretend to be angry so that no one knows what we are up to.'

'Corr,' the boy said, but she was obviously the business brain of their partnership.

'What's it wurf?' She spat out whatever she had found.

'Fourpence each.'

'Sixpence.' She watched as the boy retrieved the scrap and tried it.

'Very well, but you must shout it twice and very loudly.'

'Orright,' the boy decided as he smacked his lips.

56

Haddock and Tonsils

MRS PRENDERGAST HAD albert in her arms as her maid showed me into the sitting room. It was prettily decorated in a rosebud pattern, with bright floral fabric chairs.

'Oh, Miss Middlington,' she cried, jumping up to put Albert on a cushion. 'How kind of you to come. You must think me an awful nuisance.'

I did, but I gave her my best smile and said, 'No, not in the least.'

'Say hello, Alby,' she urged, but Alby snuggled down and ignored us both.

'I hope you enjoyed your cake.'

'Lovely,' I lied, reminding myself to remove it from the pocket of my cloak where I had stuffed it the previous evening.

Every surface was covered with china dogs – Staffordshires posed snootily, white, some with orange patches, some with black or blue, all with black noses and lips; gun dogs presented pheasants or rabbits; spaniels rolled over to be tickled; and poodles showed off their new coiffures.

'You will join me for tea, I hope.' Mrs P interlocked her fingers.

I wanted to tell her that I was too busy, but she said it so imploringly that I did not have the heart to refuse her.

'You are too kind.'

'The lovely lady is staying for teasey-weasy, Alberty-walberty.'

Alberty Walberty buried his nose under a cushion and I wondered if he felt as nauseated as I did. Mrs P skipped to turn the bell handle.

'Before I forget...' She scuttled to a little cherrywood escritoire by the window. '... I must give you your present.' She pulled down the lid and brought something out. 'Albert helped me choose it, didn't you, Alby Walby?'

Whatever the gift was, she had gone to no trouble wrapping it for she was walking towards me with a brown paper bag, with something about the size and shape of a small cucumber bulging inside it. If this was a bone, I resolved, I would thank her politely, make my excuses and leave.

'Oh, I do hope you will like it.' She came quite close, closer than I like most people to come, and held it up. 'Can you guess what it is?'

'A haddock,' I joked weakly and she gurgled in delight.

'Not a haddock! Isn't she a silly-willy, Alby?' Albert gave no sign that he cared a burned bun as she poked the bag towards me. 'Now, no cheating, have another guess.'

I had been tired of this game before it started. 'An ornament,' I tried, a little more sensibly, and Mrs P chortled. She was almost touching me now and for a horrible moment I thought she was going to kiss me. I felt whatever it was press against my stomach and she seemed to be tilting it upwards to press under her breast.

'I am sorry, Mrs Prendergast. I do not want to play any more. Please stand back a little.'

Mrs P opened her mouth so widely that I could see her tonsils. She took a deep breath and let out an eardrum-bursting shriek. For an instant I was stunned.

'What on earth is the matter?' I tried to push her away, but she grabbed my arm with her right hand and slipped it round the back of me.

'No, Miss Middlington, please do not kill me,' she screamed in my face.

Albert was yapping now.

'Let go of me,' I protested. 'I have absolutely no intention of killing anybody.'

But Mrs P threw herself on to me and I felt a sharp pain just under my ribs as her present ripped through the bag and stabbed into me.

57

The Glistening, Growing Lake

MRS PRENDERGAST LET out another scream. This one was not so loud but was all the more alarming for that. The other screams had been histrionic and annoying, but now it was a real cry of shock and her fingers hooked into my arm, hurting even through the thick fabric, but what frightened me most was the sharpness in my abdomen.

'Mrs Prendergast,' I gasped as she sprayed into my face, but her eyes were wild and unreasoning now.

I pressed my palms on to her shoulders and pushed with all my might, and Mrs P let go and stepped back so easily that I almost toppled into her. I examined the area of pain and saw a dark patch on my dress, about the size of a dinner plate. I felt it damp and my hand came away red. It was brighter than I had expected but unmistakeably blood.

'What have you done?' It dripped from my fingers, but I could not see a rip and the pain seemed to be easing. And then I saw where it was coming from. It was pumping out of Mrs Prendergast.

Mrs Prendergast was clutching at her chest and the knife projecting between her hands, and her life's blood flooded through them. She stared at it all in shock and then at me in astonishment.

'Stuck,' she breathed, and then something that may have been more words or just three short breaths.

She gripped the golden handle.

'Do not pull it out,' I warned, but Mrs Prendergast bunched herself up and with one massive effort tore the dagger away.

Three great streams burst out of the tear in her dress and she staggered forward, the blade still pointing towards her as she sagged. Albert was down off his chair and darting about excitedly. His mistress groaned and swayed, and I knew that she would impale herself again if she fell on that knife. I reached out and snatched it from her as she sidestepped helplessly like an old drunkard, grabbing uselessly at a whatnot and a revolving book-case, and bringing both crashing as she dropped to her knees and tipped face down on to the dusty-rose circular rug in the middle of the floor. Then the door flew open and the maid rushed in, slopping milk and hot water, to find me standing over Mrs Prendergast's body and Albert lapping blissfully at the glistening, growing lake in which her mistress lay.

58

Hiawatha

IN MELODRAMAS MAIDS always scream when they come across a body. In real life I had never known them to do so. This maid did. She dropped the tray and jumped back, as if it were the sugar bowl that terrified her, and screamed again and again and again. I rushed to calm her down, and it was only after she had fled that I remembered I still had the knife in my hand.

'Get the police,' I called needlessly because she was out of the door and howling for them on the street.

I threw the knife down and kneeled beside Mrs P, but there was not a moment of doubt that she was dead. I did not even trouble to check for a pulse or signs of breathing.

I heard heavy fast footsteps and the maid uttering hoarsely, 'That way, through there.' And a man dashed in.

'Strike me!' He was dressed in oily overalls, undone to the waist. 'Fetch a peeler. I saw one down Thornhaugh Street not two minutes ago.' She dithered. 'Oh, never mind.' He trod backwards on to a Russian doll. 'I'll go. It'll be quicker.' He ran out.

'Don't leave me alone wiv 'er.' The maid rushed after him. Albert was licking around Mrs P's open eyes. I pushed him away and he darted behind her to lap at the blood.

'Go away.' I flapped my hand and he scrambled on to her back and grasped her hair clip in his teeth, growling playfully as he pulled it out. 'Go away.' There was a copy of *Tit-Bits* amidst the spilled books. I whacked his hindquarters with it and he yelped but danced round to try to tug the magazine off me. I tapped him on the nose.

'Gawd, she's tryin' to kill the mutt now.' The man was back, his overall buttoned up now, with a constable at his side and the maid hanging back, crushing her apron into her mouth and whimpering as if she too had been mortally injured.

'That's 'er. Mrs Prendergast called for help and I ran in and saw 'er over Mrs Prendergast's body with a knife in 'er hand.'

I did not trouble to deny it. 'My name is Miss March Middleton,' I told the policeman. 'I am assistant to Mr Sidney Grice, the personal detective, who resides at 125 Gower Street. I expect you have heard of him.'

'Certainly 'ave,' the constable concurred. He had black stumpy teeth with the gums growing over some of them.

'We must get Mr Grice here immediately,' I said. 'He should still be at home.'

'Watch out! She's still got the knife wrapped up in that paper,' the man warned.

'Nonsense,' I said, and was about to open the magazine to show them when the constable knocked it out of my hand to land near where the dagger still lay.

'There you are.' The man danced about. 'Told you.'

'It was already on the floor where I dropped it,' I insisted, and kneeled to unroll the *Tit-Bits* to show that there was no blood inside it.

'Watch out,' the man warned. 'She's going for it.'

This policeman, it seemed, was a man of no words but plenty of action. He whipped out his truncheon and whacked into my forearm. And before I knew it I was being hauled up and my hands forced behind my back with my wrists clamped in iron manacles.

'There is no need for that,' I protested.

'No need?' the maid parroted, still hoarse from her scream-ing. 'Was there any need for all this?'

Albert was scrabbling at the hem of the rug. He was having a wonderful time.

'You're coming with me.' The policeman yanked at my hand-cuffs, able to vociferate at last.

59

The Woman from Over the Beacon

I HAD TRAVELLED IN the back of a Black Maria before but never as a suspect. The constable hauled me inside and shoved me roughly on to the bench seat.

'Have you any idea what will happen to your career when I make a complaint?' I threatened and he flopped his shoulders.

'Not much.' He smirked. 'I'm leaving next week to join the Royal Ballet.'

I tried but failed to hide my incredulity. He was a chunky, ungainly man with all the natural grace of a pantechnicon.

'As a night watchman,' he added and slammed the door.

''E's nice in't 'e?' the woman on the parallel bench remarked without any obvious irony. 'The last bluebottle wot picked me up wanted a knee trembler. I made 'im tremble with my knee, no mistake.'

'Where are you from?' I asked and she tilted her head back.

'What's it to you?'

'It's just that you have a south-west Lancashire accent but you aren't from Wigan.'

She narrowed her eyes. 'You a police spy?'

'No,' I reassured her. 'I've been arrested on suspicion of murder.'

'Freckin' Norman.' She was greatly impressed. ''Ow d'you do it?'

'Allegedly with a knife.' I clung to the bench to stop myself sliding off.

''Legedly,' she mused. 'That's a good word.' She stuck her boots next to me on the seat and I saw that she had no soles but rags wrapped around her feet. ''Cause fer all you know I could be a spy myself.'

'Appley Bridge,' I guessed and she seemed impressed but only said, 'Naaah.'

'Gathurst,' I tried again.

'Getting cold.'

'Skelmersdale.'

She cracked her knuckles. 'Third time lucky. 'Ow did you know that?'

'I come from Parbold,' I told her.

'Where's that?'

'About five miles away, the other side of Ashurst Beacon.'

'Oh.' She picked a scab on her lower lip. 'I always wondered what were there.' And she ate it with obvious enjoyment.

*

It was not far to Marylebone Police Station but the journey took the best part of an hour, though we could not see why.

The main hall was surprisingly quiet. An old woman lay on her back on the floor, her mouth opening and snapping closed like a puppet. Two youths stood with bruised faces and an enormous bald woman holding them by the scruffs of their necks.

'Miss Middleton.' The desk sergeant looked up from his register in surprise.

'Sergeant Horwich.' I acknowledged him. He had been of great help in the Ashby case.

'What the hell is she in for?' He glared at the arresting policeman. 'And this 'ad better be good, Nettles.'

Constable Nettles came to attention. 'Murder of a Mrs Philida Prendergast.'

'Did you do it?' The desk sergeant picked up his pen. He was a massive man, past his prime and gone to fat, but still an imposing physical presence with a military air about him which generally gained the respect of the men and their prisoners.

'No,' I replied.

'Take the cuffs off her,' Horwich ordered. 'She's 'ardly goin' to beat you up, a scrawny wisp like that.'

'She was found over the body with a knife in 'er 'and, covered in blood.' Nettles searched for the key in six pockets, then found it when he went back to the first.

'Bound to be some innocent explanation,' the sergeant predicted confidently as the constable unlocked the manacles.

'There is,' I assured him and he grinned, though the act was largely camouflaged by his walrus moustaches.

'There you are.' He put down his pen. 'Told you there would be.'

'And she was attackin' a dog,' the constable continued.

'What sort of a dog?' Sergeant Horwich perked up.

'A likkle 'un.'

'A likkle 'un?' The sergeant went dreamy. 'They're my faverit.'

'It was a black-and-tan Cavalier King Charles spaniel called Albert,' I informed him, 'and I only tapped him with a magazine.'

'It yelped,' the constable said and the sergeant swallowed.

'Don't suppose it takes much of a tap to kill one of them,' he pondered and puffed out his chest. 'We shall need to detain you for the magistrate tomorrow.'

A group of Irishmen came in, singing a sad song about wide oceans and pretty girls at home, and the policemen paused to listen.

'Is Inspector Pound on duty?' I asked.

'No,' the sergeant said stiffly. 'And he ain't likely to be. He's back in hostibal with his wound gone poisoned.' He sucked air through the gaps in his lower teeth.

'Oh dear God.'

'You was there when he got stabbed as I recall.' The sergeant leaned over and his breath smelled of fish.

'I must go and see him.'

'No,' the sergeant said. 'You must be booked and taken down to the cells.'

'Get Mr Grice,' I said. 'He has done you more than a few favours in the past.'

'I'm not a man what feels gratitude,' the desk sergeant told me cheerfully.

'He is also in the same club as the chief constable.'

The sergeant flicked his head at Nettles. 'Go and get him.' And the constable strolled off. 'Now then.' He dipped his pen. 'Name.'

'You know my name.'

'Name,' he insisted and there was a crash. Three of the Irishmen had thrown the fourth under a bench and were trying to kick him with their clogs. 'You stay there,' the sergeant reached for his truncheon, 'while I give those Murphies a headache to remember me by.'

He dashed round the desk and across the room with surprising agility for such a corpulent man, and I stood to one side while he and two constables flung the assailants aside and brought the affray under control.

'We'll get them in the cells first,' the desk sergeant decided, 'before they kill each other or we have to do it for them.' His face glistened with triumph and sweat.

'And they hanged him from a lamp post in the morning,' a tousle-haired young man sang in a beautiful baritone as they dragged him to the desk. His nose, I saw, had old breaks in two different directions.

It took a long time to book the four men. They kept changing their minds about what their names were and arguing with each other about it.

'Don't you be calling me Seamus, Eamon.'

'Don't you be calling me Eamon, Seamus.'

And they were just being led away when the door was flung open and Molly rushed over in a long black coat. 'Oh, miss, you ain't not been killing people, have you?'

I ignored her question. 'Where is Mr Grice?'

Molly looked up at the ceiling and crossed her fingers to help her remember. 'Mr Grice has been called away on a matter of the outmost urgentiness and he has sented me to misrepresent him for you.' She sighed in relief at having delivered her message to her complete satisfaction.

'What matter?'

'The matter is one of a delicious – no, delicate and conferential – something.'

'Does he know I have been arrested?'

Molly was flushed like a child who had been holding her breath too long.

'Do you want him to know?'

'Yes.'

'Yes,' she declared. She was hopping about and sucking her cheeks in.

'Molly, what is going on?'

But Molly was proclaiming to Sergeant Horwich, 'This woman is innocent and must be released immedantly.'

'And you are?' he enquired.

'Molly,' she proclaimed.

'And how do you know that this woman is innocent?'

Molly scratched her head. 'Because she ain't not clever enough to kill people and she don't not do lies except about smoking and drinking and her dress bill and we need her at home.' Molly clearly thought that sufficient for she was about to usher me away when the sergeant guffawed and said, 'We shall need a bit more than that before we can drop the charges.'

Something was bothering me. 'That is my coat,' I realized.

'Well…' Molly crossed her hands under her chin. 'You won't not be needing it if you're going in the jug.'

I gave my attention back to Sergeant Horwich. 'If you arrested me or Mr Grice every time we discovered a body we would never be out of your cells.'

Horwich sucked his pen. 'That's true,' he conceded, a stain

spreading from the corner of his mouth. 'But Inspector Quigley was not very happy about you being released without questioning after your uncle died and he'll be even less happy if I just let you go when we have witnesses.'

Uncle Tolly's death was not Quigley's case, but he had a grudge against me for making him look foolish in the past.

'Is Quigley here?' I asked. We may have disliked each other, but he was a logical man and might at least listen to reason.

'No,' the sergeant said, 'but you'll probably see him with his prisoners in the morning.'

'She can't not have done it,' Molly piped up, ''cause I saw her murder somebody else dead.' She folded her arms. 'So you'll have to let her go now and then you won't not be able to prove she did the other thing what I made up and you'll have to let her go for that too.' She plonked her elbows on the desk, bedazzled by her own ingeniousness, and the sergeant regarded her balefully.

'Get out before I charge you for wasting police time,' he threatened, his lips bright blue.

'If you do,' Molly tapped the desk like a debater at a lectern, 'will you let me share her cell?'

'Let me put it this way.' Horwich plucked at his mutton-chop whiskers. 'No.'

And to my astonishment Molly burst into tears. 'But there's only her and Mr Grice what's ever been kind to me, except Aunty Erica what didn't cut my throat. You can't keep her, not now of all times.'

'Molly.' I took hold of her shoulders as she sobbed uncontrollably. 'What exactly is going on?'

Molly fought to calm herself. 'I wasn't not going to tell you,' she managed at last with gasps between each word, ''cause you ain't not no use in an emergency like me and Mr Grice,' she made several horrible slurping noises, 'used to be.'

'What are you talking about?'

'Oh, miss,' Molly howled. 'Oh, miss, oh, miss, oh, miss.

Poor Mr Grice, the kinderest, gentlestest, sweetestest, kinderest man what ever ever lived, don't not lived no more. Mr Grice is dead.'

60

The Flat Stone

I WAS GOING TO *tell my father off. He had not written to me once since he had gone on his walking holiday and he was due home that evening.* Cook had roasted a leg of mutton from one of our own sheep and I had his slippers by the fire and ordered in his favourite malt. And now he had missed the six o'clock train. It was too bad.

I knew he would be all right. We had been to India and Afghanistan together. Before that he had survived wars and all sorts of scrapes. My father was indestructible. Everybody said so.

Young Sam came with a telegram.

Daddy has met with some old comrades and is stopping in his club for the night, I told myself.

But Sam was crying and did not wait for a reply or even a tip.

REGRET TO INFORM YOU...

I ran out of the house and stood on the flat stone that looked across the valley and down the hill, and a howl that was hardly human flew out to the dipping sun. It bounced around the quarry looking for escape, but you can never escape the truth.

61

The Nun with a Hatbox

I COLLECTED MY thoughts. Molly was always getting things wrong. She had explained once that men button their coats the other way because they are all left-handed, and on another occasion had given me a breathless account of how Queen Victoria had tried to assastinate a madman in the park.

'Dead?' I mocked.

'Bone dead,' she told me and blew her nose on my coat lining. 'Dead as a dormouse. Dead as water.'

I collected my thoughts. 'Why do you think he is dead, Molly?'

''Cause I've seen him.' Her eyes glowed with fear. 'I've seen him scrawled on the floor – dead as glass.'

Sergeant Horwich was listening intently. 'Are you sure?' he asked. 'I remember you coming in here saying that all London was on fire.'

'I didn't not know that was from a historitical book,' she retorted. 'But I seed Mr Grice screwn all over the floor and I took his plus in his wrist like Miss Middleton taught me and he was dead as a badger. So when the bluebottle came and said Miss Middleton – what we call old pan-face behind her back – was in trouble, I knew I had to come with my better cleverness to save her.'

The bald woman lumbered up, dragging the two youths with her.

'Now see here, my good man.' Her accent would not have

gone amiss at a royal garden party. 'How much longer am I to be kept waiting?'

Sergeant Horwich bristled. 'For as long I choose.' At which the woman let go of both her captives, grasped the sergeant by his jacket, pulled him towards her and butted him in the face.

'One moment please, madam,' he said, the blood streaming from his nostrils and through his moustaches. 'Nettles, and you, Harris, go with these two women to Gower Street at once and don't be afraid. They aren't as dangerous as they look.' He pointed at me. 'I put you on your honour to return. And you.' He prodded a finger at the bald woman who towered over him. 'Get up off the floor.'

'I am not on—' she began as he pulled back his left shoulder, feinted and knocked her clean out with one of the finest right hooks I have ever witnessed. And she fell as I have only seen an oak tree fall before, but with less grace.

'That's our mam,' one of the youths howled.

We hurried outside.

'Pity girls can't run,' Nettles said. 'It'll take forever in a cab.' He tried to wave one down but it was occupied by a nun with a hatbox. 'Hang on, wait for us,' he called as I set off, with Molly left standing.

When women have the vote and I am the prime minister I shall pass a law making all men wear dresses for a day, and see how well they can get about with petticoats wrapping around their legs and bustles bobbing up and down behind them. I was in the lead all the way up Maple Street but on the straight in University Street, Harris, then Nettles, spurted past. Harris rang the bell.

'You will have to wait for Molly,' I gasped as she opened the door.

'Got a ride with the nun,' she explained. 'Told her I was escapering from a prodingstant.'

The three of us stood fighting for breath in the hall.

'Now,' I managed at last. 'What is this all about?'

'He's in there.' Molly had taken off my coat and hung it up. There was a button hanging loose. 'Dead as clockwork. Anyone for tea?'

The policemen assented enthusiastically as she went down the hall and I led them into the study.

'Molly,' I bellowed and she came galloping back, almost colliding into me.

'I don't not want to look again.' She covered her eyes like a little girl playing hide and seek.

'I think you should,' I insisted and she slid her hands down reluctantly.

'Lord love 'im,' she said. 'He's descended into heaven.'

'Is this a trick to get your mistress out of gaol?' Harris demanded. ''cause it ain't a very good one.'

'He was here,' Molly insisted. 'I saw him dead as a pope.'

'Well he ain't 'ere now,' Nettles said perceptively. 'And where d'you fink you're goin'?'

'I am going to look upstairs,' I said.

'Not without me, you ain't.'

He followed me up and I was nearly at the top when I saw the soles of Sidney Grice's boots, toes down, then his trousers crumpled up, then him lying on his front in the corridor, arms and legs akimbo. His face was yellow and his eyes were open and misted over.

62

Flannels and Being Damned

I LEAPED UP the last few steps and threw myself on to my knees beside him.

'Open that door.'

Nettles did so and some light came in from the sitting room. I grasped my guardian's wrist. The pulse was thready and fast but definitely present and, when I brushed his eyelid with the back of my finger, he blinked.

'Help me turn him on his back.'

The others were coming up.

'See,' Molly declared. 'Dead as a cup.'

She ran her finger under the bannister rail and tutted as if it were somebody else's job to clean it.

'He is not dead.' I loosened his cravat. 'But he is having a severe bout of fever.'

'Maralia.' Molly crossed herself to ward off the evil miasmas.

'I do not think it is malaria this time,' I said. 'He caught more diseases than he will admit to when he was searching for his friend in the jungle.'

'Oh,' Molly exclaimed, 'if he wanted a friend he could have had me. I could have taken him ratting and taught him to play pinch-the-parson's-bum.'

'Haven't played that in years,' Harris reminisced as Sidney Grice shuddered uncontrollably.

'We need to get him up to bed,' I declared, and Nettles took my guardian's shoulders while Harris grabbed him under the knees and lifted.

Sidney Grice closed his eyes. He was a dead weight, limp but shivering all the while. Nettles went backwards up the stairs with Harris struggling behind. Twice Nettles stumbled and the second time he cracked Sidney Grice's head on a bannister spindle.

'Be careful,' I urged.

'Yes,' Molly scolded. 'If that barrister gets chipped it'll be me what gets the blame.'

'Don't worry,' Harris pacified her. ''E probably won't live to tell you off.'

'I wish he would.' Molly tangled her mop of red hair around her fingers. 'I wish he would wake up and say Get out, you black-headed lumpy wrench in that soft-hearted way of his.'

'Hello, Mother,' Mr G murmured. 'Shall we feed the snakes today?'

'Oh, bless him,' Molly burbled fondly.

The men reached the top and I hurried ahead to open the door. I had never seen or been in my guardian's room before – no doubt he would not have thought it decent for me to do either – and I always imagined it to be austere and cell-like but it was actually quite a cheerful room. The walls were papered in Regency stripes and there was a thick Turkish carpet for him to step on to when he got out of the bed that the policemen dumped him on to. As might be expected his bedside table was piled high with books, all with multiple paper markers jutting out of them. They were mainly anatomy and chemistry, but were topped for light relief by a volume entitled *Insoluble Mathematical Theorems and Conundrums Concerning the Algebraic Nature of Magnetism.*

'Oh, I've read one of those,' Molly said.

'Which one?' I asked automatically as I struggled to undo my guardian's bootlaces. They were tied in very complicated knots and my efforts only seemed to be tightening them.

'No, not one of those.' She wiggled her nose. 'A book about a cat what came to London but I didn't not understand it.'

'Allow me,' Harris said, unfolded a clasp knife and sawed through them.

'He won't not be happy about that,' Molly predicted. 'They were his most favouritest laces.'

I checked his pulse again. 'How do you know?' Usually I would find her chatter nearly as irritating as Mr G did but today – having been embraced by a woman impaling herself against me, arrested for her murder, been told that Inspector Pound had relapsed and seeing my guardian prostrate with a tropical fever – there was something reassuringly normal about it.

''Cause he never said he had any more favouriter,' she reasoned.

'I need some flannels and a bowl of cold water,' I told her.

'And what does Mr Grice need?' she wondered.

'Fetch his quinine from the medicine chest in the bathroom,' I told her. 'If he wakes up it will help get his temperature down.'

'You could use the flannels for that too,' Molly suggested.

There was a photograph on the dressing table of a young man. He was wearing a striped blazer, strumming a banjo and laughing, and it took me a while to recognize him.

'I tried. I tried.' Mr G stirred. 'I tried.' He clutched my wrist. 'It startled me.' He opened his eyes and focused on me. 'It was too clean under the bed.'

He tried to rise but I restrained him.

'Do not worry about that now,' I told him. 'You must rest.' I mopped his brow with my handkerchief.

Molly burst in, announcing, 'Hot water and quiline.' And I checked the bottle. At least she had brought the right drug.

'Throw that hot water away and get some cold water from the bathroom,' I ordered, 'and a cup or glass.'

'Which?'

'Either.'

'It caught me off guard.' Mr G's hand shot in front of his face.

'You are safe now,' I told him and his eyes seemed to sink back into his head, and for a while he was lost in reverie.

'Do you think it is my safety I am concerned about?' He fumbled for his watch.

Molly was hovering at my side, slopping water on his leg.

'Take this tablet,' I instructed and popped it in his mouth. There is nothing in the world more tongue-curlingly, mouth-shrivellingly bitter than quinine. It is the reason tonic was invented and the excuse we all needed in India to take more gin. 'Have some water.'

Mr G waved away the glass. 'Yum yum,' he said and instantly fell asleep.

I checked his mouth and he had swallowed it all.

'His eye needs to come out,' I said. His socket was weeping.

'Don't worry, miss, I can do that,' Molly volunteered and set to work.

'The other eye, Molly,' I told her hastily.

'Silly me.' She slapped the back of her own hand. 'I thought it felt squidgy.'

Nettles humphed. 'I am sorry, miss, but we need to go back now.'

'I can't leave him.'

'Don't worry, miss,' Molly piped up. 'I'll look after him. I'll take all his clothings off and throw pails of cold water over him. He'll like that.'

And I wondered if my guardian was right after all when he swore she would be the death of him.

'Do not do any such thing,' I snapped. 'Mop his brow to keep him cool. If he is awake in an hour give him another tablet. If he gets any worse run to the hospital and get help.'

Sidney Grice did not mind doctors experimenting on me, but he hated them coming near him.

'Dear God.' Sidney Grice clawed at his socket. 'Dear God, how I loved…'

He settled again and I bent over him and kissed his brow – the first time I had ever done so.

'Shall I do that?' Molly asked.

'Yes, please,' I whispered, and I was damned for all eternity if I would cry.

———◦•❀•◦———

63

The Diamond Dull in the Midday Sun

S ERGEANT HORWICH WAS decorated with a black eye and
had a split in his upper lip.

'Her two sons had a go at me,' he chatted merrily, 'but
they went down like skittles. Then she came back with an upper-
cut – hence the shiner – but my straight right was the undoing of
her. How's Mr Grice?'

'He has a bad fever but I think he will pull through.'

'Oh yes.' His face fell. 'I'm supposed to be booking you for
murder.' He leaned forward confidentially. 'Just between ourselves – you didn't do it, did you?'

'No,' I promised. 'Honestly.'

'That's good enough for me.' He winked and tapped the side
of his purpled nose.

'But not quite good enough for me.' Inspector Quigley mate-
rialized at my shoulder, as unsavoury as ever, a frowsy man with
dry eyes and a staleness about his person. 'Good evening, Miss
Muddleton.'

'Middleton.'

He sniffed. 'Wonder why I always get that wrong.'

'It could be because you are stupid,' I told him and Horwich
guffawed.

Quigley rounded on him furiously. 'When you have stopped
giggling like a silly schoolgirl perhaps you could book this prisoner in.'

The mirth fled the sergeant's mouth in an instant. 'Yes, sir.'

'And find her a cell for the night.'

'Yes, sir.'

The inspector turned to me. 'We will talk about this in the morning.'

'I shall look forward to it,' I assured him.

'Sleep well,' Quigley called as he made his way to the exit. 'I know I shall.'

'That wasn't very clever of me, was it?' I commented as Horwich filled out my details.

'He's a good copper, the inspector is.' The desk sergeant blotted his book. 'He usually gets his man.'

'The only trouble is,' I retorted, 'he does not always get the right one.'

'A conviction is a conviction.' Horwich shrugged. 'It's what the public want, so it's what the powers that be want and it's what they get.' He banged on a bell and shouted out, 'Harris, take this lady down. Cell three.' He picked at his moustaches. 'Busy night, tonight, Miss Middleton. You'll be sharing.'

'Not with your bald sparring partner, I hope,' I said.

Horwich's eyes crinkled. 'Would I do that to you?'

I had never been to the cells before. They were down a flight of stone steps and halfway Harris stopped.

'You don't want to get on the wrong side of Quigley,' he warned very quietly. ''E's a vicious so-and-so when 'e's roused.'

'I will use all my feminine charms,' I promised.

'That's a goodun.' Harris chortled good-naturedly. 'You ain't got none, 'ave you?'

We passed through a heavy oak door to a bare passageway with eight doors to either side, each with barred windows and hinged wooden flaps below to close them off if necessary.

Harris paused again and whispered, 'I 'ope Mr Grice will be all right. 'E 'elped me out once, but 'e made me promise not to say.'

'Will you let me know if you hear anything?'

'I'll try.' His voice rose for the audience of faces appearing in the grills. 'Saved you the one with a sea view.' He put a key in the lock.

'T'ain't fair,' an old man called from the cell opposite. 'I've only got a field of sheep to look at.'

'Yeah, but you got the four-poster bed,' Harris joked as he steered me in.

The cell was unlit except for the gaslight coming in from the passageway.

'Bloody 'eck,' a woman screeched. 'You've given me the piggin' murderess.'

'Murderess,' she hissed, the woman in the mirror.

I leaped away and tried to calm myself, and as my eyes adjusted to the dim rays I saw it was the woman with whom I had travelled there.

'They have taken my knife away from me,' I reassured her.

'Don't come any closer.'

She was sitting on the bed, crouched back in the corner, in a manner horribly reminiscent of Uncle Tolly when I had thought I'd killed him. I stood back.

'If you had never travelled as far as Parbold,' I wondered, 'how did you happen to go to London?'

'In a box,' she told me. 'Our dad packed me up in a crate and put me on a waggon that was going that way. 'E paid the wagoner three shillin' and 'e told me I could mek my fortune in London and go back in the same box when I 'ad.'

'And did you?' I asked.

The cell stank of human waste.

'Did I 'eckers.' She relaxed her arms, which had been raised to protect her from my anticipated assault. 'I lived in that box for two days and when I gor out to 'unt for grub they broke it all up for firewood. Then I got done for vagrancy, then for comforting gentlemen, then a bit of thievin' and stuff and 'ere I am twenty year on.'

'Will you go home again?'

She huffed. 'What for? I'm more comfortable 'ere than I was there.' She stuck her legs out straight over the edge of the bed. 'So why d'you kill 'er?'

'I didn't.'

'No, that won't do at all.' My cellmate rattled in mirth. 'The beaks 'ate it when you deny stuff. I've got off much lighter for admitting things what I never done. They just want a reason and then summut to feel sorry for you about. Tell them you were trying to feed your baby after your husband died for 'is country. They like that one.'

'I have not got a baby.' I sat on the end on the bed.

'Mek one up,' she urged. 'Or, better still, borrow one. Meg Turnaway is out the back most days and she'll lend you 'ers fer a shillin'. Cry a lot as well, but not loud – they don't like noisy criers, just tears rollin' down your cheeks, dignified like. Susie Veronica will lend you an onion in an 'andkerchief fer tuppence, though she might charge you more, being a toff.'

'I am not going to admit to a murder I did not commit,' I insisted and she wheezed in amusement.

''Ow many times 'ave I 'eard that?' she gurgled. ''Ow many times? But they soon change their tune when they're up in that box – 'cept fer little Queeny Dale. She stuck to 'er guns and she's doing life now.'

'But I am innocent,' I protested.

She snorted and spat on the wall, and I could just make out something gelatinous sliding down like a small slug.

'If you know what's good fer you, you'll cooperate.'

'I have rarely known what's good for me.'

'Thought so. Which end?'

'Of what?'

'The cot.'

I lay with her feet in my face. It was either that or the dripping wall. You cannot lie on your back in a bustle.

I was cold and thirsty and aching on the thin mattress, and

my cellmate was snoring while the bald woman was hollering, 'You there, is it too much to ask for tea and a few cucumber sandwiches?' And somebody else was whistling 'Lilly Bolero', and the picture flicked through my head – a man on one knee, his sabre in the dust, the band playing and the diamond dull in the midday sun.

It was the first time since you died that I had not untied the red ribbon to read your letters; nor touched our engagement ring. I said my prayers silently for you and myself and my guardian, and recited your third letter to myself, the one about the picnic. The letters and the prayers were intermingled so much now that I could scarcely tell them apart, and I could only hope the words were going to the same place. I felt George Pound's ring press into me beneath my dress. Do you know I have it? Do you hate me for it? I am not even sure what it means.

64

Imaginary Horses and Grown-up Writing

CONSTABLE NETTLES CAME for me in the morning. I do not think I slept but sleep is a great deceiver and, though the night seemed endless, I could remember little of it.

'Don't forget.' My cellmate yawned, her mouth cobwebbed. 'Susie Veronica and Meg Turnaway. They'll see you right.'

'You'll be lucky,' Nettles said. 'One's inside, the other's in a box. Don't ask me which.'

My cellmate picked something off her neck and glared as if I had given it to her.

'Good luck,' I wished her as Nettles locked her in and led me out through the thick oak door.

'Have you heard anything about Mr Grice?' I asked.

'Nothing.' He plodded up the stairs. 'Sorry.'

We went back through the reception area which was almost empty now. A new sergeant sat at the desk and two small boys galloped their imaginary horses, shooting invisible guns at him.

'Stand and deliver,' one squeaked fiercely.

'Number three,' the sergeant told my guard, and we went down the long echoing corridor to the end on the left.

I knew that interview room, with its wooden table under the tall grilled window, and I sat in the same place that William Ashby had occupied when Sidney Grice and I had questioned him about the murder of his wife, some eight months ago.

Nettles stood behind me. 'Stand up.' The door opened and I half rose, until I saw who the newcomer was and sat back again.

'I am not like Inspector Pound.' Quigley strode in, waving a brown cardboard file. 'I am not your friend.'

I sighed. 'You certainly know how to hurt a girl.'

'Oh, believe me, I do.' Quigley whipped a chair out. 'I have an interesting witness statement here. Can you guess who I took it from?'

'Mrs Prendergast's maid,' I said and he rested his foot on the chair.

'Gloria Shell.' He put his elbow on his knee. 'Pretty little thing, don't you think?'

'I had not noticed,' I lied.

'Oh, I did straight away.' He had missed a bit shaving under his nose. 'I have to in my job.' Those half dozen bristles repelled me. 'Makes all the difference in a trial. Put some eel-faced hag in the box and she could quote the Bible and not be believed. A lovely little thing like that, though, and twelve men good and true will be hanging on every word.' He leaned over towards me. 'Don't mess me about, Middleton. I've had a long night getting the truth out of some Irish bastards and if I don't go to bed soon with a nice warm signed confession I will get very irritable indeed. And I am not nice when I am irritable, am I, Constable?'

'Not nice at all,' Nettles agreed fervently and the inspector slammed the file on to the desk.

'I know you did it.' His fingerplates had been gnawed savagely back. 'Gloria Shell all but saw you do it and you went for her with the knife too. We have three people witnessed you attacking the victim's dog. Now that last part might seem trivial to you, but if we exhibit that cute little cur and tell the jury how you battered it, they won't even need to hear pretty Miss Shell before they've convicted you in their heads.' He opened the folder. 'My colleague here knows you did it and he's very good in court, aren't you, Constable?'

'Not bad, sir, but—'

'Now,' Quigley brought out two handwritten documents, 'that's enough pleasantness. I have a confession here – yours – and, just to save time, I have had it written it out already from what you told me last night. Admit to the murder and we'll drop the dog charges.'

'That sounds fair,' I said. 'Where do I sign?'

The inspector eyed me suspiciously. 'It has already been witnessed.' He jabbed the end of the document with his finger.

'Got a pen?' I asked. 'You must realize I shall deny it all later.'

'Deny all you like,' Quigley sneered. 'But me and three officers of the law heard you make it.'

I took the fountain pen from him – the nib was splayed but it still worked – and wrote in block capitals. QUI. 'I don't suppose you can do joined-up writing.'

Nettles tried to stifle a snort.

'What the—' Quigley slapped my hand, splattering ink over the table. 'Take a tea break, Constable.'

Nettles hesitated and his superior kicked back, sending the chair crashing to the floor.

'Sir, I—' Nettles began.

'Just do it,' Quigley screamed, a vein engorged on his left temple.

Nettles walked reluctantly to the door and I saw the fear in his eyes as he looked back before he quit the room.

65

Prize Fighters and Custody

N O SOONER HAD Nettles gone than Quigley was round the table and standing over me.

I looked fixedly ahead. 'If you harm me you will have Mr Grice and Inspector Pound to answer to.'

Quigley brought his temper under control and was all the more frightening for that. 'Two dying men,' he said scornfully. 'If they ain't dead already.'

'Aren't,' I corrected him. 'Your accent is slipping, Inspector.'

'Think yours will save you now,' he sneered. 'I've had women of your sort all hoity-toity and superior, but they're begging me to give them favours before I've finished.'

'The only favour you could do me is to book yourself into an undertakers,' I vowed.

Quigley grabbed my hair. My hair may be mousey but it is strong and I made no sound as he twisted me round, and his words sprayed into my face. 'Always high and mighty, and thinking you're so clever with your quips. Know what the men call you behind your back?'

'I doubt they compare my breath to horse droppings,' I retorted.

Quigley wrenched at me. 'Neither of us will leave this room until I get your signature on that confession.'

'Read it to me,' I suggested. 'We can while the hours away with a little fiction.'

'You did it, bitch.'

He ripped so hard this time that I cried out.

'No.' I fumbled for the pen and grasped it like a dagger.

Quigley cackled. 'Do it. Assault a police officer and try to talk your way out of that one.'

'You would not press charges,' I challenged. 'The great Inspector Quigley hurt by a little girl? They would laugh you out of the station.'

I jabbed. I meant to get the side of his head but he jerked back and away, and I got him under the chin. The nib sank in and, when I let go, the pen dangled like a bizarre goatee.

'Bloody bog bitch.' He ripped it out and hurled it on the floor and his hand went back. 'I'll beat you black and blue for that.'

'If you make one mark on me—'

'Good morning, Inspector Quigley.' Inspector Pound stood in the doorway.

Quigley wheeled round. 'What are you doing here?'

Pound was grey and sunken under the cheekbones. 'My turn to escort prisoners to the magistrates' court.'

'But you're off sick.'

'Well, I'm back on now.' Pound was stooped like an old man. 'This one needs remanding, I believe.'

The two men watched each other like prizefighters squaring up for a match, but I would not have given Pound much of a hope in his condition if it had come to that.

'I haven't finished questioning her.'

'I think you have,' Pound assured him, adding urbanely, 'and if there are any more questions I shall deal with it. This woman is already helping me with a related inquiry, which makes her my prisoner. We can discuss it with the superintendent if you like.'

'She's a murderess,' Quigley insisted.

'Which is why I am going to take her to court and have her properly arraigned.' Pound took a few shallow breaths. 'Otherwise she'll have her lawyer slapping writs of habeas corpus.'

'I've got forty-eight hours.'

'And the courts will be closed until Monday,' Pound reminded him.

Quigley scooped his papers back into the file. 'If you let her escape…' he warned.

'I have never lost a prisoner yet.' Pound tried to straighten his back.

'Nor me,' Quigley rejoined.

Nettles came in. He eyed Inspector Quigley warily and me with some concern.

'Except for a few who have died in custody,' Pound recalled.

'And all from natural causes.' Quigley sneered. 'Don't lose her, Inspector.'

'Oh, I intend to keep a very close eye on this one,' Pound promised and Quigley brushed past, catching Pound's stomach with his elbow.

'Oh, I dooo beg your pardon,' he said, presumably trying to mimic my accent but sounding vaguely Scottish.

Pound gasped. He stayed on his feet, but he could not hide the pain jolting through him and the blood draining from his face. I rose to run towards him but he held out an arm.

'March Lillian Constance Middleton.' A dark stain appeared on his waistcoat over where I knew his stab wound to be. 'I am arresting you on a charge of wilful murder and,' his face screwed up, 'I must ask you to accompany me…' He waved a hand weakly. 'You know the rest. Take her away, Constable.'

'I thought you had come to help me,' I said.

Inspector Pound leaned against the wall. 'I have come to do my duty,' he mumbled.

'Duty to whom?' I cried, but he closed his eyes as the constable conducted me out.

66

The Toad and the Righteous Dust

THE MAGISTRATES' COURT was a nondescript public building from the back, the stonework charcoaled by existing in the atmosphere we all breathed. Eight of us were herded out on to the street, though my recent cellmate was not amongst our number.

A small crowd of onlookers stood by.

'Jezebel.' A man in clerical garb waved a pamphlet in my face.

'And Ocabah strode in righteous dust along the path of Bababath,' I invented cryptically as I passed him by.

'Ten quid says you were with me at the time,' a shrivelled man in a crushed top hat whispered.

'Twenty says I was not,' I told him. Even a woman facing the gallows has her standards.

We were herded into a high-ceilinged anteroom with small square barred windows and made to sit on long benches, the wood worn down by countless previous occupants. I could not imagine how much misery had waited there to have more misery heaped upon it.

'I needs the privy, squire,' a merry young man declared.

'No talking,' the policeman warned.

'But I need—'

The constable fingered his truncheon. 'I won't tell you again.'

'Worry not.' The young man beamed. 'I have done the deed, indeed the deed is…' he chuckled, 'done.'

The two men on either side tried to edge away.

'You dirty prike.' The policeman retched. 'Right, you're first.'

The young man rose. 'Works every time.' He bowed to the rest of us. 'I shall bid you all a fond farewell.' He whistled as he went.

One by one my companions were called away. A girl who cannot have been more than fifteen burst into tears and tried to hold on to the bench, but she was prised away and dragged off. A tall man in a nightgown rose serenely as his turn came.

'It is all but a beautiful dream,' he assured us, shuffling out in an odd pair of slippers.

Then there was only me and the bald woman left. She had handcuffs on and chains round her ankles.

'What on earth does one do to get any service around here?' she complained. 'At last,' she exulted as he read out her name – Ann Smith. I had expected something much more exuberant than that. 'Do not drink the claret,' she advised me. 'It is filthy.'

And so there was only me and the constable, a flat-faced, well-built man, perhaps a little old for his job.

'Why am I being dealt with last?' I asked.

'No talking.' He stood eyes front like a private being inspected by his sergeant major.

'But we're the only ones here.'

'No talking.'

'Am I allowed to smoke?'

He glanced about to make sure we were alone. 'Got a spare one?' I lit my cigarette and then his with the same Lucifer, and sucked deep into my lungs. I often thought it was only my tobacco habit that stopped them getting clogged. 'Slide up here a bit.' I shuffled along the bench and he said something very quietly between clenched teeth.

'Ivanhoe?' I tipped an ear towards him, feeling like my friend Maudy Glass's spinster aunt that we always loved to imitate behind her back.

'I don't know what's going on,' he repeated a little more distinctly, 'but Inspector Pound kept telling them you had collapsed

and were waiting for a doctor to check if you were fit to be seen.'
He blew a series of perfect smoke rings. 'At least old birch-'em-
Bendrix is finished for the day. Mr Cotton is a much jollier cove
from what I hear.'

'Well, that's a stroke of luck,' I breathed, though I was not
sure what difference it would make to me. I was not being tried
today, only sent back into custody.

Something moved under the opposite bench and at first I
thought it was a mouse or baby rat, but then I saw it was a toad
shuffling along. I drew his attention to it and, before I could stop
him, the constable had pulled out his truncheon and battered it.

'That was unnecessary,' I protested.

'I 'eard that you bashed a dog to death,' he rejoined indignantly.

'You were misinformed.'

'Anyway, they give you warts.'

'No, they do not.' I was tired and hungry and more than a
little afraid, and I was probably angrier than I should have been.
'I used to handle them all the time when I was a child and it never
did me any harm.'

He inspected me. 'Didn't do much good either,' he decided.

A slender young man came in and we both hid our cigarettes.
'March Miggleton.' He spoke from somewhere deep in his throat.

I let it go in the slender hope that, if I came to trial, I could
claim they had charged the wrong person.

'Middleton,' the constable corrected helpfully and the young
man sighed.

'Good job you put that straight,' the throat speaker told him.
'It could have given us no end of problems later.'

'Thank you.' I smiled fleetingly and he propelled me out of
the room. The toad was oozing on to the floor.

It was a large courtroom and I scarcely had time to glance
about from the dock I had been directed into before the clerk was
calling for order. There was a good-sized audience. Murderesses
are always much in demand with sensation-seekers. Mr Cotton

did not strike me as an especially jolly cove. He was younger than I had expected, but his mouth drooped like the amphibian I had just seen destroyed and he viewed me sourly as I stood at the barrier to confirm my name. He glowered as the charges were read out.

'I take it there is no application for bail,' he grunted.

'The police have no objection, Your Honour.' I knew that voice, but peering across the mass of heads I could only just make out Inspector Pound, so physically diminished by his injuries. Usually he stood a good head above most men.

The magistrate found his horn-rimmed spectacles and slipped them on to examine the speaker.

'This is most irregular, to let a suspected murderess loose.'

'This is an unusual case, Your Honour.' Pound's voice was reedy and barely carried. 'Miss Middleton is a lady of the highest character, who has been of great assistance to the Metropolitan Police in the past, and is currently assisting us with a major confidential inquiry which would be disrupted if she were in custody.'

That last information was news to me.

'Who would stand surety?' Mr Cotton enquired. 'I want an independent man of good character.'

'I am sure my guardian, Mr Grice, will,' I said.

Mr Cotton scanned the crowd. 'I do not see him here.'

'He is unwell,' I explained.

'Then what he may or may not do is purely speculative.'

'I will act as guarantor.' A tall, slim, well-dressed lady jumped up, waving her white-gloved hand.

'And you are?'

'Mrs Charles Fitzpatrick of Rugby School,' she proclaimed.

And there was Harriet, sparkling and elegant.

'Old Fizzy's wife?' he asked with interest. 'We wrote a journal for devotees of Horace together.'

'He still writes it,' she informed him wearily. 'I can put my hand on two hundred and thirteen pounds, eight shillings and nine pence,' she declared. 'And, fully aware of the scandal that could stain the good old school,' she spoke with no apparent irony, though I knew she detested the place, 'I will stake my honour on the accused not doing a runner.' She coughed, suddenly aware that our shared love of sensational crime stories was being exposed by those last three words. 'As I believe they say in police parlance.'

The magistrate changed his spectacles for a larger pair. 'Very well,' he ruled. 'Bail is set at two hundred pounds.'

I was tired and finding it difficult to concentrate. 'So I am free to go?'

'For the time being.' Justice of the Peace Cotton donned an even larger pair of spectacles and intoned dreamily, 'Adhuc sub iudice lis est,' which even I knew was something to do with things being still to be judged, and was a quote, I felt fairly confident, from Horace.

67

Admiral Nelson's Hat

I WAITED ON the seat that Inspector Pound had vacated, while the formalities were gone through. Harriet was talking animatedly to the clerk and telling him how much more presentable he would be without his moustaches, and signing anything he pushed at her.

'And you really should get your hair trimmed.' She took a document that he was proffering and stuffed it into her handbag without a glance. 'At first I thought you were the wild man of Borneo.'

He snatched his pen back from her. 'Good day, madam.'

Harriet came hurrying over. 'March,' she said urgently. 'You must do something about your attire – it is as bad as that horse-blanket you arrived in last year – and then you must flee.'

'But you would lose your money.'

'Money?' Harriet piffed and floated her arm like an actress acknowledging applause. 'Do not give that a second thought. I stole it from the library fund of which I am treasurer.'

'I do not believe that for a moment.'

Harriet smiled archly. 'Paris, I think. You can live cheaply there and send me prints of all the latest fashions.'

'Oh, Harriet, you are impossible.' In spite of all that had happened, I laughed. 'But how did you know I was here?'

'That dear chunky maid of yours.' Harriet untangled a bit of my hair. 'You really must get her a uniform that fits – though I think she is probably one of those unfortunate girls that will never fit into anything. She remembered you said that I was your friend—'

'You are certainly that.' The words caught in my throat.

For an instant I thought that Harriet might cry, but she patted my hand and said, 'Anyway, while I was clipping her hair back for her and explaining that she must ask her employer for time off to have a shave, she told me about your problem and how the famous Mr Grice is incapacitated by what she called Jumbled Fever, and how Inspector Pound was in hospital – why does every man in your life seem to be so enfeebled? You must be wearing them out.' Harriet took a breath. 'So I went straight to his ward – oh, my dear, the drabness of those nurses, whoever told them they look good in white? Somebody with no taste or conscience, I'll be bound. And I appraised him of your plight. I was all prepared to harangue him for malingering, but he was calling for his clothes and a screen before I had the chance.' She leaned towards my ear. 'Obviously he is a bit seedy at the moment, but those eyes! Oh, March, I could go boating in them if he would only take them off you for one moment. And such good manners. What a pity he is not rich, for he is absolutely devoted to you.'

'I know he cares for me.' I did not tell her about the ring.

Nettles hurried across the floor and said something into the inspector's ear.

'Cares?' she repeated scornfully. 'Why, the man is head over heels – though I never understood why the expression is not heels over head, which would make much more sense, would it not? – in love with you.'

'Shush, Harriet. He will hear.'

Inspector Pound came over. 'We must leave now. I have just heard that Quigley is coming and we do not want him opposing bail before it has been processed.'

The next prisoner arrived, a huge man with a tarred pigtail and dressed in a navy frock coat with epaulettes. He sported a wild black beard and his left hand was a steel hook. He entered the dock with a swaggering, rolling gait.

'You are Jake Boatswain of Dry Dock Lane?' the clerk read from a register.

'Aye Aye, skipper.' His accent was heavy West Country.

'Occupation?'

The prisoner tossed his head proudly. 'I be a milliner, cap'ain.' The court erupted in hoots of derision and he waved his hook angrily. 'Why, even Admiral Nelson needed an 'at.'

We made our way out.

'You should be in hospital,' I told the inspector.

'You saw what the food was like and it has not improved.' Pound was shuffling in an effort not to pull at his wound. 'What would I eat if you were not able to visit me?' We went into the lobby. 'If you could wait here a moment, I just need to have a word with Constable Nettles.'

He went into a side room.

'Well-well-well, what have we here?' I knew that voice and the young man in his checked green suit and bright yellow polka-dot cravat. 'Famous Detective's Female Companion On Trial for Murder.' He painted the headline with a thumb and first finger.

'Hello, Mr Trumpington,' I greeted him coldly.

'Mr Trumpington?' He slapped his heart. 'It used to be Traf.'

'That was before you printed lies about me and Mr Grice,' I retorted.

'Lies?' Trafalgar Trumpington echoed in wounded tones. 'Show me just one dickey bird that wasn't God's truth.'

'You are clever at telling the truth in a deceitful way,' I told him.

'Deceitful?' He tipped his matching green bowler hat with the handle of his silver-topped cane.

'He is very good at repeating things,' Harriet observed. 'I bet he knows his tables all the way up to ten.'

She too had seen the articles in the *Evening Standard*, implying an improper relationship between my guardian and me.

'And who have we here?' He raised his hat, revealing his perfectly trimmed black Macassar-oiled hair. 'Beautiful mysterious consort of the famous Inspector Pound.'

'You are right,' Harriet admitted, 'in some respects. I am beautiful and mysterious. But I do not consort with anyone, and if you so much as imply that I do in one of your grubby corruptions of the English language, I must warn you that my husband is a very good friend of Mr Charles Prestwick Scott, the editor of the *Manchester Guardian*.'

Trumpington eyed her in amusement. 'So?'

'So they will print an article which I shall compose, denying that you are a regular visitor at the Blue Boy, and I am sure you do not need me to tell you what kind of gentleman frequents that establishment.' Harriet twirled her umbrella under his nose.

'Fink you can gag the press?' Trumpington sneered.

'Fink you can?' she challenged and he grimaced.

'You're wasted as a woman,' he told her. 'By the way, that fret will only work once and even then only 'cause I ain't got much of a story on you.' He primped up the white carnation in his buttonhole. 'Yet,' he gave me a wink, 'I'll be seein' you again, March, if only in court.'

'By the way,' Harriet called as he strolled away, 'those spats went out of fashion five months ago.'

He grinned. 'I'll bear it in mind.'

'You never cease to surprise me,' I said.

Inspector Pound reappeared.

'If only I could surprise Mr Fitzpatrick,' she said with a twinkle. 'I tried the other night but he fell asleep.'

'Something funny?' the inspector asked.

'No.' I composed myself. 'Just us being silly women.'

Pound's eyes crinkled. 'I doubt that very much,' he said.

68

•◦※◦•

The Hoop and the Snail

THE SUN WAS shining when we stepped outside – not in the way it would blaze in India and not even like the crisp January mornings we had in Lancashire, but the smoke-filtered ashy-ness that passed for brightness in London.

'I must desert you now,' Harriet said. 'My children will not recognize me and there is a serious risk that Charles might notice I am gone.'

'I will see you soon?' I stepped over a dead sparrow, a long fat worm projecting from its gaping beak.

'Try keeping me away,' she threatened and gave her hand to our companion. 'Goodbye, Inspector.'

'March is lucky to have you as a friend,' he told her.

'It is I who am lucky.'

'Thank you,' I said and hugged her.

'Try not to get into any more trouble.' She kissed both my cheeks. 'On second thoughts do. I have not had so much fun in years.'

We watched her go, the crowds parting as she passed through, graceful and packed with more spirit than a brigade of guards.

'Will you get into trouble for helping me?' I asked.

'I have been in trouble since the day I was born, if my sister is to be believed.'

I had met the unlovely Lucinda when Inspector Pound was in hospital after his stabbing. She was a sharp-chinned,

263

sharp-mannered woman with capillaried cheeks, her hair scraped back in a style almost as severe as her manner.

'I think I was trouble before I was born, being born and ever since,' I told him. 'But what you have done was quite legal, was it not?'

A boy in a sailor suit dashed past, spinning his hoop with a stick, shouting huzzah huzzah, and followed by an exasperated nanny.

'Little bleeder,' she cursed as she drew alongside.

'I think Mr Collins or his clerk might have told me if it were not.' He whistled for a cab and one pulled over.

'Gower Street,' I instructed.

I climbed in and Pound twisted in distress as he tried to haul himself up after me. I held out my hand and he grasped it, and I noticed with shock how cold and wet it was. I pulled and between us he got up, dropping on to the seat with an involuntary groan.

'Don't blame you,' our driver called. 'She'd 'ave 'ad a battle to get me in too.' He cracked his whip very loudly but harmlessly over his steed's head. 'She's a bit deaf, poor critter,' he explained, 'and 'er 'indquarters is gettin' stiff, but I ain't got the 'eart to send 'er to the knackers.' And I decided that I liked him after all.

Our cabby was not joking about one thing – his horse was very slow. But that was probably just as well for every bump and dip sent a deep tic running up Pound's cheek.

'I am taking you straight back to the hospital,' I told him.

He clutched his side. 'I need to talk to Mr Grice, if he is able to.'

'You need to go to bed with proper medical care.'

He bent over a little more towards me. 'Mr Grice first and then, I promise, I will go to hospital.'

'Very well,' I agreed reluctantly. 'But how did Molly know where you were?'

A snail was hitching a ride on the inside of my window.

'Constable Nettles.' Inspector Pound shifted in a futile effort to get comfortable. 'He thought Mr Grice should know what was going on, but of course Mr Grice was ill as well.'

'He was rambling when I saw him,' I said. 'Something about love.'

'Must have been thinking about money then,' Pound remarked and cleared his throat. 'When you were alone with Quigley, did he hurt you?'

'No,' I said. 'Well, not as much as I hurt him.'

'I know I can rely on your discretion.' He gripped the flap. 'There have been a number of complaints about him recently – a Member of Parliament's son who got intoxicated claims to have been beaten by him. The men are not happy. They say Quigley struck a new recruit.'

'Do you think they will get rid of him?'

'He will try to drag me down with him if they do.' He grunted as we swayed round a corner.

'I do not want you to lose your job because of me,' I said. 'I would rather go back into custody.'

He patted my hand and left his lying on it. 'Not while I have anything to do with it.' And we were both lost in our thoughts.

I climbed out first when we arrived at 125 Gower Street and went round the back of the cab to ring the doorbell.

Molly peered out before she admitted me.

'How is Mr Grice?' I enquired.

She considered the question as if it were the last thing she had been expecting me to ask.

'Oh, miss, he's really gone down,' she answered sadly.

'What happened?'

'He's gone down to his study,' she elaborated.

'Molly,' I said, 'I cannot thank you enough for what you did today.'

'You can try,' she urged.

'You showed great initiative.' I glanced in the mirror and despaired. 'I shall take you out and buy you a new dress.'

She hung up my things before asking the inspector in a stage whisper, 'Will it have to be a big brown one – to hide my big inis-inisvitive – the thing what I was showing?'

'Miss Middleton means that you saved the day,' Pound explained and Molly pushed out her ample bosom.

'Hurrah for me! Which day was it? I hope it was a Thursday. I love Thursdays more than life itself. Christmas is always on a Thursday, ain't it not?' She had another thought. 'And chocolates, I love them.'

'I shall get you a big box,' Pound promised.

'Tea would nice, Molly,' I suggested.

'Oh yes, it would,' she agreed heartily as she tried to fix her bow. 'Why don't I not go and make some?'

'That is a good idea,' I said and she wandered off.

'Oh.' She stopped halfway down the hall. 'Would you both like some too?'

'An excellent suggestion,' the inspector told her and she smirked.

'I don't not know why Miss Middleton didn't not think of it.'

'Thank heavens,' Sidney Grice cried hoarsely as we went into his study. 'You are just in time to save my life.'

69

Beef Tea and Dr Zenith

SIDNEY GRICE WAS in his armchair, a tartan blanket around his shoulders and another over his knees. The fire was blazing and his face poured with sweat. His eye was out and he had no patch on.

'What happened?' Pound asked.

'The lower orders have risen,' Mr G told him huskily. 'They parcelled me up and set me by this blaze, and when I protested they defied me.'

'They were trying to help,' I explained. 'I told Molly to keep you warm.'

'Molly tried to press her fleshy lips to my brow. It took all my strength to ward her off.' My guardian shivered violently. 'I dismissed them both but they are still here. It is the French Revolution all over again.' He mopped his brow with a hand towel. 'Though fortunately without any foreigners.'

'You seem quite strong now,' I commented as he let the towel fall into his lap.

'I do feel a little better,' he admitted, before croaking in horror, 'They tried to make me drink beef broth.'

'It might have helped,' I suggested.

'Helped?' He picked up the towel and squeezed it. 'How would cutting the throat of an animal which has more intelligence than the average curate, hacking it apart and forcing its flesh down my throat help me?'

'I wouldn't mind a mug if they've got any left,' Pound said, and despite his protestations, I settled him into my armchair and got myself an upright from the central table.

'I had a terrible dream.' Mr G took a glass of water from the lowboy beside him and I hurried to steady his hand as he slopped it down himself. 'You had been accused of yet another murder.' He took a sip and waved me away. 'But now I am not so sure it was a dream.'

'I am afraid it was not,' I admitted.

'What a relief,' he said, and I was still formulating a response when he fell asleep.

'I will go and change,' I told the inspector as Molly arrived with a tray. 'And Inspector Pound will have beef tea.'

Molly stood blankly. 'But where shall I get it?'

'Did Mr Grice imagine it?' I asked. 'He must have been even worse than I thought.'

'Oh no,' she said. 'It's just me and Cook had it all. We had so much we were sick. It was lovely – just like a Thursday.'

The inspector struggled to get up, brushing aside my attempts to help him.

'I know how you feel,' Molly sympathized. 'I have trouble getting out of that chair after I've been snoozing when I'm supposed to be working. What are you laughtering for?' She blushed. 'Snoozing ain't not rude, is it?'

'No, Molly,' I reassured her. 'It's a lovely word.'

'Oh, for a minute I thought it might be what courting couples do.' She scurried off in embarrassment.

Mr G snored.

'Where are you going, Inspector?' I touched his sleeve.

'I have a few things to see to.' He steadied himself on the back of the chair.

'You promised to go to hospital after you had called here,' I reminded him.

'So I did,' he agreed. 'But I did not say how soon after.'

I followed him into the hall and helped him on with his coat.

'You are no use to me dead,' I scolded.

I wanted to tell him that I had already lost one man I loved through my stupidity and I did not want to lose another from the same cause.

He put on his bowler. 'And we are no use to each other if you are…' He could not bring himself to say executed and tried to hide it with a cough.

I stood on tiptoe and kissed him softly on the mouth.

'I will be back in an hour.' He winked.

I went upstairs to get out of my clothes and have a cigarette and a gin and a long soak in a steaming bath. I washed and closed my eyes, and when I opened them the water was cold.

I dried myself and dressed and smoked another cigarette, and it occurred to me as I felt the effects of the gin that I had not eaten since I had picked at yesterday's lunch, so I had another tot to keep me going.

By the time I went back down Inspector Pound had returned. He had a brown leather messenger bag on his lap and both men were asleep. I felt my guardian's forehead and was pleased to find it cool. He woke with a start.

'Why is Pound sleeping in your chair? It is positively indecent.'

'You must let me get you a doctor,' I cajoled him.

'I absolutely forbid you to let one of those overpaid charlatans anywhere near me,' he fumed.

Spirit's tail waved. She had crawled under his blanket.

'You were quite happy for me to be treated by a veterinary surgeon.' I tried to take his pulse. 'Keep still.'

'I was not in the least bit happy.' He jerked away irritably. 'That man charged me four guineas when I had provided him with an experimental subject.'

Spirit poked a paw out.

'Me,' I said indignantly.

'Stop fussing, Lucinda.' Inspector Pound woke with a start and the two men looked at each other in bewilderment.

'The tea is cold,' Mr G complained, without even feeling the pot, and I rang the bell twice for more. 'So...' He unwrapped himself, emerging crumpled from his blankets like a moth from its cocoon, Spirit curled up on his lap. 'Kindly explain yourself, Miss Middleton. Do so concisely and precisely. Refrain from expressing your vaguely feminine feelings and save the apologies for later.' My guardian discarded his blankets on the floor and Spirit jumped down on to them. 'Preferably before the moderately good inspector expires.'

'I am trying to get him into hospital,' I informed my guardian, and Mr G perked up.

'When I was on the trail of the so-called Dr Zenith—'

'The Danish Disemboweler,' Pound recalled in repugnance. 'I saw—'

'I noted that there were nine per cent less patients walking out of the main entrance than had walked in,' Mr G continued. 'I did not find that statistic alluring.'

Pound brought out his meerschaum pipe and looked at it wistfully. The bowl had been carved into a woman's face with her hair streaming back.

'I shall think about going back when we have got to the bottom of all this,' he promised me. 'But I still don't know what happened when you went to Mrs Prendergast's house.'

'It was all a bit confusing,' I began, ignoring Mr G's groans. 'Mrs P said she had a present for me, but it was a knife in a brown paper bag. She held it between us and walked into it. Then she pulled it out and I took it from her so that she did not fall on to it, and the maid came in and ran away.'

'What was all that about the dog?' Pound asked.

'I tried to shoo it off because it was drinking her blood.'

'The blood was no use to her,' Mr G remarked. 'But what, in your admirably though possibly excessively abridged account, was confusing?'

'Why did she do it?' I wished I had another cigarette.

'So it is the motive rather than the sequence of events that confounds you?' Mr G got out the two halfpennies that he always kept in his waistcoat pocket.

'Well, yes,' I answered uncertainly.

He flipped the coins over in his left hand lackadaisically.

'Did she say anything?' Inspector Pound enquired.

'She screamed, No, Miss Middlington, please do not kill me.'

Inspector Pound tugged at his moustaches. 'Those words exactly?'

'I think so. Yes, I am sure of it.'

'It does not take much more than a half-hidden corner of a man's intellect to detect a pattern here,' Mr G commented. 'I begin to wonder if it is safe to be alone in a room with you.'

'That's a bit unfair,' Pound reproved.

'Life is unfair,' Sidney Grice pontificated. 'And so is death. But I am fairness personified.'

Inspector Pound and I exchanged glances, but neither of us said anything.

70

Messenger Bags and the Twickenham Triplets

INSPECTOR POUND RESTED his hands on the bag.

'I had an interesting conversation with our friend Quigley,' he announced. 'I told him that I wanted to take over your case. Needless to say he was violently against the idea. He accused me of trying to get a guilty woman acquitted because of my feelings for you—'

'Feelings?' Mr G broke in, as if even the word were an obscenity.

'Stuff and nonsense, of course,' I put in hastily.

Pound lowered his eyebrows but carried on with his story. 'And because of my indebtedness to Mr Grice.'

'You do owe me a great deal.' Sidney Grice tapped the tray for me to pour.

Pound dangled a hand to stroke Spirit but she ignored him. Mr G was always her favourite. 'I threatened to put in a complaint about his mistreatment of you.' The inspector gave up his attempt. 'But there were no witnesses and he was the only one showing any visible signs of the encounter.'

Whilst Pound was talking, my guardian put the halfpennies very carefully one on top of the other on the corner of the table. He leaned back and put his fingertips lightly together. 'Elucidate,' he instructed me.

I put down the teapot. 'He pulled my hair,' I said and saw the anger well up in the inspector, but Mr G's face was a mask of unconcern. 'So I stabbed him with a pen nib.'

'And now,' Pound rubbed his hands delightedly, 'he has a beautiful India-blue tattoo under his chin.'

'How much ink did you use?' Mr G asked with interest.

'I did not measure it.'

'That was typically remiss of you,' Sidney Grice reproved as he retrieved his coins. 'Inspector Quigley shall rue the day he abused a member of my household.' He tossed the halfpennies high into the air and caught them with a downward swoop. 'Even though it was only you. Pray proceed with your mildly interesting account, Inspector.'

'In the end I offered him a swap.' Pound unclipped his messenger bag. 'I am on the brink of capturing the Twickenham Triplets and the near certainty of three very public convictions to his credit, against one possible conviction with Mr Grice and myself opposing him, was too much to resist.'

'I thought they had already been arrested for extortion.' I lifted a black speck out of the milk with the handle of my spoon.

'So they had.' The inspector blew down the stem of his meerschaum. 'But all the witnesses were too frightened to give evidence.'

'Timmy, Tommy and Tammy,' Mr G mused. 'There is not a house of ill repute in Hounslow that does not pay them insurance. They are industrious fellows to give them their due.' Mr G rattled the coins. 'What have you got on them?'

'The murder of six people in the Bell Inn arson attack.' Pound straightened his moustaches. 'The mother of one of the victims saw what happened and is thirsting for revenge, and one of their gang has turned Queen's evidence rather than take the drop for his bosses.'

I added milk and sugar to my own and the inspector's teas. 'What a pity you will not get the credit for it.' I averted my eyes guiltily.

'The people who matter will know what I have done,' Pound said disdainfully. 'He wants to be renowned. Good luck to him. I would rather be a good policeman.'

'You are part of the way in achieving that ambition,' Sidney Grice assured him, oblivious to my indignation.

I passed Pound his tea to save him leaning over.

'Anyway,' he slipped the pipe into his breast pocket, 'I am now the officer in command of your case.'

'At least you are unlikely to assault me.' I snagged a chipped fingernail on a loose thread in my dress.

The inspector brought out a black cloth and laid it on top of his bag. 'Is this the knife?' He held it out.

I had not examined it closely before. The blade was straight, about eight inches in length and honed on both edges. The handle was long, golden and elaborately ornamented with numerous raised scroll patterns, and there was a sigmoid cross guard.

'That or a very good copy.'

'Quigley had it washed, I'm afraid,' Pound apologized to my guardian as he handed it over.

'I am only surprised he did not throw it away.' He clicked his tongue. 'But I imagine he thought it would bolster his case rather than damage it.' He turned the dagger this way and that, running his fingers along all the ridges and pressing the raised discs at the end of every swirl. 'Let us hope it does the latter.' He experimentally wiggled at the guard.

'There is no maker's name on it,' Pound observed.

'It is very poorly balanced.' Mr G see-sawed it over a finger.

'I think the handle is hollow,' the inspector suggested, and Mr G pursed his lips non-committally and passed it on to me.

'It is more like a toy than a weapon,' I commented. 'The guard is too thin. It would snap off in a fight and the handle is awkward to hold.'

'Some toy,' Pound said. 'The blade is razor sharp.'

I ran a fingertip lightly over it and nicked myself.

'And yet the tip is rounded.' Mr G took the knife back. 'There does not seem to be any mechanism for folding or retracting the blade.'

'Why would there be?' Inspector Pound queried.

'There should not be,' Mr G conceded. 'And I find the absence of such a mechanism very suspicious indeed. Remember the case of the house brick that was made of brick?'

Pound scratched the nape of his neck. 'I never quite understood your reasoning behind that,' he admitted.

Mr G sampled his tea and briefly closed his eyes blissfully. 'When you and I are old and you pay me an uninvited and unwelcome visit on my Dorset estates with your three grandchildren, we shall sit in my cherry orchard and you shall suck on your unlit tobacco pipe and we shall reminisce about it.'

'I wish I knew what you are talking about,' I complained.

The inspector smiled ruefully. 'I am glad I'm not the only one who can't follow him.'

'Only a fool knows exactly what he is talking about,' my guardian declaimed. 'Often when I listen to myself – which I always attempt to do – I am completely baffled.' He suddenly realized he did not have a patch on and produced one with a flourish. 'I do know one thing, though.' He raised the dagger like a beacon above his head. 'You did not – and I hope you will not be too disappointed to learn this – kill the abominable Mrs Prendergast.'

'I know I did not,' I said.

'How could you even think it?' Inspector Pound asked him indignantly.

'That is what separates me from the rabble, the middle classes, many travelling showmen and most of the architectural so-called profession.' Sidney Grice deftly tied his patch. 'I dare to think the thinkable.'

71

Goat Moths and Brick Dust

S IDNEY GRICE REACHED down to retrieve one of his blankets and Spirit stalked off indignantly.

'Are you cold?' I asked as he wrapped it around his chest.

'I am cold and hot in rapid alternations and intermittently simultaneously,' he explained. 'But whilst the fluctuations in my corporal temperatures are a source of endless fascination, it might be more pertinent to continue with our investigation. Do you have any more evidence in that useful receptacle, Inspector?'

Pound delved into his bag again. 'Only these.' He brought out a cardboard folder tied in a brown string. 'The statements of Gloria Shell, the maid, and Percy Brough, the passer-by who responded to her cries. And I have a report from Constable Nettles.'

He passed the folder over and Mr G undid the bow cautiously, as if afraid he might detonate an explosive device, and clipped on his pince-nez to examine a sheaf of documents.

'I was horrified,' he read out. 'Why did Nettles write that?'

'I expect he was,' I suggested. 'We all were.'

'Yes.' He turned the page. 'But why is it relevant? I detest this modern mania for expressing feelings. It is vile enough that people have feelings in the first place without parading them about like prize Norfolk geese.'

'They are men, not machines,' Pound muttered, ever sensitive about any insult to his force.

'More is the pity.' Mr G skipped two pages. 'We are given to believe that he was also shocked but,' he raised his hand as if we were interrupting him, 'it gives an honest account of his findings.' He scrutinized the second document and sniffed it. 'It appears that Mr Brough smokes whisky-flake pipe tobacco. The document must be in his own hand for it has none of the stilted style of an official document and he gives free reign to his emotions. He would have us believe that not only was he, too, horrified, but he was also shocked.' He ran his finger under a sentence. 'His cornucopia of passions then overflowed with his being appalled, shocked again and – I am sorry to relate – flabbergasted.' He turned over. 'Apparently Miss Middleton was wild-haired and frothing at the mouth.'

'I dare say my coiffure was not at its tidiest,' I protested, 'but I was certainly not frothing.'

'And you rolled your eyes,' he informed me, 'like the mad woman of Killarney with whom, I am loath to confess, I have yet to make acquaintance.'

He blew on his black tea.

'Can we go back to the first time you met your uncle?' Pound brought out his smoking tin and unclipped the lid. 'I am still not clear what happened there.' He took a pinch of honey-coloured tobacco and rolled it between his fingers.

'What happened is childishly obvious.' Mr G replaced the papers. 'Why it happened is more complicated.'

'So tell me the childishly simple part,' I invited.

'Which bit do you not understand?' He retied the string, taking great care to make the ends and the loops of equal size.

'From the moment I felt ill to the moment I ran out of the house,' I said. 'I know I was poisoned by cacti.'

'Were you?' My guardian greeted my statement with fascination. 'I must make a note of that.' He reached for his notebook. 'I wonder why Molly did not react when I gave her a sample.'

'You will kill your maid one day,' Pound prophesied.

'I tried to test it on Spirit,' Mr G defended himself, 'but she would not take any.' He picked up her ball of wool and tossed it from hand to hand.

'She has more sense,' I said. 'I hope that is how you got the scratches on your wrist.'

'It might be.' He tugged at the end of the yarn.

'Outwitted by a cat,' Pound mocked gently.

'Out-clawed,' Sidney Grice conceded, separating the wool into filaments. 'I do not know what poisoned you, and it is perhaps something that will remain occult and trouble me until the day I die. But five things struck me particularly in my inspection of that bedroom, the hall and the stairs.' Sidney Grice took up his teacup and viewed me over the rim. 'First, that there was not the slightest trace of blood, nor any evidence that it had been cleaned away.'

'You commented that there was no dust under the bed,' I recalled and he nodded.

'Second...' He sniffed the faintly rising steam. 'There was wax on the window sill.'

Just to prove he was not the only one who could play with threads, I tied a stray strand of cotton round a button on my dress. 'Colwyn said they had no candles.'

'And third?' Inspector Pound watched him intently.

My guardian tested the tea and wrinkled his lips. 'The slight scuffs on the ceiling in a room with solid walls and a locked window were highly suspicious.' He threw his head back to drain the cup, when even with milk I found mine too hot.

'Suspicious of what?' I asked, but he continued as if I had not spoken.

'And the presence of dust – which Miss Middleton so accurately identified – on the hand of that obscene and inaccurate representation of a pagan libertine was almost conclusive.'

'So what did you see in that room?' I was feeling nauseous now and hoped all my symptoms were not about to recur.

Sidney Grice sprang to his feet, though with less agility than usual, brushed past the inspector and fetched a clean white card to lay on the table. 'What do you make of that?' He had two test tubes in his waistcoat pocket and uncorked one to deposit a small brown object on to the card.

Pound squinted. 'A woodlouse but it's seen better days.'

'Oniscus Asellus, to give the creature its scientific name,' Mr G confirmed. 'And what is the most important thing about this particular woodlouse?'

'It is dead,' I guessed, but was ignored.

'What about the legs?' my guardian urged.

'There are three more on one side,' the inspector noted.

'Or, to put it another way, three less on the starboard side, and here...' Mr G tapped out another tube. '... are two of them.'

'But you found the woodlouse on the attic stairs,' I realized, 'and the legs on the undersurface of the bed.'

'So the bed was taken up and/or down the stairs,' Inspector Pound deduced.

'But there was thick dust on the steps,' I objected, 'and no footprints.'

'Could they have laid something over the stairs and then removed it without disturbing the dust?' the inspector pondered.

'I suppose so,' I said uncertainly, 'though I don't understand how they could have left no trace at all.'

'Let us take a look.' Mr G poured his sample on to the card where it formed a little grey hillock. 'What did you notice as I deposited it?'

'It did not puff up,' I said.

'And I could actually hear it,' Pound added.

'Take a pinch,' my guardian urged and we both dipped our fingers in.

'It is very gritty,' I remarked.

'And what were the walls and ceiling of that staircase made of?' Mr G clicked his fingers at me.

I thought back. 'They were whitewashed plasterwork.'

'So where did the grit come from?' the inspector wondered.

'Where indeed?' Mr G prodded around the pile with the blunt end of his pencil. 'See those red specks? They are brick dust.'

'It is more like the deposit you might find in an outhouse or a cellar,' I conjectured.

'Quite so,' Mr G agreed. 'Also dust tends to deposit more at the sides than the middle, whereas this lay very evenly on the treads and, though the goat moth must have been dead for many months, since they fly in the early summer – and I have never known one to survive beyond the beginning of September – this particular example lay on and not in the dust.'

'So you think the stairs were sprinkled with dirt more recently and the moth put on top.'

'Clever finishing touches like that are often what give the game away.' Mr G blew his pencil clean. 'Nature is not so extravagant as people are with clues.'

'What about the woodlouse?' I asked.

'That was partially covered, though it had died more recently than the moth,' he told me.

'So it dropped from the bed as the frame was carried down and before the stairs were sprinkled,' Pound surmised.

'But why were the walls not covered in blood?' I asked. 'It was everywhere.'

'Let me answer that with two questions,' Mr G countered. 'First, why was the pipe to the gas lamp so long and, second, why could Travers Smyth not reach the window sill from the position which he so obligingly re-created for you?'

'Is it possible,' Pound sniffed his tobacco longingly, 'that the room was somehow made smaller?' He shed a few strands on to his trousers. 'What about...' He hesitated to share his thought. 'This may sound fantastical, but what about if the walls were fake?'

'And the floor,' I suggested. 'That is why I tripped. It was raised. So when Uncle Tolly leaned against the false wall he could reach the window sill easily, and the gas pipe needed to be long for the mantle to be in the room.'

'A room within a room,' Pound cried out. 'Then they removed the inner room and burnt it.'

'Which is how sawdust got on the statue – they were carrying the scenery up and down – and of course…' I continued. 'Oh.'

My guardian tilted his head. 'I know that oh.'

'Uncle Tolly told me he worked in a theatre once.'

'How skilled you have become at withholding salient information.'

'I do not suppose Miss Middleton realized—'

'Indeed she did not.' Sidney Grice's voice was vinegar.

I tried to retrieve a little honour. 'So the scenery was burned in the furnace, which is why there were flecks of paint nearby and screws in the ashes… and Annie had a stiff back from helping to move it.'

Pound shut the tin lid. 'What about the wax?'

'He had a false skull,' I conjectured. 'That was why I thought his head seemed a bit flat when you knocked his smoking cap off.' I realized what I had said and added, 'No, I did not think that was important either at the time.'

'Let us put it down to your small intellect,' Mr G said benevolently. 'I knocked Travers Smyth's cap off to examine the mark on his forehead – it was a burn.'

'From hot wax.' Pound tapped the box with his fingertips. 'So presumably the smashed face and severed hand were wax too.'

It was as if a photograph flashed into my mind.

'The hand.' I clicked my fingers. 'It was not stained by ink.'

'You have a rare gift of remembering things when they are no longer pertinent.' Mr G toyed with the jackal-headed ring on his watch chain.

'But why did he spill it?' I asked.

'To destroy his family tree?' Pound suggested.

My guardian looked at the ring sadly. 'That would only have raised doubts as to its reliability.' He pushed his little finger into it. 'And it could easily have been redrawn. Most likely an accident.' He dropped the ring as if it were molten. 'It would seem that March is not the only member of her family to be physically uncoordinated.'

'But I checked for a pulse on his right wrist.' I forced myself to ignore his gibes. 'And there was none.'

'A tourniquet.' Sidney Grice grasped his own arm. 'His free left hand was under his nightgown, probably behind his back. He could tighten it at will.'

'It takes a lot of pressure to cut off the pulse completely,' I pointed out. 'That is why his arm was sore when you met him.' I refilled our cups. 'But where did all the blood come from?' I asked.

'An abattoir,' Pound suggested.

'Or the man who became a skeleton in the boiler.' I cradled my face at the thought.

'I do not know that yet,' Mr G told Pound, 'though Miss Middleton's idea is less likely than yours.'

'I am glad you do not think they were that cruel.' I yanked the thread and my button spun off. Luckily, it was purely ornamental. I watched it roll across the floor and under the desk, and Spirit darted out to play with it.

'Oh, I suspect they were much crueller than that,' my guardian said.

'They?' Pound queried and Mr G nodded.

'One man could not have done all that. It would seem that feigning murder is a team game.' He scratched at the fabric to attract my cat and she bounded over and sniffed his open hand. 'Who on earth is that at the door?'

'I did not hear the bell,' I said.

'Nor I, and my hearing is quite good,' Pound added.

'It would have to be truly exceptional to hear something which has not yet happened.' Mr G dusted his chair with the hand towel and the bell sounded. 'I saw their reflections in the window cast into and reflected off the mantle mirror, though not clearly enough to know who they are.' He dabbed his forehead.

Molly clattered up the hallway and we heard a man's voice, muffled through the door, and Molly reply and some bumping, and Molly rushed in, her apron askew and her hair even more untamed than ever.

'Why on earth are you dressed like that?' Mr G scolded.

Molly wriggled her nose. 'But this is my uniform, sir.'

Droplets were breaking out on his face again. 'But why do you look like you have been engaged in pugilistic demonstrations?'

'Is that good or bad?' Molly whispered.

'Not good,' I told her and her hopes of praise visibly collapsed.

'Why are you so dishevelled?'

'Untidy,' Pound translated for her.

'I've been fighting,' she announced, bunching up her arms as if challenging any or all of us to slug it out.

'We will talk about that later, Molly,' I assured her. 'Who is at the door?'

'There is a pair of two gentlemen come, sir.'

'Who?' Mr G snapped. 'Where are their cards?'

'They didn't not say nor not give me none, sir.' She adopted a pugilistic pose.

'Then what is their business?'

'I asked them that,' Molly unclenched her fists, 'and they told me to mind my own.'

'Then why in heaven's name did you admit them?' He gripped the air in frustration.

'I didn't not,' Molly retorted. 'They pushed past me.'

'And you just let them?' His voice rose angrily. 'You should defend the access of my house to the death, you great clumping useless slovenly sluggard. It is in the unwritten code of servitude.'

'I ain't not read that,' Molly confessed miserably. 'Shall I go out and defend your axes to the death now, sir?'

'No. Tidy all these up.' Her master kicked one of the blankets towards her. 'I cannot bear them lying around the floor like that.' He swept back his hair. 'I shall deal with this myself.'

If truth be told, I was not sure he was capable of dealing with anything. His face was drained of colour and trickling sweat.

'Oh, and one of them is all dressed up like a peeler,' she remembered as he flung open the door.

'We'll see about that.' Inspector Pound marched after my guardian. 'You,' I heard him say in surprise.

I hurried out to join them and found Inspector Quigley standing with a tall, muscular young constable behind him.

'How dare you burst into my house in that revolting neck tie?' Sidney Grice confronted him.

'My wife gave it me for my birthday.' Quigley tightened it indignantly.

'Then she must loathe you almost as much as I do,' Mr G snapped. 'Explain yourself.'

Quigley held up a twice-folded sheet of headed notepaper. 'I have here a warrant for the arrest of one March Middleton.'

Pound stepped in front of me. 'I don't know what you are playing at, Inspector, but as you are well aware, Miss Middleton has been given bail by the court.'

'For the murder of Mrs Prendergast,' Quigley agreed, 'though I have every confidence she will be convicted of that in due course of time.' He tapped Pound on the chest with the document. 'If you will step aside, Inspector, I have a job to do. This warrant is for the wilful murder of Mrs Prendergast's maid, Miss Gloria Shell.'

72

Flat-footed Peter and Her Majesty's Mail

INSPECTOR POUND WAS the first to break the shocked silence. 'Is this some sort of a joke?' He laid an arm protectively over his wound.

An odd smirk crept across his colleague's flecked lips. 'Miss Middleton is usually the comic turn, but I don't suppose she will have too much to laugh about from now on.'

'What are you talking about?' I stepped out to face Quigley. 'You interviewed that girl yourself a few hours ago. You told me how pretty she was.'

The smirk tightened tartly. 'Well, she isn't very pretty now.'

'When did this occur?' Sidney Grice had one hand on the hall table for support.

'About an hour ago.'

Pound snorted contemptuously. 'Miss Middleton has been in police custody or with me or in this house since yesterday afternoon.'

'So you say,' Quigley jibbed.

Pound stiffened. 'Are you accusing a fellow officer of lying?'

Quigley made a calming gesture calculated to have the opposite effect. 'Of course not, Inspector. It's just that you were not with the accused while you were at the station.'

'As Inspector Pound has just explained, I was here,' I said.

'And can Mr Grice vouch for that?' Quigley cross-examined me.

Sidney Grice was breathing heavily. 'I was asleep some of the time,' he conceded.

'You were in a state of disarray when I saw you last,' Quigley remarked to me.

'What has that got to do with anything?' Pound paced to and fro.

'A great deal.' Quigley slipped the document into his pocket. 'The suspect has obviously bathed and changed, which means she was by herself for some time.'

'No, she weren't not,' Molly piped up. 'I was with her the whole time.'

'Molly—' I began.

'Shut your mouth.' Quigley snapped his fingers at me.

'How dare you speak to Miss Middleton like that?' Pound rounded on him.

'I am questioning a murder suspect,' Quigley replied coldly, 'not taking afternoon tea with a duchess.' He stuck a finger in Molly's arm and she bristled as if ready for the second round. 'So did you wash your mistress's back?'

''Course I did,' Molly said defiantly.

Quigley kept his pale eyes fixed on me to make sure I did not coach her.

'And was her back still bleeding from those three scratches?'

Molly wrinkled her nose. 'A bit, p'raps, maybe, p'raps,' she decided.

Quigley's arm fell. 'Shall I get a police surgeon to ascertain whether or not you have any scratches on your back?'

'No,' I said. 'I have none.'

'Oh, miss.' Molly jiggled about. 'Of course you have. You must of forgotten.' She leaned forward and whispered loud enough for everyone to hear. 'I can scratch you good and proper before they get the chance to asser-whatever-he-said anything.'

Quigley whinnied. 'Are you aware it is a criminal offence to aid and abet a murderer?'

'Good,' Molly said. 'Whatever that means. Try to take me in and while you are doing that Miss Middleton can get out the back way and over the wall, like what I do when I sneak off at night.'

'So you are suggesting that while I was asleep, Miss Middleton went out, murdered that woman's maid, came in, bathed and changed and...' Sidney Grice's voice trailed away.

'Oh, sir,' Molly cried, 'you've gone all orange. Is it a clever disguise like how Flash-Footed Peter dressed up as a person.'

'Parson,' I corrected, as if it mattered.

And Molly wiggled her jaw. 'A parson is a person.'

Her employer nodded weakly. 'We shall take tea now... and... tea.'

'We need to get you to bed,' I said.

'I shall sit a while,' he decided, swaying like I used to after ladies' night at the officers' mess.

'Let me help you, sir,' the constable offered.

'I shall save you, March, I—' He sidestepped, 'swear it.'

The constable caught Mr G as he collapsed, scooped him up and carried him like a groom with his bride over the threshold, to deposit him tenderly into my armchair.

Quigley followed us in. 'Last time I was here you had a corpse laid out on the floor.'

'Mr Green,' I confirmed.

'Sure you didn't do him too?'

'As I recall you were adamant that it was suicide,' I reminded him and he coloured.

'You won't be so nose-in-the-sky when I have you back at the station,' he snarled.

Pound flared up. 'If you touch Miss Middleton again, I swear to God you will rue your actions for the rest of your life.'

'Threatening a fellow officer?' Quigley strolled to the desk. 'You heard that, didn't you, Bell?'

Bell shuffled uneasily. 'I did hear Inspector Pound advising you not to beat up a suspect, sir. Should I put that in my report?'

Quigley swept a book on to the floor. 'You would be wise not to make an enemy of me, Bell.'

'And wiser still not to be his friend.' I picked up the book, but the title did not register in my mind.

Quigley flicked through a stack of my guardian's postal deliveries.

'Open one,' I invited him. 'Without a search warrant, you will be guilty of interfering with the Royal Mail.'

Quigley hesitated, unable to decide if I knew as much of the law as I pretended to, and let that too fall on the floor.

'Goodness, you are clumsy today,' I reproved.

'That's because his arms is too short for his body,' Molly explained. 'I had a young man like that once. He couldn't not even do his own bootlaces. Can you?'

'Get out,' Quigley rounded on her.

Molly jutted her jaw.

'I think it would be best,' I told her.

And Molly screwed up her body. 'I just wanted to say one thing to help you with your enquirings.' She went up very close to Quigley and for some reason she was no longer comical. 'If you do hurt Miss Middleton I expect 'spector Pound will smash your face in; I know Mr Grice will put you in prison; but I ain't not so nice as what they are, Mr Quickly. If you hurt Miss Middleton, I will cut your throat.'

'Now I have you,' Quigley gloated. 'We all heard that one, making death threats to a police officer.'

'Yes, it is a lovely day, isn't it, Molly?' Constable Bell said conversationally.

Quigley went puce. 'I will break you for that, Bell.' He almost choked on his own words. 'You will be out of that uniform before this week is done.'

'Not sure I want to be in the same force as you,' the constable responded in disgust.

'I will stand up for you, Bell,' Inspector Pound vowed.

'And who will stand up for you, Inspector?' Quigley mocked.

'This girl of yours when she's in the dock? This half-blind, half-dead amateur detective?'

'I shall.' Even with her long history of bad curtsies Molly did the worst curtsy that I had ever seen.

'God bless you, Molly,' I said as she toppled over against the doorpost.

73

Prejudicial Handling and the Steel Rule

INSPECTOR QUIGLEY SURVEYED us all. 'There's not one person in this house who I couldn't arrest if I wanted to and make the charges stick.'

'Let me see that.' Pound held out his right hand and Quigley slapped the paper into it. 'It seems to be in order,' he admitted.

'That's because it is in order,' Quigley smirked.

'How and where was Gloria Shell killed?' Pound supported himself against the back of the armchair.

'Why don't you ask the accused that?'

'Because I do not know the answers,' I insisted.

'She was killed with a claw hammer.' Quigley picked up the section of mallet on Mr G's desk. 'It was a messy job, to put it mildly.'

'And what grounds do you have for thinking Miss Middleton did it?' Pound ran his thumb and first finger under his moustaches.

Quigley tapped the desk like an auctioneer.

'Please let me out.' Sidney Grice sat up, looked blearily about him and promptly fell asleep again.

'A number of reasons.' Quigley put the paperweight down. 'Motive – the accused knew that the maid was the only person to have seen her commit the crime.'

'That is not true,' I protested.

'A witness,' Quigley continued, 'heard the screams and a man shouting.'

'Definitely a man's voice?' I clarified.

Quigley nodded. 'And a tall dark-haired man was seen by that same witness and another running away from the scene.'

'So how does Miss Middleton fit into this?' Inspector Pound was very still.

Quigley picked up a steel rule. 'Because of what the man shouted: That will keep your mouth shut about March Middleton, you slut.'

'So you are suggesting that Miss Middleton had an accomplice?' Pound was poised like a cat waiting to pounce.

Quigley tossed the rule down and picked up a pen. 'That she hired or somehow persuaded an as yet unknown person to commit the murder, which makes her an accessory before the fact and therefore a murderess herself,' he confirmed.

'If that is all you've got it sounds a bit flimsy to me.' Pound rubbed the back of his neck. 'A good barrister could demolish that in ten minutes unless you find the killer and get him to turn Queen's evidence, and can show that Miss Middleton met him. I'm surprised you obtained a warrant on those grounds.'

Quigley brought out a battered silver cigarette case and I was about to tell him that Sidney Grice did not permit smoking, when he flipped it open to reveal a scrap of paper. 'Is that your handwriting?'

'Yes.'

'And what does it say?'

'I will pay one hundred pounds to have her killed,' I read out. 'But I was writing about Jennifer the—'

'Don't say any more, March,' Pound interrupted.

'Donkey,' I ended weakly.

'First-name terms.' Quigley crowed in delight. 'The men said you were sweet on that cod face.'

'Why, you—' Pound stepped forward, but I jumped in front of him and gave him my best warning look. I was quite proud of that look, though Mr G was always immune.

'Shielding behind a woman,' Quigley taunted him.

'That is exactly what you are doing.' I whirled to face him, nearly tripping on the edge of the rug. 'If I were not between you and him—'

'One punch and his guts would spill out,' Quigley jeered.

Bell ambled across the room, his bulk impressing me even more as he towered over us all.

'I can promise you one thing, sir.' His voice was a fine baritone. 'If Inspector Pound ever tries to strike you, he will have me to deal with.'

'I am very glad to hear it.' Quigley smirked. 'Though I'm not sure it will save your career.'

'Because I will be busily beating you myself,' Bell said.

Quigley breathed out hard. 'I've had enough of this.' He snapped the cigarette case shut. 'You, Bell, will report to my office at nine o'clock tomorrow morning. I shall arrange an appointment for you, Pound, to discuss your prejudicial handling of this case and you, Middleton, will come with me to the station.'

'At least you got my name right,' I said.

'Oh, Miss Middleton.' Quigley dropped the pen on to the floor, splaying the nib. 'I have got much more right than that.'

'I shall marry whom I please,' Sidney Grice shouted.

74

Pork Pies and Votes for Women

I T WAS NIGHTFALL when we left the house.

'Take good care of Mr Grice,' I instructed Molly, though I knew she would. 'And, when he awakes, tell him what has happened.'

'What has happened?' Molly screwed her apron into a ball.

'I wish I knew,' I said. 'Just tell him I have been arrested.'

'He won't not be delighted,' she warned.

'I do not suppose he will.'

'Have a nice time,' she called, and waved from the step.

'What?' Pound snapped in disbelief.

'I was talking to Fanny,' Molly said, and we turned to see next-door's maid whisk by in her best dress.

We could easily have gone in two hansoms but we waited – at Quigley's insistence – for a Black Maria. Inspector Pound gave his word of honour to accompany me in a cab but Quigley did not believe in honour. And so I was loaded into the cell on wheels with nothing for company but the sourness of vomit, stale urine and old sweat.

Almost immediately we came to a halt. I could not see what was causing the delay and I did not much care. The streets of London could not cope with modern traffic, the tens of thousands of carriages, waggons and omnibuses and the millions of people crammed into one small space, and all trying to go in different directions.

I heard a cry. 'Pork pies fresh as yer eyes, nice fick pastry ever so tastry, swimmin' in gravy 'nough to float the navy.' Sidney Grice would have been revolted, but it sounded good to me and reminded me that I was hungry. I remembered what Mrs Prendergast had pressed on me and, despite the smells, I brought the greaseproof paper packet out of my cloak pocket and opened it up. It was another slice of fruit cake, a little dried out but still quite tasty, and I consumed it ravenously, picking the crumbs and raisins from the wrapping before tossing it amongst the other detritus that littered the floor.

I wished I had brought my father's hip flask. If Mr G had been with me he would have had his patent insulated flask of tea, but he would not have shared any with me. We moved a few yards and jolted to a halt again, and I stood at the small barred window staring back along Gower Street and the children playing leap-frog on the street. A boy broke away and jumped on to the back running board.

''Ere, I know you.'

'Hello, Tommy.' I had bandaged his leg once when he had gouged it on a rusty spike.

'You taking a murderer in?' He raised himself to the opening and tried to peer past me.

'No, Tommy. They are taking me in.'

'Streuf!' His big eyes dilated. 'You ain't killed old Puddin'?'

'I have not killed anyone.'

Tommy winked wisely. His left ear was weeping pus. 'You stick to that story,' he advised.

The van started off again and he jumped down, waving his arms excitedly as he skipped back to his friends, shouting, 'Guess what, Old Plankface 'as gone an' shot old Grice Puddin' stone dead and they're takin' her off to the Tower.'

They stopped their game, but we were making steady speed now and rounded the corner, and soon we were on Tottenham Court Road and stationary again. The rain started, spraying through the bars. At first it was refreshing but then it was wet and cold. I sat down.

Somebody had carved on the bench Geezuz Loves you and I hoped the sentiment was truer than the spelling. I did not feel very loved at that moment, but I closed my eyes and opened my heart and prayed. I prayed for myself and those that I cared for, living and dead, and thought about Molly's last question. What had happened? Why did Uncle Tolly and Mrs Prendergast kill themselves? What on earth could have persuaded or terrified them into doing that? And who had murdered Gloria Shell? And again, when I needed him most, why did my guardian have to be incapacitated? I tried to pray but my mind was jumping in every direction.

Sidney Grice sat on the bench opposite, smoking a clay pipe and dressed in rags.

'I killed your mother, March.' His eyes glowed like hot coals, red then white-hot, lighting up the whole van, almost dazzling me. 'I took her by her lovely white throat and strangled her slowly, just like this.'

His arms grew longer and longer as the hands came towards me.

'You are not real,' I protested, though I was not convinced.

'Indeed I am...' The lights went out with a pop that might have been 'not'.

We pulled up outside Marylebone Police Station and we must have beaten Pound's cab to it, for there was no sign of him.

'Go 'ome,' a voice yelled. 'Filfy foreigners coming over and stealin' our jobs and our women and our...' His voice tailed off uncertainly, '... fings.'

Quigley appeared and propelled me into the entrance hall. It was packed with women wearing an assortment of hats with pink bows.

'What d'you want suffrage for, anyway?' the desk sergeant was shouting above the general chatter. 'Ain't there enough sufferin' as it is?'

'We want the vote,' a tall haughty woman replied.

'Well, I can't give it to you,' the sergeant reasoned.

'You are an instrument of the government that withholds it from us,' she informed him, 'and we intend to stay in this room until the newspapers pay attention.'

'Let us through,' Quigley snarled, pushing past a young lady who was trying to make a speech. 'This woman is a dangerous murderess.'

There was a gradual silence as word got about.

'Did he oppress and abuse you?' a little old lady quavered.

'She has killed two women.' Quigley elbowed his way past her. 'And she's thirsty for more blood. Got the strength of ten men when the fit is upon her.'

A space appeared around us and it grew as the crowd melted away.

'Oh Lord.' Sergeant Horwich picked up his pen wearily. 'Not you again.'

75

The Picnic at Jacaranda House

TRADITIONALLY, THE WOMEN and children and a great many of the men went to the hills for the summer months. Even the government relocated to Simla to take advantage of the cool mountain climate. But India could not be left deserted. Our garrison did not decamp and my father was needed more than ever after the exodus of some of his staff from the camp hospital. If he was needed, so – I insisted – was I, and, ignoring his objections, I stayed put.

It was the hottest summer I had ever known and so humid that the walls dripped, my books went mouldy and the bedding was soggy even before I lay on it. We dared not open the windows for the plagues of moths and bugs that would enter, and the bats that swooped in after them, and the punkas – flapping ceiling fans pulled to and fro by exhausted boys – did no more than waft hot air around the room.

Edward came up with the idea of a picnic. We might as well suffer outside as keep ourselves shut in our tin-roofed ovens, and so Cook packed a hamper and we lugged it through the long grass until we arrived wearily at Jacaranda House.

The house was unusual for the district in having two storeys and being constructed of stone rather than wood like the bungalows we all occupied. It had been built by Mr Rawlings, a tea merchant, we were told, to remind his wife of their Cotswold home. But after she died in a cholera epidemic, he closed the place up and returned to England. We settled on the veranda and I poured us each a warm glass of lemonade and set out our food on the blanket.

'You can see why he chose this spot,' Edward commented when he had swallowed the last sandwich, and I certainly could.

There was a faint but very welcome breeze and, if we turned our backs on the camp, we could see the hills rise until they shimmered and became one with the air.

'Someone has broken in.' Edward pointed and I saw that the front door was fractionally ajar and the hinges were damaged. 'Probably thieves, though there can't be much to steal.'

'A trinket to us may be a treasure to them,' I remarked.

We decided to take a look. The door was warped, but Edward managed to push it open just enough for us to peer into a square entrance hall with a tumbled staircase to one side.

I sniffed. 'Dry rot.'

Edward prodded the floor with his walking stick and the board gave easily. 'The structure looks sound, though.'

Through an open doorway at the back of the hall we could see a large room, the sun streaming between the planks over the windows.

'Wouldn't it be perfect?' I said.

'For what?' Edward asked blankly.

'Our school,' I explained, dismayed that I had to.

Edward looked nonplussed. 'Oh, that.'

I rammed our things back into the basket. 'I should like to go now.'

Edward shrugged but said nothing, not even when I left him to carry our hamper unaided. I marched on through the long grass, but it was not easy to keep up a pace in those temperatures.

'Stop,' Edward puffed, and I was about to make a cutting remark about him being weaker than a girl when he added, 'You are limping, March, and you know as well as I do that you mustn't get blisters.' We both remembered Mrs O'Neil, who had lost her left leg up to the knee because she got an infection. 'Sit there.'

If truth be told I was glad of a rest and sat on a log under the thin shade of a jujube tree – having checked it first for anything crawling. My feet were burning as I pulled off my boots and stockings. 'What I wouldn't give for a cold stream to soak them in.'

'I cannot provide a babbling brook but this might help.' Edward kneeled before me and began to massage my left foot. It felt like heaven but I pulled away.

'I thought you were interested in starting a school too.'

'I am sorry,' Edward said. 'I was hoping to surprise you with good news, but I do not think you will let me live that long.' He took a breath. 'I have written to Mr Rawlings to ask if he would let us use the house if we promise to renovate it. He is away at present, but his agent replied this morning that Mrs Rawlings had been very interested in educating local children and he thought his employer would look kindly upon the idea.'

'Oh, Edward.'

He took my right foot and a blue swallowtail butterfly landed on my little toe. Edward blew it away. 'Apparently there is an old stable block at the back that we could clean up for a classroom,' he said.

'Oh, Edward.' It was all I could say before we kissed. It was all I needed to say. He knew I would love him forever.

Mr Rawlings' encouraging letter and offer of financial assistance arrived three days after Edward's funeral.

76

Blankets, Buckets and Changing Walls

I HAD A cell to myself this time but it was as sparsely furnished
as before – a hard mattress with a thin blanket; and a slop
bucket. Edward often told me that public school was much
like prison with its spartan accommodation and awful food, but
at least he'd had something to eat. I had missed dinner and was
only permitted a jug of water to drink and wash in.

After I had been remanded, I would be taken to Holloway
Prison, Quigley told me with relish, and I would find that a great
deal less comfortable. He had questioned me for two hours, by
which I mean he harangued me. I had adopted a policy of listening in complete silence to his threats and attempts to interrogate
me and, in the end, he had worn himself out.

'Take her away,' he commanded the two constables who
stood behind me. He stuck a finger in front of my eye. 'Don't
think you have seen the last of me, Middleton. We'll talk again
in the morning.'

'You might,' I thought. 'But you will not get a word out of
me.'

A man was singing nearby. 'Oh, my mother was a mermaid in
the sea. My father was a captain in the Queen's naveeee.'

He held the last note for a long time, so long that I thought it
would never end, and then I heard a scream, very close by, even
longer and higher, and I wondered if it might be me because the
walls were changing, moving, alive, squealing even higher than

the scream because they were made out of rats, thousands upon thousands of them, writhing as they fought each other, clawing and biting to be the first to feed on my flesh.

There was no point in calling for help. Nobody could have heard me as the first rat broke away from the others, a giant black creature with teeth like razors hurtling through the night towards my throat.

Publisher's Note

At this point Miss Middleton was unable to continue her account and Mr Grice was persuaded to provide details of what ensued.

We experienced some difficulty in reproducing Mr Grice's notes because of his abhorrence of apostrophes, commas and quotation marks, all of which, he tells us, resemble maggots. We eventually compromised with him permitting us to insert the first two punctuations but omitting the latter.

Mr Grice refused to share any information with us about his methods of reasoning, arguing that this was an impertinent intrusion and would only serve to aid criminals in their futile attempts to outwit him.

I have removed, with Mr Grice's eventual permission, his recordings of the dimensions of every room he entered, the thirty estimated measurements of everybody he saw and the timing to the exact minute of every event. I have also omitted his twenty-eight-thousand word description of his observations on the incremental growth patterns of finger-plates. These can be found in an addendum to the limited special edition.

PART II

Extracts from
Mr Sidney Grice's Notes

77

Tuesday Morning, 23 January 1883

I SLEPT FITFULLY and, when I awoke, found myself lying on top of my bed fully clothed with a wet flannel placed over my face. I lifted the cloth away, placed it with great care on my counterpane and checked my hunter watch. Nobody had thought to wind it, I was relieved to find, for I could not bear the thought of anybody else doing so. Observing the shadows cast by the sun across my room, however, I judged it to be about nine o'clock in the morning.

I got up, feeling disconcertingly enervated, and, after ringing the bell five times to signal for breakfast, performed my toilet and went down to the dining room.

The papers had been stacked on a chair next to mine as per my usual instructions, but the pile was two and one third higher than usual, and it was then I realized it was Tuesday and I had been unconscious since Sunday afternoon. That I had not recognized this by the growth of my fingerplates is an indication of how my illness had reduced my mental faculties until they were scarcely greater than those of a highly intelligent person.

I crumpled my burned toast into my prune juice, stirred it carefully, selected three of the most symmetrical hard-boiled eggs and drank my tea. Clearly Miss Middleton's predicament required urgent attention, so I only read four of my newspapers and restricted myself to perusing the others.

Once in my study I summoned Molly and we engaged in the following intercourse.

I: You will take two telegrams to the local office.
She: But where shall I get them from, sir?
I: I am in the process of writing them.
She: But the local office is a solicitorers.
I: [with exemplary patience] The local telegram office, you stagnant dolt.
She: Dolts is pretty, ain't they not, sir?
I: I am suspicious that you are confusing them with dolls.

I printed out my telegrams, the first to Inspector Pound: WHERE IS MISS MIDDLETON QUERY; the second to Inspector Quigley, identically worded. And Molly set off with them and the correct money. I have found from experience that small change from transactions is often missing by the time Molly gets home with a brace of cream cakes inside her.

Molly in motion bears some resemblance to a steam locomotive – she is slow in building up momentum but, once under way, hurtles almost unstoppably. And she was puffing in a manner reminiscent of the aforementioned mode of transport when she returned and we entered into the following exchange:

She: Will they send your message on to Inspector Pound, sir?
I: Explain.
She: 'Cause I think he's still in hostibal. He had another turn when they took Miss Middleton away – I tried to stop them with your swordstick but it went all oily.
I: If you have broken my Grice Patent Pending Miniature Paraffin Lamp Stick I shall deduct the manufacturing cost from your wages.
She: Oh but, sir, I still ain't not finished paying for all the times you fined me for saying ain't – which you ain't not

done since Christmas when it tottered up to eight hundred pounds. Anyway, he bent over double like this. [Here I was treated to a great display of bowing and groaning.] He had all blood on his hands from grabbing himself in the middle, and they came and carted him off.

I: Why did you not say sooner?

She: I didn't not think it was my place, sir.

I: You never know your place when I want you to.

At this Molly composed her features in a fashion intended to give the impression that servants are as capable of having feelings as are their betters.

She: Oh.

I: Then I must go and see him without delay. Fill my flask and fetch me a cab.

She: But, sir, it is only three spits away.

I considered her remark.

I: Unless you have exceptional technique and a favourable wind, I would estimate eighteen expectorations from door to door. Perhaps you could test your theory in both directions on your next day off.

She: But you don't not give me no days off, sir.

I: And now you know why. The streets are filthy enough as it is.

Some thirteen minutes later I was at Liston Ward.

Matron: Visiting time is at six.

I: Have you any idea who I am?

She: No.

I: Then I suggest you find out whilst I go about my business.

I brushed past her. There is an art to brushing past people which one must adapt to suit circumstances. The Dowager Baroness, Lady Parthena Foskett, taught it to me as a special treat on my two thousandth day. I have always been a quick learner and I brushed past this officious employee before she had a chance to formulate another thought – quite a long time, admittedly.

Inspector Pound was at the far end on the left, below a window, and I was interested to see that it had been re-glazed approximately four years previously.

He: Mr Grice.

I: Inspector Pound.

He: What news of Miss Middleton?

I: None. I have only just partially regained some of my exceptional faculties.

He: If Quigley has had his way she will be in Holloway now. [He struggled ineffectually to raise himself. I considered whether to assist him but decided that to be grappling with a man in bed in his bedclothes would be an undignified process.] When I get out of here I shall kill that man.

I: First you must consider the prospect that you shall never leave here alive.

He: Thanks a lot.

I: Your gratitude is unnecessary. Second, if we are not quick off the mark, he shall have her judicially killed before you get the opportunity to be violent towards him.

He: They can't hang her, surely?

I: Juries hesitate to convict beautiful women of capital crimes and judges to pass the death penalty. Unfortunately, Miss Middleton cannot shelter under that protection.

He: Oh, I don't know.

I: I have had more opportunity to scrutinize my ward than you, Inspector, and I assure you that she is irredeemably plain.

In the mirrored surface at the back of my hunter I saw an exceedingly large and excessively hirsute man approaching, with Matron in close attendance.

Man: May I ask who you are and what you are doing here?

I: I do not need to ask the same of you, Mr O'Brian. [He raised his eyebrows, which I have oft known people to do when they are mildly surprised, and so I continued.] From the gory saturation of your attire, it is clear you are either a maniacal murderer or a surgeon, though some might argue there is little, if any, difference. Your speech betrays your Hibernian descent, though, from the way you enunciated doing, you were educated in that establishment fraudulently posing as a place of education under the name of Eton College. The way you trim your fingerplates shows that you perform the task yourself and are left-handed. The scars on the backs of both your hands indicate frequent applications of Hirudo Medicinalis.

O'Brian: [for the benefit of a puzzled inspector] Leeches.

I: From the bilateral mucocoeles on your lips it is evident that you play the oboe, and the shiny patch on the web of your right hand could only be caused by repeatedly drawing a pole-like object up and down it. And having read your excellent paper 'The Effects of Oboe Music on the Feeding Habits of Hirudo Medicinalis', I deduce that you can, therefore, be none other than the inimitable Mr S. R. O'Brian, the renowned left-handed billiard champion.

O'Brian: [chortling in delight at such childishly simple deductions] Why, sir, you must be a colleague of our detective patient here.

Pound: This is Mr Sidney Grice.

O'Brian: The author of *Post-Mortem Scrutiny of the Human Ear Lobe*? When is volume three to be published?

I: I shall send you a copy next month.

Pound: I expect the first two sold like hot cakes.
I: You have been in the company of Miss Middleton too long.
O'Brian: Miss Middleton, I know that name. [He clicked his fingers.] After this patient was stabbed last September I successfully transfused her blood into him.

I refrained from commenting: And her fondness for sarcasm, it would appear.

I: Then perhaps you would care to examine the clothing with which she is alleged to have assassinated an irritating widow.

I endured all O'Brian's tedious exclamations of surprise that Miss Middleton should find herself in such a precarious position and reiterated that this was indeed the situation.

O'Brian: I finish here at six. Shall I call on you?
I: Yes.
O'Brian: Shall I bring my oboe?
I: No.

There was the distinct perfume of a feral cat about him.

O'Brian: Then I shall not.

We shook hands, and I wiped mine and gave my attention to Matron, who had been deprived of her wish to see me evicted.

I: I am sure that you are doing your best for this patient.
She: [simpering nauseatingly] Indeed we are, Mr Grice.
I: However, it is not good enough. I must have him restored to an ambulatory condition by the end of this week. A woman's life may depend upon it. Goodbye, Inspector

Pound. Do not die. Miss Middleton will be soured by your loss, I suspect, and I have come to find her cheerfulness less infuriating than I did initially.

78

Tuesday Afternoon,

I RE-ENTERED MY Bloomsbury home and enquired of Molly whether there had been any responses, to which she replied that she did not know because no one had replied. A nice man had come offering to sharpen our knives, but she had sent him away and he was no longer nice. She chattered on whilst I occupied myself with re-stocking my satchel and selecting a cane, having first ascertained that my lantern cane had not endured irreparable trauma.

I transferred myself to Marylebone Police Station.

Sergeant Brickett was on the desk. He was a hopeless policeman, adipose and infragrant, the general opinion being that he was promoted in order to get him off the beat, where he was credited with having started an exhilarating riot. His handwriting is passable, however, and I was able (after flicking through his register to his vociferous indignation) to read upside down that my ward had been checked in three days ago and out the next morning.

He: Such information is confidenteral, Mr Grice.

I: Which is why I am reading it. Is Inspector Quigley on the premises?

He: [with a sneer] I would 'ave thought you could 'ave deducterated that yourself.

I: If all the H's you and your comrades dropped could be

swept into a pile they would fill the mouth of the Thames and bring the economy grinding to a halt. However, since you are feeling so uncooperative, I shall make my own deduction that he is.

He: And 'ow can you work that out?

[He poked the sharp end of a pencil into his ear.]

I: By using my remarkable observational powers.

I directed the officer's attention, with an elegant sweep of my cane, to the corridor down which Quigley progressed in that peculiar amphibian style with which nature had so cruelly presented him.

I: Where is Miss Middleton?

Quigley: She has been arrested, charged and arraigned, and is currently awaiting trial in Her Majesty's Prison at Holloway.

I: You are a perversion and a parasite. If the reputation of the police force has been dragged into the mud, you are that mud.

And I marched out, wishing that Miss Middleton were with me. She would have thought of something unpleasant to say about him, but that is not in my nature.

———————

79

Wednesday Morning, 24 January 1883

HER MAJESTY'S PRISON Holloway was built in a vulgar facsimile of an imaginary (though not imaginative) castle with towers and turrets and a great gateway, which no doubt Miss Middleton would have tried to make sound menacing, but bricks are bricks no matter how you pile one on top of another.

People cannot just turn up at a gaol demanding immediate entrance so that is what I did, rapping smartly eight times on the door with the silvered handle of my cane.

The hatch grated open and a warder, whom I recognized from happier visits as Grief Herriot, said: Oh hello, Mr Grice. What you doing 'ere?

I let his appalling grammar pass and responded relevantly: I wish to gain admittance.

Herriot: Not many blokes wanting to do that. In fact there's a surprising number that would rather be going the opposite way. Do you 'ave an appointment?

I: First I am not, never have been, nor ever shall be a bloke. Second, no, but if you would be so kind as to inform Mr Kindred – who, as I trust you are aware, is the governor of this penal property – that there is a green dog lurking in Pyramid Street, I would be obliged, though not so obliged as to reward you with anything more than a curt nod.

I made him repeat the sentence twice to be sure he had it right and waited for six and a half minutes, amusing myself by calculating the best way of murdering passers-by. I was just toying with the idea of dissolving an off-duty piano tuner when a door inset into the great door opened.

> Herriot: Mr Kindred says you are to come in. [Grief took my satchel, cane and the spring knife from my pocket. Did he really imagine that removing weapons would protect his governor should I have homicidal intent?] Have a care, Mr Grice. There's a few what is only 'ere 'cause of you and some of them would be only too 'appy to thank you in person.
> I: I cannot share your conviction that they will thank me for theirs.
> [This was rather droll, I thought, involving the kind of play upon words that the lower orders find stimulating, but Grief managed to keep a straight face so I decided not to trouble to give him a curt nod after all.]

Kindred was an imposing figure, six foot and three inches tall, and had boxed for his school and university – though not very well, as his visage bore witness.

> He greeted me thus: Grice. [We did not shake hands but tapped the toes of our right boots twice.] Is the dog hungry for a wasp?
> I: [wearily, for there were no secrets worth keeping in the society] A segmented worm. [Then I sat to face him across his desk.] You have lost three and a half pounds since I saw you last. [This last remark was not a code but a pleasantry, which is something ordinary people enjoy.]
> Kindred: More like seven.
> I: Three and a half. Your wife adjusts the scales to encourage you to persist with your dietary regime. Have a care,

Governor Kindred, for a spouse who deceives from love may one day do so from different motives as twelve per centum of your residents could, but probably shall not, testify.

[Grief left us, unmourned.]

Kindred: You know, of course, that the green dog code is only to be used in extremis and can only be applied once, so that you may never ask a favour of me again, whereas I may ask you two?

I: I formulated the rules.

He: I can guess whom this is about.

I: Let me save you the trouble. My ward is to stand trial for her life. I must see her and we shall be alone.

He: Alone? [Kindred cracked his knuckles twice.] Green dog or not, that would be most irregular. I could be disciplined if anything happened.

[I ran my finger over the perimeter of an ink stain on the desktop and hummed nine notes.]

I: If you cooperate I shall stand down as president of the Rigby Club and nominate you as my successor.

[The Rigby Club (which celebrates capital punishment in all its glory) was, of course, named after Elaine Rigby, who kept her mother's face in a bottle. I reversed direction and retraced the pattern, making sure that I finished at exactly the same point.]

He: President. [Kindred's battered features luminanced.] So I would get to sit on the scaffold chair. [He sat taller, no doubt imagining the prospect.]

I: Yes.

He: And wear the broken dagger?

I: Indeed.

He: And carry the ceremonial noose?

I: Yes, and silently pronounce the sentence of death at midnight.

Kindred's hands made as if to accept the scrolls of office and then he said: Very well. You may see her for ten minutes.

I: Fifteen, and I shall let you use the great seal which right-fully belongs to me.

He: Very well. [Kindred rose like a lotus-eater in one of those dreadful poems with which Miss Middleton likes to torture me.] I shall accompany you myself.

And so we set off along five corridors, through four doors which all had to be unlocked and relocked with great clamour. Kindred walked slowly for a man with such extravagantly elongated limbs and I was able to calculate that the woman in cell 314 was manifestly innocent but, since she was not my client, this was only of academic interest to me. A gentleman does not tout for business.

Kindred stopped at last and said: Here we are.

I: If you analyse that remark you will see how pointless it is. I suspect you meant to tell me that we had arrived at the door of Miss Middleton's cell.

Kindred's masseter muscles bunched, demonstrating he had reached the fourth degree of annoyance. He indicated abruptly to the perfumed warder who was patrolling the area that the same official should open the door.

80

Late Wednesday Morning, 24 January 1883

MISS MIDDLETON WAS not at all as I expected, though I should have learned from my experiences with what became known as the Beast of Buckingham Palace never to expect anything except a peerage.

My ward was seated on the bed, backed into the corner with her feet pulled up. She was clutching her knees and exhibiting, it disgusts me to relate, some three and a half inches of her left shin and fractionally under five of her right. Her hair, ever reminiscent in its coarseness of a dray horse's tail, was draped about her face so that she might have appeared to be looking at me through a shredded and dirty piece of sacking, except that she was not looking at me at all but taking a keen interest in her left hand with the digits rubbing repeatedly over each other in a manner similar to that of my mother constructing a cigarette. The door closed.

I: Good morning, March. Your presentation is worse than it was when you first arrived in London.
[Miss Middleton's hand stilled.]
I: I trust you are not being petulant because I have not visited you sooner. [Her hand formed an approximation of a claw.] I have been, as you are aware, indisposed and kept in ignorance of your plight, but you will be delighted to learn that I am greatly recovered.

[The hand rotated one hundred and seventy degrees in each direction seventeen times, as though rattling a white china handle on a satinwood door.]

I: We have limited time and I have had to promise to abdicate my presidency of the Rigby Club in order to gain any at all. [The fingers closed and the right hand enveloped it.] I have given up my chair made from the very gallows on which James Bloomfield Rush was hanged on 21 April 1849, at Norwich Castle.

[Averting my gaze, I heaved at the hem of her dress and managed to pull it down some two inches, but my ward had a tight grip on it now and I did not intend to wrestle with her.]

I: Also one of the knives used by Frederick Baker.

But it was obvious that she was not going to engage in the conversation and I began to wonder if I could trim my visit to five minutes and three-quarters, and at least retain my personal seal. I parted her hair, which I was distressed to find enriched with the exudate of sebaceous glands, and her eyes rose very slowly, rather as one's father might had he been prematurely buried in a shallow muddy grave. Her pupils, I noted, were greatly constricted, though the light in her cell was poor, and the sclera had taken on a green discolouration reminiscent of the last occasion when they had done so.

I calculated the rate of her pulse, which averaged a slow three thousand, three hundred and sixty percussions per hour. Her skin was cold and, I am embarrassed to relate, clammy. I flicked her eyelids and they rose at approximately the same rate as my green flag when one is a trifle lethargic. I pinched her ear lobes. Most people do not care to have their ear lobes nipped, but Miss Middleton did not seem to mind.

I: What have you been eating?
[I did not know if she would reply, but I thought it unlikely.

Miss Middleton chewed ruminatively at the side of her tongue without closing her mouth. Her gingival margins had also taken on a verdant hue. I examined the beds of her fingerplates, which were a striking emerald colour.]
She: Pig.

Admittedly, it was one more word than I extracted from the Marquess of Milton Keynes when we shared a lifeboat, but hardly worth surrender of the rope which strangled Elizabeth Pearson.

Not having been convicted of any crime yet, Miss Middleton had been allowed to keep her own attire. I could not view the soles of her boots (always a treasure trove of information, especially in The Case of the Four Prince Alberts, in which I played a minor role) without the risk of uncovering her lower limbs, and so I contented myself with examining her cloak which lay crumpled on the bed, used, I imagine, as an extra cover, for gaol blankets are not to be recommended for their insulating properties as I can vouch from my incarceration in Her Majesty's Prison Dartmoor.

The cloak had some bloodstains inside, which were consistent with it having been donned after the death of Mrs Prendergast. There were also two minor burns from lighted cigarettes; a slight stretch in the lining of one pocket, most probably from an ill-concealed bottle of gin; and a clue.

81

<Decorative divider>

Wednesday Noon, 24 January 1883

GOVERNOR KINDRED WAS lounging in the corridor, filling a poorly seasoned briar pipe and trying to pretend that he had not been watching me through the spyhole.

I: How long has she been approximating a stupor?
[He had freckles around his nostrils, about which Miss Middleton would have made some playful remark in happier times.]
He: I could not say, for she was in that state when she arrived.
[He tamped his shag down with an oranged first finger.]
I: Has she been attended by a doctor?
He rubbed the head of a Lucifer on the abrasive strip to ignite the former and informed me, though he must have realized that I knew: This is not a hospital. Besides, I think she is pretending.
[He sucked the flame down over the bowl, shook the Lucifer out and tossed it on the sandstone floor.]
I: Do you have a pipe knife?
He: Of course.
[He inhaled the combustion products with apparent enjoyment.]
I: Then go into Miss Middleton's cell and insert the blade under one of her fingerplates and observe whether or not

she reacts. Then try the same upon yourself and see if you can remain similarly unresponsive.

Kindred blew smoke in my face, though not intentionally, I believe, and said: We have a lot of hysterical women here.

A prisoner was being taken away. She glanced back and I saw that it was Marigold Pride, the Looms Lane Lisper.

She: Mithter Grithe. [The prisoner tried to surprise me but the warders had a tight grasp on her arms.] It'th you. [And she hithed in an almost feline manner as she struggled to break free.]

Miss Middleton would, no doubt, have had some witty retort ready, but I could only respond: I am fully aware of that, thank you, Mrs Pride.

She: Let me go. I'll kill 'im. It'th 'im what put me inthide.

I could have debated, as they dragged her away, that it was only my revelation of her actions that led to her conviction, but she did not seem anxious to enter into a reasoned discussion so I remarked sympathetically: Try to be grateful, Mrs Pride. Thanks to my investigations you will not have to worry about having a roof over your head until you are ninety-six.

Kindred: [addressing me and not the prisoner] I will show you out.

[Kindred struggled to relight his pipe and trod on a crack. He was never any good at anything.]

*

On the way home I stopped at the aptly though unimaginatively named 'Pet Shop' on Warren Street. There was a tiger cub offered for purchase under the alias of Tomass and an anonymous American alligator being promoted as an Affrikun Crockadile. Several puppies gazed at me pleadingly but unappealingly and an African Grey Parrot wondered inappropriately which of us was a pretty boy. I did not trouble to respond that neither of us were boys (though I fitted the description a little more closely than she), but I could not help recalling the case of Midshipman Alan Wilkins, whose pet bird called out Oh George yes so suggestively that he struck his wife down with a barometer. With her dying breath, she explained she had been teaching it to say Hello, Gorgeous whenever she entered their front parlour. Yet another example of the havoc created by poor articulation and the vanity of women.

I purchased a mouse. The owner, evidently a retired bagpipe repairer, assured me this was a rare specimen and very loyal.

I: It is mus musculus, the common house mouse and, if I were seeking affection, which I am not, I should not be turning to a verminous rodent.
He: If you want it for snake food I can let you 'ave them by the dozen at a good price.

I had considered getting a python as I had found one quite useful in the past, but I declined and was mortified to discover that, although the animal was only one penny, the cage which I required to convey it cost eighteen times more.

*

I regained admittance to my house.

Molly: Oh, sir, is that a friend for Mr Wispy?
I: Mr Wispy being whom?
She: Being whom what, sir?
[I placed my cane in the rack. This was not a job I entrusted to Molly since she had once positioned a stick out of line with its fellows.]
I: Who or what is Mr Wispy? And do not require me to repeat that name again.
Molly clasped her hands together and said: Oh, sir, Mr Wispy is the mouse what lives in the pantry. [She put her red-chaffed

fists over where she imagined her heart to be.] Oh, he is so sweet and brown.

I: [handing her my cloak] I shall introduce it to Miss Middleton's cat.

Molly smirked: Oh, Spirit has already metted him, sir. They snuggle up by the oven.

[I resolved to set some traps but was not in a frame of mind that equipped me to listen to her protests.]

I: Listen very carefully, Molly. Under no circumstances must you feed this mouse.

Molly pulled at a pendulous tress and asked: Under nose what, sir?

[I have heard Miss Middleton describe me as patience personified and though I suspect she was attempting to be ironic, I know it to be the case, but even I was getting a little vexed.]

I said slowly and firmly: Do not feed this mouse. If you do, Miss Middleton may die and it will be your fault.

Molly wrapped the tress around her hand: Are you getting it thin so it can crawl along a drainpipe with a key round its neck to help Miss Middleton escape? Oh, what a clever idea, sir. I told Cook you wouldn't not just let her be killed like you do all your customers.

I finally became patience un-personified and shouted: How dare you! They were clients not customers. Get back to work.

She: [sotto voce, as she lumbered off] Still dead, though.

*

I called in on Dr Crystal. He is one of the six men whose knowledge of biochemistry I respect, though not a great deal, and none can rival his knowledge of equine mud fever, but he lacks my sensitivity in dealing with humans.

He: Threw all that stuff down the sink.

I: Which might explain some of those reports of rats dying in the sewers.

He was boiling a flask of horse manure in sodium hydroxide and said: If I can turn this back into hay my fortune is assured.

[There was a member of the Atelidae family, a woolly monkey, gibbering in a tiny cage and I felt a little sorry for it, having only Dr Crystal for company.]

I: Can you make some more antidote?

[His laboratory was so untidy it made me itch on the points of my elbows.]

He: I probably could [he stirred his concoction with a tarnished silver soup spoon], given a month or two, but I feel it only fair to tell you that every dog, cat, ape, monkey, alligator or donkey to which I gave a second dose had a fatal seizure on the spot.

I left him to his ridiculous experiment, not troubling to tell him that I was having better success with my own.

82

Wednesday Evening

MR O'BRIAN ARRIVED at four minutes past six, puffing with the effort of shuffling so much adipose tissue the distance of a disputed number of expectorations.

He: [in response to my hospitable offer] Do you have nothing containing ethanol?

I told him I had some brandy which I reserved for clients who feel faint and he assured me that he felt liable to swoon at any moment, so I fetched the tray from the sideboard and he poured himself a measure at which even Miss Middleton might have baulked.

I had borrowed a mannequin from Miss Daisy's Boutique with the promise (following their frightening experiences with Mrs Juno Amplecyse) not to recommend them to any more clients. Molly had put my ward's dress on it and, as the surgeon and I stood surveying it, I outlined my conclusions.

He paced round the model and said: I can add nothing to that. [He toddled back to his Courvoisier.] Miss Middleton told me some lies when I met her but with the object of saving that fellow Pound's life. I did not have her down as a cold-blooded killer.

I: [pulling my foot away before he reversed on to it] There is little cold-blooded about Miss Middleton. She is a creature of instinct, though I have never known her impulses to be cruel. To the contrary, she is often distressingly and indiscriminately kind.

He: Pretty little thing.

[I was about to contradict him when I realized he was referring to the heel bone on my bookshelf.]

I: Indeed. That calcaneus is all that was left of Pirius Freeman, apart from some fatty sludge which is on display at the Royal College.

He: I read about that. [O'Brian poured himself another liberal brandy.] Didn't he believe that the River Styx was made of oil of vitriol and that if he dipped himself in it he would be invincible like Achilles?

I: So his brother claimed, but I believe I could have proved otherwise had anyone employed my services. Whilst we are on the subject of the human skeleton [I took the lid off the cardboard box that Pound had brought with him], what do you make of that?

O'Brian took it out and declared: I have never lost my sense of awe when I hold a human skull. To think this once contained all that was a man, this bony case of consciousness, this osseous dome, this—

I: Quite so. [There are six types of men when it comes to brandy. Some become bawdy, some maudlin, some aggressive, some docile, some silent. But the very worst kind become poetasters and the Hibernian surgeon was teetering obesely on the brink of the Shakespearean.] But what can you tell me about it?

[I have found that few people can answer a question until it is put to them in at least two different ways, Molly's record being twenty-nine before I defeated her.]

He: It was a man, to judge by the prominent glabella, supra-orbital ridges and temporal lines. The smoothness of the interior indicates that he was a creature of normal appetites.

I: Do you have any evidence for that last remark?

[O'Brian swirled the brandy in his glass as men do when trying to convince themselves they have not yet had enough. His pupils were of unequal sizes, I noted, but saw no opportunity to introduce the topic into our conversation.]

He: Professor Loredan of the University of Venice dissected the skulls of nearly a thousand effeminate men, of which there is no shortage in the Italian peninsula, and found it to be invariably the case that the surface of their skulls was corroded by the impure thoughts harboured within.

I: I believe that Loredan's diagnosis of effeminacy encompassed all men who use soap.

He: A good rule of thumb, wouldn't you agree?

I had no wish to offend my guest so I only remarked mildly: You are talking utterly inane drivel.

At which, no doubt because of the alcohol he had consumed, O'Brian took offence and snapped: Damn your eyes. [He grasped my decanter again.] Anyway, you would be better asking my colleague, the oral surgeon Mr Weybridge, for this is almost certainly one of his former patients.

I decided to exercise a little tact and said: Explain that deduction before you storm off in a childish sulk.

He: [taking yet more unintended offence] Ask him yourself. I will see myself out.

[Yet again Miss Middleton would have indulged in some repartee at this point, but I have striven all my life not to be witty and I flatter myself that I have succeeded.]

*

I had met Weybridge at a party. I hope this does not give the impression that I am a sociable or pleasant man. The hostess had received a death threat and employed my services to protect her, which of course I did to my complete satisfaction.

It interests me that surgeons, whom one might expect to have long thin fingers to perform delicate procedures, often have hands that would be useful for laying bricks. This goes some way to proving my contention that surgery is not a profession but involves the same skills of chopping and hacking that are required by a lumberjack. I said none of this to Weybridge, however. If Miss Middleton has had any effect on my behaviour it is that her lack of tact has illustrated the importance of invariably exercising it myself.

He: Grice. [Weybridge enveloped my hand in his black-haired fist.] I hear you upset O'Brian. Good for you. The man is a bully, though I would choose him every time to amputate my leg.

I: It is not an operation you can have more than twice.

[His voice was high for such a massively constructed creature and I wondered how smooth was the inside of his cranial vault.]

I showed him the skull and said: O'Brian was under the impression that you might know something about this.

[Weybridge put on his spectacles and hobbled across his laboratory to the window.]

He: Interesting. The upper-left dog tooth is displaced and completely buried, so much so that the first premolar has drifted forward to close the gap.

I: [to see if he knew the answer] Is that rare?

He: It occurs in perhaps one in two hundred people.

I: [crouching to examine a pickled baby Cyclops] Did you cause the bone damage?

He: I prefer my actions to be called surgery, but yes, it does look like one of my cases.

I: Can you be certain?

He: Fairly. It is not a common procedure as it involves cutting through the hard palate and most patients decline to have it done unless I make them.

I: Why would a man want it done?

[I scrutinized the severed head of an able seaman, which was suspended in a large jar. So much of the face had been eroded that the nasal turbinate bones and the meninges were exposed.]

He: [placing the skull fragment on a set of scales] Sometimes they are associated with cysts, which can become painful.

[It was apparent that Weybridge had been walking in Fulham within the last three days, though I doubted he would admit as much.]

I: You cannot be the only surgeon to carry out these operations?

He: I am the only man I know who does them in this way. [He ran a straight probe around a shallow concavity.] The rest of my colleagues chisel the bone away, which leaves straight lines, but I use a new electrical drill that is less destructive and leaves a rounded scar like this.

I: [admiring a foot magnificently encrusted with that delightful fungal disease, South American blastomycosis] How many of these procedures have you carried out?

He: About a dozen. Give me an evening to go through my case notes and I can give you a list. [Weybridge sniffed the skull.] Found in a fire?

I: I am interested in the condition of the dental pulps.

He: How so?

I took a probe from the marble work surface and indicated the areas I was talking about: These incisors are freshly fractured. There is no evidence of any time for repairs and the pulp has not bled into the dentine. There are still remnants of soft tissue in the depth of the chambers, as I ascertained with a fine wire. So the pulp had not the time to die. Also, the pattern of fracture corresponds with the shape of these lower incisors.

[I delivered them to him.]

He: As you say, they fit quite neatly into the upper teeth.

[He handed the skull back to me.] This man died grinding his teeth in agony.

I: Splendid.

83

⬥•⬥•⬥

Wednesday Late Evening

I REVISITED UNIVERSITY college Hospital, a massive edifice reminiscent in its grandiosity and long passageways of my parents' summer residence in Hampshire, which we had not visited since that unfortunate event which my mother ever after referred to as the incident.

The matron gave me no trouble this time. Indeed she escorted me to the bed where Inspector Pound lay sleeping.

I: Wake up, Pound.
[She glared at me, but I have only ever been interested in the emotions of nine matrons and she was not amongst that number.]
Pound: [with a start] I have already done it, Lucinda. Oh hello, Mr Grice.
I: Miss Middleton has gone mad.
He: Mad?
I: You are familiar with the word, I take it?
Pound edged up his pillows, making no end of an embarrassing fuss with his grunts and grimaces, and said: In what way mad?
I: She is almost in a trance and has an emerald complexion.
He untangled a sleeve of his nightgown and said: You think she has been poisoned again?

I: It would seem likely but I do not know for certain how, yet. I shall get Dr Villeroy of the Royal Pharmaceutical Society to examine her. His knowledge of toxicology is even more extensive than my own.

[Pound pulled his sheet down and I pulled it up.]

He: What can we do?

I: [charitably] You can do even less than usual.

He: I have been wracking my brains [Pound parted his moustaches], but I cannot understand why all this has happened. [He rasped at his stubble.] The first incident at Saturn Villa was more like a bad practical joke – pretending to be dead and making Miss Middleton believe she had done it. But why go to all that trouble to play such a prank on a complete stranger?

[I extracted my insulated bottle.]

I: We should consider the matter from a different perspective. [I poured myself a cup of tea.] What was achieved by such extravagant mischievousness?

I re-corked my flask and Pound pinched his cheek, saying: Nothing much, that I can see. Miss Middleton was upset and confused and—

I: Perhaps that was what they hoped to do... confuse her. Obviously she was drugged to abet them in that purpose, but why would you want to confuse anybody?

[I tried my tea and was pleased to find it still steaming.]

He: To distract them. [He stopped scratching.] But from what?

I put the cup on his side table and said: I do not know yet, but can it really be a coincidence that all this took place whilst I was away?

The inspector frowned and said: You are not suggesting that your abbot was killed just to get you out of the way?

He was not my abbot. Indeed I have never possessed one, but I let that pass with: Possibly but it seems unlikely – to risk being caught for murder to get me out of town. If it was just a practical joke why not just make up a story to lure me away?

He: But you think the two events might be linked. [Pound looked at my flask.] I don't suppose you've got any of that to spare?

I shook my flask and said: I have quite a lot to spare, but I never spare it.

He: What about the will? [He reached for his glass of water with another great show of discomfort.] Why make out a will in Miss Middleton's favour? It could only provide her with a motive for a crime that never took place.

I: Since you and Miss Middleton are fond of untrammelled speculation, I shall venture a little into that intellectual hinterland myself. [Something was annoying the inspector but I did not enquire what it might be.] What if they planned to put another man's body in the bed and claim that Miss Middleton had killed him, believing it to be her uncle from whom she stood to inherit a fortune?

Pound clicked his tongue annoyingly and said: The skull in the furnace.

I: Which Mr Weybridge, a surgeon in this dreary establishment, thinks he should be able to identify. [I drained my cup.] He also concurs with me that it is likely that the victim was pushed into the furnace alive.

Pound whispered: My God, what a way to die.

I: I can think of eleven worse.

[I flicked the cup dry and replaced it on my flask. Pound put his water to his lips and the dusty meniscus vibrated.]

He: But why not go ahead with the plan?

I: A germane point. By her own account, when Miss Middleton escaped from Saturn Villa the attempts to recapture her were so feeble as to be moribund. That could be because her pursuers were unfit; she can move quite quickly for a girl; or stupid, though they seem to

have exercised some ingenuity in planning and executing their scheme; or that—
Pound broke in: They wanted her to escape.

It is bad enough that I interrupt people without them doing it to me.

———◆•◈•◆———

84

Wednesday Late Evening, Continued

A NURSE ARRIVED to change Pound's dressing. I would have been interested to watch as I have written a light-hearted paper entitled 'A Few Thoughts on the Healing of Abdominal Lacerations', but the inspector was feeling coy and so I ambled up the ward, diagnosing conditions and assuring a wailing young man that his sufferings would not last much longer.

When I regained his company Pound looked distinctly the worse for his experience.

He: The wound is clean now [though I had not mentioned it], but Lord, that carbolic acid stings.
[It irritated my eye and sensitive nostrils just to stand near him.]
But I consoled him with a cheery: Pull yourself together, man [and prodded him jovially in the ear with my cane].
He: I've been thinking about motive. [Though, again, I had not asked for his thoughts.]
I: There is a lot of gibberish talked about the reasons people kill other human beings. Weighty tomes have been devoted to misrepresenting the subject but, as often, the more words people use, the less they say. [I slid the chair eleven inches further back and sat upon it.] There is only one motive for murder and that is resentment.
He: Resentment?

[There was the desiccated corpse of a house fly by the skirting board, and it had five stripes along its back instead of the usual four. I wondered if this might be a new species – Musca Domestica Gricea had a pleasant ring to it.]

I: By which I mean the wish to deprive someone of what he or she has, either because the killer wants it for him or her self or does not want the victim to have it.

He: I can see that for robbery but what about anger?

I: Is that not resentment?

He thought about it, his dark-rimmed eyes swivelling to the right, and said: What about revenge?

I: Revenge is surely based on undistilled resentment of an act performed or neglected.

[The fly's primary wings were so truncated that I wondered if it had ever flown.]

He: [tentatively] Lust.

I: We are men of the world. What is lust other than the desire to have what somebody else has, that is, their body? Possessions, carnal knowledge, status, religious beliefs. It is all as one. [A patient was trying to get out of bed and the matron was forcing him back by his throat. I crouched.] If the detective can work out what is wanted and who wants it from whom, his job becomes embarrassingly simple. [I popped the insect into an envelope and stood up.] If he cannot calculate these things he should not be a detective.

He: Do you know the answers?

I: Not yet, but I shall. [I scrutinized the fly through a small magnifying glass. It appeared to have enjoyed a natural death.] I never believe coincidences unless I can prove them to be so, and I have no reason to suspect that any are instrumental in leading to Miss Middleton's unhappy situation. [My right eye was drifting but I decided to ignore it.] It would therefore seem likely that the death of Dom Ignatius Hart, the imagined death of Mr Travers Smyth, the actual death of Mr Travers Smyth, the deaths of the over-excitable Mrs Prendergast and her reputably pretty maid were all linked by the same resentment. A person or persons unknown wanted something that one or all of them had, or was anxious that they should not have it.

He: If Miss Middleton is guilty as accused – and I can't believe that she is – what could she be resentful of?

I informed him: That is the ninetieth most difficult question you have ever asked me. Her interests go little beyond her five major vices – to wit, smoking cigarettes, drinking gin, devouring animal flesh, annoying me and being kind to people.

[Pound let out a little snigger. If he had some private joke I had no wish to participate in it.]

I sealed the envelope and pencilled the time and date upon it, then said: But let us create a mirror image of that thought. If Miss Middleton is, as I am secretly contemplating, innocent of any crime what might she have that was of interest to the murderer or murderers? It is unlikely that anybody should desire her in a physical sense.

Pound opened his mouth, but evidently changed his mind about what he was going to say and asked: What about her money?

I stood up and said: Colonel Middleton was a remarkable man, a skilled physician and surgeon, a courageous soldier, a cultured scholar and the husband of one of the twelve most beautiful women in Europe. [I went behind the chair. It had been constructed in Ipswich.] He was also irresponsible to the point of imbecility. He left his daughter to fend for and educate herself; he took her on perilous voyages to dangerous foreign climes when she was little more than a child; he exposed her to the horrors of war at an age when other girls are fretting over their flounces and eyelashes; and he gambled away – in that notorious casino known as the stock exchange – the considerable fortune generated by his own forebears and his union with the Stopforth dynasty. As a result of this the only real asset Miss Middleton had, when I tended my offer to be her guardian, was me.

Pound went back to scratching the dark spikes on his chin and said: But I understood that she has some valuable stock.

I surveyed the inspector closely. Was he feigning an interest in my goddaughter in the hope of acquiring her fortune and, possibly, even mine? But Pound was not a cynical man. He had spurned the advances of Cynthia Meadowgrass, who was worth at least six thousand a year and could have got him a promotion. So I decided to let that thought pass for the present. Normally I would not have dreamed of discussing money with a policeman, but there was nothing normal about my ward's predicament.

I: Shortly after I met my obligation to Miss Middleton, her shares in a mining company soared in price. [I ignored his muttered Damn it and continued.] In fact I allowed her to believe that this was the reason I had taken her under my roof. She has, however, made a will in which all the value of these shares should be used to start and manage a school in India.

He: She has spoken to me of the great poverty she saw there.

I: There are times she speaks of little else.

He: So the only people to benefit financially from Miss Middleton's execution would be some poor children across the world [his skin glistened with sweat and I wished it would stop doing so] – not exactly likely suspects.

I toyed with the jackal ring on my watch chain and recalled: I have captured a great many unlikely culprits in my time.

[I could not tell him that amongst those was a person given to violent attacks on prostitutes in the Whitechapel area who had only avoided arrest because of another's intervention. I deposited my elbows on the back of the chair. The young man started whimpering, rarely a good sign in young men, but the matron was telling him to shush because she knew best.]

He: What about her uncle's money?

[The inspector mopped his brow with a corner of his sheet.]

I: Assuming there is any, and I have yet to investigate that point [I pulled my lower right eyelid up over the eye], all who knew of Miss Middleton's inheritance would also have known that she had bequeathed it to a similarly wasteful cause in the East End of London, whose inhabitants can hardly communicate in grunts let alone read.

[I sat down again and poured another tea and held it out to Pound.]

He put out his hand: Why, thank you.

I whisked it away: I merely wished you to see how poorly it keeps its temperature after the bottle has been opened.

Pound looked less pleased than he had a moment ago and said: Do you think Mr Travers Smyth's death could have been accidental? [He went back to preening his point-less moustaches.] I believe the gun went off when Miss Middleton put it on a table.

I: It is unlikely to have been an accident in the sense that you mean. Until Miss Middleton fiddled – something she is always inclined to do – with the tension, the trigger was very stiff. But I am reserving my judgement until I have further information. [I drank my tea in three attempts.] I shall wish you a good night, Inspector George Henry Pound, for I have a busy day ahead of me. There are seven people I wish to see and four of them may still be alive.

There was a hush at the other end of the ward. I had heard that quietness many times in my extraordinary life and, as I passed, I saw that the young man, true to my prophesy, was suffering no more.

85

Thursday Morning, 25 January 1883

I WENT FIRST to the mortuary. In her emotional account of
the Ashby case Miss Middleton referred to it as The House
of Death and made it sound a cheerless place, but I have
spend many a happy hour there, picking at human flesh in
various stages of corruption.

Parker, the attendant, greeted me at the door with: I'm sorry,
Mr Grice [he dried his filthy hands on his filthier laboratory
coat], but I'm not allowed to show you that one.

Parker was forty-two years old but a casual observer might
easily have added a quarter of a century to that figure. He was
prematurely aged by the astonishing array of diseases that he
had acquired from his charges. This was largely due to his stub-
born and ill-informed refusal to believe in any theories of
contagion. Today he was quite healthy – apart from a virulent
infestation with ringworm on his thinly thatched pate and a
chronic case of consumption or coffin cough as it is called in the
undertaking trade.

I: Who has forbidden it?
He: Inspector Quigley says you mustn't be allowed near her
in case you tamper with evidence.
[He scratched his flaking scalp.]

I: If you let me see Mrs Prendergast I shall reward you handsomely. [I brought out my wallet.] And I am referring to paper money. [Parker twitched at this news and came up on his toes as if intending to balance it on his nose.] You can rely on me not to betray you.

He: I'm sorry, Mr Grice, but it's more than my job's worth.

I: But your job is worth very little, Parker. I probably remunerate my cook more than you are paid.

[Parker tried to push out his chest indignantly, but his ribcage was concave and the effect was not impressive.]

He: My job is worth a great deal. I get stood drinks every night of my life on account of the stories I can tell and gentry who think I will give them a tour, which I do not, on my life.

[I watched his sores suppurate and had an uncomfortable suspicion that Miss Middleton might have done better at talking Parker round. She was never much good at charm but perhaps she would have threatened him.]

I: What if I tell the authorities you have shown me around, unless you do?

He: So if I don't... [It took Parker a little while to work it out.] Then you will... [He shook his head and a disconcerting variety of particles scattered on to my Ulster.] No, you wouldn't do that, Mr Grice. You're a gent.

[I knew there was no point in denying it and that was when I really missed my ward. Few people had any difficulty in believing that she would have behaved so disgracefully.]

I dusted down my coat, put my wallet away and asked: Have you seen the cadaver?

Parker dropped on to his heels and said sulkily: Seen, stripped and washed it. [He stopped. I clinked two coins together and he started again.] She'd been stabbed once in the chest.

I: I will not pay to be told what I already know.

[He grasped a little tuft of hair and pulled it quite easily away with the attached and discoloured skin.]

He: She had two corsets on.
I: And they are worth a shilling each.

I dropped the coins into his cupped palm, taking care not to touch him. Unlike Parker, I was all too aware of the animalcula lurking in his place of work. They are more dangerous than the French and almost as treacherous as the Spanish. He bit the coins. I have seen many people do that but never known anything to result from their investigations other than the occasional chipped tooth.

I: I presume the restriction of my examination of evidence also applies to the corpse of the reputedly delectable Miss Gloria Shell.
He: I'm sorry, Mr Grice. [Parker made a strenuous but only partially successful attempt to evacuate the phlegm from his bronchi into his hand and smeared the result on to his coat.] She ain't very delicatable now, though.
I: Explain. [Seeing him hesitate, I rattled my small change.] I have other coins which, if they were capable of emotion, would be just as happy joining their fellows in your pocket as they are in mine.
[I have always found the lower orders difficult to communicate with, but I have never known them not to realize when they are being bribed.]
He: [with professional pride] All smashed in she is.
I: What do you mean by all? Are her feet crushed? What about her elbows?
He: Her face. There is more bone outside than in.
I: What a terrible pity. [I sighed.] I should very much like to have seen that. What about the back of her head?
[Parker chewed that thought, tapping the top of his encrusted dome over his parietal bone.]
Then he said: One big dent on top.
I: Describe how you think she was attacked.

Parker struck a pose and began: She was standing with her back to the murderer. [He indicated with his slime-smeared hand towards the far wall.] He crept up behind her. [He re-enacted the movement in the exaggerated way that would-be actors do in melodramas, lifting his feet high and placing them in a manner more reminiscent of a cockerel than a man with homicidal intent.] He raised an iron bar and brought it crashing down on the back of her head. [Parker obliged with an unconvincing wheeling of his arm.] She fell lifeless to the ground [he arched his foot over the slabs] and he smashed [Parker swung his arm like a town crier] and smashed and smashed—

I: I get the gist.

Parker stopped, wild with the passion of his performance, and said breathlessly: Then he whacked her dog. [He ended with a tame flick of his wrist.]

I: Mrs Prendergast's dog? You are sure of that?

Parker leaned his shoulder against the wall and wheezed: Brought it with her, they did, but I told them a human mortuary ain't no place for a dead cur.

I: So what happened to it?

He cast his imaginary iron bar aside: They dumped it here. I took it out the front and threw it in the bin.

I: How often are those bins emptied?

Parker squinted and said: I don't know that they are ever emptied. Anything the rats, cats and brats don't want just rots down.

I tossed him a florin but he fumbled and it rolled along the floor. He was still scrabbling after it when I availed myself of the exit.

I poked about with my cane. The dog, a putrescent black-and-tan Cavalier King Charles spaniel, was near the top and still in quite good condition. I did not need it all and I did not have my swordstick with me, so I took out my spring knife and cut off the head, wrapping it in a canvas bag from my satchel.

86

Late Thursday Morning

NO DOUBT MISS Middleton would have depicted Mr Reginald 'Rosie' Rosewood as an eccentric character, but there was little odd about his collection of shadows. As he himself reasoned, we are all born with at least one. It was a little unusual to find that the window of his office was boarded over, but the room was lit brightly enough by the thirty-one oil lamps placed on little tables of varying heights all around me.

He: [with great satisfaction] This is what started me off. [He touched a battered lamp with a chewed Derwent pencil.] Imagine my chagrin when I knocked this lantern over and smashed the glass.

I: I dislike imagining other people's chagrin. It is always disappointing.

[Mr Rosewood had an elongated angular skeleton enveloped in a loose-fitting epidermis, as if he had borrowed a larger man's skin. He wore a long Prussian blue coat with brass buttons.]

He: Imagine then my joy when, upon fitting a new chimney, I found that the bent reflector cast a shadow on the wall which was the spitting image of... [He paused quizzically and I glanced at the faint umbra cast upon the wall behind the lamp.]

I filled the pause: A guillotine. Now if—

[Rosewood tittered and I do not care for men who titter. All senses of humour are silly but theirs is invariably the silliest.]

He: You are toying with me, Mr Grice. Be serious.

I: [neglecting to mention that I had already conceived a dislike for him] There [for his benefit I indicated with my patent surgical cane] is the blade and there the basket.

[Apparently my diagnosis was not acceptable to Rosewood.]

He tittered again and said: It is Jumbo, the elephant. See [he outlined the details with sweeps of his attenuated digits] – the trunk and three of the legs.

I: Having seen Jumbo on six occasions, I am qualified to inform you that he and a certain lady – who must, for the purposes of this meeting, remain anonymous – were the only things I could justifiably describe as magnificent creatures, and neither of them bore more than a fleeting resemblance to that implement of execution.

Rosewood grimaced: Take a look at this one then, a particular favourite with the ladies.

[The shadow cast by the flicker of a candle on the ceiling was indeed interesting, being a vivid depiction of a Scotsman self-immolating with a garden hoe.]

I: You have some sanguinary clients.

Rosewood gibbered: The Niagara falls.

I: [playfully] Balderdash. But it is a very good representation of that enterprising Hibernian William Burke, riding a donkey.

He: [snappily] It shows the death of Cleopatra.

To which I gently replied: Utter drivel.

Rosewood's manner became distinctly peevish and he asked sharply: What is your business, Mr Grice?

I said: I believe you are dealing with the estate of the late and exasperating Mrs Prendergast.

He: You have been informed correctly. [He prodded with his quill.] Can you not see the asp poised to strike at her breast?

I: Those are the donkey's reins.

Rosewood tutted: I know you are disadvantaged by having a glass eye but—

I responded lightly: In what nine ways does having a glass eye disadvantage me? Lacking an organic eye might be of hindrance to one with such stunted intelligence as yourself, but I can assure you it has not hampered me in the least. Indeed, it was only my ocular prosthesis and startlingly quick wits that saved me from a rampaging mob eight months and one week ago tomorrow. [And, as if taking this as its cue, my right eye jumped out of its socket. I caught it deftly, not pausing in my pleasant banter.] What is the exact value of Mrs Prendergast's estate?

Rosewood inhaled sharply in the way that some men do when they have trodden on broken teapot spouts and said: Why do you wish to know?

I told him graciously: That is not your concern.

He sat even taller, though his skin still hung loosely, and said: Mrs Prendergast was my client and her financial affairs are confidential.

I: Which is exactly why you will give me all her records.

He: It is exactly why I shall not.

I looked at the silhouette of a gibbet on the wall behind him and said: If you do not pass them to me I shall denounce you as a fraud and a forger.

Rosewood: [clucking indignantly] This is outrageous.

I: Not quite as outrageous as imitating the signature of your cousin Mr William 'Woody' Rosewood on his last will and testament, and inducing two members of his staff to put their names to the document in exchange for the use of a cottage in Glasgow.

He: [ninety-four per centum less jolly than he had been eight minutes ago] You cannot prove that.

I: I do not need to because I have a disreputable acquaintance who can produce a better forgery, dated after the one by which you inherited Woody's fortune, and leaving his entire estate to the aforementioned servants. This document might be discovered hidden in your vulgar abode in which case you would be penniless, disbarred and imprisoned.

He: [crossly] This is blackmail.

I: [omitting to mention that I would be ethically unable to sanction such deceits] It would also be breaking and entering, counterfeiting and fraud.

Rosewood snapped the quill which he, but not I, had forgotten he was holding and said: Very well.

[He swivelled in his poorly lubricated chair and wrenched open the top drawer of his filing cabinet. Whilst he was rifling through his files, I put my hands in front of a lamp and cast a rather fine dove on to the side of a bookcase.]

I chatted: My father's under-butler taught me to do that.

He: What? [Rosewood spun squeakily back and witnessed the splendidly flapping wings.] Any child could do that.

I reasoned: Not all children can. A child who lost her hands in an accident with a power loom in a Lancashire cotton mill would not be able to do so.

He: If you are hoping to get hold of Mrs Prendergast's money, you will be gravely disappointed. [Rosewood held up a cardboard file in a manner reminiscent of Moses with his decade of ethical instructions.] She died penniless and in debt.

I mused: I sometimes like being disappointed, but that is excellent news.

[Rosewood slapped a cardboard file on to his desk with such violence that the lamp fell and smashed on the floor, spilling its contents over an eight-guinea circular rug from Bruges.]

He: Damn. [The fuel ignited. If I had feelings they would have been aroused by a similar incident in Highgate with an oil lamp and the flames leaping upward. He flapped hopelessly.] Help me!

[He scattered the water from his lead crystal tumbler but only succeeded in producing a little steam.]

I stood: I shall certainly assist you with some sound advice. [I stepped back.] I strongly recommend that you make strenuous and urgent efforts to extinguish that inferno before it consumes your office and your obnoxious self.

[Rosewood began to stamp on the rug, the resultant draught dispersing the oil and flames with great efficiency.]

I added: Take off your splendid coat and drape it over the fire to starve the latter of oxygen.

He: This coat cost me twenty guineas.

I: And worth every shilling, I venture. The needlework is excellent.

He: What? [And proceeded reluctantly to follow my instruction, with the result that the flames were soon annihilated.] It is ruined. [He lifted the charred remains of his attire.]

I: Indeed.

[I lingered momentarily to draw his attention to an umbral likeness of Springheel Jack.]

He: [shouting in a thoroughly unprofessional manner, which certainly would not entice me to use his services again] It is a joint of gammon.

I departed for my appointment with Messrs Griffin and Sniff to make similar enquiries about the late Mr Ptolemy Hercules Arbuthnot Travers Smyth, and on the way I posted a letter to Saturn House.

87

Thursday Afternoon, 25 January 1883

HAVING BEEN THWARTED in my attempts to view Mrs Prendergast's cadaver or the remnants of her servant, but buoyed by my discovery and decapitation of the pampered Albert and my successful solicitorial conclaves, I went home and, ignoring Molly's enquiry as to whether the dog had bitten me, deposited the head in a sealable glass jar.

Pausing only to feed the mouse and drink a pot of tea, I went up to wash and change for what Miss Middleton so coarsely calls lunch, after which I settled down with a fresh pot and a copy of the *Coroners' Monthly Illustrated Journal.*

Colwyn arrived three minutes early. He chuckled, having been announced by Molly as A man called Colin what can't not pronunciate his own name.

He: Your letter was lucky to find me in, Mr Grice. I am in the unhappy process of closing down Saturn Villa.
[He was a tall, slim man – twenty-three and four or five months (I calculated), with a full head of peculiar black hair.]
I: What is your full name?
He: Colwyn Harold Blanchflower.
I: Do you have any employment?
[I took his hand. The way a man returns a handshake can tell me twenty-four things about him. His grip was firm and dry and his gaze direct, but he had the sense to avert

it. A servant who holds your gaze for too long is trying to
be defiant.]

He: Not yet, sir. I am disadvantaged by Mr Travers Smyth
and my previous employer, Mr Fox, being unable to provide
me with a written character.

[I sent Molly to fetch tea and, at my invitation, the valet
took Miss Middleton's chair.]

I: What happened to Mr Fox?

He: He was killed by a chicken. [Colwyn rubbed the back of
his neck.] Most people find that amusing but it was a tragic
accident. It ran out and startled his horse which threw him.
He was a good man, as was Mr Travers Smyth.

I extracted my saffron notebook and asked: What took you
to Gorizia-Tyrol?

Colwyn blushed and said: Foolishness. I was young and
yearning for adventure. I joined a group of mercenaries
– the Iron Brigade, we called ourselves, but we were the wet-
behind-the-ears brigade really. We were led by a man calling
himself Captain Hazzard, a veteran of the American Civil
War, but he turned out to be Jim McAdam, a shoemaker
from Canada, who had done three months in the army and
deserted. We were going to offer our services to the king of
the Russias. Lord only knows why we thought he would
need us. By the time we got to Austria we had been robbed
so many times we were lucky to have the clothes we stood
in. Three of us got cholera and McAdam disappeared with
what little money we had left. Baron Adler-Haussmann
found me destitute and took pity on me. I think he thought
I would fit one of his household uniforms.

I extruded one eighth of an inch of the lead of my Mordan
mechanical pencil and asked: Did you speak the language
already?

He: [ruefully] Not a word, sir, but luckily the baron was
fluent in English and liked to practise it on me, and I soon
picked up the language from the other servants.

Molly brought the tea and he winked at her, saying: I'm not used to being waited on by lovely young damsels.

Molly giggled: Get away. I know I'm young and lovely but I ain't not no more a damson than you're an apple.

I: Save your vulgar banter for the servants' hall. [Molly hovered.] Go away.

[Molly left with lingering looks at our guest.]

He: After two months with the baron—

I saved him the trouble of continuing his account by remarking kindly: I am bored with that story. Where were you born?

He: In South Shore near Blackpool.

I: Indeed?

[I wrote S Shore down, followed by a symbol of my own devising meaning indeed?]

He: I have had a lot of time to think. [I had not broached the subject of how he whiled away the hours but he continued.] And I am sorry for what I said about Miss Middleton. I was upset and I do not think I was fair to her.

I was unaware that it was the place of a valet to be fair or otherwise to his betters, but I decided to exercise my usual tact and responded: Why do you say that?

Colwyn folded his hands in his lap and replied: When I heard my master cry out and heard the shot—

I interjected patiently: I know why you were unfair, but I wish to know why you have decided that you were. Kindly answer the question.

He: I have been thinking.

I: [not quite so patiently] You have already made that claim but you have yet to substantiate it.

[Colwyn reverted to rubbing his neck. People do that for one of eight reasons and I do not think the first – cervical discomfort – applied, for his upper spine seemed flexible enough.]

He said: Mr Travers Smyth was not a happy man. He was

always anxious and getting himself upset about imaginary problems. He worried for weeks once that the neighbours might say the electricity was keeping them awake, though nobody had ever complained. He was in a terrible state about Miss Middleton's visits. What if she wanted nothing to do with him? What if she hated him? Having his house searched was a dreadful shock. I don't think he slept after that. He paced the house night and day mithering about whether he would be sent to prison. I was wondering if it is possible that he got himself worked up so much that it was all too much for him. He had such a nervous personality that—

I pounced: Say that again.

He left his neck alone, contracted his nostrils and asked: Which bit, sir?

I: From the second much.

I watched him search his mind before he said: I think I said—

I: Never mind what you think you said. Tell me again what you said.

He: I'll try.

[He interlocked his fingers.]

I: Just do it.

[Colwyn cracked his knuckles, and I mentally flicked through the nine principal reasons people do that and leaned back to pull the bell.]

He: Too much for him. He had a nervous personality.

I: Once more, though you can omit the first four words.

His eyes flicked away: He had a nervous personality.

I clapped my hands and said: Excellent.

The valet tensed his lips and said: Shall I pour, sir?

I replied: You shall go.

He rose and hovered mid-air and said: Now, sir?

I: Indeed. Let me know where you are living.

Colwyn flashed defiance and said: I have been ordered to

tell Inspector Quigley, but I am not obliged to keep you informed.

I felt the teapot with the tip of the fourth finger of my left hand and said: Yes, but he does not care about you as I do.

[Molly came in. Her bootlaces were untied.]

I: Show our visitor out, Molly.

She: Yes, sir.

Molly bobbed in her best effort yet, apart from the one she had spoiled by falling backwards down the stairs.

88

Friday Morning, 26 January 1883

ANNIE, THE MAID, was a great deal more difficult to find. She had left Saturn Villa the day after her employer had died and she had not supplied a forwarding address. It was Inspector Pound, when I went to appraise him of my astonishing progress and chivvy him into getting out of bed, who made the suggestion to try Saint Zita's.

I: Who, what and where is Saint Zita?
[I put on my pince-nez to inspect the foot of the middle-aged confectioner in the adjacent bed. It was black and hanging over the side, dripping wet gangrene.]
Pound: I think she is the patron saint of servants. They run a charitable house in Highgate for domestics who have lost their jobs.
I: A great incentive to idle their lives away.
[Pound had his hand over the Bible he had been reading.]
He said: I believe they have to earn their keep doing laundry for the nuns, but I don't know much about it.
I: There is little to be gained by not knowing much. [I grasped his wrist and flipped open my hunter.] Your heart is contracting at an average rate of four thousand, nine hundred and twenty beats per hour, which is seven hundred and twenty more than I would have wished. Do something about it.

He shifted about and said: I cannot control my pulse.

[I took off my pince-nez and polished the lenses, and wondered why Miss Middleton had never suggested I used a monocle instead.]

I: No, I do not suppose you can. I shall send somebody to enquire at Saint Zita's.

[We chattered amiably for four minutes about an old case of his involving a rusty button.]

He: If it wasn't for the crossing sweeper's sharp eye we would never have caught them.

I: Indeed. [I yawned, then, in case he had misinterpreted my action, hastened to explain.] I was not yawning because I am tired. It is just that I find your anecdote tedious.

Pound seemed cross about something but I had no time to worry about that and hurried away, pausing to reassure a plumber with nine broken bones that, whilst his medication was doing him more harm than good, it was unlikely to kill him if he ceased taking it immediately.

*

I was so busy and matters were becoming so urgent that I decided to forgo my pot of tea at the cleverly named Copper Kettle Cafe and have one at home instead.

Molly skipped about excitedly: There's a special letter come.

I: The last letter you thought was special was an advertisement for a company offering to unblock my drains.

She: But this has a squashed red lump on it.

I groaned. If this was from King Ludwig II of Bavaria, wishing to abdicate in my favour, I had refused three times already.

I ordered tea and went into my study. There was a superficially nondescript communication from Messrs Griffin and Sniff, the financial investigators, with information regarding the estate of Ptolemy Travers Smyth. He had died in debt to an astonishing thirty-eight thousand pounds estimate with creditors still staking claims. That was more money than my mother had lost in a game of Baccarat punto banco against the Bishop of York.

The other letter was indeed special. It came from the Chancery division of the High Court and was addressed to Miss Middleton, and I was so angry that I marched out of the house without my tea, my flask or my satchel. I did not even wait for a hansom. I ignored the two street urchins shouting miserable old gizzard and walked.

89

T HE NEW IMPERIAL hotel was neither new nor evocative of empire. Major Gregory, I was informed by an oleaginous youth in the dreary lobby, was dining and could not be disturbed.

I: Do not attempt to deceive me, odiferous flunkey. Your resident may indeed be endeavouring to ingest this establishment's unwholesome fare but it is perfectly possible to disturb him, as I am about to demonstrate.
A burly lackey disguised as the head waiter was partially blocking the entrance: Can I help you, sir?
I: You can inhale so that I may pass.
[But the impudent fellow merely stepped nine inches to his left, rendering ingress even more difficult. I had my swordstick with me and considered running him through.]
But instead I said: I have a ten shilling note. Do you think you could take care of it for me?
[The brute's expression softened but his breath did not.]
He: Certainly, sir, but I may have to step to one side to do it properly.

He took the money from me with an alacrity which would have done credit to a judge and moved out of my way. The dining room was large, lofty, cold and almost uninhabited. Apart from two bored and misshapen waitresses, there was a camphorated lady so smothered in furs that she looked like she was being savaged by a skulk of foxes; and a gentleman in the corner, his fork poised over what he had been sold as veal but that had only recently seen the outside of a horse. I did not have to exhaust my deductive powers to calculate that this was the man I sought.

He: [without rising] Mr Grice, I presume.

I addressed him civilly: That is not the first presumption you have made, Major Bernard Samuel Vantage Gregory, but I grasp at the hope that it will be the last.

[He put down his knife but the fork still hovered.]

He: I told them to keep you away from me.

I retruded my eye and said: There is not a hotel employee in the British Empire, Europe or the allegedly United States of America who cannot be bribed for ten shillings.

Gregory: [prodding his meat aggrievedly] But I gave him a pound.

[He was the remnant of a man, shrunken by age and caved in by disease. His complexion was sallow and his eyes rheumy, with the lower lids wilting into dark purple bags.]

I: [sympathetically] Enough of your brainless chitterchat. [I pulled out the chair opposite his.] Why are you trying to abduct my ward?

He picked up his knife and sawed along the grain of his steak and said: If truth be told, March is not your ward. No court has ever made you her guardian.

[His moustaches were grey with yellowed ends from indulging in Puerto Rican cigars.]

I: She is my godchild.

He hacked a trapezium of flesh away and said: Then by all means feel free to give her spiritual guidance.

[I sat. Most men think being taller gives them an advantage. It only gives them neck ache and it is important to view people from different angles.]

I: She is under my protection.

Gregory's pupils constricted: What protection? [He impaled his meat on the tines.] The protection which led to her witnessing murders and being accused of them? The protection that has sent her half-insane into a prison full of violent criminals and placed her in peril of execution?

[I had to admire his rhetorical technique but not the way he transferred a chunk of equine muscle into his mouth. I resisted an urge to force the rest of it down his windpipe as I had choked the Prussian Colonel with my eye at Charlottenburg.]

I: I will fight you over this. I made a promise to Miss Middleton's father.

He covered his mouth with his napkin before saying: And I have a letter from him asking me to care for her if he should die or be incapacitated.

I: [arranging nine crumbs into a square on the tablecloth] I should be interested to scrutinize that missive.

He chewed another sixteen times and swallowed before telling me: The court has it.

I: [converting the square into an oblong with six more crumbs] Why did you not come forward when Miss Middleton's father died?

Gregory's head dropped: I was too ill.

I: I should not think it will be long before you are as dead as that meat.

[His head rose. There are some emotions I have never seen convincingly imitated and this was one of them. People always overplay it but Gregory was perfect – dignified suffering.]

He: At least you do not offer false sympathy.

[The backs of his hands were covered in bruises.]

I: I have only ever said one insincere thing and it haunts me to this day. What is your real interest in Miss Middleton?

Gregory tossed his napkin on to the table and said: I trust you are not implying any improper intent.

I: You should trust something more substantial, but it is fascinating that you propel yourself so rapidly to that inference. I was thinking more of the financial aspect.

[Gregory drank some '79 claret which tinted the margins of his moustaches.]

He: You know as well as I that when Colonel Middleton died his estate was in ruins.

I: [breaking a large crumb into three] I am also aware that her affairs picked up dramatically soon after she joined me. [I tidied the condiments.] My goddaughter has become a woman of some means.

[I watched carefully to see how he took the news but he did not react – not a twitch, tic or blink – and his hand, as he put the glass down, was as steady as Wellington's squares at Waterloo.]

He: Then I shall have papers drawn up to ensure that the money stays in trust for her. [He picked up his cutlery again, often a diversionary tactic, occasionally as weapons.] I have known March since she was a baby and—

I: How would you describe my personality?

Gregory looked at me blankly: What? You are worried about your personality? Arrogant will do for a start. Offensive, insensitive—

I: Excellent. [I stood up.] Please do not fancy that I am storming off in a sulk. I have many things to do and you are a dull man who does not even know when he is devouring the gluteus muscle of an aged mare.

The impression I gained was of a strong (though ailing) man, intelligent and with his own code of honour. But I learned the day before my fourth birthday never to trust one's impressions. Instinct is for the beasts of the jungles and, if it were any use, they would not be beasts; nor living somewhere so inconvenient.

90

Friday Afternoon, 26 January 1883

A MESSAGE CAME back from Saint Zita's Refuge for Domestic Servants in Penury. They had no knowledge of the whereabouts of Travers Smyth's maid but would welcome a charitable contribution. Unfortunately for them, I could not think of anybody likely to send them one.

More often than not I write messages for Molly in pencil. The writing will not run when she drops it in a puddle and she has a great gift for discovering those.

I: You are to go to these domestic employment agencies.
[Had I shot Molly, as I have twice been tempted to, she could not have reacted more violently.]
She half-spun, gasped and grasped the edge of my desk, crying plaintively: Oh, sir, please don't throw me out. Is it 'cause of me stealing that apple core what you threw away? Is it 'cause I gave the grocer's boy a glass of milk when he fell into a swooned on the floor? It was on the turn already and it made him sick. Is it 'cause I said to Cook you were a miserable old stoat when you shouted at me for spilling soup over your head? Is it because of me saying ain't? 'Cause I ain't not said ain't for hours. Is it 'cause I lost that important telegraph you told me to send to the king of Pryprus and spent the money on forty sugar mouses and didn't not never tell you?

I: [as she drew breath] No, though they are all excellent reasons.

[Molly threw out her arms and fell to her knees by my chair in the way she had seen the farmer's daughter entreat wicked Sir Jasper in a street entertainment.]

She did her best imitation of such entreatment: Oh, sir, give me another chance. You're like a mother to me. [She clasped her hands in a parody of supplication.] Nobody else would employ me. I know 'cause I've soughted other jobs.

I: It was unwise of you to make that last admission, though I was already aware that you had written to the Queen, asking to be her prursonable maid. I am not dismissing you, Molly.

[Molly looked as deflated as I have seen men do when they are reprieved. The human brain – my own and six others excepted – is a clumsy mechanism. Once it prepares itself for anything, even the worst, it does not like to be disprepared, to coin a word.]

I: But while you are down there, pick up that cinder. I do not require it any longer.

She popped it into her apron pocket and said: Oh thank you, sir. [She hauled herself up laboriously.] You're a dead saint.

I held out the sheet and said: I have written the addresses of eight domestic employment agencies on the front of this paper. Do not interrupt. And on the back is the question I want you to ask them. Read it to me.

She: [with many strenuous facial contortions] Do you have or have you reckently had a young woman by the name of Annie [she batted her bovine eyes] Grookspank.

I: Crookshank.

She: Oh, but Miss Middleton has been helping me with my reading and that first letter is a Guh.

I: It is a C, which you might know as a Cuh.

She: But it has a sticky-up bit.

I: That is just where I joined the letters.

Molly nodded wisely: Oh. It's always the joindering up that makes me confused.

I: Give it back. [I printed the name.] Try again.

She: [hesitantly] Crook-shank.

I made her repeat it four times and said: When you are asking, show them the name as well. It is very important to get it right. [I gave her a red cloth bag with a drawstring.] There are two pounds in here for you—

Molly interlocked her fingers and shrieked: Lord bless you, sir. I ain't not never had that much money in my life 'cept when I picked up that old lady's purse in Regan's Park, but then I felt bad and had to give it back with a muffin to say sorry.

I: For you to carry out your task. One pound is for a cab to take you from office to office. [I realigned my ruler.] You are to tell it to wait at each stop. The other pound is as a reward for the agent who can find Miss Crookshank. How much did I pay you last week, Molly?

Molly shifted her jaw laterally in a way that might have been the envy of an ungulate: Why, not nothing after I broke those plates.

I blew on my fingerplates and said: If you manage to find Annie Crookshank, I shall double that for the rest of your life.

[It was just as well that Miss Middleton had not started our maid on arithmetic lessons, I pondered, as Molly skipped thunderously away.]

*

The doorbell rang eight minutes later and I was obliged to answer its summons myself. It was a parcel by Special Delivery from abroad and I did not have to open it to know that it contained the case notes I had requested, and a photograph.

*

I discovered Inspector Pound propped up in bed.

He: Any news of Miss Middleton?
I dusted the chair and told him: Mr Swift, the nerve special-
ist, and Dr Villeroy, of the Royal Pharmaceutical Society,
have both been to see her and neither hold out any hope of
a cure or spontaneous recovery.
Pound inflated and deflated his cheeks and asked: Is there
nothing we can do?
I: I have petitioned Vernon Harcourt, the Home Secretary,
to have her declared mentally incompetent.
Pound's knuckles blanched: It that necessary?
I sat down: If I succeed she will be unfit to stand trial, which
at least removes the risk of a quick conviction and execution.
He: But she will be put in Broadmoor with all those dangerous lunatics.
[I discovered a piece of lint on my right trouser leg just
above the knee and speculated where it might have come
from.]
Eventually I said: I have long since come to the conclusion
that the mad are no more treacherous than the supposedly
sane, and conditions there are more humane than in any
prison I have visited or in which I have been incarcerated.
Pound squinted and said: You have been imprisoned.
I: I know. [There was an annoying asymmetry in the folds
of his blanket, but I resisted the urge to tidy his bed and
returned to my theme.] Also, the food is better than the filth
they make you eat here.
He: I would kill for a lamb chop.
I: The slaughterer has already done so.
[Two porters brought a man in on a stretcher and deposited
him on a bed. He was dead before his head hit the pillow
but they did not notice.]
Pound started fiddling with his moustaches yet again and

said: Is that all Miss Middleton has to look forward to, imprisonment in Broadmoor?

I: Of course not. [I shifted in my chair, which was rocking, with a left front leg three eighths of an inch shorter than its fellows.] I shall then have her installed in a private asylum where I may visit her when I have nothing better to do.

I watched a nurse tucking the dead man up in bed and telling him: We'll soon have you as right as rain.

[She tried to take his pulse but lost interest.]

I: Prendergast's assets are less than her debts.

He: That might be a motive for suicide.

[It struck me that he had one thing in common with my goddaughter – a capacity for stating the self-evident as if it were a thought.]

But I did not wish to annoy him so I said: If only I had your forensic experience. [He inhaled sharply.] Are you in pain?

He: Not much.

I: Then you should be up and about.

A woman in a green woollen coat arrived, bringing slices of boiled ham in a brown paper bag and a jug of beer, and the nurse showed her to the dead man.

Green-coated woman: I won't disturb you, Daddy.

Nurse: [somewhat irrelevantly] Sleep is a great healer.

I brought out a folded letter.

I: Sign this.

Pound: What is it?

I: A letter. If you wish to know what I have written upon it, I suggest you exercise your literacy skills.

The inspector read the letter carefully and said: I am not sure I can do that.

I: Do not worry. I have brought a Grice Self-Filling Flexible-Nibbed Patent-Pending Pen with me.

We then had a discussion about the laws of evidence and I reminded him that he had not been overly concerned about them in the Samuel Wesley case, attempting but failing to persuade me to say that I had found a handkerchief in the stables, so we'd had to let the man walk free, though we knew he had broken his own mother's neck.

He: Very well.

I flicked the pen to get the ink flowing and twenty-eight drops were dispersed on to the blanket, and we had a less interesting discussion about how Matron and her minions would be upset and whether I cared (the answers being positive then negative), whilst Pound appended his signature to the document.

I know that men find farewells embarrassing and so I whipped the document away, blotted it on his sheet and walked off without a word, secure in the knowledge that he would appreciate my unspoken gratitude and good wishes.

I passed the young woman.
I: You might as well give your sustenance to that patient at the end. Your father has been dead for nine minutes.

She stared at me but I am used to being stared at. It is part of the price one pays for being a man of great renown, but I ignored her. She would have been too stupid to have noticed the clink of my crowbar inside the secret pocket of my Ulster as it knocked into the bedstead.

91

Friday Late Afternoon

I HAD KNOWN Arbuckle since he was a young constable and had lifted me on his shoulders to witness a suspect resisting arrest, though quite how an unconscious woman could do so was beyond me. Arbuckle was still a constable, but time had taken most of the hair from his pate and sown it into his ears and nostrils.

He paused in his labelling of a flesh-encrusted hacksaw and greeted me amiably.

> I responded with a cheery: I have a signed authorization here.
> [I allowed him to peruse it.]
> He: That will be under P for Prendergast.
> I: Your spelling has improved.

This was intended to encourage the man but his muttered expletive indicated that my words had had the opposite effect, and I resolved to waste less of my time being kind to him in future.

Arbuckle lifted one tea chest from on top of another, and dragged the lower away from the whitewashed basement wall.

> He mumbled: Now where is...? Ah! Here we are.

He brandished a black parcel identical to the one Pound had brought to my happy home. I unwrapped the cloth and placed it on his desk, having swept half a partly devoured beef and mustard sandwich on to the floor first.

Arbuckle: 'Ere be careful. That's my breakfast.

I did not trouble to tell him that I had cleared the space with great care, but brought out my Grice Housebreaking Cane, for which I had unaccountably been denied a patent. The constable watched with interest as I unscrewed the top and tipped a tiny chisel into my hand.

He: What you up to?

I was too busy wondering where the verb had gone from that sentence to respond to it and then I was too busy running the highly honed edge of my chisel round the base of the blade.

He: 'Ere you can't do that.
I: I am often puzzled as to why people tell me I cannot do what I am in the process of doing, but I have yet to formulate a completely satisfactory explanation.
[The metal, as I anticipated, was soft and chipped easily away.]
He: It don't say nothing about you being allowed to damage it.
I: Inspector Pound would hardly be likely to sanction my tampering with evidence, would he, Constable?
[I put the first finger of my left hand to the tip of the dagger.]
He: No. [He scratched behind his right ear.] But that's what you're doing.
I: Exactly.
He: Yes but—
I: Anyway, I have finished.

I revolved one hundred and forty degrees anti-clockwise, flexed my right elbow and drove the dagger as hard as I could into the constable's abdomen, right up to the hilt.

92

A Moment Later

CONSTABLE ARBUCKLE GRUNTED. His blue coat indented under the pressure of my blow, as did his extensive waistline.

He swore and folded towards me.

I: I am glad Miss Middleton is not here to witness such language.

Arbuckle clutched himself around the dagger and gasped: Lord, Mr Grice, what d'you do that for?

[He took three short sharp breaths.]

I: To save my goddaughter's life.

[Arbuckle expelled those breaths in one exhalation and staggered two steps to his left. I pulled the dagger away and held it up for him to see.]

He: Oh God, the blade has snapped off inside me.

I: I completely understand why you made that remark but let me counter it with a simple question. How much blood do you think is inside you?

[Arbuckle rearranged his features unattractively and clutched himself tighter.]

He: I don't know. About five gallons.

[He tottered forwards, gasping, and put out one hand to steady himself against a box marked in red ink EMPTY.]

I: It is unlikely to be much more than twenty per cent of

that. And how much of it has exited your adipose body in the last three minutes?

Arbuckle patted himself and said eloquently: Oh. He considered the incident and asked: So where is the blade then?

By way of reply I shook the handle down and the knife telescoped to its full length. Arbuckle let go of himself and straightened up warily as if still expecting his intestines to become what Molly once described, on coming across a squashed common newt, as out-testines.

He: So it is a trick knife.

I: You catch on quickly.

[He grimaced at this compliment. I raised the dagger to shoulder height and brought it down into the desk where it made a gouge in the woodwork.]

He: But it didn't go in that time.

I: This raised nodule is a button which, if depressed by one's thumb, releases an internal catch. [I slid the blade inside with the palm of my hand.] The tip is rounded to avoid accidentally puncturing oneself, but the sides are well honed. We have all seen them used in stage acts where the showman will slice something, often an apple, to demonstrate the knife's sharpness.

[I chopped a corner from the other half of his sandwich to illustrate the point.]

But instead of thanking me Arbuckle merely said: Oy.

[That made him sound Jewish, though I knew him to be a Calvinist Catholic. I put the knife down.]

I: When you presented me with the weapon, however, the blade had been soldered.

He: Blimey.

[He picked the dagger up and fiddled, successfully retracting and extracting the blade.]

I: Do not attempt that trick on me. The mechanism is faulty and could easily stick.

Arbuckle gazed at me, doubtless thinking what I fine fellow I was.

———•◆•———

93

Saturday Morning, 27 January 1883

INSPECTOR POUND CAME to see me. I did not trouble to ask how he was. My first eleven casual observations (i.e. unsteady gait, stooped posture, pallor, shallow respiration, weakness of handshake, warmth of epidermis, tremor of limbs, dark patches under eyes, involuntary contractions of the orbicularis oris muscle, enfeebled voice and general lack of vigour) led me to suspect that he was not as healthy as I had instructed him to be, and my next twelve elicitations confirmed that impression.

He: I discharged myself. [Then, upon entering my study] What on earth is that?
I: It is the head of a Cavalier King Charles spaniel. I am surprised you could not work that out.
He: Mrs Prendergast's dog?
[He picked up the jar off the onyx pedestal on which I had given it pride of place.]
I: Albert.
[Molly entered with a tray and deposited it with elaborate care on the table, but still managed to tip some of the tea into the sugar bowl.]
And, though I had not invited her to join our conversation, she asked: Can Miss Middleton have visitorers, sir?
I: No. [I then addressed Pound.] Take a look at its chin.
She: Oh, because I had an idea. [And oblivious to my lack

of encouragement proceeded to explain.] We could swap clothes and she could walk out, and then I could say she had drugged me with an odium pipe like the red-hooded highwayman in The Shade of Merry Murray.

[Pound chuckled.]

I: Go away, you hare-brained sluggard and do not tell me that hares are clever.

[Molly chewed an untied apron string as something resembling a thought churned laboriously around her cerebral swamp.]

It finally surfaced as: Miss Middleton always says her hair is stupid, so some hair must be clever.

Pound laughed: There is a certain logic in that.

I: Do not encourage her.

Molly: And slag-ruds. I bet they are pretty.

I: Get out.

Molly left us with a parting mutter: Most people buy their dogs all in one piece.

Pound rotated the jar: There is some sort of dye on its chin.

[I went to the window.]

I: Though it hardly seems decent to do so, we shall inspect Miss Middleton's discarded apparel.

[I removed the sheet to reveal my godchild's dress still hanging on the borrowed mannequin, and Pound whistled softly.]

He: That's a lot of blood. [He walked round it.] But not much on the back, except for the sleeves.

I: Which would be consistent with Miss Middleton's account that she had her arms up, trying to push Mrs Prendergast away.

He: Presumably the lower stains are from kneeling beside the body.

[Pound examined the hem and I handed him my third-best magnifying glass.]

I: Have a look at the fabric there… no, there, for goodness' sake, between those clots. What do you see?

He: [after some huffing] The stain is much brighter than the blood. [He wiped the lens on his coat.] It is very like the dye on that dog's chin.

[I took my glass back, making a note to soak it in Lugol's iodine solution before I used it again, and told him about the dagger.]

He: You said the other day that Mrs Prendergast wore two corsets. Why would she do that? [He clicked his fingers annoyingly.] To protect her from the blade.

I: One corset would do that. The tip of the dagger was rounded.

More digital snapping ensued before he said: What if she had a bag between the two garments, something water-proof like oilskin, and filled it with red dye so that when she pretended to stab herself it burst to look like bleeding?

I: Which is exactly why I want you to trot down to the morgue and check her clothing.

He: [with feigned indignation] I don't go trotting anywhere.

Me: Then this is your chance to remedy that situation.

He eyed the tray: Any chance of a quick cup?

I: For heaven's sake, man, Miss Middleton's life and liberty are at stake.

He: [reluctantly] Very well, I'll go straight there.

I rang for Molly to show him out and settled back to pour myself a tea.

—◦•◦•◦—

94

Saturday Noon

POUND REAPPEARED ONE hour and forty-two minutes after setting out.

He: We were right about the bag but I couldn't bring it. The superintendent is taking a close interest in this case and he doesn't want any allegations of tampering. [He eyed my tray.] I don't suppose there's any tea left in that pot?
I: None at all.
[I tapped the drained pot with a spoon to lend weight to my statement.]
He: Only I haven't had anything to eat or drink since a very early breakfast.
[He licked his lips and waited.]
I: [wondering why we were discussing our diets] I only ate a light luncheon, as is my habit.
Pound fidgeted: I don't suppose Molly...
I: That poor girl is put upon enough as it is by my excessive demands without pandering to your every whim. [I went to my desk upon which my package had arrived from Bohemia that morning.] Besides Molly is out on an errand.

Pound peered over as I opened the box to reveal six new eyes sitting in a cotton-wool nest. They had been made under the supervision of Professor Goldman by the finest glassblowers of Egeria.

He: They're a bit gruesome staring up at us like that. Why are they all different colours?

[The front door opened.]

I: It is a trick of the light. [I shut the box quickly to protect them from dust.] It appears that Molly has failed in her task.

Pound's moustaches vacillated as he tried not to but eventually he had to enquire: How can you tell?

I: When Molly is triumphant she skips like a spring buffalo. When she is dispirited she scrapes her feet like a deep-sea diver on dry land.

[Molly dragged herself into the room, head drooping and arms dangling uselessly.]

She: I'm ever so sorry, sir, but none of those people ain't not heard nothing about her and that's the third list what I've been through.

I: This is excellent news and to show that I am not angry I would like you to have a good long rest [her eyes became fractionally less dull as I spoke], as soon as you have finished your chores.

She: Oh but, sir [her arms revived], that will never be.

I: [sympathetically] Then you had better get to it.

[Molly did not even attempt a curtsy as she trudged off. Pound took up the cage.]

He: You are very hard on that girl.

Me: It is her job to please me and not vice versa.

[He gave the cage a little shake.]

He: This mouse looks dead.

I: It is what it appears to be.

He: But why are you keeping it?

I: To show you.

He: Why should I be interested in a dead house mouse?

[He put the cage down completely out of alignment.]

I: It is not the fact of its demise that interests me so much as the manner of its death.

He: How so?

I realigned the cage and said: Use your limited detective skills.

[Pound grumbled to himself about something. He took up the cage again and peered between the bars. The creature lay supine but fell on to the roof prone when he inverted the cage.]

He: Rigor mortis has certainly set in. [He selected my second-best magnifying glass without permission.] The limbs are bent at very odd angles and... good Lord, the paws and eyes are bright green.

I: Let us go for a ride, Inspector.

I rang for my flask, gained access to the hall and ran up the flag.

95

Saturday Afternoon

SEVEN STREET URCHINS were cavorting round our hansom as we climbed aboard. They knew better than to beg for coins from me and amused themselves by lustily rendering a song that attempted to utilize rhymes of my patronym with 'Twice' and 'Nice'.

Pound smirked stupidly: Lively little fellows, aren't they?
[I refrained from commenting about the poor scansion of a stanza accusing me of having a heart of ice and a head crawling with lice.]
I: But not lively enough to work for their livings.
He: There isn't much work around for them.
[As we pulled away I mused on how I seemed to have a knack of accumulating social reformers.]
I suggested mildly: Then they should be rounded up and shipped to the colonies.
He: Miss Middleton hasn't made much progress with melting that heart of ice.
[He seemed to find his own remark amusing, which it was not.]
I: I fed that mouse with twelve crumbs that I had discovered in the pocket of Miss Middleton's cloak.
Pound: What sort of crumbs?
I: Cake crumbs.

He: Do you know where they came from?

I: Yes.

He: Are you going to tell me?

I: Yes.

He: Where then?

[He seemed a little tetchy. Perhaps his wound was troubling him for he had made a great fuss settling into the cab and was taking up more than his share of the seat, doubtless under the misapprehension that his greater bulk entitled him to do so.]

I: From Mrs Prendergast's house.

He: How do you know? Did Miss Middleton tell you?

[I extracted my Grice Heat Retentive Bottle from my full-grain leather satchel.]

I: I shall answer those two questions in reverse order. No. And because my visit to Mrs Prendergast's house revealed the cake from which those crumbs almost certainly came. The confection was stained the same rustic hue as the crumbs.

[Pound sat a fraction more stiffly whilst I was granting him that information.]

He: Hold on a minute.

I: You wish me to bring our transport to a halt?

He: No. I would like to know when you were in Mrs Prendergast's house.

I: [unclipping the tinplated steel cup from my flask] Thank you for your concern. I was in her residence from one thirty-three on Thursday night, for one hour and forty-six minutes.

He: And who let you in?

I: Why, I let myself in and, in order to abbreviate this conversation, I shall donate the following pertinent information. I gained access through the rear pantry window by committing criminal damage to it with a small crowbar known in some circles, many undesirable, as a jemmy.

[Pound appeared unaccountably surprised at this information, though he must have known that you cannot open a window with a lock pick and that smashing it would have been too noisy.]

He: I did not hear that.

I: [slowly and loudly] I gained access through the rear pantry window with a crowbar.

[Pound flopped his hands about as if there were an angry wasp in the cab.]

Driver: Next time you lock yourself out get my bruvva, Dave from the White 'Orse. 'E'll have your door open in a jiffy.

I: The last time David P. Kirk tried to access my house in a jiffy he got six months at Her Majesty's pleasure in Pentonville. Also, you may join in our intercourse when I may climb up and drive this grubby vehicle.

The driver closed his hatch with more force than was necessary to overcome the frictional forces opposing its movements.

Pound decreased the volume of his voice: I shan't insult you by reminding you what I do for a living, Mr Grice, but you must be aware that you are confessing to a crime.

I: I was searching for evidence and you were not so particular about how it was collected when we investigated the Norwood plumber.

[Pound puffed and was silent for the next two streets.]

He: But I thought Miss Middleton was poisoned by the cacti.

I: Miss Middleton was also of that opinion. I considered the theory but found myself incapable of subscribing to it.

[A blackbird trilled malignantly beyond my line of vision.]

He: So the drug was in the cake?

I: Most likely. [I reflected upon the unequal sizes of our steed's ears.] One day I shall invest in another mus musculus and feed it particles from Mrs Prendergast's toothsome gift. Without prejudging the outcome, I am fairly confident that the creature will also exhibit eccentric behaviour before having a convulsive seizure and expiring.

He: Crikey.

I ignored the coarseness of his expression and concerned myself with a fresh assault upon my olfactory organs.

96

———◆◆◆◆———

Later Saturday Afternoon

THERE IS NO better way of experiencing London than from the comfort of a hansom cab. One is raised above the unwashed herd yet not removed from it, as one is in a sealed carriage. One might still enjoy all the sounds and smells of the city and there is no shortage whatsoever of the latter. Today they were particularly malodorous as a large lorry trundled in front of us, opaque brown fluid trickling under its tailgate. Pound sprinkled camphor oil from the little blue bottle he always carried into his handkerchief.

I: I read about this. Apparently a load of horses was sent to the knackers, but the company ceased trading that night and the load sat in the yard forgotten about for five months until this morning.

He: And we had to get stuck behind it.

I: I was not aware that we were under any compulsion to do so.

[Pound crushed his handkerchief over his nose.]

I produced my own and asked: Any of that to spare?

His voice came slightly muffled: Did you spare me any tea when I was in hospital or when I came to your house today?

I: You know I did not.

[The top of the lorry was steaming, its fetor drifting over us.]

He: And will you give me any from your flask?

I: Certainly not.

He: Then why should I share my camphor?

I: To prove that Miss Middleton is not a liar.

He: How will it do that?

I: Because she has told me on three separate occasions that you are a decent man and twice that you are kind, but your current behaviour is as mean and petty as my own.

Pound laughed and said: You've got me there.

[I held my breath whilst he deposited some of the clear liquid into my handkerchief.] And, once the vapours had invaded my nostrils and subdued the stenches, I said: We must concern ourselves with four incidents: the imagined death of Travers Smyth, the actual death of Travers Smyth, the death of Prendergast, and the possible death of her maid.

He: Possible?

I: Are you happy to accept the identification of a corpse with an unrecognizable face?

He: But she was in her uniform in the kitchen. [He paused to consider the matter.] I take your point though. [He paused again.] But, if it wasn't Gloria Shell, who was it?

I: The fact that I do not know the identity of a cadaver which I have not been allowed to scrutinize does not mean that it must be the mortal remnants of the absent Miss Shell. She could be alive and giving glockenspiel recitals in the foulest corner of Guildford for all the evidence I have about her whereabouts.

He: I'll go and see her body.

I: Be thorough.

We stopped at Marylebone, he to call at his place of employment, I to the more urgent task of finding refreshment at Sisson's cafe, where I stationed myself by the window.

A snub-nosed waitress approached purposefully: I am sorry, sir, but this is a table for four people.

I: It is not necessary to apologize.

She: Can I ask you to move to a smaller table, sir?

I: You most certainly can. Indeed, you just have. If you are expecting me to do so, your confidence is misplaced. I shall have a pot of tea for two assembled with freshly boiled water and previously unused leaves, and I shall have it at my earliest convenience.

I watched a young man trying to put his hand in a woman's red handbag as she entered the premises, and I was going to warn her when she wheeled about and struck him on the ear with her umbrella. He reeled back, clutching it, before following her in.

The waitress recorded their order, which occupied four more minutes than it should have whilst they agonized over the selection of cakes. Pound arrived, his inside coat pocket slightly stiffened by the paper he had inserted into it, and the tea was delivered the moment he had hung up his hat.

He: Do you have any cake? Chocolate preferably.

She: We do have chocolate.

He: [taking off his scarf] Good.

She: [wiping her nose on the back of her hand] Or plain sponge.

He: I will have chocolate.

She: [examining the back of her hand] Or sponge with jam that tastes a bit like plum.

He: [with unnecessary tetchiness] I will have chocolate.

She: [wiping the back of her hand on her apron] Chocolate then.

I: I wonder why she has not practised her guitar recently when she has been playing it for some months.

She: How on earth did you know that?

I: I was talking about, not to you.

Pound pulled out a chair and sat on it: I think you might tell her... and me.

I: Hold out your hands. [I stifled a yawn as she did so.] The right thumb is calloused on the side as happens with repeated strumming of that unpleasant implement. The epidermis on the tips of the left fingers is also thickened in narrow bands from repeatedly depressing and sliding along the strings. All these injuries are slightly inflamed, indicating that she is new to the task and therefore still at the learning stage of being instructed, if only by herself, but the fading of the outer wheals shows that she has not played the instrument for at least four days.

The waitress scrutinized her injuries: Why, sir, you should be a detective.

I: I shall bear your vocational advice in mind.

Pound brought out his papers: I have been doing some investigation.

I: As you have for many years.

He: I mean into these murders. [He unfolded the papers.] I got my men to look into Mrs Prendergast's background.

[The waitress fetched a mud-coloured granular wedge]

She announced, as if he, not I, had done something clever: Gave you an extra large piece.

[Pound poured our teas.]

I: And did they discover anything of interest?

He: Quite a bit. [He put the papers on the table and ran his fingers down the closely written report.] The late Mr Prendergast left his widow very poorly provided for.

I stirred my tea, admiring the miniature maelstrom created by the motion: I have already established that.

Pound poured milk and shovelled two sugars into his, turning a clear elixir into a sickly off-white slurry and said: Yes, but I have found out why. [He paused in the stillborn hope of eliciting an enquiry from me.] Mr Titus Prendergast was a philanthropist.

I straightened his untidily placed spoon: This is pertinent, but why?

Pound dug a fork into his cake with some difficulty and said: Because he gave away most of his money and what little he had left he invested in an agricultural chemicals factory.

I watched him chip away at his purchase before asking: Should I be familiar with this company?

He stabbed the tines in: I thought you might be. Miss Middleton has shares in it.

I: Miss Middleton keeps her certificates in a safety deposit box. I trust you have not been taking an undue interest in my ward's financial affairs.

He: [indignantly] Of course not. She told me about it. She did not think they are worth anything because the main part of the company closed down in '74. It was starting to produce fertilizers for India, which her father had taken an interest in. The shareholders had to agree not to take any profits for the first five years.

[I sampled my tea, which was drinkable but not pleasant. The woman with the red handbag slapped her son's face and he yelped.]

I: And why did Miss Middleton feel it necessary to tell you about this?

[I made a note to scold her if she ever regained her faculties.]

Pound put down his fork: Because she had a distressing experience there.

I: I would be hard pressed to discover a location where she has not had an unpleasant time.

Pound waved his arm at the waitress: I can't eat this. Bring me something softer.

And while the inspector gorged himself on grey sponge cake, he continued with a discourse on the subject of the porcine poisonings and how Colonel Middleton put a stop to the experiments, using his majority shareholding with another shareholder's support.

I: She tried to tell me about the pigs the last time I saw her.

He: It must weigh heavily on her still.

[He washed his food down with another cup of tea.]

I: It was foolish of Middleton.

Pound dropped crumbs on the table in an interesting pattern: What kind of a father would put a young girl through something like that?

I: I was bemoaning the lost opportunity to crush the French once and for all.

Pound coughed and sprayed some more crumbs into his tea: You cannot approve of killing innocent women and children.

I covered my cup as he indulged in a small bronchospasm: I was thinking more of incapacitating their navy. We do not have Nelson to deal with them next time.

[Pound controlled his indecorous display of irregular respiration.]

He: But surely Swandale's Chemicals was created to save lives.

I: Swandale's. [I opened my satchel and brought out the file.] I was going to read this thoroughly on the way here but you were so busy gossiping that I have not had the chance. That name seems very familiar. [I flicked through the preamble about how that Prendergast woman wanted to be disposed of and ran my eye down the list of assets.] Turner's Tallow, Eagle Slate Quarries. Here it is… Swandale's Chemicals.

[I raised my brows and caught my eye just before it reached my tea. Pound winced. He was surprisingly squeamish for a man in his alleged profession.]

He: From what Mar— Miss Middleton told me, the company was divided between six people. I think she inherited a majority shareholding from her father. It was his idea to buy the company and he persuaded the others to join him.

[He devoured another piece of his cake.]

I: You must send a reliable man straight to Companies House to discover the identity of the other shareholders immediately.

[Pound rinsed his mouth with some more tea.]

He: I have already done so.

I: Why, Inspector Pound [I put the file away], you are in peril of becoming efficient.

Pound started coughing again but at last he managed: Where shall I find you when I have the report?

I: I shall be at home by six o'clock. In the meantime I am going to visit Miss Middleton.

He: Please give her my... regards.

I: They will do her no good.

I called for the bill.

———◆·❧·◆———

97

Late Saturday Afternoon

I HAD TRIED to call in favours with the Home Secretary. He certainly owed me eight, not least of which for extricating a member of his family from a scandalous entanglement. But there was talk of an election and he did not wish to fight it as the man who had overruled the courts and medical opinion to release a mad homicidal spinster into society. I reminded him of the Mystery of the White Peacock and he was shaken but would not budge. In the end he agreed to Miss Middleton being transferred to a private secure establishment off Brunswick Gardens. At least this saved me having to communicate with Governor Kindred again, or the horrendous journey out to the Broadmoor Hospital in that eleventh circle of hell known as Berkshire.

The institution was in an unimposing four-storey early Georgian detached house overlooking one side of the Foundling Hospital. It was almost indistinguishable from its neighbours except for the heavily barred windows and the sign declaring it to be the Saint Dymphna Asylum for the Incurably Insane.

Dr Hepplewhite, the hospital director, was a cheerful man and larger than he needed to be, with polished teeth and heavy caramel hair and eyes that were a comfortable hazel.

He pumped my hand effusively: Come through. Come through. You will have a Bristol Cream.

[He had an interesting white growth on a stalk on his nose, and my elbows itched to snip it off for my collection.]

I: That is either a lie or a mistake, and I am not sure I am happy that my ward should be in the care of a prevaricator or an incompetent.

He: But I was only offering—

I: Then you should learn to express yourself more precisely.

He stopped outside the open doorway of a spacious office and asked: Do you always take things literally?

I: If things are not literal, then they are not things, and if they are not things one cannot take them literally. If they are things, one must take them literally unless one wishes to be a fool, which I do not.

Hepplewhite covered his big white teeth by elevating his lower lip, then pulled it down so that his upper lip went over his lower teeth before speaking: You might be an interesting case.

I spurned the arm that tried to guide me into the room: I am interesting but I am not a case. However, I am here to investigate one and wish to see and speak to my ward.

Hepplewhite pulled his lips to the left: You will not distress her.

I: You speak the truth.

He: No, I meant… never mind. I suppose we might as well go straight there. [We continued down the white-walled corridor.] How did you get on with your father as a child?

I: I did not know him when he was one. How many victims do you have here?

Hepplewhite's lips oscillated: I prefer to think of them as patients. [He adjusted his stride awkwardly.] Twenty-four.

I: And do you treat them all yourself?

He stepped sideways. I and Dr Guess.

I: Why?

He: It is our job.

We passed a series of five doors to our left and six to the right, set twelve feet apart. They were reinforced with iron straps and there were circular viewing holes in all of them and heavy locks. Each boasted a brass number plate.

I: But the poorly lettered sign at the front of this building states that they are incurable.

He: [taking a long stride then two very short] We live in hope.

I: Is that what passes for scientific method amongst alienists?

[There was also an interesting nodular wart on the back of his neck. I scratched my elbows simultaneously.]

He: We call ourselves psychologists.

I: But surely that implies that you are following a logical discipline. [He clacked his teeth but I continued.] If you will unlock this door I shall trouble you no further.

He: But how do you know this is it?

I: You and I have four ears evenly divided between us.

He: I hear nothing.

I: Then you have much in common with this particular victim for she never listens. [It was clear that I would have to explain.] She is humming what I imagine to be a tune.

[Hepplewhite inserted a steel mortise key.]

I: I did not expect to enjoy your company and I have not been disabused. It might, however, fascinate you to know that you trod on a knothole.

[Hepplewhite's lips tightened so that I would have had trouble introducing a letter knife between them, though I had no desire to do so.]

He: Which one?

I: Sixteen inches nor'-nor'west of room nine, the imperfection shaped like a camel's lungs.

Hepplewhite crossed himself and then his arms: Damnation and botheration. You were distracting me. Thank you so much. Now I shall have to start again.

He threaded his way back the way we had come.

I straightened my hair and my eye and my fourth best blood-red cravat. There is little written about the etiquette for the ingression of madhouse cells and I resolved to produce a paper on the matter one dry Tuesday morning. I knocked three times and entered.

Miss Middleton was seated on her bed, dressed in grey sacking, with her booted feet on the floor and her hands folded on her lap.

She stopped humming and greeted me amiably: Hello. Who are you?

[I considered her question – not the answer, for I knew that, of course, but the reason she had posed it. Was this another sample of what she imagined to be a joke? She appeared to be genuinely puzzled. People who fake puzzlement generally overdo it and Miss Middleton was not an accomplished actress.]

I: Who do you think I am?

[Miss Middleton looked grave. She sucked her left little finger and was about to make a suggestion but dismissed it.]

Her eyes closed and, when she opened them, they overflowed with tears: Daddy!

[She held out her arms.]

Hepplewhite joined us: I did it.

[His face shone and he breathed fast.]

I: She is very confused. Is there nothing you can do?

Hepplewhite hooted: Of course not. She is completely mad.

[He cocked his head as if listening to something, then whispered.] I am sorry, Mummy.

98

Saturday, Early Evening

I WENT HOME and had not even started my first tea when Pound arrived.

I: An extra cup for the inspector, Molly.
He: No, thank you. I just had a mug at the station. Didn't think I'd get offered one here. [He brought a wad of documents out of his brown leather messenger bag and sat with it on his lap.] This is everything we could find about Swandale's Chemicals.

He handed it across the table, a loose sheet drifting on to my tray. The pages were unnumbered, but by the weight and thickness it was clear there were one hundred and nine of them. They were tied with a red ribbon through one hundred and nine holes in the top left-hand corner, and to judge from the smell and discolouration they had been stored in a slightly damp basement north of the river. The pages had all been written by one clerk, a right-handed widower from Notting Hill. I flicked through. Despite all my practice, I have never been able to read and completely retain more than seven hundred and sixty words a minute. It was very frustrating but I persisted. Most of the document was about the constitution of the company. Its intentions were dispiritingly altruistic, that is, to assist our Asian empire to grow more food.

He: There is a list of shareholders at the end.

I: I daresay.

[I went through its financial arrangements, which were prudent, and its aspirations for expansion, which were optimistic.]

And I said: That is interesting. The shares cannot be sold. The founders were concerned that speculators might move in and use the facilities for more commercial purposes. They can only be passed to the shareholder's child, an exception being made that Dom Hart could bequeath his allotment to his successor.

[I got to the ultimate page.] Here we are. [I ran my finger down the list.]

Colonel Geoffrey Charles Pemberton Middleton

Mr Titus Paul Prendergast

Mr Septimus Sextus Quintus Travers Smyth

Major Bernard Samuel Vantage Gregory

Brother Ignatius Anthony Hart OSB

Mr Jonathon Pillow

The document was dated 9 September 1873, which was a Tuesday, as I recalled, and five of the men had appended their signatures with Gregory signing pro persona Middleton who, a footnote explained, was in India but had written to authorize the action.

Pound reached into the inner breast pocket of his coat.

He: Why was Mr Swandale not a shareholder?

I: [smoothing out a crease on the nineteenth page]: According to the preamble, Swandale was offered a share but preferred to sell his business to the others and take a regular salary. He died shortly afterwards, gored in the thigh by a boar. Some might call that poetic justice. I do not.

[Pound brought out his meerschaum, doubtless fantasizing that I would say: By all means fill my home with noxious foul-smelling fumes. There is a shortage of those in London.]

He: I assume Septimus Travers Smyth was Tolly's father.

I: [refraining from drawing his attention to a kink in his watch chain] An assumption made safe by my already having had his ancestry analysed.

He: [glancing down to see what I was looking at, but doing nothing about it] And of course I know of Mr Prendergast and Colonel Middleton, but I don't know anything about the other three.

I: You know a great deal about them. You know their names, their professions, their addresses. You know exactly where they were three thousand, four hundred and twenty-seven days ago. You know that they were men of means to be able to finance so costly a project without making much of a dent in their own fortunes. Few men are so charitable as to spend money that they might miss. The only—

Pound chewed on the stem of his meerschaum: I meant that I don't know who they are.

I: The only exception to that rule is Mr Pillow, who was the chemist in charge of research and given a portion of the company as a reward and incentive. [Yet again I regretted the absence of my ward as I was obliged to pour my own tea.] Brother Ignatius became Dom Ignatius Hart, the abbot of Claister Abbey.

Pound whipped his meerschaum out: The monk who was murdered. We thought it couldn't be a coincidence.

I: The evidence is weighted heavily in favour of it not being one.

He puffed on his unlit unfilled pipe: What about that Major Gregory? Have you ever come across him?

[I agitated my tea. Mobile tea is much to be preferred to static. Most people do not realize that because they stir filth into their drinks.]

I: Gregory is March's enemy and therefore mine.

He frowned: How?

DEATH DESCENDS ON SATURN VILLA

I: He has applied to have Miss Middleton made his ward, and before you protest that he cannot, he can. I never had myself declared her official guardian in court for I saw no need. She was until recently, as even you must have noticed, an independently minded young woman who, for better or often for the worse, made her own decisions.

Pound slid the pipe into his outer breast pocket: But what is she to him? I understood she had no relatives until this Travers Smyth emerged.

I tried my tea. It was four degrees Fahrenheit below optimum temperature: He was a family friend and has lodged a letter with Chancery in which Colonel Middleton expresses his wish that, in the event of his death, Gregory take her into his protection.

He brought his meerschaum out again: I can certainly give evidence that she would be opposed to the idea.

I: That might be useful, but I doubt it will come to that. By the by, I am giving consideration to having Gregory killed.

He: You should not be telling me that.

I: But I must, for I am hoping you will help me.

[The mantle clock struck the hour.]

Pound rearranged his moustaches: I think I will have that cup of tea.

99

Sunday Morning, 28 January 1883

GERRY DAWSON STOPPED in response to my green flag
and he greeted us both with undue familiarity. Dawson
had been a competent police sergeant (and there are all
too few of them) before he became too interested in investigating
the contents of whisky bottles.

Dawson: Still chasing criminals, Inspector? You'll never
catch them all.
Pound: Still chasing fares, Dawson? The same applies.
A verminous boy ran alongside: 'Ave they 'anged 'er yet, the
looney woman?
I: You will be dancing on the end of a rope long before she.

He dropped back and, apart from running over and killing a
stray dog, we had an uneventful journey to the New Imperial
Hotel.

Receptionist: I'm afraid Major Gregory is no longer resident at this establishment.
I: I have ten shillings that says he is.
Pound: Save your money, Mr Grice. [He gripped his own
lapels.] I am a police officer and I must warn you that it is
a criminal offence to obstruct me in my duty or to harbour
a suspect.

The receptionist, an unfortunate young man with oily dun hair and retroclined upper-central incisors, went to fetch the manager, an equally unattractive square-jawed man with forestial mutton-chop whiskers and asymmetrically flared nostrils, who issued the same denial.

Pound glanced about: Are you aware that you are in breach of fire regulations under the 1874 Fire Safety Act, section one hundred and forty-two, subsection five, and, if you do not cooperate with my enquiries, I can close you down immediately.

The manager ran his tongue inside his lower lip and jutted his mandible: Room 24 up the first flight of stairs on your right.

I: Is the major afraid of fires?

Manager: I believe so.

I: Key.

The manager clicked his fingers and the receptionist gave him a brass-tagged three-lever key, which he slammed on to the mahogany countertop. I wiped it with a cloth from my satchel and proceeded with the inspector past the closed dining room and along the marbled corridor to the foot of the stairs.

I: [as we ascended] One of the sixty-nine things I miss about Miss Middleton is her ability and readiness to tell lies. There is no such Act of Parliament.

Pound: Perhaps I got the year wrong.

[At the top I paused and printed a message in my notebook.]

I: I wonder, and I feel confident that you will comply with my request, if you would be so good, when I tap your arm, as to knock very loudly and call out Police: open the door.

Pound glanced at me sideways: I thought you asked for the key because you wanted to surprise him.

I: [pausing to reset my eye and tidy my new lime cravat] I
think your introduction will achieve that purpose.

Number twenty-four was at the end of the corridor on the right-
hand side, as I knew it would be. When we neared it I trod a little
more heavily and, once there, I turned the handle twice.

I: [in a stage whisper] My father will never open the door to
me. Make out you're a peeler.
[In response to my signal, Pound hammered on the wood-
work and delivered his four words at an impressive volume.
I put my finger to my lips and listened.]
I: [in a faint whisper] Perhaps I could further prevail upon
you to read out this small oration which I have thoughtfully
prepared for you.
Pound took the notebook from me: We have your sin—
I: Son.
He: It says sin. There is a dot over the i.
I: That is a smudge.
He: How am I supposed to know that?
I: Kindly read it.
[Another reason I missed Miss Middleton was that I could
have scolded her, but policemen tend not to care for being
treated like silly girls.]
He: We have your son and he has told us everything. I have
a warrant for your arrest.
[I banged on the panel five times with the side of my fist
and was rewarded with the many sounds of scuffling, e.g.
drawers opening and closing, a suitcase being dragged out
and dumped on a bed.]
Pound: Use your key.
I: When the time comes I shall.
He: But he might jump out of the window.
I: He will not need to jump. There is a fire escape outside
the window.

He: So he will get away.

[I have long thought that the only point of the obvious is for people to state it.]

I rapped smartly and said: He is taking an unconscionable time in doing so. I shall give him ten seconds more. [A sash window slid and I held up the key.] Would you care to do the honours?

Pound huffed and put out his hand: For heaven's sake.

I: Or shall I? [I unlocked the door.] Are you armed?

He: You know I am not allowed to be.

I: You are also not allowed to falsely claim to have a warrant before entering the premises.

I wondered at his limited repertoire as he huffed again: No, I am not.

I: I only ask because when Marcello Jones made noises which suggested he was climbing up a chimney, he was really waiting for me with a Samurai matchlock known, I believe, as a tanegashima.

Pound showed six physical signs of pent-up frustration: Why are we standing here talking while our suspect is absconding?

[I depressed the handle and stepped aside, extending my cane to push the door open whilst remaining out of the line of fire.]

Pound charged straight in: Gone. He has gone.

The room was as dreary as I had imagined, small and poorly lit, and sparsely furnished. The Welsh wool rug was frayed along one edge and pocked with seventeen cigarette burns.

I: I am disappointed that he was unable to deceive my senses.

Pound marched to the window: He has wedged it from the outside.

[I picked up the ashtray from the badly veneered dressing table. The inspector wheeled round. His complexion had adopted a ruddier hue that did not really suit him.]

His voice took on an accusatory tone: You let him get away.
[I prodded a cylinder of cigar ash with my left second fingertip and the ash fell apart, still warm.]

I: Of course I did.

Pound pushed his bowler back and rubbed his brow: And
they say March is mad.

I: Miss Middleton to you, Inspector. [I replaced the ash
tray with a little less care than is my habit and opened the
side-table drawer.] Do you not see the position he has put
himself into? I had no evidence against him and, until now,
no evidence that he even had a son.

[He rattled at the window again. I handed him my spring-
loaded knife, made in Toledo by José Miguel Armando.]

I: Slide this along the gap.

[He rammed the blade in and sawed it to and fro without a
thought for the craftsmanship.]

He: That's done it.

I watched the wedge fall and said: Besides, I think Dawson
will be more than a match for an elderly infirm man.

Pound wrenched the lower sash up and leaned out: You
crafty...

His last word was inaudible above the hubbub of my city but I
did not trouble to ask him what it was.

100

Two Minutes Later

O N THE WAY down Pound asked: How did you know there was a fire escape?

I: Dawson checked the building for me yesterday.
Pound: We could do with him back on the force.
I: He is far too useful to me in his present role.

But we both knew that a dismissed policeman is never reinstated. We returned to the lobby.

There I addressed the manager: I am a private citizen and you were ill-advised to give me this. [I placed the key in a shabby leather tray on the countertop.] That is very lax security indeed.
Manager: But the policeman—
I: Did not ask for it.

A door opened at the far end of the hall and Gregory entered with Dawson behind, obligingly carrying a heavy suitcase.

Pound: Major Bernard Gregory, I presume.
Gregory tried to adopt a military posture but he was too stooped to achieve his purpose: What is the meaning of this – hammering on my door and frightening me? I thought you were a murderer.

I spoke very quietly: And so you quite reasonably made your escape, pausing only to pack your calfskin-covered portmanteau.

Gregory blew and blustered: I thought there might be a fire.

Pound chuckled: What exactly did I say to make you believe that, sir?

Gregory: I am partly deaf. It comes from standing too close to a cannon.

I said softly: How unfortunate.

Gregory: Yes, it was, and why are you mumbling?

I: To disprove your lie.

I watched a young couple enter from the street, arm in arm, the man carrying a new calfskin valise, while Gregory ranted about outrages and how he had fought for the empire.

I: By all means come in, but I feel it only fair to warn you that there is a suspected murderer in this building.

He: Oh.

She: Oh my goodness.

[They hurried away.]

Manager: You cannot do that.

I: If you do not wish me to make a habit of the practice, I suggest you grant us the use of a chamber where we can conduct our business in private.

[He coughed without covering his mouth and I hastily shielded mine.]

Manager: [flapping limply] Through there. You can use the Green Lounge.

I: And we shall have tea.

Manager: [spluttering] You most certainly— [the front door opened] will [he added hastily as a tall lady entered, wrapped in the outer membranes of Canadian beavers].

I: You have done sterling work this day, Dawson. And, if

you take a seat, these gentlemen will arrange for you to be
brought tea and Dundee cake.
[Gerry Dawson grinned. He had lost eleven teeth arresting
a mathematician on Sunday the ninth of July, 1871.]
Manager: [appreciatively] My favourite.

Dawson took a copy of the *Sporting Times* from his overcoat
and settled down to peruse it.

I had no great trouble calculating why the Green Lounge was
so named. Everything from the wall hangings to the large square
rug to the upholstered armchairs and sofas had been garishly
painted or stained the colour of bile. Pound closed the door
behind us.

Gregory: Where is your warrant?
Pound: You must have misheard me. Shame about that
cannon.
[We settled round a table near the incinerating coal fire.]
I: Where is your son, Gregory?
Gregory cast his gaze down and his shoulders rounded: I
have no son. Barney died at the age of fourteen of consump-
tion.
I: And your daughter when she was five.
Gregory nodded miserably: Daisy was born with a weak
heart. It failed her, the doctor said.
I: And that doctor's name was?
Gregory discovered an undone button on his waistcoat:
What exactly is all this about, Grice?
I: Colonel Geoffrey Charles Pemberton Middleton exam-
ined your dead daughter.
Gregory fumbled with the button: He wrote the death cer-
tificate. So much is public knowledge.
A waitress came to the door: Is it all right to come in, sir?
Pound beckoned her over: Just leave it on the table, thank
you.

[He slipped her tuppence and she fluttered her eyelashes before quitting the room.]

I: You lived in Parbold at the time.

Gregory: Have you dragged me here to recount my life's history?

I: No. [I set to work straightening the contents of the tray.] That would be ghastly. You were on holiday at the time of your daughter's death in Southport. Why not call a local doctor?

The major gripped the arm protectors of his chair: Middleton was a close friend. Daisy was dead so there was no urgency, and Parbold is only a twenty-minute train journey away.

I: Not at one o'clock in the morning. Middleton also diagnosed your son Barney's illness, did he not?

Gregory crumpled the protector: Yes.

I: Two days later.

Gregory: I assume March told you all this.

I: If she did I was not listening and, as you are aware, she is in no condition to discuss anything at present. [I was not entirely happy with my rearrangement but decided to let it stand for the moment.] For all her vices, Miss Middleton has one great virtue, i.e. she is an inveterate chronicler. There is hardly a day of her life since she entered her second decade which she has not recorded in minute, often tedious, but rarely turgid detail. One of my eighteen greatest virtues is that I am incurably curious.

[I felt the pot, took off the lid and stirred, and was depressed to discover how little steam escaped and how few leaves swirled as I did so.]

Gregory: So you read her diaries. Is that why I am being chased down fire escapes?

Pound poured out three dismal, cloudy cupfuls: Your actions were not those of an innocent man.

I: Miss Middleton is also a prolific letter writer and she

makes copies of a great deal of her correspondence. She wrote to Barney at least six times.

[Gregory steadied his right hand with his left to pour the milk and I covered my cup to stop any splashing into it.]

He: They were great friends when they were children.

I: She never received a reply.

Gregory helped himself to the sugar, showering some into the spilled milk: He was probably too ill to write.

I: Or not allowed to. Miss Middleton's letters were addressed to the Friedrich Abbing Hospital, Rotschau, Bern, Switzerland.

Gregory mopped at the mess he had created: Then there is your explanation, not that I can see how it matters since it is not yet a crime to fail to answer letters. She sent them to the wrong place. Barney was at the Rotschau Respiratory Clinic for the fresh mountain air.

I repeated firmly: The Friedrich Abbing Hospital, Rotschau, Bern, Switzerland. Please do not embarrass us all with any more prevarications. I have telegraphed Dr Abbing and he has confirmed that your son was a patient there.

Gregory had lifted his cup an inch and three-quarters but he put it back on the saucer: I remember now. Barney was at the clinic for a while, but we transferred him to Abbing's because they had more advanced treatments.

[I stirred my tea energetically but the water had been boiled at least five times. It was dead]

I: The Friedrich Abbing Hospital specializes in the treatment of neurasthenic disorders.

Gregory: Daisy's death, his own illness and being so far from home proved all too much for Barney's system. He had a nervous collapse. People do not understand these conditions and so we kept it quiet.

Pound drank his tea with no apparent displeasure: I can understand that. I had an aunt who—

I: Yes, yes. We can reminisce later. Unfortunately for your

story, Major Gregory, the Friedrich Abbing Hospital has confirmed that Barney was admitted on the day after he arrived in Bern and that they only take patients who they describe as having undergone complete moral and rational... the closest translation I can come up with is implosion. Pound dabbed his moustaches with one of the silly little napkins provided and said: In other words, a madhouse.

101

Immediately Afterwards

GREGORY STOOD, AN arm protector clutched in his left hand.

Gregory: I do not have to put up with this. My family is none of your concern.

[Pound had risen at the same time, needlessly ready to block the major's escape.]

I: Drink your loathsome beverage, Gregory, and I shall divulge more of the Middletons' chronicles.

[Gregory fell back into his chair but Pound stayed on his feet.]

I: It was Colonel Middleton who arranged the unhappy Barney's transfer to Switzerland, was it not?

Gregory only said: Yes.

And so I continued: I have read five of Dr Abbing's treatises in various medical journals. These are so delusional as to make one wonder if he should be admitted to another hospital. He claims that he is capable of reconstructing shattered minds and therefore effecting cures. [Gregory had his head in his hand as if he had a migraine.] And in May 1881 he wrote you a letter, saying that he believed your son to be completely healed.

Gregory kept his head down: That is true.

Pound: [standing at ease] And was he?

I: That is what Colonel Middleton intended to judge for himself when he made his journey to the Bernese Oberland. [I opened my satchel.] He arrived in Rotschau on the fourth of July, an unhappy anniversary if ever there was one, intending to visit Abbing at his hospital the next day. And that is the last entry in [I produced a tattered black leather-bound book] his secret diary.

[I held it up for both to see.]

Pound strolled over: Why was it secret?

I: It is really a casebook and was written in code because it contains highly confidential information about Barney James Gregory. I do not think that Miss Middleton has managed to find the key but it was a simple enough cypher, little more than a personal shorthand.

Pound sat: And does it tell us anything else?

I slid the saucer out and placed it over my cup, weary of being confronted by its murky contents: There is a fascinating entry in May 1872 and I believe I shall read it aloud.

[I opened the journal where I had marked the page and stood up to declaim its contents.]

Thursday, 12 May 1872. A truly appalling day. Groggy sent a messenger to summon me to the Clifton Hotel. Dear sweet little Daisy had been taken from him. Marjory was in a terrible state. It was she who had discovered Daisy dead. I gave her a good shot of morphine and she was soon sleeping peacefully, but I knew that I could not relieve her pain forever. Groggy was very shaken. From the froth around Daisy's mouth and bleeding from her nose, it appeared she had had a fatal convulsive episode. I was concerned, however, to notice petechiae in her conjunctivae and then a stain on the lower edge of her pillow. When I raised her to turn the pillow over, I found it had blood and vomit on the undersurface.

[Gregory hid his face in his hands, breathing slowly and deeply.]

I closed the journal: I shall precis the rest. Colonel Middleton very reluctantly told you that there was evidence of deliberate suffocation. Naturally you violently disagreed with him but, in the midst of the argument, you heard something and went to check your wife, only to find Barney pressing a pillow over his mother's face. She survived another one thousand, six hundred and eighty-nine days, but never spoke again.

[Gregory's chest heaved in and out as he struggled to inhale.]

Pound reached out as if to pat his shoulder but checked himself: Dear God.

[I had never known a policeman so readily moved to emotion. It was probably his greatest weakness and possibly his greatest strength.]

I: Colonel Middleton did not want you, his best friend, to have to undergo the horrors of having your son declared criminally insane, and even to say that Daisy had died of a fit could cause people to spread rumours about congenital idiocy, so he agreed to sign a death certificate for heart failure on condition that Barney was sent to a mental hospital. He had read Abbing's papers too and been more impressed than I. Plus Rotschau is far enough away for staff not to gossip with anybody who knew the family. Your wife, it was declared, had been prostrated by the shock.

Gregory clenched his fists in front of his eyes: I lost my little girl and my wife, and my son was revealed as a monster.

Pound leaned towards him: Did you have no inkling that anything was amiss with him?

Gregory lowered his fists to chin height and I saw that he had been weeping: Not until he was nine. He was always a happy affectionate boy, but then he had a bad fall playing near the quarry. March saved his life by climbing a hundred foot cliff and sending her friend Maudy to get help. I wish to

God she had not. [At this point Gregory broke his account to make an emotional display.] He was unconscious for four days and when he awoke he was a different child, sly and cruel. I found him torturing a mouse once. But I never thought he would do anything like that. [His arms fell.] He took a knife to Middleton on the train to Dover and managed to cut the side of his neck, though fortunately not deeply. From then on he was restrained, my beautiful son, in a straitjacket.

[Gregory fell back, his chest quivering.]

Pound waited for him to regain some of his composure before saying: Let us leave that aside for the time being. What can you tell us about Swandale's Chemicals?

The major replaced the arm cover: Swandale's? Why do you want to know about that?

[There was a minor commotion coming from the lobby.]

An elderly man was protesting: But I want to read my paper in there.

I: Swandale's.

Gregory shook his head as if he imagined the action would clear his thoughts: It was a small company set up to make bleach, but there was too much competition and it was going bankrupt. Middleton had seen for himself the devastation caused to crops and grassland by locusts and the famine that resulted, and he was eager to find some means of destroying them. He could not afford to purchase and run the company alone and so he gathered like-minded men to support the venture. I could ill-afford to do so but he was a very persuasive man. [Gregory stopped to regain some of his breath.] Even so, he ended up providing the greatest part of the money and so he took the most shares. He had come across Jonathon Pillow in his army days. Pillow was an explosives man originally, but he could turn his hand to anything in the chemistry line. We gave him a ten per cent holding as an incentive to join us. Pillow experimented on cockroaches and grasshoppers. They were the closest we could get to locusts but they proved remarkably resilient, and then he came up with his gas. I assume you know about that.

[Gregory stopped, his energy evidently sapped.]

Pound: I know about the experiments with pigs from what Miss Middleton told me.

Gregory's voice was getting hoarse: It was a gruesome sight and Middleton had not the sense he was born with, to let a child witness such carnage, but he was adamant that the experiments be stopped immediately. I was in two minds. I thought we could make a great deal of money out of his invention and put that to good use.

I: You thought it right to massacre people in order to provide funds to save people?

Gregory sagged wearily: I believed that it would help protect the empire and that, if we did not equip our army with the weapon, sooner or later the French would invent it and use it on London. In the end it was irrelevant. Brother Ignatius Hart was against the idea and between them they had a majority holding, and so the project was quashed.

Pound refilled both their cups: How did Pillow feel about his work being abandoned?

[I reflected silently that he had something in common with Miss Middleton, i.e. the belief that people can accurately assess the emotions of others.]

Gregory blinked paroxysmally: He was furious. He threatened to go elsewhere with his formulae. Middleton went straight into the laboratory, gathered all the papers he could find and went to thrust them into an iron stove in the corner. Pillow was like a man possessed. Four of us had to physically restrain him. He would never be able to recall the formula as it had taken several complex mixtures in precise conditions to create it. [Gregory put his right hand to his left breast.] In the end Prendergast and I prevailed upon Middleton. At least he could keep the documents safe so that, if the French did discover the gas, we could match their threat.

Pound poured the milk, untroubled by its curdling in his beverage: Lord, what a world we live in. As if there are not enough horrors already.

[I got out my flask. The tea would be cool but at least it would be drinkable.]

I: Let us move on to May 1881. You received a letter from Dr Abbing, saying that in his opinion your son was cured and fit to rejoin society.

Gregory turned his face away: We never told him the full extent of Barney's actions, only that he was cruel to animals and had tried to hurt his sister. Abbing put it down as a morbid jealousy, which Barney would grow out of when he was old enough to appreciate the consequences of his actions. Every sinew of me wanted to believe that and I knew I could not bring myself to condemn my son to further confinement. [He patted his own right knee hard, three times.] And so Middleton offered to go and assess him on my behalf. According to Abbing, the first impressions were favourable. Barney was calm, contrite and charming – he could always be that. Middleton took him for a walk on the mountains near Rotschau.

I unclipped my metal cup: And neither of them ever returned.

Gregory slopped tea down his front but did not appear to notice: Geoffrey Middleton was found dead the next morning on the rocks at the bottom of a waterfall. There was no sign of Barney, but a young man answering his description had been seen running away. [He clattered his cup on its saucer.] My only hope was that it had been an accident and that Barney had panicked.

Pound produced his pipe: Doesn't seem likely, given his past history.

I: History is, by definition, past. [I pulled out the cork from my heat retentive bottle.] But it seems even less likely given his present behaviour. It was not us you were running from, was it, Major Bernard Samuel Vantage Gregory?

[Gregory sank lower in his chair but did not reply.]

Pound opened his tobacco pouch: Who then?

I took a drink straight from the bottle: Why, Barney James Gregory, of course, currently posing as Colwyn Harold Blanchflower, valet to the late Ptolemy Hercules Arbuthnot Travers Smyth.

102

Immediately Afterwards Again

MAJOR GREGORY DROPPED his cup. It fell on his knee and bounced to the floor.

He reached for it but the handle snapped and it rolled under the table: No.

Pound rubbed a twist of tobacco between his palms: How can you be sure?

I recorked my flask: Three reasons. First, he was transparently not a valet. No servant would be permitted to wear personal jewellery, yet Colwyn sported a signet ring. He did so to provide evidence that he had lived abroad, where he had picked up his faintly Germanic inflections. A stupid over-egging since nobody would have asked for evidence. Plus no valet would lay out odd socks for his master, especially not such a well-presented intelligent young man as Colwyn. Travers Smyth must have dressed himself in his typically haphazard way. Second, Colwyn gave me a cock-and-bull story about his time in Gorizia-Tyrol, though he said Merci Vielmol for thank you. No Austrian would use that phrase, though a Swiss German from Bern most certainly would. Say personality for the inspector please, Major.

Gregory snorted: What on earth are you playing at, Grice…?

Oh, very well… personality.

I: You heard that, Inspector Pound?

Pound dipped his meerschaum into the pouch: I heard it but I don't see—

I: Third, I am afraid Colwyn's accent let him down again. Even the most skilled of actors find it difficult to remove all traces of their origins. It is like trying to alter the pattern on whorls on your fingertips. [I put my flask back into the satchel.] People unfortunate enough to hail from the northerly regions of England have a number of unpleasant vocal traits. The lower orders, as most people know, drop their H's, though they are not unique in this. As they rise a little from the dregs towards the scum they reapply this letter but, in their anxiety not to forget, tend to add it to any word starting with a vowel. A little higher up they manage this without too much effort but there is usually a slightly greater emphasis than is required.

[A clinker cracked in the fire and they both started in surprise.]

I pressed on: What interests me more is that they complete some words. Let us take happy as an example. I have classified the vowel E into twenty-six different sounds and Lancashire is especially rich in the variety of ways it is presented.

Gregory's left arm rose as if on a string: Just get to the point.

I: All people from that region overemphasize and elongate the al, shorten the Tee and cut it off with an aspirant – the lower orders say person-al-it-teh. Those who imagine they know better over-correct so that teh becomes tey. Those who know best clip it to person-al-it-ih. I have oft known Miss Middleton slip into that speech pattern when she is overwrought. I noted that you did too, Major Gregory, when I watched you devour that over-boiled slab of equine buttock.

Pound laughed, though I had not invited him to share the joke and concluded: One's speech patterns are a gazetteer of one's life – a pocket of south-west Lancashire within six miles of Parbold, formalized Swiss German from Rotschau, Bern. [I took a brown cardboard folder from my satchel.] These are strong indications of who we are talking about. [I undid the brown string.] The Friedrich Abbing Hospital may not know that insanity is incurable but they do keep detailed records, including [I opened the folder] this.

[Gregory froze, as much as his involuntary trembling would allow.]

I: It is not a good likeness. Dr Abbing explained that they had to hold the patient still whilst they stimulated the chemicals on this photographic plate. So you can see the nurse's hands, and the face is quite blurred.

[I passed it to Pound.]

He held it at arm's length: That's him all right. [He held it out to Gregory, who waved it away.] So where is your son now, Major Gregory?

Gregory rubbed his chest: As God is my witness, Inspector, I do not know.

I took the likeness back. Colwyn was strapped into a chair. The sterno-mastoid muscles were splayed on either side of his neck, showing the huge physical effort he was making to resist. His mouth was open and his tongue extruded, and the eyelids were retracted.

I: God is frequently summoned as a witness. I have yet to see him in the box. Your son wants to kill you.

[Gregory struggled to rise.]

He was very short of breath and his complexion was grey: You cannot know that for certain.

Pound rose to block his escape, though Gregory was hardly capable even of walking unaided: Then why did you try to run away when we knocked on the door?

Gregory grunted in pain: I was confused. Let me be.

I leaned back to scrutinize the major: I am not a medical

man but I have seen death in many guises and, if you do not sit and try to calm yourself, I shall expect to be witnessing it in this room very shortly.

Pound held up his hand: Please sit down, Major.

Gregory took a step towards him: My son, the only child I have, is a murderous madman. If I knew where he was I would shoot him down like a rabid cur.

[The major was swaying in a manner resembling that of a drunkard.]

Pound reached out to steady him: Shall I get you a brandy or a glass of water?

Gregory staggered diagonally and grasped the back of his chair: Too late for that. [His voice came in faint gasps.] Too late. He has killed my lovely girl, my loving wife and my one true friend. God alone knows who else he has killed.

His legs buckled and Pound grabbed his sleeve: Come on, sir. Sit down.

The major fell to his knees, clutching his chest: And now, God damn his soul to hell, he has killed me.

Gregory fell forwards and it was only the inspector's quick action that stopped the old man's face smashing into the tea tray. Pound laid him on his back on the floor and went to tug out Gregory's right leg, which was trapped under him.

Pound put an ear to the supine man's nose: Dead. [He got to his feet.] I shall get his body taken away and then I shall have to write a report. [He rubbed the back of his neck.] It does not look good when a witness dies under questioning.

I tied up the cardboard folder and put it away before I stood up: Who will complain? His son will not.

Pound: Quigley will make as much as he can out of it. [He wiped his hands on a handkerchief.] I shall put out a description of Barney Gregory and we can have copies made of that photograph.

I fastened my satchel: And I must go in search of a drink-able pot of tea.

Pound gazed at me: But we have work to do.

I: My work is finished here, Inspector.

He: We have a maniac to catch.

I: When I said I wanted you to help me kill Gregory, I meant the major's son, judicially. [I crossed the room to survey the street and the anonymous masses making their ways towards their graves, and I spoke with my back to him.] But I have failed. You must do what you think fit, Inspector Pound, but neither you with the large but inept manpower at your disposal nor I with my colossal intellect shall ever find Barney James Gregory.

103

The Aftermath

THE POLICE WENT through a simulacrum of the motions of looking for Barney Gregory. Copies of his photograph were sent to police stations around the kingdom and the port authorities were alerted, but I knew from personal experience how easy they are to evade.

Pound came.

He: One thing I was wondering. Why did Barnaby or Colwyn, as we knew him, answer your summons to this house? He must have known you might catch him out.

I: [stirring my tea] It might have looked suspicious if he had refused to answer any questions but, more importantly, Barney James Gregory suffered from something you and I find difficult to understand – that is, arrogance.

Pound coughed and, not for the first time, I refrained from advising him to quit his tobacco habit: So he thought he could outwit you?

I: Many have tried but most have ended up being tried.

[Pound had developed a habit of looking at my teapot like a puppy wanting chocolate, but I had developed a habit of ignoring his habit.]

He: Why do you think Travers Smyth and Prendergast got embroiled in it all?

I: [patiently] Few things incite the desire for money more than having had but lost it. [I sampled my tea with mild pleasure.] They probably thought they were merely assisting in a ruse to make Miss Middleton seem incompetent. This would allow them access to the fortunes they believed to be theirs by right. They may even have told themselves that developing the poisonous gas was a patriotic duty.

He: [swallowing ostentatiously to draw attention to his lack of anything to swallow] And I do not suppose they knew that anyone would die, least of all themselves.

I: Indeed.

Pound took me to Mrs Prendergast's house and I spent five days searching it, but found nothing to contradict the story that her maid, Gloria Shell, and her dog, Albert, had been beaten to death with a claw hammer in the kitchen. The attacker had been a tall, right-handed man with fair hair and wearing clumsily made hobnail boots with one of the iron heels missing, I surmised, but the two witnesses were able to add nothing more. The one who claimed to have heard something was a local wine merchant of good reputation and insisted that the killer had used the exact words: That will keep your mouth shut about March Middleton, you slut.

I could not find a cab driver who had taken anybody to or from the area of the house around the time of the murder. I spoke to all the local constabulary, neighbours, every tradesman, every street urchin and every crossing sweeper I could find, and nobody gave me any further information.

Weybridge wrote. He had identified the man whose skull was recovered from the furnace. I did not trouble to read it.

At the end of three weeks I suffered the heaviest blow I have ever received. Vernon Harcourt, the Home Secretary, had bowed to pressure from Her Majesty's vile Prime Minister, William Ewart Gladstone, and declared that Miss Middleton was mentally competent to stand trial on the capital crime of murder and must be transferred to a prison immediately.

Pound came round as soon as he heard.

I told him: She is lost to me. I swore to protect her and I cannot.

Publisher's Note

At this point Mr Grice ends his account.

The following extracts are based upon the more coherent of the many notes made by Miss Middleton whilst in detention and discovered hidden in her mattress after she was taken from her cell.

PART III

Extracts from
March Middleton's Notes

The Lost Ones

———◆◆◆———

MY ROOM IS quite agreeable, as far as any cell can be. It is certainly better than the last condemned cell I visited. I have an iron bed with blankets, which is comfortable enough, though very chilly at night; a wooden table and a chair; and they have provided me with writing materials. I expect my guardian persuaded the governor to grant me that. He has influence in many quarters – either by having helped people or having knowledge of their secrets – and is never shy about calling in favours.

The guards have been very kind. They bring me books – I hope they do not get into trouble for that – and they are generally courteous and considerate. I am not allowed newspapers, though, and when I ask if there is any petition for my reprieve they pretend not to understand and tell me not to worry about such things.

The doctor comes daily. He asks how I am and I tell him I am well, though I am developing a rheum in my chest. It hardly matters to me, but it seems the authorities prefer hanging a healthy woman to a sick one.

The lost ones have not visited me as often as they used to and I know how to deal with them now. I can get rid of Mrs Prendergast just by hiding behind a screen of my hair. She will cluck and fuss and try to tempt me out with cake but if I ignore her long enough, she will go away. Uncle Tolly is more persistent, though. He will sit in his own armchair for hours, watching me balefully, and I have to go inside myself to hide from him. But

427

Dorna is not so easily avoided. However deep I go she follows, always beautiful, warm and sympathetic; always whispering into my soul.

I am afraid for you, March... Sidney Grice will destroy you, just as he destroyed me and just as surely as he murdered your mother.

Silence

WHY CAN I remember nothing of the trial? I asked the padre if I had given evidence and he said I had not. Was that because I would condemn myself? Sometimes it is better to be quiet. I am quiet most of the time. I lie on my bed, my arms crossed over my breast and block out all the noises of my prison – the shouts and echoing clatters – and then I listen to myself. I slow my breathing and make it so shallow that I can no longer hear it. My heart steadies and the roaring blood dies down, creeping noiselessly through my ears, and even my thoughts begin to murmur, so low that I cannot hear them. I turn the images off, one by one like a series of Chinese lanterns, and then there is not a darkness but a lack of light and, for curled slivers of time, silence, all is silence.

The Unredeemed

—◆◆◆—

SIDNEY GRICE CAME this morning. He had his eye patch on and was pale and haggard and physically diminished. He was a small man but his erect posture and dominant manner usually made one forget it. Today he was hunched and the way he had of holding one's gaze with his was gone.

I asked if he would be here when they take me out and he told me that he would always support me.

'I am frightened,' I said and he squeezed my hands. 'So frightened,' I whispered.

'I'm sorry, Mr Grice,' the warder said, 'but I have strict orders.'

My guardian leaned forward. I thought he was going to whisper but, to my astonishment, he kissed my cheek. 'God bless you, March.'

Dorna laughed when she heard that. '*You do not believe in God*,' she said.

My guardian let go of my hands and stood up, his face to the wall. 'Somebody must be to blame for all this.' He slipped a coin into the guard's palm and was gone.

I listened, but I could not hear his soft footfalls above the clang of the door and the clatter of the lock and the cries of those who are also damned.

Every Night

EVERY NIGHT I wonder if this is my last. At first I hope it will be. The reality can be no worse than the fear of it – though I have heard first-hand accounts from Inspector Pound and Mr G of so many botched hangings – but the longer they delay the more I realize something.

I know I should not be loath to meet my Lord and Saviour but it is growing inside me, undeniable and inescapable, this knowledge of myself. And my prayers for a quick release have been replaced by a new supplication.

Above all things, I do not want to die.

A thousand times a day, kneeling by my bed or lying on it, sitting at my desk or standing under the window, I send my petition. It flies to the heavens and is caught and carried by the angels.

Another sunrise and another sunset; please God, grant me one more day.

The Carpenters

T HE CARPENTERS ARE here. I hear them hammering and sawing and one of them sings, happy in his work. I know what they are building but I dare not give it a name.

'Is it for me?' I ask the doctor and he pats my shoulder.

'Not just for you.' He has gentle grey eyes, but they are heavily underlined by black bags. His work must be a dreadful strain. He has to tend the living and witness their deaths.

'My father was a doctor,' I tell him. 'Colonel Geoffrey Middleton.'

'I am afraid I never came across him.'

'After my mother died he rejoined his regiment and, when I was fourteen, he was stationed in India and Afghanistan.'

My father's face appears on my sheet like Veronica's miraculous image of Jesus on the cloth with which she wiped his blood away, but it dissolves in the weak rays struggling through my window.

Only light and the noise of construction come between those bars and nothing gets out but my prayers.

'You must have missed him.'

'I went with him. We worked together.'

His brow wrinkles as it rises. 'But you were a child.'

I think about his words. 'Until the day I helped hold a man down as my father sawed his leg off.' But it was before then. I was a mother to my father at the same time he was a father to me. 'We looked after each other.'

His hand goes out to me, but falls away before it has even travelled half of its journey.

'*You were like a child to me,*' Uncle Tolly sighs, '*the daughter I could never have.*'

'Do you have a daughter?' I ask and the doctor nods.

'She is about your age, a little younger.'

'Love her,' I say and he whispers something, lost before it reaches me.

He goes and I think about it again.

I remember playing with Maudy Glass and Barney, running up Parbold Hill and rolling down it, scattering the sheep and spinning until we were dizzy, and afterwards being told off by Mrs Leyland, my father's housekeeper, for getting grass stains on my dress. I suppose I must have been a child that afternoon. But at the end of that same day, I took the tumbler from my father's loose grip in his lap and fetched a tartan blanket to cover him as he slumbered fitfully by the dying fire.

'Do not let this happen to her,' I said, forgetting my visitor had gone.

'*A child, yes, a child,*' Uncle Tolly moans.

When will the blood stop pumping – pumping from his ripped-open chest?

Repentance

I HEARD SCREAMS this morning – not unusual here, but these screams went on and there were sounds of a struggle and a man saying:

'You will only make it worse for yourself.'

It comes from the cell next to mine and I have heard her before, praying loudly or sometimes shouting obscenities.

She howls. 'No I'm not ready. You should have warned me.'

And the chaplain – I know his voice – says, 'Come on, Maggie. You will only get hurt.'

There is a dull crash and a clattering, and I know her table must have gone over with her tin wash jug on it. My jug has not come yet. I suppose she is more urgent. They don't want to hang a woman with a grubby face.

They are coming past. I hear scraping and feet drumming, and so they must be dragging her.

'You should have told me.' She is crying. 'I had no time to prepare myself.'

'They're never ready,' a warder says. I know his voice too and I do not like him.

Dorna opens the door so suddenly that I jump. I have no chance to shut her out.

This is what you did to me, she says sadly.

She comes in, dragging her right leg, and then I remember that it was snapped when she died.

'All those people,' I try to explain.

I wonder why her neck is not broken, but then I realize that it is and that her head is lolling loosely as she tells me, *'They were nothing – nothing to you – but I loved you, March… and him.'*

The chaplain tries to reason with Maggie. 'You knew it was coming.'

'But not today.'

Maggie starts to sob and cannot speak. The chaplain murmurs something. He is probably quoting scripture – a verse about repentance, I imagine.

I imagine so many things as the gate slams. And the sounds fade in my ears, but they are trapped inside my head by the hands which must be mine crushing my ears. Round and round they go, bouncing off the walls of my skull until I am quite dizzy. They would drive me mad if I were not mad already.

The Remains of a Life

I HEAR THEM later, clearing out her cell. One of them says something. I cannot hear what, but the tone is mocking and the others laugh.

'You wouldn't've credited as she could fight so 'ard,' a whining voice said. I know him, a sniffy little Cockney barrow boy made important by the uniform he cannot fill. 'Gawd but she didn't want to go. Gave Eustace a real shiner she did. 'E won't see out of that eye this side o' Christmas.'

They laugh again and I decide there and then I will really give them something to laugh about – no demurely climbing the scaffold steps and tipping the executioner for me. I shall fight tooth and nail for every extra beat of my racing heart.

'What shall I do with that?'

A slight pause while they examine it. 'Frow it away.'

In a land where people live by collecting scraps of bones from gutters what could have remained of a woman called Maggie that was so completely worthless?

The Dark

THE LIGHTS WENT out last night. There are none in the cells.

The corridors are lit by gas mantles and the beam they project through the spy hole in my door casts a yellow disc on to the wall by my head. I can reach out from my bed and see my hand illuminated, alive. I wriggle my fingers and watch the shadows dance on the whitewash. I make birds and an elephant, just as my father taught me with his magic lantern, when I was a child in The Grange. For the first time in my life I am glad he is dead. I cannot bear to think what the shame and shock would have done to him.

Last night I touched the disc and it vanished as if I had snuffed it out, and my whole world became black. It was then that the screaming started. I think it was the Irish major's wife three cells away who started it, but screaming is more contagious than scarlet fever. Few have any natural resistance. I do. Screaming annoys me as a rule. It is almost always done to gain attention. But these were cries of fear, and fear is more contagious than screaming.

I never understood how a crowd could panic so quickly until I was in a single-storey theatre in Bombay. In the interval a chai wallah knocked his charcoal burner over and the curtain burst into flames. There was a stampede to the exit at the front, people pushing, elbowing and clawing at each other in their desperation to escape the spreading conflagration, trampling wild-eyed and high-pitched over their fallen fellows. The British press printed accounts of white men trying to calm hysterical natives, but I saw

Europeans fighting their way through the scrimmage and a military policeman using his truncheon, not to restore order but to effect his own escape. I watched from the back in horror. The exit was blocked with a terrified writhing mass and I was just about to cry out when Edward took my arm.

'I shall not let you die in this place,' he vowed and I believed him. There was a planked door at the back, hardly discernible in the poor light, and it was locked. He drew out his revolver and shot off the padlock, kicked the door and it flew open.

Edward ushered me out and told me to stand back and then, as the smoke poured out of our escape route, he kissed me. There was blood on his face, but it could not mask the fear as he went back in. The screams were awful. I stood in the street and put my hands over my ears. An age later he reappeared with a bawling Indian girl under his arm and leading her mother by the hand. He was shouting: 'This way. This way.' And people began to follow. The mother kneeled and kissed his hand, but he pulled away in embarrassment and told her to get up.

Four people died, all natives. My father told the colonel-in-chief that Edward should get a medal, but Sir Terrence guffawed and asked, 'What for? Helping old ladies cross the road?'

A splinter of wood had flown up when Edward fired his gun. It cut his cheek quite deeply and he was delighted later, hoping that it would look like a duelling scar, but it healed with hardly a trace.

Drowning in the Dark

———◆◆◆———

I LAY IN bed, forcing myself to breathe slowly and deeply, and telling myself that the dark is not a thing. It cannot hurt me. It is just an absence of light. It cannot crush my chest and suffocate the life out of me.

But the dark has a cruel sense of humour and what I know to be logical is no longer true when my eyes might as well have been plucked, like one of Sidney Grice's, from their sockets, for all the use they are to me. Even though I feel my ribs rise and fall and the cold damp air being sucked into my lungs, I cannot truly breathe. The oxygen is not getting into my blood or being circulated by the rapid percussive shocks of my heart.

My lungs are filling. I held a man once while he drowned in his own fluid and watched his eyes locked on mine in helpless desperation until I could no longer support him and he fell lifeless into my armchair. We hanged his murderer. I try to rise to relieve the congestion but I am strapped to the bed by terror and nothing can snap the bands whilst darkness rules my earth.

I have a pain in my chest and I cannot even cry out except in my mind. 'Not yet, Lord, and not like this.'

Waiting

———◆———

WILL YOU BE waiting for me and how will you be? Happy to see me? Ashamed of how I got there? Angry that I took another's ring? Or will you enfold me in your arms?

What am I thinking of? I shall be cast down where the flames shall lick my bone and the worms eat my flesh.

I remember a man being eaten alive by worms. I remember him picking maggots out of his face. He found hell long before he died.

Lancelot

I AM HUMMING the tune that the mice sang so long ago in Uncle Tolly's house when the visitor comes, his broad-brimmed hat in his hand like the shield of Lancelot in a poem.

'Hello,' I say. 'Who are you?'

He looks very familiar but people have a habit of looking familiar – even that valet once – when they are not.

'Who do you think I am?' he asks unhelpfully.

I suck my little finger to help me concentrate and almost make a suggestion. Something tells me it can't be him but I can't remember why. I close my eyes but when I open them he is still there and the word sobs out of me. 'Daddy!'

I hold out my arms but another man rushes in, panting for breath. 'I did it.'

'She is very confused,' my father tells him, though he looks nothing like my father any more. 'Is there nothing you can do?'

But I shoot back inside myself before he can reply for I realise that this is not my father come for me, but the man who murdered my mother.

Gloves and Dead Mice

----◆-◆-◆----

SIDNEY GRICE HAS a new eye: limpid blue, but with a golden glint to it. He sits on the end of the bed.

'You seem more lucid,' he observes.

He is always observing things. Sometimes I find that inspirational for I want to follow in his footsteps or even walk alongside him, but mostly it irritates me, especially today.

'*Tell him,*' Dorna urges.

I try to shush her. 'Not now.'

He takes off his gloves as if it were a surgical procedure to do so. 'Why not now?' And places them on the bed by my feet, like Spirit offering me a dead mouse. I make a mental note to ask him about her, but Dorna nudges me.

'*Go on.*'

'Very well.' I fill my lungs with air and say, 'One thing troubles me.'

'Only one?' The gold vanishes from his eye. 'What a delightful life you must lead in here.'

'His cane rests across his knees and I wonder which one he has brought. The Grice Patent Get Your Ward Out Of Gaol Stick?

I pounce on a glove. 'When I last spoke to *her*,' I still did not dare speak the name, 'she said that if she were reprieved she would be unpicking ochre. She must have known that it is oakum.'

I was so busy trying the glove on and finding that it fitted – but not like a glove – that I did not notice the silence at first, but as it lengthened I glanced up. Though Sidney Grice hastily composed his features, I had glimpsed something. I did not know what, but it involved suffering.

'She said that?' His voice was unsteady. 'You are sure?'

'Does he think you are stupid?' Dorna is indignant on my behalf.

'Of course not,' I tell her. To him I say, 'Of course... but I did not see any point in correcting her.'

My guardian's fingerplate beds are blanched as he grips his cane like a bicyclist about to crash.

'It was a message.' He stares at something behind me. 'Dear God! If I had known.'

I would have asked what he meant, but he was up and muttering something about an appointment and the door was locked between us before I realized that I was still wearing his glove.

Follow

———◆◆◆◆◆———

'ARE THEY TREATING you well?' Sidney Grice asks and his face tics – a spasm of emotion from the man who prides himself in having none. In happier times I would have teased him for that and he would have got all stiff and starchy.

How strange to think of them as happier times, the days we dealt with death, and yet in an odd way they were. I witnessed people being murdered. I saw things more horrible than my worst nightmares. I helped send murderers to the gallows. And yet I was happy. I was the avenging angel, the righter of wrongs. How did the huntress become the hunted? Perhaps it will always be so.

'They are very kind,' I tell him, and the thought of kindness makes me want to cry. But I have no tears left for myself, I hope.

'And how are you?' I ask.

'I am always well.'

'Except when you have your fevers.'

'Except then,' he concedes.

'Or the time you had an upset stomach from those unripe peaches.'

He shifts on the rickety wooden chair. 'Then too.'

'As I recall I advised you not to eat them,' I remind him.

'You did.' He is getting annoyed now.

'But you did not listen,' I point out and his irritation bursts to the surface.

'Oh, for goodness' sake, March.'

But I am so happy to see him not gazing at me as if I were a dying kitten.

'How is Spirit?' I ask and he blinks.

'As mischievous as ever. Yesterday she plucked my Versailles rug.'

'Did you punish her?'

He looks sideways. 'I did not speak to her for nearly an hour. And I ignored her attempts to get me to play with a ball of wool.'

'You talk to her and play with her?'

Mr G touches his glass eye and says gruffly, 'Only for your sake.'

'Thank you.' I burst into a deluge of tears and throw my arms round him.

'Rules,' the guard grunts, but makes no attempt to separate us. And my guardian holds me closer, I should think, than he has ever held anyone before.

'I am sorry.' I unfold myself from him.

'You have always been over-emotional.' He is taking out his handkerchief and I think he is going to offer it to me, but he blows his nose and stuffs it away.

'I am sorry, sir, miss,' the guard says, 'but it is past the hour.'

'When the hour comes…' I whisper. 'When they take me out, will you be here?'

Sidney Grice inhales and looks me in the eye. 'I shall always support you, March.'

And I shiver. 'But I am going where you cannot follow.'

I cannot stop shivering for a long time after he leaves. I have never seen him looking helpless before.

The Rainbow

———◆◆◆———

SIDNEY GRICE COMES. He was always a natty dresser but today he is exceptionally spruce. He has forsaken his usual Ulster coat for a long black cloak and I might have thought it was for a funeral were it not for the sheer scarlet lining. He carries a top hat – silk brushed to a high sheen – with white gloves, which he deposits inside as he places the hat on the end of my bed.

'Good morning, March.' This must be the most civil greeting he has ever given me. Normally he can hardly be bothered to grunt from behind his newspaper. 'I trust you are well.'

I sit on the bed and he on the wooden chair, dusting it first with a flourish of his red handkerchief, and hitching his trouser legs a little to stop them bagging.

'Tolerably,' I respond.

'How long have you known me, March?'

'It must be about nine months, I suppose.'

He clears his throat. 'And what opinion have you formed of my sense of humour?'

'It is like the unicorn,' I tell him. 'A lovely idea but I have given up any hope of finding it.'

For some reason this remark pleases him. 'Then you will know that I am completely serious in what I am about to say.' He puts his hands on his knees. 'I should like to show you something.' From his inside coat pocket he brings out a box. I have seen that shape and size before, but obviously it cannot contain what would usually be expected. 'This belongs to my mother.' He flipped open the lid and I saw it, rose gold with a tear-shaped diamond that coruscated even in the weak light of my cell.

'Then why is she not wearing it?'

'Her finger joints are swollen with rheumatism. She can hardly remove it and she hates the idea of it being cut off.' A rainbow flashes from the gemstone. 'So she wanted me to have it,' he grunts, 'now that I require one.'

I lean forward. 'You are planning to get engaged?'

His irises are violet as they flick towards the bars and back at me. 'I hope to.'

'Have you been courting long?'

'No time at all.' His cheeks colour a little. 'But my mother insists that, if I am to do it, I must do it properly.'

'Well, of course you must,' I agree.

And my guardian coughs. 'I know that I am not the sort of romantic hero you read about in that mawkish drivel you are so fond of dribbling over, but my finances are solid – I can produce my last three years' accounts should you wish to examine or have them audited – and for all my sixteen faults I am a steady fellow, honest and superlatively intelligent.'

'And I am sure you will make an excellent husband.'

Mr G looks at me uncertainly. 'You think so?'

'I have little doubt of it.'

For an instant I think he has slipped off his chair but Sidney Grice is falling on to one knee and, before I know it, he has my hand in his and is gazing up at me. 'March Middleton, will you marry me?'

I stare at him. 'But you do not love me.'

'That is true but do not take it personally. I love no one and nothing except the truth and possessions.' His right eye has drifted inwards. 'You need not worry about – how can I put this delicately? – physical matters. You may rest assured, March, that I find you just as unattractive as any other normal man.'

'*He should have asked my permission.*' Uncle Tolly puts a hand to his shattered head, but I shoo him away.

'If not more so,' Sidney Grice added.

'That is of great comfort to me,' I say.

And I whisper to Uncle Tolly, 'I told you to go away.'

'So you could keep your own bedroom and I my own,' my guardian continues doggedly.

'Why?' I demand and could have sworn that he blushes.

'You cannot imagine I would want to share.'

'No,' I concur. 'Even my imagination does not have such fancies. But, if I am mistress of the house, why should I not have the bigger bedroom?'

'Mistress?' He puts a finger to his eye but it stays obstinately fixed on the tip of his nose. 'The arrangement is purely one of convenience.'

'Whose convenience?' I ask. 'Go away, Uncle Tolly.'

'Why, yours, of course.' He holds up the box. 'It would be nothing more than a nuisance and an embarrassment to me.'

'No,' I say.

'Are you talking to me this time?' Sidney Grice asks.

'Yes.'

'No, what?'

'No, I shall not marry you.'

Mr G grimaces. 'I am deeply hurt, March.' He lets go of my hand. 'That you should reject me so peremptorily. Have you any idea how repellent I find the whole idea?'

'For once I can entirely empathize with you.'

My guardian scrambles to his feet, levering himself up on my knee. 'I receive proposals of marriage by the Royal Mail every week.' He beats the dust from his knee. 'Why, only this morning I had one from a Russian countess.'

The ring flares in his hand for the last time before he snaps the lid shut and blots it out forever.

'Then I suggest you accept it.'

I nearly add that I cannot give my life to the man who took

my mother's, but Dorna appears at his shoulder and puts a finger to her white lips – It is our secret – and Sidney Grice glances back, wondering what I am staring at. How can he not see her – this man who sees everything?

The Night of the Storm

WHAT NIGHT IS it? Friday, I think – the night of the storm. The tempest that has been slumbering in my mind finally stirs and bursts out in an uncontrollable rage. Lightning forks, thunder shakes the window of my cell and a howling gale hurls oceans of water to burst against the glass.

I have always loved storms. When I was a child I would stand on a chair to watch the sky split and the world light up with jagged bolts of electricity, but tonight I am frightened. The power of it makes me feel so small and weak. I lie back in my bed and clutch my pillow, and the moment I close my eyes the door flies open.

'Edward!' He stands tall, backlit by the gas mantle, and at first I think I must have imagined him, but the storm lights up my cell and there is Edward, splendid in full uniform, his boots gleaming, his spurs glittering. 'Is that you, my darling?'

'*Dear March.*'

His eyes are golden and flash through the chaos.

'But how did you get in?'

He grins boyishly. '*Love knows no locksmith.*'

And I remember how he scaled the old fort wall, heedless of the rows of spikes in the dry moat forty feet below him, to pluck a wild rose. I was furious but I took it from his mouth and I have it still, crushed and dried in my journal.

I get up and try to run towards him but we are drowning in the thickening air. It holds me back and, as I move forward, he drifts away.

'Wait for me, Edward.'

'*Wait?*' He unsheathes his sword. '*But you have another man now. You wear his ring, not mine, next to your heart.*'

'Only because…' But I cannot speak the reason why. I am not sure that I believe it anymore.

'*You promised to love me forever, March.*' He holds his sword out, straight-armed. '*You swore it.*'

'I do love you,' I protest. 'I never stopped.'

Edward's voice rises. '*I cannot compete with him, March. He is alive and warm. He can hold you and dance with you and make you laugh,*' his voice is failing, '*while I lie cold and rotten in the earth far away… far away.*' He slices the air with his sword and the lightning cracks and a long flame sizzles around the blade. '*You must choose between us, March.*'

The flame dies.

'You,' I cry. 'You every time.'

Edward turns away. '*But you are not ready.*' His voice is growing weaker. '*When will you be ready to come with me, March?*'

'Now!' I scream. 'For the love of God, now!'

I am tossed helplessly in the turbulent air but Edward stands firm, a rock in the tides of time. I flail frantically and, just as I think I am sinking, a rolling wave propels me towards him. I strain and my fingertips almost touch him.

'Edward!'

He spins back, the man with no face, my name spraying out in droplets of the blood he shed for me.

'*Murderess,*' he hisses as I shoot up in bed.

The Shadow of Sadness

———◆———

SIDNEY GRICE VISITS me, grey with exhaustion, and semi-sits on the edge of my table.

I watch him for a while, staring at his open snuffbox as if waiting for something to happen.

'How did my mother die?' I ask, so suddenly that I take us both by surprise.

My guardian shuts the box. There is an enamelled figure of death on the lid and I hate it.

'That letter,' he says simply.

I gape at him. 'You knew what it contained?'

'Of course.' Sidney Grice flips the box open, clicks it shut and puts it away. 'I knew the hand and so I read and resealed it.'

I gasp. 'Then why did you let me see it?'

'It would still have been there.' His left eye glances outwards then back at me.

I jump up. 'You could have destroyed it and I would never have known.'

'I would have known.' My guardian pinches the bridge of his nose. 'Sit down, March.' He says it so gently that I go meekly back to the bed and Sidney Grice crouches at my side and takes hold of my hand. 'Your mother died of complications in giving birth to you.'

'So you did not kill her?'

He does not flare at the accusation, but a shadow of sadness falls over him and he answers quietly, 'No.' He looks at me directly. 'I did not.'

'You are lying,' I blaze and he bridles, but even then only a little.

'If I live to be a hundred,' he vows, 'you will never hear me tell a lie. I did not kill your mother, March. She was a wonderful woman, quite wonderful. Your father adored her and he was devastated when she died – that was why he rejoined the army – but he still kept in contact. He wrote me letters as a friend. Would he have done that if he had held me responsible?'

That seems an odd way of declaring his innocence and yet it is difficult to imagine he was guilty and yet...

'There is something you are not telling me,' I accuse, and my guardian lowers his gaze and then his head.

'You are right.' His hand tightens on mine and he falls silent for a while. 'And you have every right to know.' He clears his throat and looks up again. 'On 5 November 1862—'

'The day of my birth.'

'Quite so. My father was shot. I shall not go into the details now but he suffered two wounds – one in his left arm and the other in his chest. It lodged just under his heart. My parents had a house in Bedford Square and yours had taken one nearby for the season. I ran across and asked your father to help. I did not need to beg. Your mother was healthy and with friends, and you were not due for another three weeks. Your father saved my father's life – there is no doubt about that – but when he got home he found that your mother had gone into a sudden and very difficult labour. Her friends did not know where I lived to alert him and had called upon a highly successful surgeon who lived next door. His name was Cunningham and he was fortunate to die from a heart attack two days later before your father recovered his faculties. I do not say that he killed your mother – nature did that – but he tried to delay your birth with catastrophic results. Some people blamed me. I have always had many enemies and it is conceivable that, had I not called upon your father, he might have saved his wife, but he did not think so.'

'If my father did not blame you, you cannot blame yourself,' I say. 'And neither do I. But why did you not tell me this before?'

Sidney Grice shrugs and his head goes down again, but he does not reply.

'You are hiding something from me,' I say and Sidney Grice shakes his head.

'No,' he tells me very quietly. 'I am hiding a great many things.' He rubs his injured shoulder. 'If ever you get out of here, do you want to leave our home?' he asks at last. 'I will assist you in any way I can.'

'Where would I go?' I respond. 'You are my protector and you called it our home.'

My guardian pats my shoulder awkwardly and shivers, and I look down to see a drop of water on the back of his hand.

And, as I lie in bed that night looking out into the starless sky, I think about that shadow on my guardian's face. The sadness has been there since the day I met Sidney Grice and I cannot imagine it will ever go away.

Publisher's Note

This was the last note written by Miss Middleton before she was taken from her cell.

PART IV

Extracts from the Journals of March Middleton

104

The Last Day

IT WAS A sunday morning when they came for me. I heard the bells of the city peel and the one bell of the chapel toll its measured beat.

The padre was there and two guards, one the little man I did not like and the other a fat middle-aged man who had been kind to me.

'Is this my last day?' I asked and the little man bowed his head. 'It is.'

'I am not ready,' I protested. 'You should have warned me.'

And the wan-faced chaplain said gently, 'Come along, March.'

'You should have told me,' I protested. 'I have had no time to prepare myself.'

'They are never ready.' The little warder smirked.

The kind guard put a hand on my arm. 'Surely you knew it was coming.'

I nodded. 'But not today.'

We walked to the wooden platform set up in the courtyard and I glanced up to see the two other prisoners watching from the laundry-room window. We went around the platform.

'Pity you will miss our concert,' the padre said.

We went into the office and the governor rose behind his desk.

'Hello, March.' Sidney Grice stood by the unlit fire. 'I told you I would be here.'

'Is this my last day?' I asked.

'Yes,' he said. 'It is time to leave.'

'Leave?' I took hold of my sleeves above both elbows.

Sidney Grice came up to me.

'All charges have been dropped.' The governor beamed. 'And the doctors have pronounced you cured.'

'Of what?' I looked from face to face.

Mr G brushed my right hand as lightly as one might a cobweb. 'I will explain it all.'

''Ere's your 'andbag,' the mean guard said. 'And we ain't taken nuffink from it.'

I rooted about and shook my father's hip flask. It was empty as was the silver cigarette case.

'Have one of mine.' The nice warder held out his pewter case and I picked one out. He lit it for me.

My hand was steady, I was proud to note, because my insides were fluttering like a caged crow. I inhaled deeply and the effect was immediate. I felt dizzy and sick and absolutely wonderful.

Mr G watched disapprovingly but I did not care.

The governor grasped my hand. 'I wish you well.'

For a moment I felt I should say how much I had enjoyed my stay or thank him for having me but, even in my confusion, I knew that would not be fitting.

They stood round me, watching me smoke as if I were an entertainment.

'You'll soon be back,' the mean warder forecast.

'May I shake your hand too, miss?' the nice warder asked and wrapped his fist so hard round mine that I felt my bones shift.

I tossed my cigarette into the fireplace and straightened up.

'Thank you for what you have done.' The remark was only intended for one of them, but the other two assured me it had been their greatest pleasure. 'Give me your arm please, Godfather.'

Side by side we walked out of the office, down the hallways and through the doors until at last we came to the iron-studded outer door, and then we were on the street. I glanced back at the sign over the gate: The Ambrose Hospital For Mental Diseases.

'They left you here when the election was postponed,' Sidney Grice told me, as if that meant something.

Ahead of us Gerry Dawson waited by his hansom with his old piebald mare, Meg, in harness, and I wished I had an apple core for her.

There was a little bouquet of dried flowers on the seat.

'Welcome back, miss,' Gerry called and I mouthed thank you dumbly.

I do not remember the journey. We were on the pavement and Mr G had yet to ring the bell when I burst into tears, and for the first time ever my guardian put his arms round me, holding me so tightly that I could hardly catch my sobbing breath. And I buried myself deep in him and wept some of my agony into his embrace.

He stroked my hair. 'Oh, my dear, dear March,' he murmured, and the front door opened.

'Oh flip.' Molly touched a gash on her cheek. 'I was just sneaking out to post that letter that you tolded me to last week.'

105

The Ring in the Flames

I HAD CHICKEN. It had been run over by a bicyclist in Leicester Square, Sidney Grice assured me, and so he had only five objections to me eating it. I had become repulsively scrawny, he explained, and needed building up, but he would not put any in his mouth. Cook had boiled the poor bird until the meat was disintegrating and it was served with her usual vegetable gruel, but I could not remember when I had relished a meal so much.

And I was allowed red wine to strengthen my blood. I would rather have had gin but consoled myself with the knowledge that Molly had sneaked some into my room.

Mr G recounted what he knew about Groggy and Barney and what he had surmised about the death of my father – but I was too numb to cry again.

'Then we must find him.'

'I cannot.'

I had never known him to admit defeat before and I did not know what to say. I sipped my wine. 'Why did you ask me to marry you?'

My guardian picked something brown, about the size of a plum stone, off his plate. 'To gain control of your financial affairs before Gregory did.'

'But surely no vicar would have officiated whilst I was legally insane.'

'You were relatively lucid for a time.' He scrutinized his find. 'I intended to have you declared competent, marry you and have you recertified again.' He analysed its aroma before adding hastily, 'Needless to say, the offer is withdrawn.'

'But I never accepted it anyway.'

'No.' He tugged at his scarred ear lobe. 'But I am terrified that you will.'

Out of the depths of my misery I managed a wry smile. 'Would it have been that awful?'

'Try to imagine how bad a wife you would make.' He held the lump out at arm's length. 'You would be much worse than that.' He pushed it back into his food and announced, 'Quigley came to tell me that you were being sent for trial, but really to gloat. He was lucky to be carried on to the street alive.'

'Carried? You did not—'

Sidney Grice waved a hand. 'Molly set about him with as fine a flurry of punches as I have ever witnessed.'

'Is that how she got her face cut?'

'That was when I took the carving knife off her. No doubt I shall regret my action one day soon.'

'She did threaten to cut his throat.' I took a glass of water. 'Did he press charges?'

'Would you, a police inspector with a reputation for toughness, announce that you had been beaten up by a maid in a fair fight?'

I laughed. 'Perhaps not.' I searched my mind. 'I do not remember my trial.'

'There was none.' He put a finger gingerly under his patch. 'And you were only back in prison for nine days before they sent you to the Ambrose Hospital.' His voice became gruff. 'You have Trumpington to thank for that. He ran a campaign on your behalf.'

The doorbell rang.

'So he was my friend after all.'

The front door closed.

My guardian puffed. 'Do not be too grateful. First, he did it, as he does everything, to sell newspapers. Second, he ran it along the lines of would a pretty girl have been treated so shabbily?'

'Oh.'

'And you have Pound to thank for your acquittal, but I shall leave him to explain that to you.'

He returned to his meal as Molly clomped up the stairs.

''Spector Pound is here.'

'I am going to have some more of this delicious turnip,' Sidney Grice recited as he went to the sideboard. 'You had better go and see what he wants.'

It was with a heavy heart that I rose and made my way down the stairs.

Pound stood in the middle of the room. 'Hello, March.'

'Inspector.'

'I wish you'd call me George when we're alone.' He was drawn, bloody-eyed, and his walk was flat as he approached me.

'George.' It was the first time I had addressed him by his first name.

I went to the window and he followed, standing behind me. The street was dark, the gaslights no more than feeble beacons for the few pedestrians.

He grunted. 'They would not let me visit.'

'I would not have wanted you to see me like that.'

He touched my shoulder and I put my hand to his.

'I would not have cared how you looked if I could have been with you.' His hand squeezed me gently.

I turned so that I was side on to him. 'I am not a pretty sight at the moment... my hair...'

Pound ran his fingers down it and let them rest on my cheek. 'When I first met you I was unforgivably rude.'

'No worse than any other man.'

'I called you a mere girl.'

'I remember.'

His deep blue eyes were bloodshot and underscored with dark crescents. 'And I said that you were plain.'

'I remember that too, but you meant it kindly.'

'I was a fool, March.' He took my hand. 'And blind. I look at you now, worn out by your ordeal but still with that spark inside you, and I see that you are the most beautiful woman I have ever known.'

Another man told me that once in another country and, it seemed, another life. I still have the letter to prove it.

'I believe you were instrumental in having me set free.'

He took my fingers one by one. 'It was my sister's idea.'

'Lucinda?'

Lucinda did not like me and made no bones about it.

'When Mr Grice gave up, I got drunk,' Pound confessed. 'It wasn't the first time and it won't be the last, but it was one of the most stupid things I have ever done. Can you imagine what it is like being ill while your insides are trying to burst out of you?'

I knew all too well what a hangover was like. 'I dread to think.'

A dray trundled by, carrying a mound of something covered in sacking.

'Lucinda does not approve of drink and she has good reason not to but, equally, she doesn't like to see her younger brother so miserable. She had a long think and asked if I was sure that Gregory had not said anything else that might help us.'

'And had he?'

Pound folded my hand in both of his. 'She asked the question in a very pointed way and I was a bit slow on the uptake, but then I realized what she meant.' He looked at the floor. 'It was then I told her that I "remembered" that, as I put my ear to Gregory's mouth, with his dying breath he told me he had attacked Gloria Shell with a claw hammer.'

'How extraordinary.'

The inspector looked up but past me. Outside the girl with one ear was selling noo lied th'eggs.

'Not only that but he described the unusually shaped jelly mould hanging over the dresser. Nobody could have known about that unless they were in the room.'

I stared at him, this new, troubled man.

'But did nobody ask why you had not reported this earlier?'

'I said that I was too ill.' He exhaled. 'But as soon as I told your guardian he paid the Home Secretary a visit and then he called in a favour from Chief Superintendent Butcher.'

'To do what?' I put my other hand on top of his but he did not seem to notice.

'To get Quigley out of the way for a day or two. He was sent to assist investigating a death in Devon.'

I managed to catch Inspector Pound's eye but I could not hold it.

'I had a lot of time to think in that place – once I was capable of rational thought.' I swallowed. 'When you gave me your mother's ring to wear around my neck, I thought you had given me your heart.'

'I had, my dearest.'

'But I cannot give you mine,' I said and his grip crushed my fingers, 'not while I wish in every waking moment that I could still wear somebody else's.'

'There is another man.' He was hurting me.

'There was but I cannot have him.'

Pound darkened. 'Is he married?'

I took a breath. 'We were engaged when I was in India but he was killed.'

I did not add by me but I could not meet his eye.

Pound took his hand away. 'I cannot compete with a dead man. I will make mistakes. I will be tired and sometimes I am grumpy. He will never put a foot wrong.'

I reached behind my neck and a shaft of pain shot up him as I pulled the cord over my head.

'If it were not for Edward…' I put it in his hand. 'I am truly sorry.'

'I perjured myself for you.'

'I wish to God that you had not.'

'Damn him.' Inspector Pound made a tight fist and pulled it back and a rage burst out that I had not imagined he had in him. 'I hope he is in hell.' His arm whipped forward and he hurled his mother's ring into the glowing fire.

'If he were I would be seeing him now,' I whispered, but George Pound had wrenched open the door.

'Leaving so soon?' Sidney Grice called down.

'I should never have come,' the inspector shouted as he rushed outside.

106

Beside the Grandfather Clock

A FTER MY APPOINTMENT with Trafalgar Trumpington and meeting with Harriet I went back to Parbold. The lease had fallen through before the new tenants had even moved in. They had second thoughts about the amount of work needed to make the property comfortable but I was not seeking comfort, only solace and what was mine.

George Carpenter, the old gamekeeper, met me at the station with Onion, his ageing donkey, to haul my luggage up the steep hill.

Maudy Glass came that evening.

'I am so sorry,' I said, 'but I need to be alone.'

For her own sake I could not tell her why. Maudy's neck reddened and she marched away.

I ate the steak and kidney pie Mrs Carpenter had baked for me and raided what I still thought of as my father's cellar for an old claret.

The next morning there was a mist over the valley but it cleared as I walked into the village, down the hill to Station Road and sent a telegram. There was only one person I trusted to help me now. On the way back I stopped at the church on the hill and visited the graves – Daisy Gregory was laid to rest near the entrance. Her mother had been denied a Christian plot.

In the far corner, a little way down the slope, was the Middleton Plot – twenty-four graves in the shade of a yew tree, eight of them being my father's siblings who had died in infancy, the most recent being my mother's and his. I could not get flowers in the village but my father would not have cared. He never saw the point in visiting his own parents' graves. I bowed my head and prayed.

The next two days passed slowly. I tried to read but could not concentrate. I walked the old walks and threw sticks in the brook. I made a lackadaisical attempt to tame my old herb garden. But mostly I sat staring across the Douglas Valley to Ashurst Beacon and smoked and drank too much.

I adopted a stray cat. It was a flea-bitten tabby with too few teeth to catch its own food and had come scavenging round the kitchen door. I called it Juniper but, from the lack of response to my clicking my fingers behind it, I could have called the old creature anything.

I remembered my father telling me that the greatest problem they used to have with troops awaiting action was not fear but boredom. Juniper at least gave me an interest in life, and I was just looking for my favourite carving knife to chop her food when I heard a thud. Juniper must have knocked something over.

'Silly boy,' I called as I went into the hallway.

'Is that any way to greet a friend,' the man I had known as Colwyn said from beside the grandfather clock.

107

Goldilocks and the Man in the Furnace

'BARNEY! YOU MADE me jump.'

He came into the hall, his hands behind his back, and my first thought was of the missing carving knife. 'You know me this time then?'

'We were children when I last saw you here.' I moved back a little. 'And you had beautiful blond hair.'

Barney came towards me. 'You called me Goldilocks,' he recalled. 'And that vulgar Glass girl took it up. Goldilocks Goldilocks Goldilocks,' he chanted bitterly.

He stopped about a yard from me and I backed away a little more. He was very elegant in his black coat and grey trousers and his cravat arranged like a double pink camellia.

'I was jealous,' I admitted. 'But I did not mean to hurt you.'

I set another foot behind me and then to the side, but Barney shadowed every move.

'Your tongue was always too sharp for your own good.' He sniffed. 'That was my greatest fear, that you would recognize me, but it is incredible what time, torment and a bottle of cheap dye can do to a man.'

We continued our bizarre dance.

'But how did you get in?'

'I know this house,' he reminded me. 'And love knows no locksmith.'

I fought the temptation to run and said, 'I almost knew it was you from my first visit.' Backwards and sideways we went. 'Something flitted through my mind but I did not believe it. Then when you told me Jennifer was a donkey...'

'What about it?'

'The way you said it to rhyme with monkey.'

'Oh yes, I remember.' Barney flicked his head bitterly. 'You mocked me about that too.'

I tried to pacify him. 'I laughed because I thought it was sweet.'

'Sweet?' He chewed the word over.

'You used to be so kind.' I felt the mantelpiece in my back. 'And brave. Remember how you rescued Jumble from the canal?' I slid to the left. 'And when that mastiff escaped? It killed poor Jumble and was turning on me before you beat it away.'

Barney tittered. 'Who do you think threw your mutt into the water in the first place? And who do you think set that hound on you?' He came close. 'Go on, Marchy, reach for the poker.'

I glanced down and saw that he was producing it from behind his back.

'What is all this for?' I asked as Barney raised the poker to face height, like a dragoon presenting his sabre on parade.

He sniggered meanly. 'Have you and your sickly lover not guessed?'

'He is not my lover.'

Barney grinned and for a moment I saw the happy boy, but the grin curdled as he said, 'Neither is he your guardian.'

There was a scarred lead cannonball on the mantelpiece to my left. I had found it in a ploughed field near Cromwell's Forge when I was eight. I shuffled a fraction towards that.

'Why did your father want me for his ward?'

Barney shouldered the poker. 'To protect you, March, to get you away from Gower Street. My father genuinely believed that Grice was destroying you, just as strongly as he had argued with your father about the things he put you through. He would have liked to apply for adoption when your father died – you were always the daughter he lost – but he knew he would not have the time.'

I shook my head. 'There was more to it than that.'

'He was persuaded by Mrs Prendergast. She said she knew you well and was shocked by the way you were being treated – though she had never met you at the time.' Barney put one hand to the chimneybreast to stop me edging any further along. 'Cromwell will not save you.'

'I still do not understand why.'

Barney giggled. 'Oh, Marchy, you used to be much quicker than that.' He was very close to me. 'The object of it all – Tolly's fake death, his real death, Mrs P, Annie the maid—'

'But I thought—'

'Oh, you sweet innocent.' Barney toyed with my hair. 'Of course it was Annie, poor harelipped stupid Annie. When she saw me sneaking down to swap the ammunition in that gun, she believed my story that it was the skeleton. She was so grateful to have a man court her that she would have died for me given the chance, but I never gave her that choice, Marchy. She knew too much and, when she caught me with Mrs P's maid, Gloria, she threatened to go to the police. Gloria was the one who gave me the knife and put it back in the drawer after I had jammed the trick blade. I knew that Prendergast would be too lard-brained to double-check it.'

'Is that how you burned your hand – with a soldering iron?'

'It is nearly healed.' He pressed the blister to my lips and I forced myself not to recoil.

'You used to love making things in Groggy's workshop,' I recollected, in the hope of rekindling affectionate memories, but Barney's mood changed in an instant.

He whipped his arm away. 'Groggy,' he raged. 'I called my father Puppa when I was little and he adopted the name quite happily until you came along.' His left cheek ticked rabidly. 'Then it was Groggy this and Groggy that, and the next time I called him Puppa he told me to grow up.'

The words sprayed in dark droplets.

'So is Gloria still alive?' I asked as calmly as I could.

The tic slowed and Barney giggled again. 'She was until last night, but I had to give Pound and Grice something to occupy them while I was here. I watched them go to examine the body – what there was left of it – before I set off for Euston. Even if they realized immediately, they could not get here for at least another two and a half hours.' His finger ran round the rim of my ear. 'The aim was never to have you hanged, Marchy. You were no use to us dead. We had to drive you mad, or at least convince the courts that you were.' He went round again, very slowly inside the rim. 'But you recovered from Tolly's fake death and so I had to devise his real murder in a way that only a lunatic would have carried it out.' He rested his forehead against mine. 'Your damned godfather saw through that one and so Mrs P had to go.'

'Luckily for you, Mr Grice and Inspector Pound were both too ill to help me by then.'

'Quite so.' Barney straightened up. 'Then, once you were made Father's ward and declared mentally incompetent, he could have controlled your shares.'

'The Blue Lake Mining Company? You did it all for that?' I asked incredulously.

'I know nothing of any mines,' he pinched my lobe gently between thumb and forefinger, 'though that might be a bonus. This...' His arm swam about. 'Swandale's is what I am after.'

'So it was all just for money?' I could not look at him.

'Only a rich girl would say that,' Barney spat. 'Just money?' He flushed. 'Have you any idea what rival governments would bid for the means to obliterate their enemies' armies or extermi-nate their populations? We could have held the whole world to ransom.' He was crushing my lobe now in his excitement. Then his expression hardened. 'But even with Dom Hart disposed of, the new abbot was just as much against the project. So we still needed your vote to go ahead.'

'You killed Dom Hart?' I fought down an urge to push him away. 'Mr Grice accused Brother Jerome of that.'

'Oh, Jerome did it.' Barney shrugged. 'All men have their weaknesses and the abbot's was his taste for Communion wine. But your detective should have delved a little deeper.'

'He had no time,' I said. We both knew why Sidney Grice had been called back to London. 'But what should he have found?'

Barney grinned. 'Mr Prendergast's cousin, Francis, was a noviciate at Claister Abbey. That was how Prendergast met Dom Hart and told him about Swandale's. In a world where men are supposed to be chaste they very often find themselves being chased. Fortunately for us, Brother Jerome took an... interest in young Francis.' Barney leered. 'Francis was shocked but, being new to the monastery, he did not know whom he could trust and confided in his cousin, who told Mrs Prendergast, who told me. Jerome was given a simple choice – adulterate his detested superior's wine or let the relationship be exposed and be defrocked and cast out of the abbey to face criminal charges.' He kneaded on my lobe.

'It cannot have just been a coincidence that Mr Grice was called away for that case,' I reasoned and his grip slackened.

'Of course not. Once Jerome had committed murder he was in my power. As temporary head of the monastery, he did as I instructed and summoned your godfather.'

'That was taking quite a risk,' I observed.

Barney tilted his head. 'Not really. Jerome does not even know who I am.'

'That was clever of you.' I leaned my head a fraction into his hand. 'But surely, even if your father had gained custody of me, he was always against the project.'

Barney cupped my ear. 'Papa was in two minds. He was a good-hearted man and did not care for the idea of gassing people, but equally he did not want any other country to steal the march on us. We were going to convince him that Jonathon Pillow had managed to re-create his work in Paris. He would have given the work his – and your – full blessing then.'

'So what happened to Jonathon Pillow?' I shivered and saw a thrill run through him.

'Johnny got greedy.' Barney ran his hand down to the side of my neck. 'He thought that we could not manage without him and tried to get a bigger cut of the profits.'

'The man in the furnace,' I guessed.

Barney's voice rose excitedly. 'Lord, how he sobbed and begged before I had even lit the fire. Oh, Marchy, if only you could have seen him trying to stamp out the fire, dancing about like a cat on pins, how he tried to beat the flames off his trousers, how he climbed up a pile of clinker and how he screamed when it collapsed and he fell over into the flames, rolling around like a pig on a spit.' Barney quaked with laughter. 'His face went like crackling, Marchy, all bubbled and brown while he was still,' Barney fought for breath, '… alive,' he managed at last.

I put my hand over his. 'I never liked that man.' Barney raised his eyebrows as I continued. 'The shame of it all, Barney,' I inter-twined my fingers with his, 'is that, if anyone had asked me, I would have given the production my full support.'

He snorted. 'But you were horrified by that demonstration. Pillow told me all about it,' Barney smirked, 'while he was still raw.'

'I was a child then.' I leaned my head back. 'But, in case you have not noticed, I am a woman now.' I put my hair behind my ear. 'You said you would marry me, Barney.'

Barney's eyes flickered. 'And your father mocked me.'

'He just thought we were too young to think that way.'

'He despised me,' Barney burst out. 'You had The Grange while we just had the Old Hall House. Your family had been there for centuries while mine were newcomers. Your father was a magistrate. Mine was not. Your father was a colonel and mine just a major.'

'No, Barney, my father had a great respect for yours and he always liked you.' I put my left hand on his sleeve. 'And so did I.' I squeezed his arm. 'I waited for you.'

He caressed my cheek. 'Made a bit of a mess of your face, didn't I?'

'So that was you who put the sack over me?' I nuzzled his palm.

'Me.' Barney toyed with my ear. 'And Tolly. He excelled himself that day, doing two voices arguing with each other. We rehearsed the part for hours.'

'I heard his knees double-click when he tied me in the stable and when he kneeled to untie me in his study,' I realized.

'Pity you did not put two and two together then.'

I closed my eyes very briefly. 'You were always good at acting. Remember how you took the role of my beau in that play?' I stroked my left hand down on to his right. 'No need to pretend anymore.' I felt the poker. 'And you will not need that to get me to,' I sighed and drew him to me, '... cooperate.'

'Perhaps not.' I could feel his breath on my face. It was soft and fresh. His nose nudged mine. 'But why...'

'Why, what?'

'Take the risk?' I saw the poker rise. There was what sounded like a gunshot and the world went out.

108

The Rope and the Number

I DO NOT know how long I was unconscious but when I awoke my head was pounding and my arms were raised high, and as my eyes began to focus I found that we were in the meeting room next to the laboratory of Swandale's Chemicals. It must have taken Barney at least ten minutes to carry me there, out of the house and along the path across the fields. I had not been in that building since the day they gassed the pigs but little had changed, and nothing for the better. There were cobwebs over the portholes now and thick dust on the oval conference table, the chairs pushed back as if Jonathon Pillow had just finished addressing us, and I found myself standing, propped against the same pillar where I had sipped my lukewarm lemonade all those years ago.

I drifted but was brought back by a sudden sharp pain in my wrists. There was a thin rope round them and Barney was passing that rope through a metal lamp loop on the ceiling, and standing on a scuffed desk.

'Don't have much luck with pokers, do you, Marchy?' he remarked happily. 'It was a nice try.' He jumped down and hauled on the cord, pulling it tight so that, even when I stood on tiptoes, the knot dug in. 'But why would I let you seduce me when I can have you anyway?'

He tied the free end round the pillar.

'Have you forgotten what friends we were?' I asked. 'What happened to the boy I played with?'

Barney screwed up his face. 'He was smashed on the rocks.' Barney glanced over his shoulder edgily and his voice grew ragged. 'The Quirry got me, Marchy. While I lay there broken and helpless, it scrambled down the dark side of the cliff.'

'That was me, Barney,' I told him. 'I climbed down to help you.'

He laughed mockingly. 'No human could have slithered like that.' Barney stared as if still seeing the object of his delusion. 'It waited behind a boulder for the sun to set and crept towards me along the lengthening shadow, and when the darkness reached me so did the Quirry. I saw it, Marchy, scuttling like a gigantic loathsome spider, rearing up with its moth's head.'

'You were confused,' I reasoned. 'The Quirry was just a story, Barney.'

His head went slowly from side to side. 'I am proof that it was not.'

Barney shuddered. 'It plunged its proboscis into the wound in my belly and sucked my innards out, just like you said.' His whole body trembled with the memory. 'Can you imagine how that feels, Marchy – lying there paralysed, not even able to scream? But you went for help, didn't you? And when they came – our fathers who art now in heaven – they took the Quirry by surprise and so it crawled inside me and hid in my shell like a hermit crab.'

'Maudy went for help,' I explained. 'I tried to staunch the bleeding in your stomach with part of my petticoats.'

But my words went unheeded and all despair of the earth broke over Barney. His face and body sagged under its weight.

'What you see and hear is the body that Barney wore, a glove puppet, moving at the whim of the Quirry.' His voice, so dry and hollow, seemed hardly human now. 'The little boy you knew died in that quarry, and you should have left him there but, no, you saved the body and so the monster dwelled in me and became me.'

His breath was short and fast.

'No,' I protested. 'You lived, Barney.'

'The Quirry,' he insisted fiercely. 'This is the Quirry.' He thumped his chest. 'The monster who killed my sweet sister and our doting mother.'

'But your mother survived.'

'She had a temporary reprieve,' he corrected me. 'Five years ago I found a sympathetic pock-nosed nurse to comfort me. Helga thought it was awful that I was not allowed to communicate with my mother and smuggled a letter out for me. Luckily, she couldn't read English.' Barney began to recite in a little boy's voice. 'Darling Mummy, I hope you can forgive me for my botched attempt on your life. Rest assured, as soon as I get out of here I shall make amends and finish off the job. Your loathing son, Barney.' He flicked his head back. 'Soon after she received my message my mother did the job for me – hacked herself apart with a carving knife in her stupid studio.'

I shall never forget the horror that had swamped me when I heard that news. 'Have you no remorse?'

Barney stopped and chewed a fingerplate. He was breathing normally now. 'Oh, Marchy,' he said sadly, 'I shall never forgive myself for not being there to watch.'

'You cannot mean that. Your parents loved you.'

He tugged with his incisors at a skin tag near the cuticle. 'I was very upset when my father died,' he admitted, 'before I had the chance to kill him myself.'

His words whipped into me.

'Instead you killed mine,' I cried out.

And he wagged his finger. 'Not I, Barney; I, the monster.'

'I know you, Barney.' I struggled with my bonds but they only cut deeper into my wrists. 'You are still not so depraved as to force yourself upon me.'

Barney howled with merriment, his shrieks echoing round the bare brick room. 'Who do you think undressed you, Marchy; took off all those petticoats you were always complaining about; put your nightgown over your nakedness? I would have taken you there and then, but Tolly was such a prig.'

He leaned on the cupboard, watching me twist about.

'Why was Uncle Tolly so afraid of being murdered?' The knot was burrowing into a tendon in my right wrist, making my thumb hook into my palm.

'The only thing Tolly was frightened of was being poor,' Barney snorted. 'He told you he would be murdered to make you more receptive to the idea when you found him.'

'I was inconsolable when I thought you were dead,' I told him.

Barney came up to me. 'Then rejoice that I am not.'

I ran back and swung my boots at him with all my might but he stepped easily aside, watching me cry out as my arms were nearly wrenched from my body and I struggled to get back on my feet.

Barney chuckled. 'Still the fighter, Marchy. Still the little girl who gave that boy from the mill a bloody nose. I was going to torture you,' he informed me matter-of-factly, 'but you seem to have done that very well yourself. In about twenty minutes you will lose both your hands. See, they are already going blue.' His eyes glinted steel. 'What is the combination number, Marchy?'

'You do not imagine the formula is still in there?'

'Yes.' He came up close, tongue out a little, like Spirit when she was sleeping. 'And, if my fool of a father had told me about it, I should not have troubled with all this charade but gone straight to hurting you. Still, it has all been a great deal of fun and I have been able to hurt you anyway.'

'Fun?'

He giggled again. 'I would not have missed it for all the steam treatments, straitjackets and bromide in Switzerland.' Barney stood against me and lapped the blood from my temple, but I refused to react. 'The number, Marchy?' He ran his tongue from my chin to the bridge of my nose.

'Six-two-three-four-four-three-nine.' I lost my footing and yelped, and I almost wished that Sidney Grice or George Pound could have been there. They would have slain him where he stood, leering and slathering like a filthy mongrel.

'Tell me again – and it had better be the same.'

'Six-two-three-four-four-three-nine.'

He strolled towards the inner room. 'If you are lying, March, I shall do things to you which you cannot have imagined in your most terrible nightmare. You would not credit how long it took the lovely Gloria to die. She was all over the room by then.'

'Five-one-one-one-eight-six-two.' I struggled to keep upright.

Barney depressed the corners of his mouth. 'I might have guessed.'

He went down the steps into the laboratory and slid aside the panel that concealed the safe, and I thought, If I die today I shall never be able to put things right. I took a deep breath. Let me live for the living.

'Now!' I screamed. 'For the love of God, now!'

The cupboard flew open and there was a rush of body and red, and Barney whirled just in time to see the door crash and hear the bolt slam, and there was the flash of a long steel blade hurtling towards me.

'I thought you would never call,' Harriet gasped.

109

The Sunset

HARRIET FITZPATRICK SAWED at the rope.

'I wondered where that knife had gone,' I said shakily. She glanced at me grimly. 'You would not have been the only one seeking revenge,' she loosened the last knot, 'if I had not got to the door in time.' She broke the last strand. 'I would have run him through.'

I forced my fingers to bend and the blood scorched back into them as they straightened stiffly. 'What is he doing?'

We went to the barred window and saw Barney turning the dial to and fro. He wrenched at the lever.

'Bitch!' he shrieked. 'You didn't even give me the right number.' His voice came through the one open porthole high over his head.

I cleared my throat. 'That is because I do not know it, but it makes little difference. My father destroyed the contents years ago.'

'You are lying.'

'He did not want to risk a falling out with your father,' I rubbed my wrists, 'and so he never told him, but he was not going to risk that safe being broken into.'

'But there was an account in the *Bloomsbury Times*.' Even as Barney spoke, his voice betrayed his growing doubt. 'A man was coming from Berlin to open the safe and retrieve important documents.'

'Mr Trumpington wrote that article in exchange for being able to describe how he helped to capture a murderer,' I explained.

Barney tried to stand on a rusty wastepaper bin but it buckled under him and he nearly toppled over.

'He would probably be snooping around here now if I had not given him a sensational story about an incident in Rugby.' Harriet put the knife down. 'And told him we were coming here tomorrow.'

'Who the devil are you?' He kicked the bin across the room.

'It is not I who is the devil,' she retorted.

Barney charged up to an outer window and hammered on it with his fists.

'The glass is six inches thick for safety,' I told him.

'You think it will hold me?'

'I should imagine so,' Harriet told him, and I said quietly, 'You had better leave us, Harriet.'

She squeezed my hand. 'You will be all right?'

'I am safe now, thanks to you.'

'Goodbye, Mr Gregory.' Harriet put on her gloves and gave Barney a wave. 'By the way, I love your cravat.' She went reluctantly.

'What?' Barney ripped his collar open in a frenzy, but Harriet had already gone.

'Did you really think I was so helpless?' I addressed Barney. 'I who rescued that calf from the bog; I who climbed down that cliff to help you? '

Barney paced the room, rifling through a filing cabinet for something to aid his escape but it had been emptied long ago.

'I was not waiting for Mr Grice and Inspector Pound to rescue me,' I told him. 'I was hoping they would not arrive in time to save you.'

He wrenched a wooden drawer out and hurled it in a wind-milling motion to bounce uselessly off a skylight and fall shattering on the floor. 'What the hell are you talking about?'

'Revenge,' I replied. 'You thought you were hunting me but I was hunting you.'

'You are talking rubbish.'

'I knew you would come,' I continued, 'with the bait of the formulae and knowing I was here without a man to protect me.'

Barney unclenched his fist. 'Things got a little out of hand, that's all.' He forced a travesty of a smile. 'You know I have always cared for you, Marchy.'

'Pay close attention, Barney,' I instructed. 'There are two bottles on the ceiling right above your head. One is filled with the chemicals that make yellow smoke. Remember that evening on Southport Pier? The other is filled with the last sample of liquid for the gas. Let us call them left and right for identification purposes. Look carefully and you will see the little hammers, which are activated by two levers in here. If I pull a lever it will smash a bottle. You must choose which.'

Barney sneered. 'You are not a killer, Marchy.'

'The little girl you knew was not,' I agreed. 'But then you murdered her father, the one man she had left to love.'

It took every fibre of willpower not to pull both levers there and then.

'He slipped on the wet grass,' Barney insisted desperately. 'I risked my life getting down that waterfall and I did everything I could for the colonel, but his head had hit a rock and he died instantly. I knew I would be blamed and sent back to that hospital, and I could not bear the thought of being imprisoned again. So I took the only course left to me and ran.'

'Stop it! I cannot listen to any more lies.' I clutched at my head. 'All those other people, were they accidents too?' Barney exhaled dumbly. 'And for what?' I demanded. 'For that vile poison?' I gripped my hair in wretched frustration. 'Is that what I saved you for? Dear God, Barney, if you had only heard those poor animals squealing and seen them burn and blister and how they frothed in agony, even as you have become, you might have thought better of your plans.'

Barney hung his head. 'I did not know what it did,' he protested with an innocent lift of his shoulders. 'I thought they would just fall asleep.' His shoulders dropped. 'That is what I was led to believe.'

I had trusted those words the first time I had heard them on Southport Pier, and I ached in my desire to believe that Barney had not understood the consequences of his actions. But a tiny twitch at the corners of his mouth betrayed Barney's soul and I knew then, beyond doubt, that there was no redemption for my childhood friend.

'Perhaps you will find out for yourself in a moment,' I said. 'I shall count to five and, if you have not chosen, I shall pull both levers. One.' I held up my fingers to count off the numbers.

'I know you too well, Marchy. You are bluffing.'

'Two.'

'Look at me, Marchy. This is Barney. I would never really have hurt you. All that stuff with the axe – it was just a trick.'

'Three.'

'They let me go too soon. Let me live and I shall go back and be cured, and then we shall be married just like we always planned.'

'Four.' I put my hands on the brass levers.

'Left!' he shrieked. 'Left! God rot you, you stinking bitch!'

I slammed the porthole and pulled the lever and a wire twitched on the laboratory ceiling but nothing else happened. Had I connected it wrongly? I could not go in to fix it.

'Help me,' I whispered to the man who could not be there.

Barney looked up at it and then over to me. 'I knew you were bluffing,' he crowed.

'Do not be afraid.' It was a voice I thought never to hear again, inside and all around me, and I could almost feel my father's strong hand wrap round mine as I pulled again.

The wire straightened and tensed so hard I thought it might part. The hammer went up and dropped back a fraction. It stuck but, as we watched, the hammer fell and the bottle exploded into a cloud of yellow. And even through the wall I heard Barney, or the monster that he became, scream, one cry of agony and despair amidst the countless he had wished for.

I hurried from the room to the lobby, where Harriet waited for me, and we went out into the chill wind, shutting the door behind us. But still I heard him – whether it was through the thick walls, or across the many years, I could not tell.

'Don't leave me, Marchy. Don't let me die.'

But this time I could not take his hand, nor swear, I won't.

'Which one did he choose?' Harriet asked.

'Left.'

'Oh, March,' Harriet whispered, and we clung to each other, and afterwards we walked along the path to the top of Parbold Hill. A family of pigs snuffled in the ploughed remains of a turnip crop.

'If you had not answered my telegram…'

'How could I not?'

I pointed. 'That is Maudy's cottage where the smoke rises. I sent her away.'

'She will understand.' Harriet slipped her arm through mine.

'I sent somebody else away.' I fought back the tears.

'You will not find it that easy to be rid of him.' Such suffering broke her voice that it startled me.

We went over and stood at the tumbled fence by the edge of the quarry, each staring over her own chasm.

Harriet grasped the splintered rail and shivered. I kissed her cheek and went to the flat rock where so often I had waited for my father. I looked down the road. Past the church and grave-yard came George Carpenter, urging Onion at a pace I had not thought possible, and on his cart sat two figures, shadows in the sunset, but unmistakeably those of the two men I loved.

Postscript

———◦•◦•◦———

SIXTY YEARS HAVE passed and, as I look back on those events, we are embroiled in the most terrible war in history. But at last we have some grounds for optimism. The seemingly invincible German forces have been dealt a crushing blow with the surrender of their 6th army at Stalingrad, and one can only hope and pray that the tide is turning in our favour.

*

Shortly after we returned to London, it became apparent that I was not so completely recovered from my ordeal as I had imagined. The poisons which had upset the balance of my mind took a long time to be flushed from my nervous system and I was not able to work effectively with Sidney Grice for several months. Those wishing to know more of his work in that time, his handling of the notorious Mystery of the Creeping Women, for example, will have to look for sources other than my journals.

That summer I was sent on a long holiday and Harriet Fitzpatrick came with me, more than a little dispirited by the ease with which she managed to convince her husband that he could manage just as well if his sister came to look after the house.

We had a pleasant tour of Britain, the August sunsets being especially gorgeous because of the eruption of a volcano at Krakatoa. The sunrises, we were given to believe, were equally dramatic but we never managed to see any of those.

Our tour was not entirely hedonistic, however, and one day I hope to be able to give an account of our visit to Scarfield Manor where we helped to investigate a particularly loathsome crime.

Saturn Villa still stands, I believe, though I shall never visit it again except in my dreams.

I did not go back to see what had happened to Barney Gregory that fateful night in Parbold but left him to Sidney Grice and Inspector Pound, for I knew that, whichever bottle had been chosen, the result would have been the same.

M.M., 19 February 1943
125 Gower Street